NICK LOUTH

THE BODY ON THE ISLAND

© CANELO CRIME

First published in the United Kingdom in 2020 by

Canelo
31 Helen Road
Oxford OX2 0DF
United Kingdom

Print ISBN 978 1 80032 110 6
Ebook ISBN 978 1 78863 762 6

This book is a work of fiction. Names, characters, businesses, organizations, places and events are either the product of the author's imagination or are used fictitiously. Any resemblance to actual persons, living or dead, events or locales is entirely coincidental.

Map @ Alessandra Thorbjorn

Look for more great books at www.canelo.co

Printed and bound in Great Britain by Clays Ltd, Elcograf S.p.A.

For Louise, as always

When you stare into the abyss the abyss stares back at you.

Friedrich Nietzsche

Chapter One

Tuesday, 14 May 2019

The prisoner being transported in the back of the Serco van was having a laugh and joke with the two fresh-faced young prison officers sitting with him. He was being escorted from the high-security wing of HMP Wakefield to HMP Spring Hill, an open prison in Buckinghamshire, to complete the last few weeks of his six-year sentence. They chatted about last night's Manchester United game, the sending-off and the high tackle that caused it. The two officers, Steve and Aaron, new recruits to the outsourcing firm, were relaxed. It was the last trip of their working day and this pension-age prisoner handcuffed to Aaron wasn't going to be any trouble.

Neil Wright was a wiry little guy with red Ferrari brand glasses, a soft white beard and just a few tufts of snowy hair. The paperwork gave his age as sixty-seven, but he looked well over seventy. He was described as a low-risk offender unlikely to reoffend. The crime he'd committed back in 2013 was listed as manslaughter.

He barely looked capable of swatting a fly.

Towards the end of the journey, Steve had asked him about the crime, something he wouldn't have dared with a more intimidating villain. Wright took a while to reply. He eventually said he had accidentally killed his wife during an argument. She had threatened him with a kitchen knife, and during the struggle to disarm her she had tripped. She fell and banged her head on the stone-flagged floor of their cottage. Manslaughter. The two officers were quite understanding of Wright's explanation and his regret for what he'd done. Steve, the older of the two, was divorced, and he admitted his own relationship had verged on violence during its breakdown. We've all been there, he told the prisoner. Could have been any of us. Wright smiled. Aaron, just twenty-two and unmarried, listened to the conversation. He was a tall, well-built lad, with a soft innocent face and a snub nose. The prisoner, sitting right next to him because of the cuffs connecting them, asked him a few questions and listened carefully to the answers. Aaron volunteered that he was a Crewe Alexandra fan, and lived just around the corner from the ground. He liked techno music. He admitted that he and a girlfriend had just broken up. The prisoner nudged his elbow and told him to cheer up. Plenty more fish in the sea, eh? Then the prisoner held Aaron's lanyard, and commented on the picture. What a friendly guy, Aaron thought. He hadn't expected how normal some of these prisoners would be.

The van arrived at the gatehouse of the new jail, Steve passing across a clipboard holding a stack of documents, including the prison escort record and its matching risk assessment document, all neatly filled out. After being checked through by the gate officer, the barrier was lifted and the vehicle made its way into the courtyard. Other more detailed documents had been emailed to the prison governor, ahead of the arrival. Everything appeared to be as it should be. Bureaucracy doing its job.

Almost every word of it was fiction.

The prisoner they were escorting was sixty-three, not sixty-seven. He had served thirty years, not six. He had not killed his wife.

Neil Wright didn't exist. It was a pseudonym.

The prisoner was Neville Rollason, a notorious child-murderer. He had at the Old Bailey in 1989 been given an indeterminate sentence for the killing of at least five boys between the ages of ten and seventeen over a period of four years. The judge had described him as: 'Perhaps the most wicked, bestial and cold-hearted killer ever brought before me.' The decades in various segregation wings across the British penal system had gradually changed his appearance. The grinning, muscular, tousle-haired goblin of thirty-three, a staple of the 1980s tabloid press, had gradually transmuted. He had aged. Wiry now and almost bald, he affected a stoop that added more years. Only the dark watchful eyes, now behind the red-framed spectacles, were the same.

Only one thing on the false documentation was correct. The release date of Tuesday 2 July 2019, when this criminal, known in his heyday as the Bogeyman, would be released back onto Britain's streets. He'd had more than thirty years away from his passion, and after working hard to fool the shrinks and officials on the Parole Board, he was anxious to get started again. He'd already started compiling a mental list, the most recent addition to which was the name of the young officer escorting him. Aaron Jenkins of Crewe. He'd read it from the lanyard. But that was for pleasure. All in good time. There was more serious stuff to be planned. Like revenge against those who had tormented him. The friends and families of his victims. And, of course, the young fit policeman who had chased him down in the street in Croydon on that fateful day in

1988. Drawing the knife, and getting it knocked from his hand. Inside, he had replayed that moment in his head a million times. An exaggeration? Not much. There are 950 million seconds, give or take, in a thirty-year sentence. That's a lot of time to plot revenge. To envisage all the details of what can be done to a bound and helpless victim. Blades, acid, drugs. Eyeballs, genitals, fingernails.

It helped to have a fake identity.

Neville Rollason's fake identity was neat and flawless, utterly professional. It was not the result of some cunning sleight of hand by the prisoner himself or any of his associates. It was far too comprehensive for that.

It was created by a senior officer in Special Branch, under instruction from the Home Office. The British state that had jailed him was now slipping him back, invisibly, into society.

Thank you.

Chapter Two

Michael Jakes liked to cycle down to the river during the summer nights, but the summer solstice was always special. There were a lot of thoughts that he needed to get straight, and somehow he couldn't make sense of them in the daytime. But in the coolness after midnight, with the shade of the trees above him, he'd pedal miles along the southern bank through Hurst Meadows park near Walton-on-Thames. Although it was part of London's south-west suburbs, and still within the great arc of the M25, the park felt far more rural and tranquil than its location might indicate.

There he would lie down and listen to the sounds of the waters, the ripples and the rills, the raucous noise of the ducks and geese foraging on the grass. There were narrowboats moored here too. From them came the sound of laughter or music, muted lights, and often nearby the silhouettes of lovers, drawn to the water. Just before two, with the dew beginning to soak through to his back, he stood and clambered back on his bike. He set off to complete his circuit, riding past East Molesey Cricket Club, across Hampton Court Bridge, then along the north bank on Hampton Court Road, a permanent daytime traffic jam and never quiet even in the small hours.

On a whim, he turned off across the narrow bridge to Tagg's Island in search of solitude. He'd not been onto the private island for years, and was surprised that, beyond the houseboats that ringed the shoreline, there were many wooden homes, some quite luxurious. In the distance he could faintly hear many voices, laughter and music. A party. He abandoned his plans to explore any further, turned off his head-torch and sat on a small grassy hillock by the water's edge. The sky was mottled with clouds but stars were faintly visible.

Perfectly peaceful.

A splash came from his right. A big 'thwock' like someone diving in from a high board.

Jakes stood up and looked towards the bridge in the direction from which it had come, a hundred yards from him. In the water he saw ripples, echoes of the disturbance, but there was no sound to disturb the distant rumble of the traffic. He turned his head-torch on and began to cycle up the gentle slope of the narrow road bridge until he got to the middle. In the distance were the faint brake lights and indicators of a vehicle turning right, exiting the lane that led from the bridge to the main road. Looking over the railings, he could see nothing in the water except a faint shadow, but the reflection from his head-torch dazzled any details.

Turning back towards the island, he saw a man walking towards him, silhouetted in the lights of a large two-storey houseboat. He was slim, with a long ponytail like frayed rope. Beyond him a woman was lit up in the doorway. 'Did someone just jump in?' she called.

'I can't see anyone,' the man yelled back, then turned as he approached Jakes, his hand lifted to shield his eyes from the head-torch beam. 'Was that you?' the man asked. 'Did you chuck something in?'

'No. Not me. I just heard the noise and came to look. Maybe it was someone from a car.' He pointed north towards Hampton Court Road. 'I thought someone was going for a swim, but whoever it was hasn't surfaced.'

'Maybe that was the BMW that was parked here earlier with its stereo pounding out,' the man said.

Jakes drew away from him, not wishing to be properly seen. He had learned not to approach others at night. People sometimes thought him strange, especially when they saw his eyes, afflicted by nystagmus. He was hard for some people to look at, he knew that. It wasn't helped by his dark unruly hair and beard, often still spattered with plaster. Strangers had suspicions about him, he was aware of that, even though almost no one knew the awful truth.

He wanted people not to look at him, but at his work. The smooth, perfect finish, not the merest ripple, product of a steady swing of the forearm. Jakes could make a ceiling flatter than the Thames, a straight horizon in any dimension. An unconscious skill, honed over years. Other people had bad ideas about him. But then he had bad ideas about other people.

Bad ideas. Someone jumping in the water. And then not swimming a stroke. Not calling for help. Just ripples, disturbing the surface. Finally smoothed over by the flow of the Thames. Leaving one world and entering another. Insightful as ever, Nietzsche had once said: *There are no beautiful surfaces without a terrible depth.*

-

Elvira Hart loved living on Ash Island. She had bought a houseboat there years ago when she retired. The 260-

yard-long teardrop-shaped mound was largely wooded, unlike its immediate upstream neighbour Tagg's. She prized its seclusion. The only access was by boat or along the footpath along the top of the East Molesey weir to the southern bank. Unlike Tagg's, there were few homes on Ash apart from the houseboats. It was a close-knit community and the only significant business there was a small boatyard on the southern shore.

Ash Island was usually a peaceful place, but last night had been different. The party on Tagg's she had been to earlier was still continuing, loud conversation and music drifting down. It was too hot to sleep inside the houseboat and she had considered sleeping on the deck. It was something she often did in the summer heat, lying naked on a beach lounger, with just a sarong over her to keep the midges away. But last night there had still been too much racket. She had decided instead to take a short run. Across the weir, along Hurst Meadows park to Walton and back again. She hoped it would restore her equilibrium.

If only she had known what she was to discover. She would have stayed at home.

It was four a.m. when she saw it. Just after dawn. She had stopped running at the weir, walking over to avoid generating a metallic thrum on the walkway that might wake others in their houseboats. She saw something bobbing between two of the boats. Going over to take a closer look, she did a double-take. And then screamed like she had never screamed before.

It was a body, a swollen purple-faced horror, with bulging bloodshot eyes staring back at her. It resembled nothing so much as a medieval demon. That it was a man, naked and dead, was in no doubt. She couldn't imagine what had happened to him.

Stumbling backwards, she fell against a fence. Reached for her phone and, fingers trembling, tapped out three nines.

Chapter Three

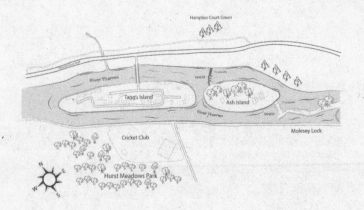

There were several more calls in the next hour, from those whose homes backed onto the river. Surrey police were soon on the scene, the islands taped off, uniformed officers assembling by a van, getting ready to fan out for door-to-door. Standing away from the senior officers, PCs Jim Cottesloe and Andrew Wickens stood on the Tagg's Island bridge, now blocked by their patrol car, and awaited a fire service recovery boat.

'Looks like a lovely day to kill yourself,' Cottesloe said, squinting into the sunrise. He was a thick-set fifty-year-old with a shaven head, twenty-seven years on the force.

'Not a bad day to be murdered either,' Wickens replied. He was thirty-two, a lean and angular individual, a keen runner. 'Could be an accident though. Messing about on the river.'

'You're a bit young to remember the song,' Cottesloe said, turning to him.

'What song?'

Cottesloe didn't reply but began to hum the tune.

Wickens checked his watch, and sighed. 'CSI won't be able to set up a tent, will they? They'll just have to lug him aboard the boat and into a body bag.'

'That's right. No dignity or decorum for him, whoever he was. Poor sod.'

The call from the uniformed inspector brought them back to the group. A search for evidence along the shoreline. Wet feet guaranteed.

–

Detective Chief Inspector Craig Gillard was the overnight on-call detective. It was almost seven o'clock on the Saturday morning and, as he prepared to finish the shift, he reviewed the incident log: domestic abuse resulting in an arrest in Redhill, criminal damage at a car park in Woking, two road rage incidents and an aggravated burglary. No stabbings. He'd spent much of the evening on the Redhill case. The woman knocked unconscious by her partner, but so far refusing to press charges.

Averagely busy for an overnighter. But quiet by Midsummer Night standards.

One new report had come in since he last checked at four a.m. A body found washed up on an island in the Thames at East Molesey. It had already been transferred to the mortuary at Kingston Hospital. The CSI initial report included some rather graphic photographs. The man's face was an extraordinary puffy purple, his eyes wide and bloodshot with swollen eyelids. It almost looked like one of the masks worn by the Indian Kathakali dancers he and Sam had gone to see a couple of weeks ago. The poor woman who found him must have been given a terrible fright.

After reading the CSI report Gillard rang Yaz Quoroshi. The CSI chief would be able to give him a heads-up if this death was an accident, or suspicious and thus likely to turn up in his in-box. After they'd greeted each other, Quoroshi said: 'I'm no forensic expert, but something terrible happened to this guy before he fell or got chucked in the water. The cyanosis is so extreme. I've never seen anything like it.'

'Any ID on him?'

'Nothing. Stark naked. If you've seen the pictures, it's obvious he's Chinese or some other East Asian. To me it looks like a case of massive high blood pressure. Maybe there's some kind of drug abuse that does this to you, but if there is it's not something I've ever come across.'

'Well, it was Midsummer Night. People do a lot of strange things at the solstice, including consuming a lot of strange things.'

'That's certainly true.' Quoroshi laughed. 'One other thing – I'm sure Dr Delahaye will be fascinated by the strange impressions left in his flesh. It looks like the guy got trapped in a fishing net.'

Gillard clicked through the photographs until he saw what Quoroshi was referring to and agreed the Home Office forensic pathologist would be captivated by these unusual injuries. There were two or three images of a kind of a mesh pattern, pressed deeply enough into the corpse's shoulders, chest, buttocks and legs to leave deep bruises. Quoroshi's idea about a net was compelling. The impressions were all across the man's body, even on his sides. It was as if he'd been wrapped tightly. Gillard could buy that – except for one thing.

Where was the net? And who cut him out?

Those distinctive injuries put paid to any hope that this case would not require his attention. One, if it was an accident, it was certainly a weird one. Two, most accidents happen to those wearing clothing. Three, no one had so far reported him missing. He decided to try to get some of his paperwork done on some of the other incomplete cases, to prepare for the inevitable call from Chief Constable Alison Rigby telling him to drop everything for the new case. Rigby had come to the job three years ago, bringing a stellar reputation from the National Crime Agency. Part of the new wave of assertive female senior officers, she had an unerring eye for detail, and a keen political antenna that few of the old-school men seemed to have. She demanded utter dedication from her subordinates, but it was nothing she had not done herself. Rigby worked phenomenal hours and would back her officers to the hilt if she was sure they were in the right. If they weren't, she was terrifying to behold, aided by her six foot one height. Gillard got on well with her, and the respect was mutual, but he wasn't immune to the frisson of fear felt by all officers in her commanding presence.

Gillard checked his watch. It wasn't yet eight o'clock, and there was a lot he could get done by mid-morning, assuming he was left alone to do it. But he had barely opened the first page of the domestic violence case when Rigby rang him from her home number.

She'd clearly been looking at the same CSI pictures that he had.

'Craig, I know you've got a lot of preparation to do for some other cases, but I do want you to take a look at this for me. We've been lucky in that Dr Delahaye will be free to begin the post-mortem this afternoon.'

'Yes ma'am.' His instinct had been right. But at least an early glimpse at the corpse from an expert should quickly answer some of the questions.

Cottesloe and Wickens allowed Elvira Hart a few hours to regain her composure before going to visit, which required negotiating the walkway over the East Molesey weir. Her home turned out to be an emerald green house-boat, adjoining a gaily painted raft crowded with planters of irises and gladioli. A dining table and chairs were set out among the greenery, beneath a parasol. The two constables crossed the gangplank from the shoreline and tapped the brass knocker on a door small enough for a Hans Christian Andersen tale. The woman who answered the door was what Cottesloe would have called a glam-orous upper-class granny. Tall and slender, with refined features and clear blue eyes. She had evidently once been very beautiful. Her thick, shoulder-length, silvery hair had been expensively cut. The two officers were shown into a small but exquisitely furnished lounge, in which the morning sun reflected off a range of antique silverware. The two sat side by side on the chintzy settee, sipping proper coffee and eating artisan biscuits, as Ms Hart moved gracefully around them, plumping cushions and brushing imaginary specks from the arms of an antique chair before she sat in it.

'You must have had an awful shock this morning,' Cottesloe began, biscuit poised in front of his mouth.

'It was horrible, actually. It was only just light, and this bloated, ghastly purple… *thing* floated up. I have no idea what must've happened to the poor chap.'

'Well, we'll leave that to the pathologist,' Wickens said. He got out a printed map and asked her to show exactly where she'd found the body. The point she marked was exactly where CSI were now examining the scene.

'Did you see anybody else around?' Cottesloe said.

'On the island? No.'

'Ms Hart, in your initial call, you said you had just got back from a run,' Wickens said.

'That's right.'

'Do you normally go out jogging in the small hours?' Wickens was a keen runner himself, but didn't like to run at night.

She smiled. 'Not normally that late, but it was the solstice and I was too hot to sleep. It was a beautiful night and I felt full of energy.'

'And do you feel safe at that time of night?' Cottesloe asked.

She laughed, an infectious tinkle. 'Well it's your responsibility to keep me safe isn't it? No, I've never had any problems. I take a small torch with me. I can run quite fast, and have a loud scream, should I need it. There are plenty of houseboats around if I do need help, and a boyfriend lives on the next island.'

Wickens noted the phrase *a boyfriend*, leaving room for more. 'Ms Hart, honestly we wouldn't advise running in darkness. There have been incidents over the years.'

She smiled again. 'Your advice isn't surprising since you're a policeman. Every day you are surrounded by evidence of the worst that people can do.'

'Well, you may have just seen it yourself,' Wickens said.

'Possibly. But the risk is that fear informs a life of constrained choice and curtailed freedom. By contrast I have lived my entire life sustained by a belief in the best that people can do, the best that they can be. I am rarely disappointed.' She reached for her own coffee, and the long sleeve of her sweatshirt rode up for a couple of seconds before she brushed it down.

'When you were having your run, were you aware of anything unusual? Were there other people around?' Wickens asked.

'Yes, there were a surprising number of people around in Hurst Meadows park, considering the time. Late-night picnics, carousers, young lovers. It made me think of Sisley's paintings, you know.'

'The French impressionist?' Cottesloe asked. 'I think he's the best of the bunch.'

Wickens glanced at his colleague appreciatively. Hidden depths. First obscure songs, now this.

'He was British, actually, though he lived most of his life in France. He lived around here in the 1870s. I've got a delightful print of his Molesey weir painting in my bedroom. It's a gorgeous melange of aquamarine and whites, with a thick impasto sky. Take a look if you like.'

Cottesloe paused, his eyes unfocused as if considering.

Wickens jumped in: 'Anything else unusual you noticed, Ms Hart?'

'Yes, there had been some noise. There was a party on the other island...'

'Tagg's Island?' Cottesloe asked.

'Yes. I'd been there earlier myself. It was the usual Kretz solstice bash and carried on a bit after midnight. As I was on my way home I also heard some awful music pounding out of a car on the bridge. That racket must've lasted until almost two. That's really why I decided to go for a run.'

'Did you get a look at the car?' he asked.

'Well, it was a white BMW with a personalised number plate.'

'Did you write it down?' Cottesloe said.

'No, but I might recognise it again if you showed me. There were three people there, in the car with the doors open.'

'Can you describe them?'

'The two in the front were black, one was quite a big guy.'

'Did you approach them?'

She shook her head. 'No. I wasn't angry or anything, I just thought it a little inconsiderate.'

Wickens said: 'How do you get back from a party on Tagg's Island? There's no bridge between the islands.'

She laughed. 'By boat. I have a little motorboat, although in the past I have swum it. It's only fifty yards. When there is a drought you can even wade it.'

The two policemen finished writing down her statement and offered it to her to sign. They were shown out and made their way back over the weir and the rickety metal walkway across the lock gates to the southern bank. Once they were solidly on dry land, Wickens turned to Cottesloe and said: 'Did you see her arms?' Seeing his colleague shake his head, he continued: 'They were criss-crossed by scars, lots and lots of old scars. Self-harm. I think there's evidence of mental health.'

'Interesting,' Cottesloe said. 'Did you see the date of birth on her statement?'

'No.'

'Born in 1938. Eighty-one years old. I'd reckoned sixty-five.'

'No way! And she still wanted you in her bedroom.' Wickens nudged him in the ribs.

'You, young man, have a one-track mind. She clearly loves living here, and I can see why. It's beautiful, which is why painters like Sisley were drawn to it.'

'So what about the car that was drawn to it? Making all that racket on the bridge.'

'Probably nothing. If you're going to dump a body in the water, it sounds stupid to draw attention to yourself.'

'Double bluff,' Wickens said. 'That's just what they want us to think.'

Cottesloe grinned at his colleague's easy certainties. 'Let's see if any of the other witnesses can fill in the blanks.'

–

Cottesloe and Wickens finally had something to get their teeth into. Elvira Hart's report about a party led them back to Tagg's Island. It was eleven a.m. The *Drifter* was a large, white two-storey clinker-built houseboat moored on the island, right by the southern edge of the bridge. As the two officers boarded the large exterior deck, they took in the smoked-glass picture window over the water and the roof terrace filled with pot plants and strung with decorative lamps. The door was answered by a slim blue-eyed man in his sixties, face screwed up against the light. 'Yeah?' He looked horribly hung-over.

He had a ponytail of iron-grey hair and was wearing a leather waistcoat over a partially unbuttoned white shirt. Tight black jeans, no shoes and a large mug of black coffee in his hand. Behind him, a thirtyish woman with bed-hair of tabby shades and a resentful expression tightened the belt on her thigh-length white kimono.

While Cottesloe made the introductions, Wickens' eye strayed to the woman. She had long tanned legs and shapely feet with red varnished toenails. The rustle of silk as she showed them in enticed him to imagine her naked.

'We've come to take a full statement from you both about last night,' Cottesloe said.

'What about last night?'

'The body that was discovered this morning just down-stream.'

'Christ, so that's what Elvira was on about,' the man said to the woman, then turned back to the cops. 'Our neighbour left us a garbled message about it.' He led the two policemen to a low and expensive-looking black leather sofa, which hissed as they settled in. The man slumped onto a director's chair with his back to the picture window, a leg folded horizontally across his thigh. The woman arranged herself on another, a tantalising glimpse of thigh again beckoning Wickens' gaze.

'So let's take down your full names,' Cottesloe said.

'I'm Brent Kletz, and this is Juliette.'

'Full names please.'

'Brent Oswald Kletzmann.'

'I'm Juliette Aquaria van Steenis,' she said, her voice betraying the husky tones of a lifelong smoker.

Cottesloe looked up quizzically. 'You mean aquarium as in fish tank?'

She rolled her eyes, then spelled her name. 'As in the feminine form of Aquarius, the sign under which I was born.'

'Right, I see,' Cottesloe said, exchanging a glance with his colleague. After the formalities of name and permanent address were completed, Cottesloe came to the point.

'We understand you had a party yesterday evening.'

'Is it that obvious?' Kletz said, holding his head with both hands. 'Did someone complain about the noise?'

'No.' Cottesloe smiled. 'What time did it finish?'

'Not late. People drifted away from about one a.m. but the last guest didn't go until three.'

'Can you account for all your guests?' Wickens asked.

'Account for them?' Kletz asked. 'It's not a nursery class. Their parents don't come to collect them.' He shrugged at Juliette, who was quietly killing herself laughing. 'Fuck, there might still be a couple hiding under the bed in the spare room,' he said, playing up to her.

'Have you spoken to any of them this morning?' Wickens asked. 'A man is dead. He could have been one of them.'

Kletz shrugged. 'Look, we've not been up long. I think if it was one of our lot, Elvira would have recognised him and said so in her message.'

'We'll need the contact details of all your guests,' Cottesloe said.

Over the next few minutes, and with the unfamiliar deliberation of a toddler learning to write, Kletz compiled a list. 'There's twenty-two names on there,' he said, passing Cottesloe's notebook back. The list was barely legible.

'You know, we did hear a splash,' Juliette said. 'Like someone jumping in.'

'What time?' Cottesloe asked.

The couple looked at each other.

'Half one?' she said.

'No,' Kletz said. 'It was later. Must have been two-ish?' he asked, turning back to Juliette.

'The cyclist!' she said, her memory sparked again. 'You spoke to him.'

'Yeah, I came out to take a look.' He described walking up to the bridge and encountering a cyclist.

'What did the cyclist look like?' Cottesloe asked.

'I couldn't really say. I was being dazzled by his head-torch the whole time, but he was pretty tall and slim, and a bit shaggy.'

'Shaggy?'

'Unkempt hair and probably a beard.'

'And how long after you heard the splash was this encounter?' Wickens asked.

'A couple of minutes, wasn't it?' Kletz said, turning to Juliette for affirmation. She nodded.

'Definitely not before?' Cottesloe asked.

'No. I only came out onto the deck when I heard the splash, looked around, saw this light, which turned out to be the head-torch, and then called out to the bloke.'

'So what do you think caused the splash?'

Kletz shrugged. 'I thought someone had jumped in for a joke, but I changed my mind when I couldn't hear any further noises. You do get people messing about but there's usually a bit of shouting and laughing along with the splashes as they chuck each other in. There was none of that.'

'Did you hear anything else?'

'There was some music from a car stereo a bit earlier. We get a bit of that from time to time too.'

'Was that nearby?' Wickens asked, remembering that Elvira Hart had referred to that.

'The same place on the bridge. It was interfering with our own music, so I just slid the window closed for a while.'

'What time was that?'

'Not sure, really. But maybe half an hour before I heard the splash.'

'Did you see anything else suspicious earlier that evening?'

'No.'

Wickens asked if he could use the toilet. 'I'll show you,' Juliette said. She led the young constable into a large and untidy bedroom, strewn with lingerie. 'Sorry about the mess,' she said. Wickens' gaze was drawn to the woman's shapely posterior as she padded through the room, but he was professional enough to take in a few observations that were more in the line of duty.

Back in the lounge Cottesloe said: 'As you may be aware, there is a public appeal for information over the body. So perhaps you could ask your friends and neighbours if they saw anything, and to ring Crimestoppers. The incident number you should reference is 196.'

Wickens' return was Cottesloe's cue to stand, ready to leave. But the younger officer said: 'I couldn't help noticing that you have a cannabis pot plant sitting on the cistern of your toilet.'

'Fuck,' breathed Juliette, letting her face fall into her hands.

'And there is a strong smell of cannabis in the bedroom.'

'Juliette, I told you to shift it out of there,' said Kletz, turning to her. 'They can't help themselves.'

She leaned back in her chair and stared at the ceiling. 'I can't believe it.'

'It's *illegal*,' said Wickens, as if the two had never heard the word before. 'I think we can refrain from ordering a search, but I wouldn't be surprised to find a few more plants, a good bit of wacky baccy, on your boat.'

'I thought you wanted our help,' Juliette said.

'And right now we are giving you ours,' said Wickens. 'And here it is: we would be perfectly entitled to issue a penalty notice for disorder on finding even modest amounts of cannabis. It would be a warning, effectively...'

'I know how it works,' Kletz replied.

The two officers looked at each other. 'Do you have previous convictions?' Wickens asked.

'A few, nothing serious.'

Juliette laughed. 'He shared a cell with Hugh Cornwell in 1980.'

Kletz turned to his partner. 'Thanks for that.'

Wickens looked baffled.

Cottesloe whispered to his colleague: 'Lead singer of the Stranglers.' The younger officer didn't seem much enlightened.

Kletz turned to the cops and shrugged. 'It was only three weeks. But Pentonville back then was the worst place in the world.'

'That's as maybe,' Wickens said. 'We'll take no action so long as you are straight with us, okay? But I strongly suggest that you don't flaunt any of your unpleasant personal habits if we need to speak to you again.'

The two officers signalled the end of the interview and were shown to the door. Once they were standing outside on the deck, Wickens said: 'I saw some signed posters in the bathroom. This bloke used to be a session musician. Played with Jeff Beck, Jimmy Page and Eric Clapton.'

'He told me he played bass,' Cottesloe said. 'Must have seen some parties back then.'

'They might well still be having them,' Wickens said. 'Pound to a penny it was snowing cocaine last night.'

'Yeah, you're probably right.' Cottesloe squinted into the sky and wondered whether if he had pursued his own musical studies with a bit more effort when he was at school it could have been him.

–

Once the cops had gone, Kletz turned to Juliette and said: 'You've got to be more careful. It could bring the roof crashing in.'

'It'll be fine,' she said.

Kletz then went to the kitchen, brought out a biscuit tin and took off the lid. Inside were lots of small polythene bags with tablets inside. 'What about these? When were you going to tell me about this?'

'Jesus, Kletz. Give me a chance. It was a last-minute opportunity.'

'But what if the police come back for a search? How on earth are you going to explain them?'

Juliette looked heavenwards. 'I'll take them to Matt's this evening, okay? I don't know why you feel the need to panic.'

Kletz shook his head. 'What if he did kill someone? Sitting there with his music blaring out, like he owns the world. What if they discover your connection to him?'

'Are you ever going to put a sock in it?' she said, angrily. 'Such a worrier!'

'Yeah well, Juliette, the difference is that I have done time inside. You never forget the noise, you never forget the fear, and you never forget the smell of the shared bucket.'

Chapter Four

It was five o'clock in the afternoon when Cottesloe and Wickens arrived at the terraced house in Walton-on-Thames where Michael Jakes lived. It was their second attempt to visit him that day after his call to the information line. They needed to ring the doorbell several times before a dishevelled figure emerged to let them in. Jakes was about thirty, tall and skinny, his greasy shoulder-length hair and untidy beard flecked with what could have been paint. He ran his hands through his locks as he turned away and tried to find somewhere for the two officers to sit. He had clearly been asleep. He offered coffee and they accepted.

His eyes unnerved them. One seemed to continually drift upwards, and then jerk back to its original position. The officers must have been staring because Jakes said: 'I suffer from vestibular nystagmus. It affects my left eye. People often think I'm looking at something over their heads. It doesn't affect my vision too much because I rely on my right eye.'

'Is there no cure?' Wickens asked.

'That's an interesting philosophical point. I would say it's the attitude of others that needs curing. As I said, my vision is largely unimpaired though I do suffer from vertigo from time to time. I'm luckier than many others who have a similar condition.'

The two police officers then asked what he'd seen the other night, and he gave them as detailed an account as he could. 'So just to be clear,' Cottesloe said. 'You saw a vehicle leaving the bridge shortly after you heard the splash.'

'Yes.'

'Can you describe it?'

'No. It was quite far away by the time I saw it. I just saw the rear lights and the right indicator, which seemed a bit fast.'

'Malfunctioning, you mean? Flashing at a higher than normal speed.'

'Yes. Perhaps its own version of nystagmus.' He smiled.

'And this vehicle was not present when you arrived on the island?'

'No. I would have had to walk past it on the bridge.'

'And what time was this when you arrived?' Wickens asked.

'I don't know. All I remember is the time of the splash because I looked at my watch. It was 1:56 a.m.' He tapped his wrist.

'How could you see?' Cottesloe asked.

'Head-torch.' Jakes touched his own forehead.

'How long after you arrived on the island was that, would you say?'

'Ten minutes, fifteen perhaps.'

The two officers were briefly stuck for further questions. 'So you do a lot of late-night cycling, I understand?' Cottesloe said eventually as he cast a jaundiced eye over the untidy living room. There were books everywhere, more than the home-made plank and brick bookcases could hold, plus a few dirty dishes, one of which was being eaten from by a small grey cat.

'I think better at night,' Jakes said. He went out and brought back two grubby mugs of black coffee. 'I like to go somewhere quiet, and the riverbank is normally pretty empty at that time.' His voice was cultured, and thoughtful.

Wickens stroked the cat, which was purring contentedly, and took a quick glance at the statement that had been taken over the phone. 'You say on here you talked to one of the houseboat residents?'

'Yes. He seemed to have heard something too.'

'What is your occupation, Mr Jakes?' Wickens asked. He was expecting something academic, given the house and the accent. The answer really surprised him.

'I'm a plasterer.'

The two policemen looked at each other. At least it explained the blotches in his hair and on his fingernails. They had both assumed he was working on a DIY project.

'Would you recognise the houseboat resident again?'

'I think so.'

Once they were on their way back in the patrol car, Cottesloe tuned into the radio news. There was a report about the impending release of Neville Rollason from prison.

'That's so wrong,' Cottesloe said. 'After what he did.'

Wickens flexed his fists. 'I'd kill him given half a chance. Give me half an hour in a cell with that bastard, and it would all be over. I need my kids to be safe.' He tapped the centre of his chest.

Cottesloe shook his head. 'Yeah, but you won't even know where he is. They're bound to give him a new identity to fox the vigilantes.'

'Why are they protecting him?'

'Oh dear, Andy. How long have you been a cop? Since when has the criminal justice system ever listened to the likes of you or me?'

–

Gillard called an initial incident room meeting for three o'clock and roped in Detective Constables Carl Hoskins and Carrie 'Rainy' Macintosh. Rainy was fascinated by the tale that Gillard told as he presented the witness statements collected by Cottesloe and Wickens.

He dealt the photographs of the dead body out to the two detectives. 'There's plenty to look at, I think you'll agree. What most interests me are these mesh marks, which he's got all over. To me it looks a little like a fishing net or maybe chain-link fencing, but I'm open to other ideas.'

'That's fantastic cyanosis,' said Rainy, pointing to the purple stain visible across the face, neck and upper chest. 'The guy is almost incandescent. It's like he's a wee toothpaste tube and all the blood got squeezed to the top.' Rainy had been a junior doctor in Glasgow for several years before finally throwing in the – presumably bloodstained – towel in search of something a little less stressful and with significantly shorter hours. The fact that she chose to become a police officer caused some of her colleagues to question her judgement, but in the six months she had been with the Surrey force, she had proved diligent, intelligent and marinated in the same kind of dark humour as theirs, required to get through the worst shifts.

'What does the pathologist say, sir?' Hoskins asked.

'I'm waiting for his call. It may be hours yet.' Gillard looked up at the clock.

'Well, I'm no pathologist, but I'd say this wee fella was asphyxiated. He didnae drown.'

The two other detectives stared at her.

'Och, I'm just gassing, sir. But when I was training in Glasgow we had an exam question about the Ibrox disaster back in 1971. Sixty-six dead, crushed when a terrace collapsed. I saw the photos. I was only twenty-one. You dinnae forget them in a hurry. Some of them looked a bit like this.'

Gillard pursed his lips. 'Okay, that's interesting. Any ideas, Carl?'

Hoskins inclined his head, and said: 'Could it be, sir, that this is some kind of industrial accident involving an illegal immigrant? The body being dumped, simply because that's the most convenient way to be rid of him without any awkward questions being asked by the authorities.' Hoskins was shaven-headed and over-weight, with a weakness for the stodgier offerings at Mount Browne's cafeteria. Consistently underestimated by colleagues, his diligence on the boring hours of CCTV checking, the bedrock of modern detective work, was valued by Gillard. It more than balanced out the off-colour jokes he was prone to letting slip.

'It's entirely possible, Carl. As I say, we've had no one report him missing, which might well indicate he was here illegally.'

'So what's the next step, boss?' Rainy asked.

'I've got an underwater search team looking around both Tagg's Island and Ash Island, to see if we've missed anything in the water, particularly netting. They are also going to check if there are any industrial water intakes nearby on the river, anything industrial that might be connected to this.'

'What about us?' Carl asked.

'We need to speak to the witnesses again,' Gillard said. 'There seem to be some inconsistencies. Rainy, I'd like you to follow up on the public appeal this evening, and feed back useful information to the officers going door-to-door. Carl, I want you to look at the ANPR.'

Hoskins was not enthusiastic. 'There's bound to be thousands. That's a heck of a busy road.'

'I know but we can narrow down the time slot. And I have a couple of ideas for which hits will be relevant.'

–

Gillard and Hoskins sat side by side at twin computer terminals, scrolling through pages and pages of registration numbers, hits that had been made on the two number plate recognition cameras on Hampton Court Road. The detective chief inspector sorted it by the timestamp on the left of each entry. 'I want you to check every hit from half eleven at night until three the next morning.' He scrolled up screen after screen. 'Okay, that's twelve pages of records. We've got one camera a mile to the left of the Tagg's Island turn-off, and one on the Hampton Court bridge 400 yards to the right.'

Hoskins sagged at the prospect as he hit the print button. 'That's over 600 records, sir. What are we looking for?'

'Ignore any vehicles that hit both cameras in quick succession, that's through traffic. Prioritise any that tripped only one camera. The best would be two hits on the same camera pair, once in each direction. That might indicate a there-and-back journey to the island, or somewhere close to it. We may pick up some residents too, but that's no bad thing. Anyone about at that time might have seen something.'

Hoskins nodded. He never failed to be impressed by his boss's analytical mind. There was a tool on the system that would flag up vehicles that had hit two specified cameras. Gillard showed him how to use it, and clicked search.

'That's not so bad,' Gillard said, as a result came up. 'You've eliminated 579. That's only twenty-seven to check. Bear in mind that some of these will only have hit a single camera once, but it could still be through traffic.'

'Yeah, the A308 continues north from the roundabout, and those vehicles would miss the camera on the bridge.'

They both squinted at a Google map that showed the three main arterial routes joining at a roundabout. 'Anyway, see how you get on with that,' Gillard said.

—

Six o'clock on Saturday afternoon. The lurid photographic enlargements from CSI were laid across Gillard's desk, like a pack of horror cards, eight inches by ten of glossy gore. A life ended, presumably, in terror and agony. Someone nobody missed, and somebody hated. Disposed of like rubbish, tossed into a river. What had caused that diamond pattern on his body? In any criminal investigation there are theories and speculation, ideas and hunches. None of it gets you anywhere until you have some firm facts, some clear evidence, to act as foundations. All he had so far was a splash.

The ringing phone rescued him. Dr David Delahaye.

Gillard was always glad to speak to the Home Office forensic pathologist. On every cadaver he cut through to demonstrable fact, separating assumption from observation.

'I've had a quick look at the chappie,' he said. 'My report won't be ready for a couple of days. But here's what you need to know to begin your other enquiries.'

Gillard reached for a notepad. 'Go ahead.'

'The deceased was probably mid-fifties or so, and seems to be of East Asian origin. Chinese, Japanese, Korean perhaps. In my opinion he had already been dead for several hours before he found his way into the River Thames.'

'What about those impressions on the body?'

'I'll get to that. First things first. What I can tell you for certain is that he didn't drown – there was no evidence of significant liquid in the lungs, nor of the characteristic foam that one gets in the airways. The cause of death was almost certainly compressive asphyxia.'

'You mean he suffocated?'

'Yes, a particular form of suffocation. He simply couldn't expand his lungs enough to breathe. The symptoms were quite clear, indeed spectacular: profuse petechiae in the conjunctiva and strong cyanosis in the head and neck. Pressure on the thorax was sufficiently intense to reverse the blood flow in some important veins and arteries, some of which can be seen in the upper body. There was also a distended jugular vein in the neck, which again would be caused by excessive pressure. Those conclusions are reinforced by evidence of damage to the body. A broken collarbone, two cracked and one detached rib, plus extensive evidence of bruising on the thorax.'

'Did the netting cause that, do you think?'

'Hold on. I think you're jumping to conclusions, Craig. Let's disentangle, if we may, those two observations. We cannot automatically assume the marks on the body were connected with the cause of death.' Delahaye's habitual caution was informed by knowing that any conclusion needed firm forensic foundations. They might have to be defended under the most rigorous cross-examination.

'Sorry, David.'

'Let's start with what the body is telling us. Compressive asphyxia. The best-known examples were those in the Hillsborough disaster, fans crowded against others for several minutes. The only case I have personally dealt with was in Southwark in 1993. An arrested youth dying when a large police officer knelt on his chest, making inhalation impossible. It usually takes some minutes to kill this way. There are numerous high-profile arrest death cases from the U.S. The literature is extensive. However, although I haven't yet had chance to review it, I have to say at the outset that the trauma to the body appears to be so severe that I suspect it is beyond human agency.'

'You mean an accident?'

'Possibly. Industrial or mechanical, almost certainly. Now that would be unusual for machinery. We must be careful to distinguish between compressive asphyxia, the kind a python would use on its prey, and its cousin traumatic asphyxia. Road accidents, where a vehicle occupant is crushed, say, underneath a lorry, are usually traumatic asphyxia: catastrophic pressure to the chest. The classic cases of traumatic asphyxia are seen where victims are trapped under vehicles that fell off hoists or ramps. In such cases you tend to see other crush injuries, which are not present on this victim. Gouges, grazes, puncture wounds as well. But in this case I would provisionally lean towards some kind of gradually applied but sustained mechanical force.'

'I keep thinking of the victim being trapped in a net at a weir, or some industrial water intake,' Gillard said.

'I did too, initially. But there is no water in the lungs. As I've said, he didn't drown. Despite the alluring fishing net ideas, we have to follow the forensics. While he may have still been alive when he was in the water, if so his head must still have been above the surface at the point of death.'

'And he couldn't shout for help because he couldn't breathe.'

'Precisely. But, as I say, that is just one possibility. He may well have been dead before his body hit the water. There is no way of knowing, forensically.'

'The lack of clothing is interesting though,' Gillard said. 'If he wasn't swimming, why wasn't he clothed?'

'Not my job to speculate,' Delahaye said. 'Now, about those cyanosed contusions. The mesh pattern, as you will have seen from the photographs, is pretty extensive. Whatever it was, he seems to have pretty much been wrapped in it. The pattern is regular and found on most parts of the body.'

Gillard said: 'Trying to think about death prior to the river: maybe he was gradually rammed by a car into a chain-link fence?'

'Possibly, but presumably there would be fence marks only on one side of him. Anyway, that's your job to figure out. I can only describe to you what has happened to the body. I found quite an array of textile fibres in the nose and mouth, which I'm going to send off for testing.' He paused and then asked. 'Any progress on who he is?'

'None at all that I'm aware of,' Gillard replied. He pulled up the rather sketchy details that Cottesloe had produced so far. 'He doesn't tally up with any of the existing missing persons in our area in terms of appearance, and no one has called in to say he is missing in the last twenty-four hours. I suppose I had better order a mitochondrial DNA test so that we can look for relatives.'

'If no one comes forward to claim him, you might want to consider stable isotope analysis, which should narrow down where he had originated from even more closely.'

Gillard nodded, recalling that a hit-and-run case that he had been involved with was partially solved by this technique. Stable isotope analysis examined the isotopes of carbon, ingested with food and drink and then trapped in hair, bones and teeth. These are cross-referenced to the geology of particular areas of the world and give a surprisingly accurate trace of exactly where a particular person lives. Only a few universities had the facilities to undertake the analysis, and it always took several weeks to produce results.

'One other thing, Craig. I found a tumour in his liver the size of a cricket ball. Poor chap might not have known, but wouldn't have lived long anyway.'

'Not much comfort in that. All right, I need to get the ball rolling on the tests.'

Gillard knew that Rigby had ordered a public appeal for witnesses this evening and that would be followed up by a door-to-door. The Thames is home to hundreds, particularly in this bucolic locale. Narrowboats, houseboats and barges, as well as some glorious riverside properties. It wasn't called the Thames Riviera for nothing. There was money here, and power. Motive, maybe. Quite a few who lived along this desirable stretch of river had heard something. A splash. Someone must have seen it.

Throughout the evening, when he had a spare moment, Gillard dipped into the evidence file as the control room collected the reports from the public. Going back to the previous evening, the first logged calls for the Tagg's Island area had all concerned loud music that had been heard during the small hours of Saturday morning. Several residents had already called the local authority to complain about the racket and now, following the plea for information, renewed their complaints to the police. One late-night dog walker recalled seeing a white car, a BMW, parked on the bridge to Tagg's Island a little after midnight, corroborating the witness statements from the houseboat residents Elvira Hart and Brent Kletz.

Hoskins' work had borne fruit too. He'd found five one-way trips, and just three there-and-back-again journeys. One of those was by a BMW 7-series, the same type of car identified by several witnesses. That seemed the one to concentrate on. The detective constable had forwarded to Gillard the addresses corresponding to each car registration. They were all within five miles of the crime scene. He in turn forwarded them to PC Cottesloe, who was coordinating the door-to-door enquiry.

Gillard couldn't get the image of the dead man out of his head. Extraordinary injuries, something squeezing the very life out of him. Hoskins' contention that it might have been an accident of some type, someone working illegally, had much to recommend it. The fact that no one had reported the man missing, too. That he or someone else had removed his clothing before he got wrapped in the mesh. That spoke of a certain level of preparation. But then chucking a body into the Thames in that area wasn't the smartest idea. It was probably the most packed part of the river in terms of houseboats and barges. There were hundreds of them. If the man was killed nearby, okay, that might explain why the body had been quickly disposed of at that point in the river. The Tagg's Island bridge was one of the few car-accessible routes to the river in that area. But if he had died some distance away, it wouldn't make much sense to transport him here, where there were so many eyes and ears.

There were plenty of suspicious ingredients. Bizarre injuries on the body. No clothing. No one reporting him missing. Add a splash, give it a quick stir, and you are halfway to a cocktail of murder.

Chapter Five

At the same time, less than a hundred miles away in the village of Grendon Underwood in Buckinghamshire, the man now known as Neil Wright sat alone in his new room at Spring Hill open prison, practising a signature to match his new identity. Born left-handed, he had spent every spare moment since arriving at the jail practising writing with his right. He admired his handiwork and had to admit it was now pretty neat and bore no resemblance to the left-handed scrawl he had used for most of his life.

Neil Wright Neil Wright Neil Wright

He hoped it would fool the graphologists once he started spreading a little bit of terror, getting even with those who had put him away. What he had to do now was to make it second nature, so that every time he picked up a pen he picked it up in his right hand. That would take a bit longer to perfect. But after all, time was something that a prisoner has plenty of. He recalled, years ago, before he went permanently into Wakefield's segregation wing, spending eight months working on a blade to defend himself. It had originally been a DVD from the prison library, and once bent in half and snapped it had a vicious edge. But to make the most of that edge it needed honing, and a strong and reliable handle. That was where the work came in, cutting and then filing a slot in a toothbrush to hold it, chewing jelly sweets to make a glue that would harden when dried. He had been particularly proud of the home-made sandpaper. Sand collected from the edges of the exercise yard, glued to a paperback book cover.

Neil Wright. After penning it twenty times, until he was satisfied the style was consistent, he ripped up the thin page of the notebook on which he was practising. He stuffed it into his mouth, chewed and swallowed. It tasted of nothing. He didn't want to leave even a shred of his writing practice in the wastepaper bin. No one must know what he was doing.

He looked around him. The room was comfortable, like a budget hotel bedroom, except with more space. A glorified Portakabin in construction, it had a TV, a washbasin and a private toilet, a single bed with sheets and blankets and a small wardrobe. For the first time in decades he was not in a segregation wing. And unlike most of the other prisoners, he had a room to himself.

Spring Hill was small, with just 335 inmates, most there for a short time. It was a perfect place to be anonymous. It looked less like a prison than a static caravan park, the buildings arranged neatly among gardens and vegetable patches. He loved the fact that there were no bars on the windows and that the door was generally unlocked. To step outside whenever he wanted, for the first time in decades, was a wonderful feeling. On his first evening he had stood outside in a downpour for half an hour. He listened to the pattering of rain on the leaves of the bushes, inhaled the aroma of wet grass, and delighted in the icy rivulets that ran off his scalp and down his neck and trickled down inside his shirt. Being out in the elements thrilled him. Only when he was chilled to the core and shivering did he retreat to his room for warmth and shelter.

Before, being sheltered had had no meaning for him. He had been moved numerous times over his decades inside but had never been in a category D open prison before. Cat D prisons were designed to prepare felons for returning to society. No one was moved there unless the Parole Board was happy it was safe to do so. Wright was perfectly aware of the outcry about his impending release. He was originally sentenced, in 1989, to life with a tariff of twenty-eight years. After he had completed half his sentence he applied every year for parole, but was consistently refused. In 1991, after reading a psychiatrist's report presented at a parole hearing, the Home Secretary increased his term to a whole life tariff. Then, having served more than the entire original sentence, he applied to the Parole Board again. With the application he offered to identify the burial places of two victims, if he could be released. He had always admitted killing three but had been convicted of murdering five. There was also suspicion that he was involved in two other unsolved killings in the south of the country, which matched a time when he was away from his native north-east. That made a total of seven.

The Home Office had made no promises, saying only that it would look leniently on his application if he co-operated prior to the decision. As a result, he had spent several enjoyable weeks, accompanied by police officers, on the North York Moors trying to locate the burial spots. He made a big show of not being sure, so that he had day after day out in the open, being fed pub lunches and cafe meals, and generally getting a bit of fresh air. He had after five weeks led officers to a small burial mound, now overgrown, near a stream, where he had placed the bodies of one of the two. He claimed not to recall where the other was because of the change in tree cover and bushes. In reality, he had a very clear picture in his mind, but pretending to be uncertain meant he retained his trump card. For weeks a senior probation manager had ferried messages backwards and forwards between Rollason and the Parole Board. The prisoner's message was uncompromising. I've given you one burial place. I'll give you a second only in exchange for a release date.

He'd been aware that the mother of his second victim was dangerously ill in hospital, because he'd read about it in the *Daily Mirror*. Mrs Rita Hollingsworth's dying wish was to be able to bury her son, Gordon. For three weeks last winter, nothing happened. Then the Home Office finally relented, approved the parole application and confirmed Rollason's release date. Tuesday 2 July. The week after, Rollason had indicated he was willing to keep his side of the bargain. He was taken back to the North York Moors and led police to a patch of bracken by a tree stump, in the shadow of a large rock. That was where he had buried Gordon Hollingsworth. The later recovery of bones made national headlines. He was miffed not to be given a shred of recognition in the media for his part of the bargain. Still, at least he would be released.

He picked up his notebook and wrote the precious date down: Tuesday 2 July. Just ten days away! He fantasised about what he was going to do. The first pint of beer, the first meal out, Thai red curry with saffron rice with an ice-cold lager. His first bout of sex, with anyone other than his own left hand. Perhaps most prominent of all was his list of acts of revenge, planned over many years, a campaign to be conducted with the utmost care.

Those who had put him inside would suffer retribution, and those who had written him hate mail while he was in prison would get their comeuppance. He had a few addresses, mostly of those who were friends or relatives of the victims' families. Then there was one police officer, Gillard, now a detective chief inspector in Surrey. That was definitely a case for vengeance. There wasn't going to be anything too high-profile to start with, just some subtle psychology. Vandalised cars, graffiti, short messages by letter and by phone. The easiest approach was to adopt the tabloid description of him from 1987, when his crimes first came to national prominence. The Bogeyman. That's what they'd called him. He'd already written his first letter and popped it into the letter box in the village in Grendon Underwood, yesterday. It was in his new handwriting, written with forensic caution in a gloved right hand, on a sheet torn from a new notebook. It was addressed to one of his most persistent and irritating correspondents. It just said: *Are you afraid of the Bogeyman?*

Chapter Six

Following up the list of party guests, Constables Cottesloe and Wickens drew their patrol car up to the imposing wrought-iron gates of the Holdersham Estate. Straight ahead was a half-mile tree-lined avenue leading to Holdersham Hall, where party attendee Gus van Steenis was manager. Cottesloe leaned out of the window to press the intercom button set into a metal column, and the gates slowly parted.

'I remember when this place was a preparatory school,' Cottesloe said, as they rumbled down the rough driveway towards the gigantic three-storey honey-stone hall. 'But it's been owned by some sheikh from the UAE since the mid-1990s. This private zoo of his must cost a fortune.'

Wickens' eyes glittered. 'I'd love that kind of cash. Private plane, my own Caribbean island.'

Cottesloe stared at his younger colleague. 'You're in the wrong business if you want to be rich.' He chuckled. 'There's too many dangerous temptations. You have to be incorruptible.'

'Like you?' Wickens said sceptically.

'That's right. Never taken a free pint or a free meal in all my twenty-seven years on the force.' Cottesloe pointed left out of the window. 'That's the zoo.'

'What's he got?'

'No lions or tigers. Crocodiles, I heard, lots of reptiles and a rhino.'

'So what's the point if it's all private?'

Cottesloe turned. 'Conservation. The sheikh is a big donor to conservation societies, the fight against ivory poaching, that kind of thing. Very progressive chap. There's an old white rhino here. I saw an article about it in the paper. Shot and injured by poachers in Kruger National Park. Had its horn chainsawed off, then was left for dead. Still got a damaged leg.'

Wickens stared out the window, as if expecting to see the benighted animal. 'Perhaps they should put the poor bugger out of its misery.'

Cottesloe shook his head. 'Never underestimate the power of a good story, Andy. It's fantastic PR for the sheikh.'

The patrol car came to a halt outside the grand portico, next to a battered olive-green Land Rover. Wickens and Cottesloe headed up the steps to the main door, but a greeting from below drew their attention. A man had emerged from a basement door and climbed a short flight of steps to the gravel. Wickens now recognised him from the local paper.

Gus van Steenis was a ramrod-straight septuagenarian of grizzled features. He was wearing a faded short-sleeved brick-red shirt and muddy green shorts, and looked like he hadn't shaved for several days. A battered bush hat sat on his head, giving him the appearance of a long-retired Indiana Jones. 'I'm Gus. Good day,' he said, thrusting out a hand. His grip was strong, and he made eye contact. 'Terrible business about the body.' He showed them in through the basement door, which led along a low dark corridor to a small 1960s-type kitchen with pale green glass-fronted cupboards. The remains of a meal could be seen on a yellow melamine plate on a Formica-topped table. 'Excuse me, gentlemen, I was just finishing my scrimbled iggs.' His accent sounded South African to Wickens.

He arranged wooden chairs at the table, and dumped the plate and cutlery in a big enamelled sink. 'So what can I do to help?'

'We believe you were at a party on Friday night on Tagg's Island.'

'Yes, absolutely cricked.'

'What time did you arrive?' Cottesloe asked.

'At 11:50 p.m. I left at 1:30 a.m.'

'Did you see a white BMW parked on the bridge?'

'Yes. I had to ask the two gentlemen to move it so I could pass.' The word came out as 'jintlemin' and it didn't sound like he meant it.

'Did they co-operate?'

'Eventually, yes. I also mentioned to them that their music was excessively loud.'

'And how did that go down?'

He laughed. 'Badly. There was a bit of a staring contest between me and the big black fella who seemed to be in charge. But I've had decades of dealing with that kind of thing back in Rhodesia. Eventually he turned the music down very slightly and reversed the car enough to let me past.'

'Was there anyone else in the car apart from the two men?' Cottesloe asked.

'I think there was a woman, also coloured.'

'Did you hear a big splash at any time, either when you were approaching the white BMW or afterwards?' Wickens asked.

'No. As soon as I passed them, I drove off home. Parties like that are okay if you're young, but I need my sleep.'

'What did you think they were doing, the black guys on the bridge?' Cottesloe asked.

For the first time van Steenis seemed to hesitate. 'I have no idea.'

'Were they at the party?'

Van Steenis looked into the air as if this was a difficult question. 'I didn't see them.'

'So how do you know Brent Kletz?' Cottesloe asked. 'Unreconstructed hippies don't seem like your kind of people.'

'True, I suppose. But Juliette is my granddaughter, and works with me here. That's why I was invited. They all seem nice enough people to me.'

'Were there any drugs at the party that you are aware of?' Wickens asked.

'Ach, no. Look, man, I'm really not sure. I didn't see any. But then an old stick like me, well I'm not sure I would recognise any.'

'Did you use the bathroom?' Wickens continued.

'I'm sure I must have.'

'Did you not see the cannabis plant on the cistern?'

'I don't recall it.'

'So you don't take drugs, Mr van Steenis,' Wickens persisted. 'But you drink alcohol?'

'On occasion, yes. But I didn't drink that night, because I was driving.'

The Zimbabwean had successfully headed off their next question. The two policemen thanked him for his time. Wickens, who had been making notes, read them back and asked if he wanted to add anything.

'No, that's fine. Look, I was just going to give Dinnis his dinner, would you like to come?'

'Dennis?' Cottesloe asked.

'Our rather sick rhinoceros.'

'Yeah!' Wickens said, earning himself a cool glance from Cottesloe, who added, 'I suppose we do have a little time left.'

The two constables piled into the Land Rover with van Steenis driving. The ancient diesel roared alarmingly as they headed at excessive speed over a meadow towards a collection of buildings. Van Steenis described how the estate had been rescued in the early 1990s during a property collapse, and when the private school on the site was having financial difficulties. 'I was recruited in 1995. It's the best thing I ever did,' he said. They passed numerous paddocks, and a large newly constructed barn-like building, which van Steenis said would be his herpetology centre. 'Reptiles and amphibians,' he said into the puzzled silence. 'They're currently housed in the old barn. Juliette looks after them for me. She's got a PhD in herpetology.'

'The study of her pets, that's what it means,' Cottesloe said, with a wink to Wickens.

They pulled up outside what would have been once a stable block, enclosed within a small paddock. There were two fences, one a chain-link external fence and the other a more substantial inner bulwark of motorway-style crash barriers. 'This is where the old boy is,' van Steenis said, getting out and unlocking a door into the stable. The building was dark, and smelled intensely of animal. A heftily barred enclosure gave a view into the main part of the building, where on a bed of straw lay an enormous leathery creature. The rhino's small dark eyes reflected what little light there was and, having scented the visitors, he blinked and shifted his huge weight.

'He's a splendid old fella, aren't you, Dennis?'

As their eyes became accustomed to the light, the two constables could now see the bandaged right foreleg, and the scarred nose where the horn had been.

'We have a video camera outside, so that those who helped Crowdfund the rescue can watch him recuperate. Sadly, I think he's a bit down. He seems to prefer to spend time in here in the dark. Maybe a bit of food will cheer him up.' Van Steenis took a bucket from the wall and filled it with some kind of dry food from a sack. 'Rhinos in captivity don't need much extra food if they can forage, though Dennis has put on a lot of weight because of his mobility difficulties. But he's always glad to see me, aren't you Dennis?' He jangled his keys. At the sound of the iron gate being unlocked, the huge animal rose ponderously to his massive feet, snorting enthusiastically. Van Steenis slipped into the enclosure, immediately closing the gate behind him. He wafted the bucket under Dennis's snout and patted the beast vigorously on his huge leathery flank. 'Who's a good boy then?'

The rhino followed as van Steenis led the way to the open-air enclosure. Directed by van Steenis, the two policemen moved along a sloping walkway that climbed out of the stables and circled high above the edge of Dennis's compound. Van Steenis continued to chat to the animal as if he was a domestic pet while he chewed through a bed of hay on which the food supplement had been emptied.

'Isn't he dangerous?' Cottesloe called across.

'No. Dennis is as gentle as a pussycat. White rhinos like him are much more placid than the smaller black rhino species, except when calves are about. Besides, he knows me and his other keepers by our scent.'

'You know that dead body,' Wickens muttered to Cottesloe. 'Wasn't it wrapped in wire?'

'That's what I heard. But I haven't seen it.'

'See over there?' He pointed to a hefty roll of wire mesh fencing stuffed down behind metal railings at the far end of the rhino's compound. 'What if the bloke had been caught in that, and the rhino leaned against him?'

Cottesloe turned to him, a sceptical smile on his broad face. 'You fancy yourself as a detective, don't you?'

Wickens shrugged. 'There's a lot of ways of being squashed in a zoo, that's all.'

'Sure, but mostly accidental. If that happened I can't see they would just dump the victim in the Thames.'

They left the walkway as van Steenis made his way back into the stable block. He led them out towards the herpetology building. They passed a rough concrete pool, wired off from the track.

'I'm going to build a roof on this in the next couple of years, so we can make a tropical crocodile pond.'

'Where do you get the crocs from?' Wickens asked.

'We got some young Nile crocodiles rescued from a French zoo that went into bankruptcy. They need special certificates to be moved, but it was a lot easier within the EU because there is common certification. They are microchipped, like dogs, believe it or not. When they've grown a bit I shall put them in here.'

'It'll be carnage,' Wickens said, with boyish enthusiasm.

'No. It's much easier to have a gang of Nile crocs than salties, because the Nile boys have a clear pecking order and don't fight among themselves. That really helps at feeding time.' He stared over the railing reflectively. 'Boy,

I learned my lesson with Australian saltwater crocs. I had two females, Betty and Nora, but Nora bullied the other, bit her tail, and then chewed off a foreleg. Eventually she killed her. Nora now has to have an enclosure on her own, over the back.' He gestured with his arm. 'She is nearly ten feet long now, must weigh half a ton, and I wouldn't trust her an inch.'

He then led them on foot into the herpetology building. 'Only the gharial will be inside this building, with the monitor lizards and snakes. I suppose I shall put the scorpions and tropical spiders in here too because they like the warmth.'

'Are you going to open it to the public?' Cottesloe asked.

Van Steenis blew a long sigh. 'Well, maybe one day if the sheikh can be persuaded. We've already got planning permission for a bigger visitor centre, but it might lapse. You see, many of the buildings here would not pass the zoo licence requirements. I'll have to rebuild them first, and then there is all the woodland we would have to lose for the car park, which would break my heart. Finally, there's the great undisciplined British public, tapping on the glass, disturbing the animals, chucking litter and bottles into the enclosures, all that stuff. I don't know, the sheikh quite likes it as it is, and I'm sympathetic to that view.'

Cottesloe checked his watch and told van Steenis that they should be going.

'If I've answered all your questions, I've got one of my own.'

'Go ahead,' Cottesloe said.

'Perhaps it's not quite on the point, but I have to say I am outraged to hear that the police are going to release from prison one of the worst murderers in British history—'

'Ah, it's not the police who were releasing him,' Wickens said. 'In fact if it was down to me—'

'Not only that, but if the newspapers are cricked, public money will be spent giving this man a new identity. So he will be invisible in our community, ready to strike again.'

'Your concern, sir, is noted,' Cottesloe said, getting into dealing-with-the-concerned-public mode. 'The Parole Board in its wisdom makes its decisions only when an offender is considered to be safe to release.'

'May I remind you that the Bogeyman used to torture his victims, most of whom were adolescent boys,' van Steenis continued.

'Yeah, he's evil personified,' Wickens said, eyeing his colleague. 'He should have been kept inside for life.'

Van Steenis shook his head. 'No, PC Wickens, not so. He should not have been kept inside. He should have been hanged. It isn't fashionable to say so, but execution has much to recommend it these days. Miscarriages of justice are much less likely because of the power of DNA evidence, which neutralises the one powerful argument against the gallows. It would save the great British public a lot of money too.'

'You've got a good point there,' Wickens conceded. 'You really have.'

'I looked it up. It costs £26,133 per annum to keep a prisoner. Times thirty years and that's over three-quarters of a million pounds. Multiply by the number of murders each year, say 700, and that's half a billion—'

'Well, thank you for the tour.' Cottesloe stood up to bring the discussion to a close. He thanked van Steenis for his views, which he promised he would pass on to his superiors.

'It's a hot topic, Andy, death penalty. Always has been,' Cottesloe said to his colleague as they got back into the patrol car.

'Not surprising. It's a bloody outrage. Bastard gets out a week on Tuesday.'

'Well, relax, he's old now. Pretty harmless too, I expect. A bit like Dennis.'

Wickens snorted his disagreement.

Chapter Seven

Sunbury-on-Thames was a typical piece of London suburbia. Not wealthy, not poverty-stricken, not in any way distinctive. Gary Tilling's home in Linden Avenue was a scruffy 1930s former council house, which had been gradually extended over the years. What had been the front garden was now tarmacked up to the enlarged porch with its flat roof and leadlight effect UPVC windows. As PC Andrew Wickens parked his patrol car outside, he checked for the car whose number had shown up on the ANPR. Yes, there it was, parked in the street outside. A ten-year-old Volkswagen Golf, black, short of two hubcaps and a section of rear trim.

Wickens rang the doorbell and waited. The chime was one of those electronic tunes that seem to go on and on. He could see through the glass the approach of a sizeable figure. The door opened to reveal a paunchy man of perhaps thirty, six-one, in a black T-shirt and stained baggy joggers. He had straggly dark hair around a balding pate, and a slice of toast jammed halfway into his mouth.

'Gary Tilling?' Wickens asked.

The man nodded and mumbled something through his toast. *What's it about?* Wickens guessed.

'May I come in for a minute?'

The man nodded and gestured for Wickens to enter. They both stood in the hallway. The TV was on in the background, some kind of soap opera, enveloped in the aroma of toast.

'You may have heard about the appeal for information. Over the body discovered in the River Thames.'

'Yeah, I think I heard something about it.' He had a loud voice, but didn't make eye contact.

'According to our records, your car was on Hampton Court Road late on Thursday night.'

Tilling didn't say anything, but the tip of his tongue moved out slightly and along the edge of his lip, as if searching for the last fragments of jam from his toast.

'Is that correct?' Wickens pressed.

Tilling nodded. 'Is that from a number plate camera?'

'Yes, sir.'

Reluctantly Tilling beckoned him through. A glance at the place showed why he was so reticent. The carpet was grubby and threadbare, mended in places with gaffer tape and littered with crumbs, dust and hair. The place smelled of body odour; sour and enduring. It felt like the windows hadn't been opened in years. Dust lay thickly around the edge of the room, with just a well-trodden footpath past a builder's jack right in the middle, bracing a metal joist against a cracked ceiling. Wickens took in a leather-effect three-piece suite, extensively repaired with tape, behind which stood a bald car tyre and some tools, balanced on a badly scratched and oil-stained sideboard. The only well-cared-for object was the wall-sized flat screen TV, on which *Emmerdale* was showing. Wickens was finding the noise of the TV distracting, and said so. Tilling picked up the remote and muted it.

'Take a seat. Want a coffee?' His voice was deep and rough.

Dragging his eyes away from the domestic drama portrayed in larger than actual size, Wickens looked again at the grubby and sagging sofa, and eyed the unspeakably filthy kitchen off to the right. 'No, I'm fine thanks. This won't take long. So may I ask what you were doing by the river at that time of night?'

Tilling scratched his head, sending a shower of dandruff onto the well-dusted shoulders of his T-shirt. 'I was hoping to spot an otter.'

'Are there otters in the Thames?'

Tilling nodded. 'One or two. I've got pictures,' he said proudly.

There was a voice from upstairs. Wickens didn't catch what was asked, but Tilling clearly did. 'It's the police, Mum. About some dead body in the river.'

Straining for the reply, Wickens heard a little better. *I told you to call them.*

'But why? I didn't see anything,' he called back up. 'I didn't see anything,' he repeated to Wickens.

'You mean otters or people?' Wickens asked.

'There were people. Too many for otters to show themselves.'

'Can I get some details down about timings?' Wickens asked.

'What do you want to know?'

'What time you arrived at the riverbank, and what time you left.'

Tilling scratched his head again. 'Won't it be on the cameras you recorded my number plate on?'

Wickens sighed and looked at his notebook. This was like pulling teeth. 'Yes, sir, but I'm anxious to get your own estimation.'

'I'm not sure,' Tilling said. 'It was after midnight. I got to the bridge, and it was noisy. Rap music or something like that, coming from a car parked in the middle of the bridge to Tagg's Island. I waited on the north bank, unpacked my kit and waited for them to go. I couldn't decide whether to drive around to Hurst Meadows park on the southern bank. The park is bigger, so it's easier to get away from people, but the parking would be shut there, and it's further to lug the kit.'

'What time did you leave the north bank?'

'I gave up before two a.m.,' he said. 'They showed no signs of leaving.' Wickens looked at his notes. The western camera had recorded the Golf passing eastbound at 00:47 a.m. and returning westbound at 2:07 a.m.

'Can you describe the vehicle that was on the bridge?'

'It was a white BMW.'

'Did you see the occupants?'

'There seemed to be several, because of the conversation. There were two black guys stood looking over the water, but they were also talking to somebody inside the car.'

Wickens felt he was really getting somewhere now. 'Can I ask why you didn't call us with this information? It could be quite important.'

'It was just some people on the bridge,' Tilling said, looking at his hands. 'I should have listened to Mum. She said to ring in.'

Wickens could see that Tilling's departure time didn't quite tally with the camera record. There would be nearly ten minutes unaccounted for after Tilling said he'd left. Yet it would only take a minute to drive that distance from the Tagg's Island bridge to the western camera. He decided that it was probably nothing. The white BMW was a more interesting prospect.

'Do you want to see the otters?' Tilling said.

'Why not,' Wickens replied. At least it might explain Tilling's motive for being there.

Tilling led him to the sun lounge at the back of the house. 'This is my office,' he said unnecessarily. The room was packed, but markedly less neglected than the rest of the house. Computers, laptops, screens, modems, keyboards on and under tables, resting in heaps on chairs and boxes. The whole floor was criss-crossed with networks of cables, over which plywood duckboards had been laid. The electrical sockets were crowded with plug adapters. The whole place had fire hazard written all over it. Tilling picked up a large camera with a telephoto lens attached and, after fiddling with the screen at the back, showed it to Wickens. A five-second video clearly showed an otter sitting on a riverside log. It preened itself, before staring in the direction of the lens and then sliding sinuously into the water.

'You took that?' Wickens asked.

Tilling nodded. 'Last year, in the winter. You have to be very patient. They've got very keen senses.'

'What do you wear for these otter trips?'

'Camouflage jacket and trousers and a woolly hat.'

'In the summer?'

'Yes. I don't get hot. I have a small tent that I use as a hide. Do you want to see pictures of egrets?'

'No, thanks. Did you see anyone else?'

He thought hard. 'There was a man on a bike. He had a head-torch, which annoyed me because it might have disturbed the otters. But he rode onto the island and I didn't see him again before I left.' Tilling started playing with the camera. 'I've got some water voles if you want?'

Wickens, trying to avoid being drawn into Tilling's hobby, asked to use the toilet. He was directed upstairs, first on the left. He negotiated more threadbare and grubby carpet, and squeezed past an old stairlift, clearly not in use going by the fractured seat. A smell, worse than stale, assailed his nostrils. On the landing he noticed a tea trolley on which several dirty plates were stacked. Wickens stepped back from the stench, and banged into the trolley, setting off metallic clinks. He opened the bathroom, took one look and thought better of it. Turning to come down-stairs, he ran into Tilling, who was coming up the stairs.

'You didn't wake Mum up, did you?'

'Wasn't she awake already?'

'She has sleep apnoea, among other things. She's not well. She's been bedridden for years, and now she's got problems with her spine. It's gradually crumbling, and she's in pain.'

Tilling escorted Wickens back to the front door. The PC escaped gladly to his car, breathing in some fresh air. It was only when he was safely inside and had already started the engine that he looked up at the gable. That would be the room Tilling's mother was in. The curtain was drawn but between it and the glass, moisture could be seen running down the inside. Poor Mrs Tilling, being looked after by a man like Gary. Not the most natural carer.

Unless you were an otter, perhaps.

After the policeman had gone, she called loudly again from upstairs. He never had any trouble hearing her.

'Did you discover why they came here?'

'I think he was interested in otters. But not egrets.'

'I don't think so, Gary.'

'It was the car registration. Got caught on a camera.'

'You've got to be careful,' she said.

'Yes Mum.'

'You're a good boy, Gary. You're a great comfort. And there aren't many of them left for me in this world.'

'No Mum.'

'Can you fetch me some of the new painkillers? It's bad again.'

'Yes, Mum.'

-

Kletz was strumming his Alvarez classical acoustic gently, sitting on the deck of his houseboat. It was nearly midnight and the river was quiet, just the lapping of the water, the quacking of foraging ducks and the distant hum of traffic on the Hampton Court Road. Juliette had already gone to bed, and he was thinking of doing so himself.

A light on the bridge drew his attention. A head-torch, casting its searchlight erratically over the river, towards him and then back, then down to the water. Kletz muttered to himself about LED lights, far too powerful and dazzling, even at a hundred yards. When his eyes had readjusted he again saw some activity, the light being partially masked by the railings.

Then there was a splash.

Not as loud or as big as the one he had heard two nights before, but enough to stop him playing. The head-torch was now pointing down into the water, the guy leaning over. He realised who it was. That peculiar cyclist again. His suspicions were confirmed by the speed of the man's departure, and the whirling reflectors on the bike wheels.

He wondered whether to call the police. It was the kind of thing they might like to know, but then judging by previous experiences they would spend half their time sniffing round his own home looking for drugs and leering at Juliette.

No, he'd give it a miss.

Still, he was curious as to what had been tossed into the water.

Chapter Eight

Monday 9 a.m.

Anton St Jeanne was annoyed but not surprised to be pulled over by uniformed police as he was driving across Kingston Bridge. Being a youngish black guy in a new white 7-series BMW, he was never surprised. He had lost count of the number of times he had been stopped over the years. But today he was in a hurry, already running late for a meeting with a supplier at his restaurant *J'adore Ça*. Anton knew from long experience that arguing just slowed the process down, so he swallowed his irritation and co-operated when they asked him what his number plate was and demanded he produce ownership documents. Again, from long experience, he had the papers to hand. Only when the young female officer had finished establishing his credentials as a legitimate car owner did she ask him what she really wanted to know.

'So, sir, can I ask you where you were last Friday night?' The officer was among a group of six checking traffic at the bridge.

'I was at my restaurant until one a.m.'

'Your restaurant?' There was just the hint of a smirk. Perhaps it was the fact that he was casually dressed in a short-sleeved white shirt, jeans and high-top trainers that fuelled her scepticism. He had always tried to make mental space to understand the narrow exposure that most cops had to people of his ethnicity. Too many white police officers never met black or Asian guys except on the wrong side of a charge sheet. Their idea of society was colour-coded: law-abiding whites, dodgy Asians and crooked black guys. He'd considered inviting all the local cops to his restaurant for a free buffet to meet all his friends, all young, all intelligent, mostly professional, with skin colours between ebony and latte. But he knew it would take weekly meals for several years to erode the ingrained stereotypes and he had neither the time nor the money to make it happen.

'Yes, I am the proprietor of *J'adore Ça*.' He produced a business card. She took it, then asked him to repeat the phone number printed on it. He did so, while wondering how many white guys would be tested over the authenticity of a business card.

'Can I ask you, sir, about where you went after that?' Her tone was now just marginally more courteous.

'I drove with my girlfriend Leticia down to the river.'

She nodded. 'Are you aware that a man was found dead in the Thames, not very far away?'

'Really? I'm sorry, I work very long hours and the news passes me by.'

'I'm afraid we're going to have to ask you to come to the station for an interview,' she said. 'It shouldn't take that long.'

He blew a sigh. 'Come on, can't I make an appointment to do it later?'

'I'm sorry for the inconvenience.' Now, she genuinely did seem apologetic.

Anton shrugged and smiled. It was the default setting for his face. He had smiled his way through a lot of adversity in his short life, and this shouldn't be the worst. 'Okay. I have to make a couple of calls first.'

–

Less than ten miles away, in the probation service office at Swan House in Staines, Leticia Mountjoy was in the ladies' toilet when she took Anton's call. He sounded unusually anxious 'What is it?'

'I'm on my way to Staines police station.'

'Why? What happened?'

'A dead body's been found in the Thames. Somehow they seem to know where we were parked. I'm sure it's just the usual shit. Makes me sick. It's putting me behind on the refurb too.'

'I'd offer to help, but we've got a really big case management meeting in a minute.'

'Don't worry, babe. I'm sure it's just a formality. If we've been seen, I'll mention that you were in the car. But please don't say anything about Leroy being there.'

'But Anton…'

'Shh. You know what they'll say if Leroy is ID'd. Look, I've got to go, see you.' He cut the call.

Leticia shrugged, finished up in the cubicle and washed her hands. She looked in the mirror and freshened her make-up before heading off to the meeting. It was a big one. As well as six of her colleagues, Leticia recognised senior psychiatrist Dr Ronald Golob, who had a reputation for being slightly weird. Beyond him was social worker Margaret Chan and at the end, a shirt-sleeved policeman she had never met before, Detective Inspector Graham Morgan from Special Branch. The one unoccupied chair belonged to Verity Winter. As so often the senior resettlement officer was a few minutes late to the meeting. As was usual at Swan House, Leticia was the only black person in the room. That didn't include those meetings where offenders were present; then she would often be one of two. She had got used to black offenders staring at her as if she was a turncoat.

Jill Allsop emerged from her office, finished a call on her mobile and called the meeting to order. At fifty-three, and just five foot three, Jill compactly wrapped a lifetime of probation experience in a humane and unflappable personality. She ran the local branch of the National Offender Management Service, which occupied the second floor and whose sixteen staff looked after the most serious offenders in the area. Kent, Surrey and Sussex Community Rehabilitation Company, on the first and ground floors, handled the vast majority of more minor offenders. The private firm's plastic sign was the only one on the outside of the building, and Jill liked it that way. Confidentiality was vital to offender management.

Ten minutes late, Verity slid silently into the room, with only the slightest nod of contrition to her boss. Preternaturally pale, with hair the colour of weak tea, she was a Pre-Raphaelite ghost, with her pea-green eyes encircled by translucent lashes. The high cheekbones and graceful nose hinted at beauty, but were let down by a prim, permanently downturned mouth. Tina, a long-serving admin officer, had once memorably observed that Verity always looked as if someone had just crapped on her bathmat.

That image remained with Leticia as Jill summarised the issue.

'As you all know, Neville Rollason is due for release on licence in two weeks.' There was a general muttering around the room at this unwelcome turn of events. 'He's being resettled in our patch, even though his offences were largely committed in the north-east.'

'Why exactly have we inherited him?' asked Adrian Richards, Jill's deputy.

'Quite simply for his own safety. Graham, do you want to explain?'

Morgan steepled his fingers. 'The Home Office in its wisdom agreed to create a new identity for Rollason on his release. There are credible threats to his safety from some of the vigilante organisations.'

'Should we care?' Richards asked. There were some uneasy looks around the table. The psychiatrist, Golob, shook his head in mute disagreement.

Morgan ignored Richards' comment: 'As you know, the nature of his crimes was quite extreme, but the quid pro quo for his co-operation in recovering some of the bodies is that he will be put in a place of safety. He was ghosted into a category D prison for the last month of his sentence, under a pseudonym, with a fictitious criminal record to match.'

'What's the new name?' Jill asked, pen poised over her notes.

'I'm afraid I can't share that in an open meeting.' His eyes flitted from face to face around the table.

'Which prison is he in now?'

'That's confidential too. We can't take any chances.'

'All right, we'll see who needs to know,' Jill said. 'Carry on.'

'We have learned that it is often prison officers who tip off inmates about a particularly unpopular offender within their ranks. Having him living under the false record in the last few weeks of incarceration protects against that.'

'Won't he be recognised?' Leticia asked. Rollason had been sentenced before she was born, but in the recent news coverage about his impending release there were numerous versions of the original scowling dark-eyed mugshots, with his thick quiff of greasy black hair and satanic eyebrows.

Morgan smiled. 'We are hoping not. All the photographs in circulation are of him in his late twenties. He is now sixty-three, has lost most of his hair and what remains is white. At our suggestion he has trimmed and bleached his eyebrows. He now has as forgettable a face as you will ever see. Since an attack by his cellmate in 1994, he's had false teeth too, and some further dental work recently. Given the amount of time he spent in segregation, we're pretty confident no one in this neck of the woods will recognise him.'

'He had a lot of tattoos,' Verity said.

'Well remembered,' Morgan said, his eyes lingering appreciatively on her face. 'He's had them removed entirely, painfully, by laser. It was part of the deal.'

Richards shook his head, his thick grey moustache bristling. 'Personally, I'm not entirely happy about the public purse funding this kind of thing.' He was a bear of a man, a former prison officer in his fifties who had brought with him some of the old-school thinking that was now decidedly out of fashion in the probation system.

Jill Allsop snorted. 'Well, I'm sure most of us agree with you, but we have to maintain a professional detachment. The bottom line is that his false identity may work for him, but it makes it more difficult for us to do our job. Though we may think it beyond our ability to reintegrate someone like him into society in any meaningful way, we have to remind ourselves that our job is to rehabilitate. It is equally obvious that if he was identified and hounded, then any chance of reintegration would be lost, and the chance of reoffending increased.' She looked around as if inviting disagreement. None was voiced, though a great many faces were staring sullenly at their paperwork. 'Now. Inevitably, there will have to be a certain element of subterfuge, given that there will be weekly visits to his home.'

'So where will he live?' Verity asked.

'The Home Office has rented a flat for him, which we need to inspect,' Morgan said. 'But this is important. Only two people here can see that address, or his new name, apart from me – the probation officer appointed to oversee him, and one supervisor. We have learned a lot since the Bulger case.'

Everyone remembered the shocking murder of two-year-old James Bulger in 1993 by two ten-year-olds. They were given new identities when they were released from prison as adults in 2001, but somehow these became known to the press. The publicity was disastrous to the cause of rehabilitation, compounded by news that one of the two had reoffended.

'Who's drawn the short straw, then?' Morgan asked, looking around the table. All eyes were drawn towards Verity, the only one of them who had dealt with a serial killer before. A slight smile played across her pale lips as she turned to Leticia.

'It's you,' she said.

'Me?' Leticia exclaimed.

'Gill and I think you are ready for a challenge of this magnitude. You'll do an excellent job.' It was definitely a smile. Her teeth were visible. Maybe nobody had crapped on her bathmat today.

Leticia didn't know whether to be excited or worried. Rollason would be by far the most high-profile offender she had ever managed. She really didn't know what to expect. For the next hour she basked in the congratulations of her colleagues. However, at the end of the day, when she looked through the files, read the details of his crimes and saw the full depravity of the man, she started to get nervous again.

She went to the bathroom to splash some water on her face and banish some of the images that the court documents had thrown into her imagination. There were three cubicles, of which one was taken. Someone was being violently ill. Initially she was tempted to leave whoever it was to her privacy, but the sheer anguish of the retching made her a little worried. 'Are you all right in there?' Leticia asked. She had to repeat the question once more. There was a short gap in the wheezing and retching, and a ragged voice gasped: 'I'll be fine, just leave me alone.'

'I'll get you a glass of water, that always helps.'

'I've got one in here with me. Just go.' The woman was out of breath, but Leticia now recognised the voice, for all of its edge.

It was Verity.

She left her boss to her anguish, but on her return to her desk sent a private screen-top message to Tina.

Just seen Verity throwing up in the ladies'.

Tina looked across the top of the computer screen at her and raised one eyebrow. She began typing.

She has an eating disorder. Can't keep stuff down. Feel sorry for her.

Leticia typed another message. *Unusually charitable for you*.

> Tragic background, emotional baggage and a
> nasty divorce. I'll tell you all about it one day,
> but she doesn't like people knowing.

Leticia had had no idea that her workaholic boss was struggling with personal issues. In the eighteen months she had been working there she had gathered that Verity was divorced and childless, 'married to the job' as Adrian put it. From the acid comments she let slip about some of their male clients, Leticia assumed that her boss had not been treated well by men. None of that was surprising. The world is full of damaged people. Verity was one of those who seemed to keep aloof, which often indicated buried problems. She didn't socialise with the team. Come to think of it, Leticia had never even seen her eat.

A few minutes later Verity re-emerged into the office, looking even paler than usual. Leticia caught her eye, and the slightest inflection of her eyebrow communicated a very clear message: *don't you dare say anything*.

Leticia gave a small smile. It was meant to be reassurance, but it was freighted with guilt. She felt anyone could read it: *Too late, Verity. Sorry*.

–

Anton sat in Staines police station with his arms crossed opposite PCs Cottesloe and Wickens. To the chef they looked like the classic white British bullet-headed bobbies. Cottesloe looked at the statement in front of him.

'So Mr St Jeanne, your version of events is that you and your girlfriend were sitting in your car on the bridge, listening to music, between roughly half past midnight and quarter to two on the night in question.'

'That's right.'

'And you say that you didn't hear anything during that time, because of your music.'

'Yes.'

'Did you see anybody else, wandering around on the shore of Tagg's Island for example?'

'I didn't notice anybody, but then I might have been busy.' He smiled.

'Because of your girlfriend, do you mean?' Wickens asked.

Anton shrugged, but left the grin in place.

'Are you an exhibitionist?' Cottesloe asked. 'We have a witness who says that there were three people sitting in your car, not two.'

'No that's wrong. It was dark, after all.'

'One of the doors of your BMW was open, the interior light was on,' Cottesloe continued.

'Sorry, what are you trying to say?'

'I need you to be straight with us. Three people were seen in your car. Two black guys in the front, someone else behind.'

'Says who?'

'Witnesses, that's all you need to know. So is your girlfriend actually a big black bloke?' Cottesloe asked.

'Obviously not. Your witness was mistaken.'

'Witnesses plural, which means more than one.'

'I know what it means,' Anton said. 'Don't insult my intelligence.'

There was a pause and then Wickens leaned across the table, his chin jutting. 'I understand you're a chef. Bit of a dab hand with the frying pan,' he said, looking across at

Cottesloe. 'I looked him up on the website.' He turned a belligerent gaze back to Anton. 'Perhaps I should bring the missus around for a meal.'

'You'd be very welcome,' Anton said, and tried to make it sound like he meant it, which he did not. 'Do you enjoy Creole creative fusion?'

The two cops shared a derisive snort. 'Bit posh for the likes of us,' said Cottesloe. 'Fish and chips. That's what I like. Solid British grub.' He locked eyes with Anton.

Anton laughed. 'Fish in batter was brought to the UK in the sixteenth century by western Sephardic Jews who had been living in Holland, having gathered the *pescado frito* recipe from Portugal. With *French* fried potatoes, of course.'

'Bollocks,' said Wickens, folding his arms.

Anton shrugged. He had vouchers in his jacket for a free starter at *J'adore Ça*, but he was damned if he was going to give these two any.

'Do you like Chinese food?' Wickens asked.

Anton stared at the ceiling, wondering how much more of his time they were going to waste.

'He asked you a question, sonny boy,' Cottesloe said, folding his arms to match his colleague.

'Is that relevant to the inquiry? Should I get a solicitor before I answer?'

'Do you or did you ever by any chance employ a Chinese chef?' Wickens asked.

Anton waited a few seconds just in case there was a punchline, but then decided to take it as a straight question 'No, I'm the chef. I have a female sous chef who is from Guyana. But I'm sure she could rustle you up some pork chow mein.'

Cottesloe took over the running. 'See, the thing is, our dead body is Chinese or thereabouts. Maybe there was a Chinese man sitting in your car just before two a.m., before going out for a splash.'

'An involuntary splash from which he never returned,' Wickens added.

'You cannot think, surely—'

'We don't think, we follow the evidence.' Wickens grinned. 'We'd like you to hand over your car keys, so we can see if there's any trace of Chinese. And while we're at it, we want to swab your gob too. Might get the DNA of some of your recipes, eh?'

Chapter Nine

Detective Chief Inspector Craig Gillard sat in the meeting room with PCs Wickens and Cottesloe to go over the witness evidence they had collected. 'So you've found a surprising number of people about along the edge of the river in the small hours, but what in the end was it that they were witness to?'

'Not sure what you're driving at, sir,' Wickens said.

'Okay, a lot of people seem to be aware of a large splash. But there's nothing here to say what that was. It surely is quite possible that it was nothing whatever to do with the body we have found, isn't it?'

'I suppose so,' Cottesloe said, eyeing Wickens.

'I mean it's entirely conceivable,' Gillard said, 'that the body was slipped into the river more quietly at another place, a few hours earlier or later. The splash may simply be irrelevant, and a distraction that wastes time and resources.'

The two uniformed officers said nothing, but Gillard could see an insolent set to their jaws. They clearly didn't appreciate having their assumptions unpicked.

'I'm not saying that you are wrong, but I don't want you to close off your minds to other possibilities.'

'We've only been going where the evidence is leading,' Cottesloe said.

'Speaking of which, did the divers find anything, sir?' Wickens added.

'Nothing of interest so far. They've still got another day.' Gillard looked down at the statements again. 'I see that you have dug up quite a few criminal records and were particularly interested in Anton St Jeanne. He had a few minor skirmishes with the police in his teens. A bit of drug possession, but nothing for over a decade.'

'There were three people seen in his car by a witness,' Cottesloe said. 'He claims there was only him and his girlfriend. I still think we need to get to the bottom of that.'

'The guy on the houseboat has a few convictions and his girlfriend had a police caution a couple of times, all cannabis possession,' Wickens added.

'It might be that whoever was in the car was at the party,' Gillard said, looking through the printouts. 'Gary Tilling is clean. He runs a laptop repair business from home, and perhaps you don't know this, but he has helped us on a few occasions over child pornography that he has spotted on customers' machines. He's mildly autistic, as you may have gathered.'

'I thought it was something like that,' Wickens said.

–

Gillard sat in his office with DC Macintosh. Spread out over the desk were all the photographs that had been taken of the body by CSI as it was recovered, and by Dr Delahaye while conducting the post-mortem. 'Okay, Rainy,' Gillard said. 'Seeing as you are a former medic, I'd like to pick your brain. We know that a lot of force was exerted on this man, something that stopped him breathing. We also

74

know that there are deep impressions on him all over, like he was caught in a net. But Delahaye is insistent he didn't drown.'

'But why was he naked if he wasn't in the water?'

'It's a great question. Along with, why wasn't the net or mesh found wrapped around the body?'

'Someone tore it off?' She was tapping a biro against her teeth.

'Absolutely. And that could only have happened before he was chucked in.'

'So it proves the poor wee bastard was dead before he hit the river, right?'

'Proves is a strong word at this stage. Delahaye has been at pains to stress how many ways there are of dying in water aside from drowning. But yes, unless the netting is found in the river, we're going to assume he was already dead. That would accord with the splash, heard by so many, and the vehicle on the bridge.'

Rainy was now sucking the biro. Gillard could see a fleck of ink on her lip where the top seemed to be leaking. He had heard on the grapevine that Rainy's partner Ross had stayed in Glasgow when she moved down to join the police training scheme at Hendon two years ago. She had brought her fourteen-year-old son Ewan with her. He didn't know exactly whether the relationship was in crisis or not, but either way it must be tough for her. She was a real asset, one he wanted to nurture. Far too many female officers dropped out early in their career.

'I can't think of it being an accident,' she said.

'Neither can I. But let's concentrate on what we can see in front of us. I quite liked the idea that this was a net, but there's a problem.'

'Something fishy?' she asked, grinning. There was a smear of ink on her incisor. Gillard pointed it out, and she laid down the leaking pen and got a tissue from her bag.

He passed across one of the 8 by 10 inch enlargements of the victim's torso. 'Think about any net, around its catch, so to speak. If the force is applied at one end, it wants to equalise the stress by enclosing a sphere. On a body, which has odd shapes, there will always be parts of it slack and parts taut. Some parts of the net would be stretched. Yet this is different. It has a certain rigidity. There's some distortion, but not much.'

'Maybe it is chain-link fencing, that's more rigid.'

Gillard nodded. 'Okay, that might fit the bill. The problem with the fence idea is that neither the gauge nor the pattern of the impressions here matches the most common chain-links. It's typically 50 mm gauge, but the marks on his flesh are smaller and a different shape.' He pointed to one picture of the victim's upper arm, which showed a very deep cyanosed indentation, a tracery of purple. 'Chain-link is a diamond pattern, but not this elongated.'

She looked closely at the photograph. 'Aye, sir, you're very observant.' She continued to dab at her lip with the tissue. 'So maybe it has the tensile characteristic of chain-link, but not the pattern.'

Gillard looked at her appreciatively. 'We're getting somewhere.'

'Are we? I'm just confused.'

'Think about it. This mesh doesn't distort much, so it might be wire or plastic-coated wire.'

'Or rigid plastic.'

76

The detective nodded, and slid her another picture, of the back and buttocks of the victim.

'Although the deepest indentations are on his front and back, there's clearly enough to go right around him. Under his arms, inside of the thighs there are some fainter indications. But nowhere do we see any overlap, with two or more sets of impressions superimposed.'

'That's a canny observation.'

'If he'd stumbled into this mesh, somehow, or been casually chucked in a roll of this stuff by an assailant, however it's done, it would be messy, wouldn't it?'

'Aye, sir. So you're saying it was like a wire body-stocking or something.'

He nodded. 'Made to measure.'

'Fuck, that's scary, sir.'

Gillard nodded, his speculation reaching a terrifying conclusion. 'Gangland punishment, something like that. Ever heard of the iron maiden?'

Chapter Ten

Leticia Mountjoy came to the station at five p.m., just an hour after Anton had left by taxi. He had rung her to tell her what he had said and that she should expect a fairly hostile reception.

'Anton, I'm a probation officer,' she'd said. 'I cannot perjure myself. You have to understand that. I've got a really big case coming up that could be great for me.'

'Tish, please. Don't drop Leroy in it. We're in the clear anyway, it just risks complications.'

Leticia was totally stressed out by the time she walked into Staines police station. Anton and Leroy had a friendship going back to childhood. He was a big guy, charming but intimidating, and she had never trusted him. When Anton had set up his restaurant he'd admitted he'd borrowed some money from Leroy. Leticia really wanted Anton to succeed but there was some kind of taint about Leroy and some of the unsavoury characters he hung around with. She had brought it up with Anton, who had become quite defensive. Her fear was that Anton's loyalty to his childhood friend was stronger than his connection to her.

Now, she really didn't know what to do for the best. The same two uniformed police officers that Anton had mentioned, PCs Cottesloe and Wickens, were there. They offered her coffee, which was vile, and took her into a rather pleasant interview room, all pot plants and fabric settees, which sounded quite different from the dark basement in which Anton said he'd been questioned.

'Ms Mountjoy,' Cottesloe began. 'Thank you for making time to help us try to get to the bottom of what happened to this unfortunate man in his last few hours.'

'No problem, happy to help,' she said. This wasn't at all what Anton had described happening to him.

'I understand you are the girlfriend of Mr Anton St Jeanne?' Cottesloe asked.

'Yes.'

'May I ask for how long you two have been going out together?'

'About eighteen months.'

The two policemen went through the arrival and departure times of the car, which Leticia knew only hazily, and then asked her whether she had heard a splash just before two a.m.

'I can honestly say that I didn't. The music was quite loud.'

'What was playing, do you remember?' Wickens asked.

She hadn't expected this. 'I couldn't tell you, to be honest. It wasn't my kind of thing.' It was a lie, but a harmless one surely. She just couldn't be sure what if anything Anton had been asked about this.

'Where were you sitting, Ms Mountjoy?'

'In the front seat, next to my boyfriend.' A small lie, but surely not important. She had been sitting in the back, behind the driver's seat.

Cottesloe was reading a handwritten document in front of him and looked up. 'Had you met the Chinese man in the back seat before?'

Her look of bafflement must have been obvious. She had no idea what Anton must have said. After what seemed an age she said, 'There was no Chinese man in the back seat.'

'You don't seem very sure,' Cottesloe said.

'It's a pretty simple question, wouldn't you say, Jim?' Wickens asked, earning a nod from Cottesloe. The cops both stared at her, looking down at the papers in front of them and up at her. 'No one in the back seat,' Wickens began to write.

She licked her lips. Perjury starts with small beginnings.

'That's right,' she whispered.

She submitted to the cheek swab and gave various details about her address and contact numbers. 'I'm sorry to have to ask this,' Wickens said, finally. 'But may we borrow your mobile phone for half an hour?'

'Why do you need it?'

'It's actually to help you,' Wickens said, with a smile. 'We'll use cell site analysis to prove your location. It just helps us be sure that you have been telling the truth.'

'But you only need the number for that. You want to look at my messages and emails as well, don't you?'

'No, of course not,' Cottesloe said. 'But it would make things faster.'

Leticia looked from one to the other. Anton hadn't mentioned having to hand over his phone, so she didn't understand why they would pick on her. She brought out her phone, and then realised that she couldn't hand it over. She had exchanged a couple of emails with Jill Allsop about Neville Rollason. She was pretty certain that those emails didn't include any of the confidential details, but she was going to try something.

'I'm sorry, I can't give you my phone.'

'That's very unfortunate, Ms Mountjoy,' Cottesloe said. 'It doesn't look good does it? What have you got to hide?'

Leticia delved into her handbag, and finally found the business card that DI Morgan had given her. 'Ring him first, he'll explain.' She hoped that she had done the right thing. The card mentioned his rank but made no mention of the fact that he was Special Branch.

The two police officers looked at each other and, excusing themselves, walked out of the room.

—

'She must be a snitch, and Morgan is her handler,' Cottesloe said, as he took out his phone.

'That makes me more suspicious, not less,' Wickens said. 'I don't know what she could be doing that is more important than us investigating a dead body.'

Cottesloe made the call and got straight through to Morgan. 'Sir, sorry to bother but can I just ask whether you are running an informer called Leticia Mountjoy?'

Morgan seemed confused for a minute. 'The name's familiar, hang on. What's it about?'

Cottesloe explained where she had been seen. 'She may be a witness to a death, you know that body in the Thames, but she doesn't want to hand over her phone.'

'I remember now. I'm sorry, Constable, you have to lay off her. Let her keep her phone.'

Cottesloe tried to suppress his groan of disappointment. 'Sir, may I ask what your interest is in her? It's just that it may impede our investigation.'

'I'm not at liberty to tell you why, except to say that it is a Special Branch matter. I'm not sure who you are reporting to, but if you want to contest this, it needs to go up to the chief constable.'

Gillard, tipped off by the two PCs, had emailed a request for details of the Special Branch interest in Leticia Mountjoy from Chief Constable Alison Rigby. If there was something bigger going on involving her, he needed to avoid treading on any sensitive toes. He assumed it was unlikely to concern her involvement in probation work, but couldn't imagine what else it might be. Witness protection was a possibility, perhaps. He waited in his office doing paperwork after the end of his shift, hoping for a reply. It was gone seven and he was about to give up when the chief constable rang him. 'Craig, I'm sorry I can't give you the information you requested. But trust me, it's much less exciting than you might imagine.'

Feeling frustrated and dissatisfied, Gillard logged out, locked his office and drove home. When he got there at eight o'clock, Sam was sitting in front of the TV, fully dressed. This was good news. The last few times he'd come in at this hour, she'd been in a bathrobe with little sign she'd strayed far from bed. 'How was your day?' he asked.

'It was good. I've been to the gym, and my one-to-one psychotherapy was really helpful today. Have you made any progress on the dead man in the river?'

He was pleased that she had begun to ask about his work again. Sam's near-death experience in an abduction a few months ago had put her into a very dark place mentally. The psychologist said that her therapy was going well, and the group PTSD talk sessions were certainly helping to exorcise her personal demons. He had noticed that she seemed a little less clingy than she had in the early weeks, too. He adored holding her, and feeling her close, but sometimes her need for it had been a little too intense.

'Are you feeling well enough to come with me to see Trish tomorrow?' he asked. Gillard's elderly aunt had been in a coma in Redhill Hospital for weeks. The bleed on her brain had been stopped, but she was still in a critical condition. Although the nursing staff said she was completely unaware of her surroundings, Gillard had found time to drop in to see her twice a week. She wasn't his favourite person, but even when unconscious she managed to exert a powerful feeling of guilt over him.

'Yes, why not?' Sam said. 'I'm prepared for horror stories. I'm going to watch *Panorama* tonight, about Neville Rollason,' she said proudly.

'Are you sure you're going to be okay with that? He's a nasty piece of work. I read what he did to some of his victims and believe me you don't want to know the details.'

'It's BBC One, it's not going to be too graphic,' she said. 'But I'm amazed they're letting him out.'

Gillard sighed. 'The canteen is full of talk about it. In the end it's a question of quid pro quo. If a killer finally decides to let a family know where their child is buried, there has to be some kind of reward.'

'But to let him out!'

'I know, I know. The Parole Board say he's better. Won't reoffend. But who knows.'

Sam harrumphed, and pulled her knees up onto the settee. 'Come and watch it with me.'

When the programme started it showed a presenter standing before the brooding front gate of HMP Wakefield in West Yorkshire.

'Later this week, from this grim high-security prison behind me, one of the most notorious killers Britain has ever seen will be released. Neville Rollason, now in his sixties, will once again be free to roam the streets of Britain.' A black-and-white mugshot of Rollason filled the screen. It was one of the many pictures taken at the time of his arrest, and showed his lips curled and dark eyebrows flexed as if in some private joke.

'The question has to be: is there ever a right time to release a prisoner like this?'

Chapter Eleven

The man now known as Neil Wright was watching the same *Panorama* programme at Spring Hill open prison and enjoying it. On the screen were his own features from decades before. The presenter then described several of the murders of which his alter ego Neville Rollason had been convicted. Images of the streets in the north-east of England from which the victims disappeared were shown, streets that were still familiar to him. Places that he visited frequently in his dreams, where he found himself cleaning away in retrospect the forensic clues that in the 1980s had sunk him.

The presenter was now in full condemnatory style. 'Is it right to release this man, a man who has only recently shown any remorse for the brutal killings he committed more than thirty years ago in a different century? I put this question to a senior retired judge, Lord Waverley, who as Mr Justice Waverley put away many of Britain's most notorious criminals.'

'Not that idiot,' the prisoner muttered to himself. He toyed with muting the TV so he didn't have to listen again to the voice of the appeal court judge. Waverley had chaired the Parole Board hearing in Wakefield Prison in 2004 that quashed his first appeal for release. He was on his little list, near the top. Wright knew the chambers in London's Lincoln's Inn where Waverley had worked and still occasionally returned for drinks and meals with former colleagues.

The patrician features of the elderly lord showed him sitting in a book-lined study. 'It's entirely understandable that many people say that a dreadful offender like Rollason should never again see the light of day. However, we have to balance society's need to punish this man against the important goal of rehabilitation. We must hold out the hope of release for those who admit their crimes and show some remorse. It may not be the most important point, but it is still essential to note that Britain's overstretched prisons would become ungovernable if those within were offered no hope of release.'

'Too bloody right,' muttered Wright. He didn't yet have a residential address for the noble lord, but once he got to use the Internet, that shouldn't be too hard.

'But for some,' the presenter said, turning back to the camera, 'revenge is much more important than rehabilitation.' The screen then showed a silhouette of a man against a drawn curtain. He appeared to be wearing a jacket and a baseball cap. The presenter's voiceover lowered to a conspiratorial whisper: 'This man, who we are calling Dave, is a vigilante. He belonged for several years to one of many organisations that are involved in the entrapment of child abusers. These organisations normally pass on information to the police. However, Dave and some of his friends have a more radical agenda, one which would put them the wrong side of the law. I arranged to meet Dave in the back room of a pub in the Midlands. His words are spoken by an actor to protect his identity.'

'It is wrong that evil men like Neville Rollason should ever be released from prison,' the actor's voice said, softly. 'He's never really been punished, has he? Prison isn't really a punishment any more. Those segregation cells are luxury, really. They have TV and books and everything.'

'What are your plans?' the presenter asked. Wright thought he detected a note of eagerness in his voice.

'Well, let's put it this way. After we've finished with him, he won't be up to any more of his old tricks.'

'Is that a threat of violence?'

There was a laugh. 'You can take it any way you want. But it will be justice.'

Wright snarled and pointed a finger at the screen as if the vigilante could hear him. 'You'll not get me, mate.'

The presenter said: 'In Mr Rollason's case it seems that his release by the Parole Board is closely tied to his agreeing to identify places where he buried the bodies of two of his victims. So what do the families of the victims think?' The TV cut to a living room, where a frail elderly couple sat on a settee, the woman holding a handkerchief close to her nose. 'Mrs Cooper,' the presenter intoned. 'Describe what it's been like for you to deal with the knowledge that the killer of your son will be released in a few days.'

'I can't believe it,' she said. 'My Daniel is lost to me for ever. He's got no life, and we've only got grief. But somehow this… beast is to be let out.'

'Was it not a comfort to you to be told of your son's final resting place?'

The woman's already-lined face folded in upon itself even further at the question and she was unable to speak. But her husband, his arm squeezing tighter around her shoulder, said: 'It's true, it gave us some comfort, but if we knew that the murderer would be allowed out, we would never have agreed. It's barbaric.'

Wright rocked back in his chair and laughed at the screen. One week and one day, that's all he had to wait.

'I understand you were notified of the release date by the Ministry of Justice only last week,' the presenter said.

'That's right,' Mrs Cooper said. 'It's a horrible shock. I just hope no other mother has to go through what I've been through over the last thirty-five years. My son would be nearly forty-seven now.'

'I tell you what else,' her husband said. 'I don't agree with Rollason being given a new identity. That's just not right. That means he could soon be anywhere.'

'That's right.' The prisoner chuckled, turning off the TV. 'That's absolutely right. Anywhere I bloody want.'

—

Elvira Hart was just getting ready to go to bed when she heard a noise like footsteps outside on the gravel path. Nudging aside the lace curtains and peering from her houseboat window, she couldn't immediately see anything. She was moored on the northern side of Ash Island, and though it could be quite busy with pleasure craft during the day, this late at night it was very unusual to hear anything nearby apart from ducks and geese. Neither of the neighbouring houseboats were occupied. The owners were abroad and had both left her keys. As far as she knew she was the only one currently resident on this side of the island. She checked the brass clock on the mantelpiece. It had just gone midnight.

She opened the casement window in the lounge a crack so she could hear better. There was nothing to be seen in the river itself. She thought about opening the front door to look out on the path but felt a cord of fear in her gut. The dead body on the shoreline just three days ago had overshadowed her dreams ever since. She was just about to close the window when she heard more footsteps – and something else. It sounded like the low whirr of a bicycle being wheeled. She crossed to the other side of the room, switched on the porch light and looked out of the tiny leadlight window next to her front door. Yes, there was a man, with a bike and a head-torch. This was a private island, and he shouldn't be there, especially at night. Elvira tried to pluck up courage to open the front door, to chastise this person for scaring her. But as the seconds rolled by she found she didn't dare.

Things had changed in the last three days. She had told the two policemen who had come to interview her that she never worried about her safety. It was true, when she herself had walked or run in parks alone at night, that there had never been any frightening incidents. She had always projected self-confidence and capability. But things were different now. Suddenly she realised that the discovery of that poor man's body had robbed her of a freedom. A freedom from worry and anxiety. She just hoped and prayed that this didn't cast her back to the dark days, to the terror that had almost destroyed her. She was eighty-one, but she could fight.

She took a deep breath, pulled open the door, and went out to confront her fear.

Chapter Twelve

Tuesday

It had been a quiet night at Staines police station, that's what the duty log showed when Sergeant Vince Babbage arrived at Kingston Road to start his shift on the desk at seven a.m. For once there was no one in the cells. He was just thinking about going to get a coffee when a call was passed through from the control room. A report of a suspicious intruder on private land.

'Righto,' Babbage said when the call was patched through.

'Hello. My name is Elvira Hart, and I'd like to report an incident from last night.' In cultured tones she went on to describe the noises she had heard and then how she had opened the door to confront the intruder.

'Madam, I really don't think that was a good idea,' Babbage said, scratching at his ginger beard. 'You shouldn't put yourself at risk. You should call 999.'

'And wait half an hour for you to arrive? Well, I did open the door and I saw this rather scruffy individual with a bicycle and head-torch. I asked him what he thought he was doing terrifying residents at this time of night.'

'What did he say?'

'It was most peculiar. He said he had come to lay some flowers on the water for the dead man.'

Babbage put down his pen. 'Sorry, I'm not with you here. What dead man?'

'I told the operator. I'm the woman who discovered the dead body here on Ash Island three days ago. I was interviewed by your colleagues about it. It was just by my houseboat. Now I have this strange man coming along late at night, claiming to lay flowers for the victim.'

'That's very distressing for you,' Babbage said.

'Well indeed, but don't you think it might be pertinent to the case? As I understand it no one has been arrested for this murder, and whoever this person was knew exactly where the body had been found. I don't think that had been publicised.'

Babbage conceded the point, thanked the lady for her public-spirited intervention and said that an officer would be round to interview her later that day.

–

Gary Tilling heard the letter box clack and shuffled out to the front door in his slippers. There was a sheaf of post. Not normal for a Tuesday. More like a Thursday delivery. Opening the envelopes, the first thing he saw was that the service was due on the stairlift. He'd ring them up today and make an appointment, even though she'd not been able to use it for five years. He sometimes wondered if her mobility would ever improve. Mum's health had got worse and worse over the years. Osteoporosis, type two diabetes, and now ankylosing spondylitis on her spine. Some days she could hardly move. Looking after her had occupied more and more of his time.

Fortunately, she had found a surprising array of new hobbies over the Internet, things that with his technical knowledge he had been able to help with. A bedridden woman thirty years ago would have been able to do nothing but watch TV. But now she was able to roam the world, talk to people and even earn a kind of living. As the kettle boiled, he picked up the teapot and warmed it carefully, then poured boiling water over a scoop of lapsang souchong leaves. He then picked up a large package, the size and weight of a bale of toilet rolls, which had come from South Korea yesterday, the usual Monday delivery. He broke open the package and pulled out a crisply wrapped cellophane packet, one of a hundred within. This was a new flavour. He couldn't read the Korean script, but the picture of what looked like a sea vegetable made it clear. He wondered how his mother would get on with it. He looked at his watch. She would do a little practice this morning and then was due on screen this afternoon at what she called Chinese dentist: two thirty. It was her little joke, one that she never ceased to find amusing.

There was one final letter, a small, neatly handwritten envelope, posted in Buckinghamshire on Friday. It was addressed to his mother using her old married name. That was weird. After the divorce the whole family had gone back to her maiden name. He took it up to her, with her tea, and went downstairs.

The scream he heard from her a minute later had him racing back up to see what was the matter.

–

Detective Inspector Claire Mulholland had set off earlier than usual for her shift at Surrey Police's Mount Browne headquarters. After setting a breakfast for her teenage kids, she had to give her plasterer husband Baz a lift to his first day on a new contract, while his van was being serviced. 'I've been booked for a week on this job,' Baz said, as they skirted the high brick wall encircling the Holdersham Estate near Walton-on-Thames.

'I didn't realise you meant here. So you're working for the sheikh?'

'Yep. It's billionaires' alley round here. It's a bit of a rush job, and they're paying double time. It's got to be done by this time next week. Jakes recommended me.'

'Ah. He's the eccentric one, isn't he?'

'He's all right. Hadn't seen him for months until this. Dead easy to work with, if a little boring. Never get a peep out of him. He's got them things in his lugs all day. Classical music. He let me listen to it once. Sounds like an orchestra tumbling down a hill.' He laughed.

'So do you have to keep your radio turned off?' Baz's own device, a much bespattered item, was sitting on a dust sheet in the boot, along with his tools.

'No, but I keep it low.' Baz turned to her. 'I forgot to mention. Jakes was interviewed by some of your lot last week.'

'What do you mean "some of my lot"?' she asked in mock offence.

'You know, the filth, the Old Bill, the pigs.' Barry grinned at her. It was part of their family repartee for Barry to slag the police off as corrupt while she denigrated him as an unskilled labourer. The kids loved it. When they were younger they would, at her instigation, pile on him on the sofa while he was watching TV to make an arrest, with nee-nah siren noises and the aid of Dexter the overexcitable Irish wolfhound. Barry, affable as ever, always agreed to be locked in the cupboard under the stairs with the vacuum cleaner for a couple of minutes.

'It's about this body that was found on the island in the Thames.'

'Ah, Craig's just been given that case. Did Jakes see something?'

'Nah.' Baz crinkled his face sceptically. 'Jakes never sees anything beyond the edge of the trowel. He's away with the fairies half the time, I tell you. Did you know that he's got a master's in philosophy from the Open University?'

'What's he doing as a plasterer, then?' she asked, taunting him again. 'Playing with the great unwashed.'

'He went bonkers for a while,' Baz said, picking from the back of his neck a dried lump of plaster that he'd missed in the shower. 'Couldn't hack it.'

'Bonkers: you are so PC, Baz. The full empathic mental health lexicon.'

'I love it when you use big words, Claire.' He laughed, and kissed her on the cheek. 'Okay. Technically, Jakes was doolally at first, then he went bonkers, and now he's just fucking mad.'

Claire laughed as they arrived outside the gatehouse, guarded by ten-foot-high wrought-iron gates and stone lions on plinths.

'Right, this is me.' Baz turned to her. 'Jakes does have a bit of an excuse, though. His family fell apart. No mum or dad, just a mad sister.'

'When was that?' Claire asked.

'Long time ago, when he was little.' Baz got out of the car and picked up his tool bag and radio from the boot.

'Be kind to him, then,' Claire called through the open window.

'I am,' Baz replied over his shoulder as he strode up to the gatehouse. 'I always am.'

Half an hour later Baz was standing in the shell of a newly constructed single-storey building. Jakes told him that it was to be a reptile house. The building was partially divided up by numerous stud walls, each of which had a large low window-hole. Baz guessed that those apertures would house glass tanks for the creatures.

'Is he turning this place into a safari park, then?' Baz asked.

'No,' Jakes replied. 'He said it's not going to be open to the public. It's mainly for conservation.'

'So what do you know about this van Steenis bloke?'

Jakes chuckled. 'Quite a lot. I read about him. Born in Southern Rhodesia, as it was then, now Zimbabwe. He founded his own bunch of mercenaries and made friends with some dodgy dictators.'

'That's a good way to get rich.'

'Yeah, but he doesn't own this place. He just manages it. He used to be employed by Mobutu Sese Seko, the Zairean ruler, to eliminate his political enemies.'

'Jesus!'

'That was decades ago,' Jakes said. 'Having met van Steenis, I find it hard to believe. He really cares for animals, you can see that.' He turned to look at Baz. 'Back in the early Eighties, this used to be a preparatory school called St Thomas's. I went here for a term when I was six. Awful place.' He cringed as if in remembered pain. 'The old swimming pool I tried to learn to swim in is going to be part of a covered enclosure for the Nile crocodiles.'

The plasterers worked hard without a break until early afternoon. Baz watched in admiration as Jakes strode about in his stilts, covering up the ceiling fibre-tape between the plasterboard prior to the main skim. Baz had never got on with stilts. He had tried the two-foot-high metal platforms, which are clipped to the boots and secured by retaining straps to the calf. They had made him feel clumsy. Still, seeing Jakes, he had to admit it was hard to beat for quick work on ceiling scrim. Baz, doing the main overhead skim, worked off a more laborious framework of inverted milk crates with planks on them. Jakes was a bit of a prodigy with the trowel, Baz had to admit. Just the right amount of pressure, just the right forearm movement. Barely a ripple disturbed the surface. From his apparently effortless rhythm, it was hard to guess that Jakes suffered from tennis elbow, caused by the relentless weight of the wet plaster on the rectangular hawk, held always in his left hand, ready to be scooped up and trowelled on.

It was gone two when Baz called a halt and burrowed into the plaster-spattered knapsack containing his packed lunch and flask. He went outside and lay on a patch of grass, soaking up the sun. Jakes, who never ate while working, wandered off, still wearing his earbuds. Baz had just finished the last of his coffee when he saw Jakes running back. He looked distressed, his gangly arms and legs disordered.

'What is it, mate?' Baz asked.

'You've got to come and see this,' Jakes said, clearly a little out of breath. 'You're not going to believe it.'

Chapter Thirteen

Detective Chief Inspector Craig Gillard had been stuck at the computer all morning. He had been puzzling over the discrepancy between the number of people who had been seen in chef Anton St Jeanne's white BMW by witnesses – three – and the claim by the man himself that only he and his girlfriend Leticia had been there. Did Mr St Jeanne have something to hide? The search of his car had turned up nothing of obvious interest. The boot had contained some decorating materials, and an unopened wine box. There was no trace of human hair, blood or anything else that would get a crime scene investigator excited. Samples from the seats were currently being tested to see if there was any match to the DNA of the dead man. That would take another day to come through.

The detective often took an elliptical approach to a difficult problem, so he had spent quite a while on Companies House, looking up the details of ASJ (Kingston) Ltd, the company that owned the restaurant *J'adore Ça*.

The listing details showed it had been incorporated four years previously, with Mr St Jeanne as sole proprietor. It had made a loss of increasing size every year, starting at £25,000 and finally exceeding £75,000. Gillard was no expert on corporate finance, but it seemed to him that unless something improved, *J'adore Ça* was heading for bankruptcy. There was something else significant too, perhaps the most interesting information he had gleaned so far. Just over eighteen months ago, an additional director had been appointed, with a forty-nine per cent share in the business. His name was Mr L. Churchill Jenkins. That name didn't flag up anything significant in Gillard's mind, but the address of the director certainly did. It was Effingham House, a notorious tower block in south London, rife with drug dealing. When Gillard checked across on the Police National Computer, he found that the flat number mentioned corresponded to a known gangster by the name of Leroy Churchill Jenkins, better known as Leroy Ceejay, a man with ambitions in the world of rap, but more significant achievements in the arena of drugs. Cross-referencing to the man's criminal record, he saw that Jenkins was thought to be head of the Mambas, an organised crime group with its own amphetamine-manufacturing operation.

He sat back in his chair with his hands behind his head. Leroy Ceejay was making a heap of money, that much was clear. To make it clean wasn't easy, and probably a bit more complicated than actually manufacturing the required chemicals. But a business like a restaurant, with high overheads, a lot of them in cash, would do the laundry trick just fine. Gillard could imagine how it would work. Leroy has £100,000 of cash gleaned from drug sales. He uses the cash to pay some of the legitimate bills the restaurant has incurred: local food suppliers, drinks wholesalers, casual staff. Meanwhile, Anton would use his legitimate bank accounts to pay Leroy a hefty salary for recruitment, for security services and so forth, equalling the amount that Leroy had put in. Whether the restaurant made an overall profit or not was less important than the amount of dirty money it made clean.

Of course, none of that would necessarily mean that Anton St Jeanne's late-night party on the bridge, whether two people or three, was connected with the death of a so far unidentified Asian man. Gillard decided that he would get his financial specialist colleague Detective Sergeant Shireen Corey-Williams to examine the books. He meanwhile was going to take a closer look at the restaurant itself.

Could the Special Branch interest in Leticia Mountjoy be connected to an inquiry into her boyfriend's business partner, Leroy Ceejay? It was an intriguing idea. There was no point asking the chief constable. He would instead make some discreet enquiries with the NCA. The National Crime Agency, Alison Rigby's old stamping ground, had first dibs on all the major criminals operating in drugs, trafficking, weapons and cybercrime and would know if some major operation was being undertaken on Leroy Ceejay. They had a tough job to do and were often reluctant to share information with what they called plods, which basically meant anyone else in the police.

–

In the mist of a summer's morning Ash Island was like an imagining from Arthurian legend. The tree-clad slopes rustled faintly in the breeze, and quicksilver ripples bounced between the many houseboats and barges. A single heron flapped lazily into the air, turning west away from the sun, as Gillard and Rainy Macintosh crossed from Hurst Meadows park on the walkway that ran across the East Molesey weir. Only the faint hum of traffic on

Hampton Court Road on the other side of the river intruded on the bucolic image.

The detectives were following up on a report from the divers. They had found nothing of significance in two days of searching both sides of the river. They had covered a half-mile upstream down to where the body had been found, and fifty yards beyond. No point going below that. Dead bodies may drift but they don't swim. There was plenty of junk and detritus, but most of it was clearly old. Too old, rotted or weathered to have found its way into the water in the last few days. No netting or mesh, no recently discarded clothing or footwear. The weir was clear, the flow only a trickle with the recent lack of rain. There were no industrial water intakes or other fast-water sources nearby that could be implicated in the injuries found on the victim. In the entire two days, the only thing of interest wasn't in the water, but above it. The team leader had emailed a photograph to Gillard.

Gillard and Rainy crouched on the aluminium walkway that ran along the top of the weir to Ash Island and stared at the pattern. It was diamond shaped, with a 2 cm by 1 cm gauge.

'It's not this,' Gillard said. 'Wrong size, and too rigid.'

'It couldn't be wrapped around him either,' she said.

'There are no factories or workshops nearby with the kind of equipment that could have been used on our victim. Uniforms have done a thorough trawl.'

'It doesn't have to be local, does it?'

'No. If he was chucked out of the car, he could have been killed anywhere.'

'Aye, but in that case why ditch him, here, on Midsummer's Night of all times. He's bound to be seen.'

'Okay, it was worth a try. Now to take a look at the body. Maybe that will clear some of the fog surrounding this case.'

–

For Rainy Macintosh a trip to the mortuary was like a reprise of her previous job. As a junior doctor in Glasgow she had on occasion escorted those unfortunates who had died either in theatre or on the ward and passed them over to the technicians who would allot them space in the huge chilled storage unit. She and a colleague would agree the cause of death and write up the death certificate. That was usually the end of the story from her perspective, although she had often to talk to bereaved families. But now, visiting the dead was the start of a process, and one with a very different end in mind. To find out how this person had died, and if it was accident or an act of malevolence.

Walking into Kingston Hospital mortuary with DCI Gillard, she felt quite excited at the opportunity to deploy some of her medical knowledge, and to meet the rather forbidding Dr David Delahaye. A technician showed the two detectives into the examination room where the consultant forensic pathologist was bent over a gurney, looking into a partially opened body bag.

He looked up at their approach, brief introductions were made, and they turned their attention to the corpse that three days previously had been found washed up on an island in the Thames.

The photographs had not prepared Rainy for the shock of seeing the victim, cartoonishly swollen into an incandescent blimp of fury. She was astounded by the intensity of the cyanosis that still marked the upper body. The man's chest, shoulders and face were a livid mauve overlaid with a regular purple diamond pattern, so precise it looked almost tattooed into the skin. His eyes were so swollen they had almost popped out of his face. Combined with eyeballs rimmed in blood from broken capillaries and the laugh-like grimace, he had a demonic appearance. The pathologist's Y-shaped chest cut and the ear-to-ear scalp incision, performed as part of the post-mortem and now roughly sewn back, were bloodless by comparison.

'So Ms Macintosh, in your previous life dealing with the living, have you ever seen anything remotely like this?' Delahaye asked.

'No, nothing.'

'What actually causes these purple marks to remain in the skin after death?' Gillard asked.

'Thousands of ruptured capillaries, what we call petechiae. Leaking blood, basically. It produces a rather graphic lividity, doesn't it?'

'Designer contusions,' Rainy said. 'Even more impressive than my own varicose veins post-pregnancy. But I cannot imagine what crushed him to produce this.'

'That indeed is the $64,000 question,' Delahaye said. 'The detective chief inspector and myself have been whizzing emails back and forth for several days on this very subject. I do think the idea of an industrial element is quite persuasive given the amount of force that must have been used. I've been reading around in the literature, and there are chest-compression injuries here that easily exceed those caused by Hillsborough, the crowd crushes at Mecca during the haj, and similar events.'

'Have you been able to calculate the force?' Rainy asked.

'It is not so easy. Human ribs are not made in a factory, and do not have a standard tolerance. Detaching them through gradual pressure, as appears to have happened here, would depend on numerous bodily factors in addition to the force applied. However, I am reasonably confident that nothing less than half a metric tonne could do this damage. A car toppling from a jack, that kind of thing. Of course, that is most unlikely in this case. Very little car maintenance is undertaken in the nude, or so I am reliably informed.' His eyes twinkled as he looked at Rainy.

'What about this mesh suit he seemed to have been wearing?' she asked.

'Ah yes, Craig's idea of the iron maiden. A medieval instrument of torture.' He glanced at Gillard, his indulgent smile conveying scepticism.

'It's possible isn't it?' Rainy asked.

Delahaye laughed. 'Well, I suppose so. I looked it up last night after Craig first suggested it. The first references were in the nineteenth century, of medieval iron coffins lined with iron spikes. However, historians reckon they are mythical because of the lack of contemporary mention in the medieval era. Of course, just because they didn't actually exist doesn't automatically mean no one could invent one now. Certainly, the pattern and depth of contusions indicates that pressure seems to have come from above and below – assuming the victim was prone. It would have been nasty. However, I'm less convinced that this mesh is the source of the force applied, rather than having merely transmitted it to the body. It's quite possible the netting was just being used to restrain the victim while he was crushed.' He looked at the two detectives, his metal-framed glasses glinting in the cold clinical lights.

'It's your job to ascertain whether it may be a gangland punishment of some sort. That's beyond my remit. All I would do is to point to the absence of any conventional signs of violence. Punches, kicks, stab wounds and so forth. A very disciplined gang, I would say.'

'What about the broken nose?' Gillard said.

'Sustained pressure not trauma,' Delahaye replied. 'You get a nosebleed either way, of course. Gangland or not, I'd be happier to know what type of machine did this, whether it be hydraulic press, stamping equipment or something else, before passing judgement.'

'Rainy, perhaps we can make that a project for you,' Gillard said. 'Research the type of industrial machines that can cause this injury. Everything, from forklifts to hydraulic presses, where gradual pressure is possible. Maybe start with the Health and Safety Executive, see what guidance they can offer.'

'That sounds like quite a wee task.'

'I'm sure you can get me some ideas by tomorrow morning.'

'Oh aye, and I'll have figured out cold fusion by teatime,' she muttered.

Gillard shared a look with a smirking Delahaye, then asked: 'Can we have a look at the rest of him?'

'Of course,' Delahaye said, undoing the zip on the body bag to the bottom.

The florid mauve patches were less marked further down the body, but the tops of the thighs and both kneecaps bore vivid purple diamond-shaped impressions. 'You may recall from my report that the pressure on this kneecap was enough to snap the patella. That takes quite some doing.'

'Whoever did this to him was very imaginative about it,' Gillard said.

'I do agree,' Delahaye said, then looked to Gillard. 'So have you made any more progress on finding who it was?'

'A little. We have evidence of a splash, a little upstream from where the body was found, witnessed by a number of people at around two a.m., which is three hours before he was found. The location of that splash would be a possible site for a body to be thrown out of the boot of a car. We have a number of active leads we are pursuing—'

'Right, so not actually much progress then,' Delahaye said, grinning conspiratorially at Rainy. 'Let's turn him over, shall we?' He called over a technician, who helped turn the body face down. The cyanosed impression of a diamond grid on his back, shoulders, buttocks and thighs was extremely clear. Whatever it was he had been crushed against had broken thousands of capillaries across his body.

'There is one idea I had, which you will probably consider is stupid,' Rainy said. 'This could have been a sex game gone wrong.'

'Very wrong, I would have thought,' Gillard said.

'Och, you'd be gobsmacked what we saw in A&E. You can never say anything is too extreme for people to have a go at. The items they will insert, the inventiveness. You wouldnae believe it.'

'Yes,' said Delahaye with unusual enthusiasm. 'When I was a medical student, I was present for a champagne celebration. Including the removal in theatre of the empty Krug bottle from a middle-aged woman.'

'Aye, I've done a couple of those,' Rainy said dismissively. 'You have to drill through the bottle to break the airlock—'

'Then squirt some baby oil into the vaginal canal so you can ease it out,' Delahaye said.

'No, this is much more extreme,' Rainy said, shaking her head.

Gillard, open-mouthed, looked from one to the other. 'You're not kidding.'

'What I'm thinking,' Rainy said, 'is that partial asphyxiation is a known method of enhancing the power of an orgasm. So the victim dresses up in his own mesh playsuit—'

'—and gets crushed to death,' Gillard said. 'What fun! And then gets tossed into the river by someone else who, incidentally, pinches his playsuit.'

'Aye, sir,' Rainy said. 'I said it was stupid.'

—

Claire Mulholland knew that Baz had enjoyed an interesting day from the texts he had sent her. When she arrived to pick him up, shortly after six, he was full of the story of the large reptile house that he and his colleague were preparing. 'That is going to be some serious zoo,' he told her, as he sat himself down in the passenger seat of her car, his dusty overalls and a large plastic carrier bag between his knees. 'But it's just for the sheikh's own pleasure.'

'What did you see?'

'Well, by trespassing a bit, we saw the crocodile pool, and an enclosure that was marked up for a Komodo dragon. They are supposed to be eight feet long, but we couldn't find the bloody thing anywhere. There were lots of dead hollow trees for him to hide inside. But the thing that Jakes got deranged is that under one of the older buildings he went back to, a basement room that he had plastered last week…' He stopped and looked at her. 'Actually, I'm not supposed to be telling you any of this. Van Steenis made us sign a non-disclosure agreement.'

'Why?'

'He's frightened of animal rights activists getting wind of what he's doing.'

'He'd have to have permission for the animals he's bringing in anyway,' Claire said. 'If what he's doing is legal, he shouldn't have anything to worry about.'

Baz inclined his head in agreement. 'Okay. Well, this basement room has now got a big lock on the door, and a kind of sliding hatch, so you can see in from outside. And a kind of urinal-type gulley leading to a drain.'

'Sounds like a zoo enclosure to me.'

'Except there is a brand-new mattress, still in its plastic, on the floor.'

'What are you saying, Baz?'

'It's a prison cell, that's what Jakes thinks.'

–

When Cottesloe and Wickens arrived at his home, Michael Jakes came to the door in a scruffy threadbare bathrobe. He had clearly emerged from the shower to answer the doorbell and, by the lumps of plaster still visible in his hair, was only partway through the process.

The two constables sat in the same places on the settee as before, but this time the small grey cat decided to snuggle up between them. 'Mr Jakes, have you been wandering around at night on Ash Island?' Cottesloe asked.

'I tied a bunch of flowers on the bridge for the man who died.'

'That's the bridge to Tagg's Island. I'm asking you about Ash Island, the next one down. We had a lady complain about an intruder.'

Jakes nodded and scratched absent-mindedly at a lump of plaster on his cheek. 'She had a go at me, yeah. I told her I was sorry.'

'Why were you there?'

'I'd made a little paper boat and wanted to set it in the river at the place where he was found. I'd already thrown in a home-made wreath, off the bridge.'

The two officers briefly glanced at each other. 'But why were you doing it at night?' Wickens asked.

'I work during the day.'

Cottesloe chuckled sceptically. 'Come on, you don't work until midnight, do you?'

'I think better at night.'

'Doubtful,' Cottesloe said. 'If you did, you would realise that going sneaking about on a private island at midnight would give the residents the heebie-jeebies.'

Jakes stroked his chin thoughtfully. 'I'm going through a difficult time,' he said. 'I've got personal issues.'

Wickens rolled his eyes. 'Haven't we all, matey boy? Look, in future keep off private property, and don't go scaring people. All right?'

Jakes looked away. 'Okay.'

The two officers wound up the interview. Jakes watched from the lounge window as they walked to their patrol car. They were laughing and joking, playground bullies who never grew up. Wickens pulled a face at his colleague, gurning like an idiot, with his tongue out. Jakes reflected that, as so often, Nietzsche had said it best: *Man is the cruellest animal.*

Once the car had gone, Jakes went upstairs to the spare room, seeking some comfort in a familiar although secret routine. There, spreading beyond the original corkboard to the wall, were pinned or taped hundreds of newspaper articles about the murderer Neville Rollason. Many of the pieces were new, speculating where he might be or what this dangerous man might look like now, with the aid of software and artists' impressions. But others were older, from decades ago, sun-bleached and curling, showing the glowering eyes and dark devilish eyebrows of Rollason in his youth. In the centre of the bedroom mirror was taped a new enlarged photo of a mild-looking pensioner, with dark eyes and a swirl of snowy hair around his balding pate. To Jakes this rare image was both precious and repulsive, already seared into his mind through familiarity. The thought of this man leaving jail terrified him. He was certain that once he did, Rollason would once again seek him out. On a desk was a pair of scissors and sheaf of fresh newspapers awaiting scrutiny. Each new snippet, a repeating pattern, a texture in the tapestry of terror Jakes had created for himself.

Chapter Fourteen

It was just PC Cottesloe's bad luck that he was standing in front of Vince Babbage at Staines police station when the desk sergeant took a call. Cottesloe was waiting to have his overtime request authorised when Babbage put his hand over the receiver and said: 'I'll be with you in a moment, Jim.' He grabbed a notepad and pen and said: 'Yes, madam.'

Cottesloe could hear from where he was standing that the woman was hysterical but couldn't make out exactly what she was saying. Babbage waggled the biro between his fat fingers. 'And you just received this today? So what did it actually say?'

Babbage rolled his eyes at Cottesloe as the torrent of words poured into his ear. 'Well, it's not exactly threatening in its own right is it? It's the kind of thing you say to children.'

That was clearly the wrong thing to say. The woman's reply caused Babbage to remove the receiver a couple of inches from his ear. 'Ah, I'm afraid the control room didn't pass that element of it across to me. Yes, I see what you mean now. And your name is? I'm sorry, I know you told them, but they didn't tell...' He wrote down what she said. 'And how many years ago was that?'

Cottesloe could see a certain element of contrition in the way that Babbage was now speaking to her. The constable decided to retreat to a bench, where there was a copy of *the Sun* beckoning. He hadn't even reached a juicy story before Babbage had ended the call.

'What was all that about?' Cottesloe asked.

Babbage blew a sigh. 'Some poor old dear has had what she considers a threatening letter. Naturally, it's unsigned. Her son went missing back in the 1980s, never been found, and she thinks it's relevant to that, because of the impending release of Neville Rollason.'

Cottesloe shook his head. 'Everyone's got an opinion on him.'

'You couldn't print mine, even in there,' Babbage said, indicating the tabloid newspaper in Cottesloe's hands. 'Life should mean life.'

'What did the letter say?'

'All it said is—' Babbage held out both his arms and bugged out his eyes—'"Are you afraid of the Bogeyman?"'

Cottesloe rolled his eyes. 'For God's sake, is that all? It could be anyone.'

'I said I'd follow it up,' Babbage said. 'Like we need another wild goose chase, given the body found in our patch.' He mimed screwing up the report just written and chucking it over his shoulder. They both laughed.

–

Rainy Macintosh sat in the cramped lounge of her one-bedroomed flat in Reading, her laptop balanced on her knees, and a cup of coffee getting cold on the end table next to her. It was eight p.m. and she was frustrated. Her fourteen-year-old son Ewan was upstairs in his bedroom playing computer games. She wasn't entirely convinced by his claim that his homework was finished, but she had too much of her own to start policing him. She'd been working away all evening on Gillard's project, trying to figure out the types of industrial machinery that could cause compression asphyxia. She would have preferred to work on finding the culprit, the 'who', rather than embark on this wild goose chase about 'how'. Her boss was convinced that cracking the second would lead to a breakthrough on the first. She wasn't so sure.

She had twelve search tabs open, covering everything from industrial cranes, statistically the most dangerous type of construction equipment, right through to stamping machines for car panels. Her initial calls that afternoon to the Health and Safety Executive hadn't been much help. They didn't have statistics sorted by machine type, only by industry. As far as accidents were concerned the construction industry was clearly the most dangerous, but again that didn't help her. A really well-designed, modern machine was only safe when it was used in the way it was intended. If a bunch of people decided to use it as a weapon against a helpless individual, then that was different. The only progress she had made was on the size of equipment. An image search had allowed her to disregard many different types of presses, moulders, extruders and so on as not having the scope to accommodate anything as large as a man's torso.

Perhaps a bit of outsourcing would be useful.

She got up and made her way to Ewan's bedroom door. It was quiet, but there was still light coming from inside. She tapped on the door and walked in. The place was an absolute tip, but she knew she had to bite her tongue if she was to get what she wanted. The boy, all gangly arms and legs, was lying on his bed in shorts and T-shirt, looking at his phone.

'I've got a wee project for you, son,' she said. His bright blue eyes flicked up to her briefly before returning to the video he was watching. He made no reply.

'A little bit of detective work.'

That seemed to grab his attention. 'What?'

'A piece of Internet research, right up your street. I want your ideas on the types of industrial machinery that could be used to kill people—'

He launched right in: 'Drill through the head, burned in a steel furnace, crushed by a bulldozer...'

'Whoa, hold your horses. It's quite specific. It must be capable of gradually suffocating someone by pressing their chest, so it must be big enough for a person to fit inside.'

His eyes widened. 'Wow, like a horror film.'

She gave him the minimum context, knowing that the idea alone was enough to inspire him. She returned to the lounge and looked at her home with fresh eyes. She needed somewhere bigger, where she didn't have to sleep on the settee. But she couldn't afford a place with a second bedroom, since she hadn't got a penny of child support money from Ross. Ironic that her former partner, a paediatric critical care consultant, was blind to the needs of the one child he was truly responsible for. He just couldn't stand it that she'd decided to put her own life first. For a decade she'd followed Ross, moving round Scotland from one hospital to another, always several rungs lower, always having to do the killer hours and the childcare while he got the glory and the money. Now at least she was her own mistress.

Poor but happy, and finally appreciated for her work.

She went into the kitchen, to the fridge, and helped herself to a glass of wine. Her first of the evening. Now that was a success. When she'd been working eighty hours a week in Glasgow it had often been a bottle at the end of a shift. She had frequently gone back to work in the morning a little tipsy. Not now.

'Here's to profiting from murder,' she said to herself, raising her glass.

On Wednesday morning, just after eight, Gillard was sitting in his office when he spotted Rainy Macintosh walking into the CID block. As always, she was in a generously cut dark trouser suit that hid her plus-size figure. She had a Thermos flask in hand, which she set on the desk while she shrugged off her jacket and hung it on the back of her chair. He stood in the doorway and watched as she logged on, skimmed her emails, then helped herself to a coffee from her flask. He knew, from previous observation of the crumbs on her jacket, that she would have eaten a croissant sitting in traffic on the congested route from Reading to Guildford. Not the best commute in the world. He had sensed real potential in her right from the beginning. Something about the way she could turn round a problem in her mind and examine it from different directions. She had been allotted Colin Hodges' old workstation, with its smeary screen and crumb-filled keyboard, and the dubious pleasure of sitting next to Carl Hoskins. She had gelled pretty well with Carl, which was more than could be said for most of the female members of his detective team. She could match him filthy joke for filthy joke, swearword for swearword. For all that, there was some melancholy in her, some dent in her confidence. He had asked Claire Mulholland to act as her mentor, woman to woman, and make sure she could ride out any early difficulties.

'How was the homework, Rainy?' he called.

'Dog ate it, sir,' she said without even turning round. Gillard made his way over to her desk, a great deal tidier these days than it had been in Hodges' day, notwithstanding the croissant crumbs.

'What have you got?'

She rotated on her typist's chair, feet off the ground. She was wearing tiny black patent leather shoes, with little bows on them. She pulled them in just before she scraped his shins.

'I put the problem on the family supercomputer and ran it overnight.'

Gillard laughed. 'Glad to hear you have that kind of resource.'

'Yes, my laddie Ewan. As long as it involves murder and death, he's onboard. I've now got a list of fifty manufacturers of hydraulic presses, non-heat based moulding, and other kit. He's pulled together 150 pages of photographs of machinery big enough to contain the human body, and eliminated many others. He's dug up the contact details of the companies that maintain and service them, so we should be able to get a client list pretty quickly.'

'Fantastic work. How old is he?'

'Fourteen. He loved it. He's been badgering me since then to know what the case is. I said I'd tell him at the end, when it's solved.'

'Hope he won't be boasting about it to his friends.'

'Aye, well he's got nae friends. Just like his mam.'

The revelation took him aback. 'I'm sorry to hear about that, Rainy.'

'Mine or his?'

'Both, actually.'

'Forget I said it, sir. I've got a big gob and stuff just falls out.'

A text to Gillard's phone drew his attention. Dr Delahaye had forwarded the results from the textile analysis. He made his excuses to Rainy, and returned to his office to look at the report on his screen. There was real progress. A series of cotton fibres, recovered from the mouth and nose of the dead body, had produced some interesting results. Though the fibres were of fairly generic manufacture, they were contaminated with two human DNA traces, only one of which matched the victim. Under a microscope, the presence of dust mites was noted, and a separate DNA test confirmed it. A couple of hairs in his mouth yielded a third DNA trace, also human. Bar the victim's, none of the DNA was on the national database.

Gillard picked up the phone, punched out his number and got straight through.

'Craig. I'm in the car.' The background roar confirmed it. 'Well, we seem to be back in more familiar asphyxiation territory, don't we?'

'Do we?'

'Yes. Dust mites. Indicative of the involvement of bedding or a pillow. At this concentration, those textiles had been in use for some time. However, I would be cautious about linking the pillow to the death. He could simply have been sleeping in someone's spare bed before the attack on him took place.'

'Am I missing something?' Gillard asked. 'I don't see it helps very much.'

'No, I agree. But any extra data is a help.' There was a noise in the background and some uncharacteristic cursing from Delahaye.

'You all right?' Gillard asked.

'Got to go, Craig. I've just knocked a cyclist off.'

'Ambulance required?'

'For me, possibly. The guy is huge and seems really quite upset.' The call ended.

Gillard punched out the control room number and reported the incident, telling them to trace Delahaye's mobile number to get a location. From memory, the forensic scientist always used a hands-free set in the car. There would be serious trouble if he hadn't.

—

Leticia had arranged to meet DI Graham Morgan in a cafe on the corner of Wexford Road in Staines.

She was ten minutes late because of the difficulty of finding somewhere to park in the crowded terraced streets and had in the end squeezed her Mini into a small space, half of which intruded on a single yellow line. There was no sign of a traffic warden, and she hoped she would be in and out within half an hour anyway.

Morgan was already there, reading a paper, dressed in a rugby shirt and jeans, his greying hair neatly combed. He pointedly looked at his watch. 'We've got official permission for a bit of subterfuge here,' he said, as his coffee and bacon sandwich were brought to the table. 'When we meet the landlord's agent, we will explain that the new tenant is my brother, who is just emerging from a period of mental health difficulty. I'll do the talking, though we shouldn't encounter any difficulties because they've already got copies of all the relevant paperwork.'

'What's my role?'

'You don't really have to say anything.'

'Okay, but who am I actually meant to be?'

'I was thinking that you are my girlfriend,' Morgan said, with a smile that was intended to be reassuring. 'I know there's a bit of an age difference – it's not too much of a stretch is it? I've always liked black women.'

Leticia tried to wipe the revulsion from her face. Morgan wasn't her type at all, and she didn't like him even imagining them as a couple. He wasn't exactly creepy, not like the shrink Golob, but a bit too cocksure. The kind to boast of imagined conquests to his mates down the pub. Quite apart from that, he looked at least a decade older than she was. 'All right, but don't try too hard to make it convincing, okay?'

Morgan held up his hands. 'I'm not the affectionate type, don't worry.'

Once she had finished her coffee and watched him demolish the remains of his sandwich, they headed round the corner to the Victorian terraced house. It was quite a neat place, with a small bay window overlooking a tiny patch of paved front garden. The agent, a woman of perhaps twenty-five with her dark hair in a ponytail and a navy blue trouser suit, was waiting outside and greeted them enthusiastically.

'I think your brother is really going to enjoy this place,' she said to Morgan, with vowels as polished as her patent leather shoes. 'I know the rent is a little bit high for the area, but there are quite a lot of extra facilities. There is even a secluded garden to the rear, which catches the evening sun.' She selected a key, unlocked the front door and let them in. The house was light and open-plan; there was a modern kitchen with fan oven and microwave. The agent showed them throughout the house. It looked like a perfect home for a small family.

'It's very nice,' said Leticia. 'I'm sure he'll like it.' It was way better than any of the halfway houses, hostels or other accommodation that she had ever seen offered to newly released prisoners.

'The landlord is quite relaxed about some of the… special situations, especially as you've been kind enough to act as guarantor,' the agent said. 'The references all seem to be in order.'

'Thank you,' said Morgan.

Once they were out on the street again, and the agent had returned to her car, Leticia turned to Morgan and said: 'That is bloody luxurious. It's way better than *my* house. It's massive. I've seen entire hostels to sleep half a dozen that are smaller. And none are this well equipped.'

Morgan held up his hands. 'I know, I know. If the tabloids ever get hold of it there will be hell to pay. I looked initially at a flat in a conversion. But the guidance is clear that we can't have him sharing a hallway with some unwitting family. Besides, we've got valuable information for the families of the victims, to ease their pain and give them closure. Rollason held all the trump cards and knew how to negotiate. Sometimes you just have to hold your nose and make the deal.'

Leticia shook her head as she walked back with him to her illegally parked car. 'I'm meeting him this afternoon at the prison for the first time.'

'Be careful. He's very slippery, and deceptively charming. I would come with you but having two of us there would just draw attention to him among the other inmates. We've got to keep it low-key, understand?'

'I know. But I'm really nervous.' She pressed her key fob and the orange light of her Mini flashed its greeting.

'Good luck,' he said, resting his hand lightly on the small of her back. For a moment she thought he was going to kiss her, and she ducked rapidly into the safety of the car.

–

Leticia sat down opposite the anonymous-looking prisoner and wondered if she had been paired up with the wrong offender. The man, perhaps only five-six, balding and skinny, looked utterly harmless. He had trendy red-framed glasses, a sparse swirl of fluffy white hair and a neatly trimmed beard. He looked considerably older than his true age of sixty-three. Though she had been emailed a picture of Neil Wright's face, in the flesh she had still expected to detect an aura of evil and had fully antici-pated being unnerved by the man, given his reputation. But Neville Rollason now seemed transformed into Neil Wright, as if the pseudonym was actually a whole new personality. She introduced herself, and with a smile he held out a hand to shake hers. She made brief contact, and it was nothing remarkable. Soft, dry, warm skin. She could have been shaking hands with a colleague at work.

'I'm very glad to meet you, pet,' he said, with just a trace of a north-east accent.

'And you, Neil,' she said. 'So how are you finding it here?'

They were in a bright and airy interview room at HMP Spring Hill. It was painted in pastel blue and yellow, with matching plastic furniture and a potted plant in a corner. She could see a prison officer in an adjacent office through an internal window, but there was no one else in the room with them.

He laughed, showing what were clearly bleached as well as reconstructed teeth. 'A proper soft bed, much less racket from the corridors and a civilised class of neighbour. Even the screws are nice and young, with downy little moustaches and lovely long blond eyelashes.' He licked his lips. 'And they call us men, not prisoners.'

Leticia felt a pulse of anger at this man's sense of entitlement, the way he felt he could still broadcast his proclivities even to a probation officer. She suspected he knew he had more power than she did. Even if she recommended that he not be released, at this late stage she would probably be overruled. The Parole Board machinery had ground out its decision after considerable deliberation and wasn't likely to reverse it easily, especially as DI Morgan still had hopes of extracting from him the location of the final victim.

'I've been made aware, of course, of your full background,' she said. 'We've no need to go into any of that at this meeting, which is mainly about the practical arrangements of your release plan. We will however still need to see you quite regularly to assess how you are meeting the objectives we set in this, and to action any additional requirements.' She tapped the document in front of her.

'That's fine by me.' He folded his arms behind his head and leaned back, a picture of relaxation.

'I believe you have seen the listing details of your new home?' she said.

'It looks good. It's a long way away from my old stamping ground, which suits me just fine. No one will recognise me.'

Leticia ran through the minutiae of the release plan, but realised he was barely listening. Finally, she tried a bit of small talk to spark some re-engagement. 'So what's the first thing you'll do when you're out?'

'Well, I could *murder* a pint of proper English hand-pulled bitter. It's been a few years since I tasted any, I can tell you. Someone told me that you can pay a fiver for a pint down here. Five pounds! When I went away, well, up in Newcastle it was only just over 75p.'

'That was a long time ago.'

'Before you were born, pet,' he replied, with a wink. 'Long before you were born.'

'I just have to remind you of a few things,' she said, having got his attention back. 'On the morning of your release you will be given a package, which will contain a phone, your discharge cash and the keys to your new home. Look after them. There are no spares.'

'I'm not a child, pet.'

'There will also be a map showing the bus route to get to Staines. It's quite long and involves several changes. You should be able to get there by ten thirty a.m. I will meet you at the house by eleven thirty so that we can review your release plan and see which initial objectives have been met. You must be there punctually. That's very important.'

'Okay. I'll be there, don't worry.'

She looked down at her papers. 'There will be another meeting after four days to set further rehabilitation targets, and then it will be once a week for the first year. You also have to attend a weekly therapy course.' She looked up at him.

'That's fine, pet.' He leaned the chair back so it was balanced on just the two rear legs. He seemed perfectly relaxed. 'But if I'm in therapy under my bogus name, I presumably have to talk about bogus crimes.'

'I'll have to ask my manager about that,' Leticia conceded, then referred again to her papers. 'If you form any kind of relationship, a girlfriend or anyone else, you must tell them about your background, and you must inform us. You understand?'

'I understand that right enough.' He was looking at the ceiling.

'We would have to do a risk assessment, if this person had children.'

He nodded.

'You must not under any circumstances contact either directly or indirectly any members of the families of your victims, nor go to within five miles of any of their homes.'

'I wouldn't want to do that, anyway.' He was still studying the ceiling tiles.

'Now, about your own adult children.' She looked through the document in front of her.

'I haven't had any direct contact with them since their mother died.'

Leticia read a little further. 'They were brought up by your sister-in-law.'

'That's what I heard,' he said. 'She hasn't spoken to me either.'

'Now, since you've asked if you can make contact with them, we've tried to find out whether they are agreeable. As far as your daughter Susan is concerned the answer is no, I'm afraid. We weren't able to find out where your son is living.'

'Right.'

'It would show considerable maturity on your part if you respected her wishes. It would look good on your rehabilitation plan.'

'Right.' He was inspecting his fingernails now.

'There are some additional conditions here about the use of the Internet, which I want you to read. I can't stress enough the fact that if you breach any of these regulations, even once, you will be called back to prison immediately. There will be no second chances.'

He leaned forward. 'So what about these death threats? Vigilantes threatening to kill me. I need twenty-four-hour protection.'

Leticia had expected this question. 'I think you've been told that won't happen.'

'So you'll just let them murder me?'

She stared at him and choked back a retort. *It would be no more than you deserve.* She took a deep breath and said: 'Look, you should get this in perspective. You are not a gangland supergrass and the vigilantes are hardly professionals. Besides, we've gone to enormous trouble to give you a new identity, and put you into a new location. Keeping your identity secret is mainly down to you. The evidence is clear that in most cases where a new identity was broken it was because of carelessness or boasting by the offender. My advice is, be cautious. However tempting it is, don't get drunk or stoned. Stay off the spice.'

'Are you finished?' He folded his arms.

'We'll never be finished,' Leticia said. 'You were sentenced to life imprisonment, and you are released now only under strict licence. That means we can call you back even twenty years from now. We'll be watching you, every step of the way.'

'Is that right, pet?' The murderer turned his gaze on her. Now she felt the coldness of those small dark goblin eyes. A momentary shiver ran down her spine, as if someone had just walked on her grave. The evil was there, all right, well-hidden but unreformed, disguised with the aid of the public purse. Suddenly repulsed, she couldn't get out of there fast enough. What on earth were she and her colleagues doing, letting this man loose on British streets?

Chapter Fifteen

The Red Lion Inn had been bypassed by the gastropub revolution, just as it was bypassed by the M3. Deep within the Surrey countryside, the brick-built tavern was a mouldering relic of 1960s modernisation and needed serious money spending on it. The bar as usual was bustling. But on this occasion two of the regulars were sitting at the back of the lounge, where the lights were dim and the tables still sticky from lunchtime. Terry Dalton, self-employed air-conditioning engineer, and Nigel Chivers, one-time nightclub bouncer, were excited about a secret project they had been working on for a while. Now they were waiting for the man who could make it all happen.

'We'll get one chance at this, and we'll have to go in hard,' Chivers said, examining the heavily bitten nails on his giant fists. 'We ain't going to film this one, and we ain't going to post nothing online, right?'

'Yeah, we should keep it low-key,' Dalton replied. 'I'd say zero publicity. Just the three of us. I'm not gonna tell the others, particularly the women. Careless talk costs wives.'

Chivers sniggered. 'Just give me five minutes with that bastard. Five minutes, that's all.' He ground one fist into his open hand.

'Save some for me,' Dalton said, eyeing the doorway. 'My cricket bat's getting itchy.'

'Fuck that,' Chivers said. 'I'm not wasting my time with injuries. We've got to sort him for good.'

Dalton turned back to his mate. 'You better keep quiet about that when his nibs arrives. I said it was just gonna be a going-over. Andy might get cold feet if we kill him. And we need him on our side.'

'I'm not so sure,' Chivers said.

'Nige, he's the only one who can get the address. You've got to be on the inside.'

'What about Len? You remember, the screw at Wakefield.'

'I told you. Len says Rollason was ghosted to a category D more than a week ago. They're keeping a lid on where. So Len's no use to us no more.'

They both turned to the window at the sound of a car pulling into the car park, and waited for the crunch of boots on gravel. The man who walked in was wearing a scruffy donkey jacket and a baseball cap. More used to being here in uniform, Andrew Wickens scrutinised those at the bar carefully before making his way through to the back of the lounge.

'Hiya guys, sorry I'm late. Only just got off duty.'

'Got what we need, Andy?' Chivers asked.

'Not yet. It wasn't on the local database that I have access to, nor the Police National Computer. They're being very careful with this. Special Branch is running it, and I think I know which officer.'

'Bastards!' Chivers banged the table with his fist. 'Why are they wasting public money protecting people like that?'

'Keep your voice down,' Wickens said. 'I'm already taking a huge risk. Don't go getting gobby on me, all right?'

Chivers nodded in contrition. 'Sorry.'

'There's another avenue I could pursue,' he said. 'I know Morgan has been working with probation in Staines. I may be able to find out who the case officer allocated to Rollason is. My feeling is that it's going to be a woman called Verity Winter.'

'Why's that then?' Chivers said.

'Because she's the most experienced. Here's her car details.' Wickens passed across a scrap of paper. 'If you follow her, she may lead you to him, or at least the place where he'll be staying.'

'Can't you do it?' Dalton asked.

'Well, I'm on duty most of the time, aren't I? And half the probation team know me.'

'That gives you cover doesn't it?' Dalton persisted.

'It gives me cover for being in the office with them, but I'd look a bit suspicious if I was spotted following her car, in uniform as well.' He looked at Dalton as if he was an idiot.

'Fair point,' Dalton conceded.

'Look, I know how the probation team works. They'll want a face-to-face meeting with him on the day he gets out. But you can take your time. Do a bit of surveillance. You don't have to grab him on day one.'

'I suppose not,' Dalton said, looking at Chivers.

'The big question is where we take him,' Wickens said. 'You haven't told me what the plan is. I take it there is a plan?'

'We've got a plan. But we've got to be very careful,' Chivers said. 'Sworn to secrecy on this. It's best if you don't know.'

'I do have to know that it isn't something stupid,' Wickens replied. 'Something that is gonna come back and bite me on the arse.'

'Anaconda has it all arranged,' Chivers said. 'You just get us the bastard, we'll sort the rest.'

'Who the fuck is Anaconda?' Wickens asked.

Dalton rolled his eyes and inclined his head towards Chivers. 'The code name was his idea. Anaconda is the backer, the guy who has got somewhere to keep him sorted.'

Wickens realised immediately who it might be. 'It's Gus van Steenis, isn't it?'

Dalton let his head fall into his hands. 'See, Nige?' he said to Chivers. 'Didn't I say it was a stupid name?'

Wickens rubbed his forehead. 'It's not just the fact that he's the only bloke in the area who might own a fucking anaconda. Van Steenis was gobbing off to me and Cottesloe about what an outrage it was that Rollason was being released.' He looked around the pub, checking that nobody was listening to them. 'I mean, can't anyone keep their mouth shut? Am I surrounded by idiots?'

'You mind what you say to me,' Chivers said, pointing a fat finger at the cop.

Dalton grasped Chivers' hand and eased it down to the table, unclenching the fingers one at a time. 'Look, we've got a plan. Andy, you let us know who the probation officer is. We'll follow, find out where Rollason lives, and nab him. Your involvement ends there. All right?'

'You're going to kill him, aren't you?' Wickens asked.

'No, no, no,' Dalton said. 'Just rough him up a bit.' He turned to Chivers. 'Aren't we?'

Wickens shook his head. 'I can't be part of murder. If you kill him they'll only get fucking Gillard onto the case, or maybe even someone more senior. Then we're all screwed. Keep it low-key, right? Not too many visible injuries. Warn him not to report it. Keep it off the radar. Think smart.'

'Right,' Chivers said, and gave a quick wink to Dalton.

Wickens looked at his watch and said: 'Look, I've got to go. Promise me you won't do anything stupid.' Without waiting for a reply, he made his way out to the door.

'I don't know what he is worried about,' Chivers said, as he watched Wickens get in his car. 'There won't be a body. All those hungry crocodiles.' He laughed.

–

Even in normal times Sam Gillard had only rarely been able to go out to dinner with Craig during the week. His shifts often spilled over into hours of unplanned overtime. So she had made other evening arrangements: badminton, a book club, and every other week a girls' night out with her colleagues from the police control room. But since her kidnap ordeal, she hadn't been out of the house much at all. She had been diagnosed with PTSD and had two months left of sick leave. Her most regular outings had been to the twice-weekly therapy sessions. But now she was beginning to feel a little stronger, and chafed at her domestic confinement, even though it was medically recommended. She missed the busy camaraderie of the control room, the buzz and the excitement, the fact that every day was different.

At home, every day seemed the same. For the first time in decades she had completed a jigsaw. It was four p.m. and she had just fitted the last piece of sky when her husband rang to ask if she wanted to accompany him, tonight, to

J'adore Ça, one of the trendiest restaurants in the area. He had managed to secure a nine p.m. booking that evening. Even though it was quasi-official business, Sam could not quite believe it.

'You do know it's a very upmarket place, don't you?' she asked him.

'Yes, I looked at the website. A lot of Cajun and Creole food, but supposedly with a French twist. Which I guess means the portions will be small, even if the bill isn't.' He laughed.

'What exactly are you hoping to find out?'

He told her about Leroy Ceejay. 'He is one of the partners in the business, and it could be a money-laundering outfit.'

'How will you be able to tell just by eating the food?'

He laughed. 'That's a good question. Clearly, if the place is full of disreputable-looking types that will be a clue. It would be a good opportunity to speak to the owner if he is there, too.'

'Well, I'm getting dressed up for this. I hope you will too.'

'Suit and tie is all I've got to offer. I've got permission from Alison Rigby to expense my meal, and I'll pay for yours. No wine for me.'

–

J'adore Ça had famously taken over a car showroom on one of the smartest streets in Kingston-upon-Thames. Its Grade II listed Art Deco features, including curved metallic windows, gave the dining area a spaciousness and a light that made diners feel like they were on a film set. Anton St Jeanne had hung the place with iridescent kingfisher-blue silk curtains, which absorbed the echo of the wood-panelled floor and the usual crockery and kitchen sounds. The Gillards were shown to a secluded table a little way back from the windows, and Craig sat so that he could see the entire sweep of the dining room.

A stunningly attractive black waitress with a shaven head brought their menus. Sam ordered a Kir Royale as an aperitif, while her husband settled for a mocktail of fruit juices. It didn't arrive as Sam expected, as some great confection with a paper parasol stuck in it, but in a tall slender glass, more like a vase, with rainbow colours visible through the side. Earlier research online had prepared them for the prices, and Sam craned her neck to see what was being served on other tables. She had spotted a fillet of blackened catfish, and a seafood concoction crowned by a crayfish. When they ordered she chose a remoulade of shrimp with horseradish celery and a mild mustard sauce. Craig chose the Creole oxtail with okra and was complimented by the waitress on his choice. 'That's my favourite. It's a long, slow cook, which brings the richest flavours from the bone to the gravy.' Sam chose a glass of Chardonnay to accompany her dish.

While they waited for the food to be served, Gillard eyed the other diners. Middle-class white well-to-do, for the most part, as befitted the prices. No one there seemed to be overly familiar with the staff. The detective had familiarised himself with the appearance of Anton St Jeanne. It wasn't until after ten o'clock, when the Gillards had finished their delicious main courses, that he emerged briefly from the kitchen, to talk to the small Asian woman at the front of house. He was dressed as if he was doing the cooking, and the beads of sweat on his forehead seemed to prove it.

A few minutes later, a large black guy in a tightly fitting suit and wearing braids rolled in from the street. Gillard watched carefully as the front-of-house woman greeted him deferentially and picked up a phone. The man oozed physical capability, shoulders never quite still, jaw high and to the front. Two minutes later Anton emerged from the kitchen. The body language between the two was fascinating. The big guy was largely impassive, while Anton was expressive. His face animated in a rapid succession of smiles, and he gripped the large man's hand between the two of his. It was easy to see who was in charge. A glass of wine was produced by a waitress, while the visitor carefully ran his cold dark eyes over the diners.

His gaze stopped on Gillard's table. The two made brief eye contact, which the detective broke. 'I've been recognised,' he told Sam.

'Is it okay?' she asked. 'Do we have to go?'

'It's fine. I think the guy who saw me is Leroy Ceejay, the guy I told you about.'

She started to look over her shoulder, but Gillard held her hand and said: 'Not now, wait till you go to the ladies'.'

'Have you ever crossed swords with him?'

He chuckled. 'I was once in an unsuccessful drugs raid targeting him and his then boss. Neither were there when we kicked the door down. But that was quite a few years ago, and Ceejay has struck out on his own. Still, I'm a little surprised he knows me.'

Leroy Ceejay's approach to their table was slow, deliberate and a little intimidating. His huge shadow fell across the dessert menus that they were studying. Gillard looked up, to see a slow but restrained smile. 'Detective Inspector Gillard, what an honour.' He extended a meaty paw that swallowed the detective's own up to the wrist. 'I hope you're enjoying your meal.'

'I am,' Gillard said.

'It's delicious,' Sam said hurriedly.

'How was your oxtail?' Ceejay asked. 'Don't you think it's amazing that poor man's food has got so damn trendy?'

'It was always neglected. Unjustly – unlike lungs or tongue,' Gillard said.

Ceejay laughed. 'I'm not a fan of those either. I hope you will accept a complimentary dessert with me, and perhaps a brandy on the house too?'

Gillard knew that taking freebies from anyone, let alone suspects, was bureaucratically a tricky area. Even trivial and genuine acts of generosity could be misinterpreted in the black-and-white of an expenses claim or, worse, a courtroom. But now was not the time to demur. They plumped for brown-sugar cookies and crêpes à l'orange. Sam accepted a double brandy, while the detective ordered a coffee.

'So is this your restaurant?' Gillard asked.

'No, no. It was set up by my good friend Anton.' He turned and called loudly for Anton across the dining room, a *faux pas* which had other diners looking up.

Anton emerged from the kitchen, wiping his hands, and approached the table. 'I'd like to introduce you to Detective Chief Inspector Craig Gillard,' Ceejay proclaimed loudly, before turning to the detective and asking: 'Are you here on business?'

'No,' lied Gillard. 'This is my wife Sam. I just heard great things about this place.'

'I'm sure you did,' Ceejay boomed. 'Delighted to meet you, Mrs Gillard.' He rested his hand briefly on her shoulder.

Anton St Jeanne looked embarrassed, as did Sam. Gillard could see other diners staring at them, no doubt discussing the fact that a senior policeman was among them. The desserts arrived, and Ceejay and Anton left them to it. Sam's fork was shaking in her hand over her crêpes, and Gillard now regretted having brought her here so soon after her trauma. Even this mild piece of intimidation was too much for her at this stage.

Gillard called for the bill but when the waitress approached she was empty-handed. 'I'm afraid your bill has already been settled, sir.'

Gillard shook his head. 'I don't want to be given a free meal because of who I am.'

'I completely understand, sir. But your bill was settled by another guest, not by the restaurant, so I'm afraid there's nothing that we can do.'

'Which other guest?'

'I apologise but I'm not at liberty to say.'

Gillard looked up and could no longer see Leroy Ceejay. 'Was it Mr Ceejay?' he asked.

The waitress shook her head. 'I'm sorry, that's all I was told.'

'Okay, thank you.'

The waitress walked away to another table.

'You can always leave a big tip,' Sam whispered.

'I will,' he replied. 'But they know full well that I can't show an audit trail. And they only have to say I was given a free meal, and I'll have questions to answer.'

'It seems that Leroy Ceejay is a pretty clever guy,' Sam said.

'Yes, he certainly is.' Gillard considered that further research might be a good idea. Cracking Ceejay's amphetamine business was definitely on the National

Crime Agency's agenda, but if he could find a connection with the dead body in the Thames, that would help. As they got up to go, Gillard spotted Anton peeking out at him through the little glass window in the kitchen door. No doubt he was a subject of extended conversation in that private enclave.

—

Anton St Jeanne watched as the detective and his wife left the restaurant. 'What was all that about?' he asked Ceejay.

'I'm not sure,' came the reply. 'But it's useful to have a heads-up when the fuzz are after you.'

'Do you think someone on the island dropped you in it?'

He turned to Anton. 'It would be pretty stupid if they did, wouldn't it? I think I need your help, Anton.'

The restaurateur shrugged. 'I've got five covers that still haven't had their dessert.'

'It's not just them that haven't had their just deserts.' He laughed at his own joke. 'Can I have your car keys?'

Anton rolled his eyes. 'Why can't you use your own car, Leroy?'

'Because the police know all about it, don't they?'

'They know all about mine too, remember? I only got it back this morning.'

'What about Leticia's car? That's not on the list.'

'Jesus, Leroy.' Anton heard his own tone of voice, a supplicating whine rather than a firm refusal. 'Can't you borrow one from one of your own guys? I'm serious, she could lose her job.'

'No one is going to find out, Anton. Not even her. I'll come around in an hour, you leave me the keys under the mat outside. She'll be in bed asleep, she won't even know it's gone, I'll be back in an hour.'

Anton shook his head as he prepared a serving of pecan pralines with whipped cream. After arranging the three biscuit-like confections on a large white plate he drizzled a semaphore of raspberry sauce back and forth across the plate. He used the tip of a damp cloth to remove a couple of specks that were in the wrong place, before passing the dish across to the serving hatch.

'Okay, but it better not be longer than an hour,' he said. The fig-leaf demand that barely covered his abject surrender.

–

Two hours later Leticia's car made its way slowly across the bridge to Tagg's Island. Leroy Ceejay was behind the wheel. He parked in a small pull-in just by the houseboat, left the car and went and knocked on the door. Kletz opened it. He seemed surprised, but invited Leroy in with grudging acquiescence.

'Juliette,' he called. 'It's for you.'

She emerged from the bedroom, her kimono loosely tied. 'I've got it,' she said. 'Hold on a minute.' She disappeared back into the room and re-emerged with a fat brown envelope. 'Mine and Matt's. It's all there.'

'Need any more gear?' Leroy asked.

Juliette's glance strayed to Kletz, who looked tense. 'No. Thank you, that's fine.'

The big man nodded, looked Juliette up and down deliberately and slowly, and let his gaze wander to Kletz and back again. *You and him, really?* his look seemed to be saying. He said a brief goodbye and slipped out of the door, back to the borrowed car.

Chapter Sixteen

Thursday

First thing Gillard went to see Chief Constable Alison Rigby and told her about the previous night's experience. She listened carefully, her powerful blue eyes focused on his.

'I can see why you did it, Craig,' she said. 'But you don't need me to tell you what an awkward piece of potential evidence you have created for a defence team should Mr Ceejay be brought to court.'

'Yes ma'am,' he said.

'So what did you learn as a result of this rather fool-hardy reconnaissance?'

'Well it's clear that the restaurant is controlled by Ceejay. You can see it in the body language between the two principal shareholders. Filings at Companies House show that Anton St Jeanne is the majority owner, but on the ground it looks the other way round. Ceejay was confident enough to be able to offer me and Sam a complimentary dessert without having to check it with anyone.'

'Are we thinking money-laundering?'

'That's my guess, but of course it's so hard to prove.'

Rigby sighed, and looked out of the window. 'Any link to our mystery body?'

'None whatever. I had intended to casually ask a wait-ress about recent staff turnover, but once my cover was blown there was no point. I wouldn't have got a straight answer. So I think we are now waiting for the mitochon-drial DNA results, which I have been promised for this afternoon. Stable isotope analysis, which tells us exactly where this person has lived, is going to take another couple of weeks.'

'Okay. Are there any leads coming from overseas?'

'No, ma'am. As you know, there is no international missing persons database, except for those concerning war, human rights violations and natural disasters. Interpol has a few cases notified, but there is no apparatus to pursue them. If we knew the country he came from, we'd be able to narrow it down. That's why I'm putting my hope in the stable isotope analysis.'

'Good, that should get us a definite answer.'

'On another subject, ma'am. It's about Anton St Jeanne's girlfriend Leticia Mountjoy, who has the Special Branch contact.'

'Yes, Craig,' she said wearily.

'It's come to my attention ma'am that she is a probation officer. She wouldn't by any chance be working on the Neville Rollason false identity, would she? He is due to be released on Tuesday. Rumour has it he's in our area.'

'Craig, you know better than to try to get confirmation from me.' She smiled, which seemed to be a recognition of his powers of deduction.

'You do know that it was me that apprehended him, don't you?' Gillard said.

'I had no idea, Craig. Weren't you a little young?'

'I was twenty-one. It was 1988 and I was a uniform working in the Met Police in Croydon, on my first week.

I was standing by a police public information caravan near the Whitgift Centre handing out leaflets as part of the public information campaign on drink-driving. I spotted a registration plate that matched a nationally notified vehicle of interest. It was a car stolen in Newcastle, which was where Rollason's family originally came from, and had been seen near the place where one of the missing teenagers up there had vanished. I phoned it in, but before anyone arrived I saw a guy coming back to the car. It was Rollason. I approached, and he ran off. I was pretty fit in those days, and caught up with him in an alleyway. It was quite a ding-dong battle before I subdued him. He's a wiry little bugger, well he was. I got a commendation for it.'

Rigby looked at her subordinate with amazement. 'The most surprising thing about that, Craig, is that you remembered the registration number.'

'Well, ma'am, I've always had that kind of memory, I suppose. And of course it's only the new recruits that ever read all the circulars.'

'Okay. Stay away from the probation officer and from DI Morgan, who is handling her. They both have a job to do. I don't suppose for a minute that Leticia Mountjoy is involved in anything criminal herself, but if you have suspicions come to me in the first instance, okay?'

'Yes ma'am.'

'And one more thing Craig, given what you've just told me. I shouldn't have to remind you of course, but I think you should keep a careful eye on your home. I don't imagine for a minute that Rollason is going to be a serious threat to you, but I know Sam is still going through a rough time, so it's up to you to take care of her.'

'Absolutely. Thank you for your concern, ma'am.'

'Well it's more that I'm trying to kick-start *your* concern, Craig.'

'If it was down to me, ma'am, I'd not let her out of my sight. But then I couldn't do my job.'

Rigby nodded. 'Well, we certainly don't want to stop you doing that, do we.'

-

Leticia Mountjoy was running a little late. Too many appointments, not enough time. She slotted her Mini into the car park outside Swan House and hurried into the building with a cheery wave to the ground-floor security guy. She was beginning to understand why Verity never made it anywhere on time.

She had only just got to her desk when she saw at the far end of the office a uniformed police officer talking to the receptionist. Ah, that's why a patrol car was parked right outside. There was something familiar about the man, which was immediately apparent the moment he turned towards her. *Shit!* PC Wickens, one of the cops who had interviewed her about being in the car last Friday. She ducked down into her cubicle, her back to him, and picked up the phone. Face close to her screen, she pretended to make a call, while praying he wouldn't see her. She felt her face go hot with embarrassment as she heard the approaching sound of heavy male feet. *He can't be here for me, can he?*

Wickens walked past and spoke to Tina in the cubicle opposite. 'I'm looking for Verity Winter's office,' he said. Tina pointed out Verity's glass-fronted office a few yards further on but added. 'I'm not sure she's here yet. I've not seen her.'

Leticia blew an enormous sigh of relief. The palpitations she was suffering began to lessen, although she still didn't want to risk being seen or be caught up in any embarrassing conversation.

'I'll just go in and wait for her,' Wickens said and, opening Verity's door, went and sat in the room.

Tina caught Leticia's eye and they exchanged helpless shrugs about the effrontery of the officer. 'I'm going to ring Jill,' Tina said. It was only one minute after the admin officer had put the phone down when Jill Allsop, only five-five even in her heels, marched into Verity's office and asked PC Wickens to leave and wait in the reception area. The constable meekly followed as the probation manager politely but loudly put him in his place. 'The receptionist asked you to wait there for Verity, and police officer or no police officer that is where you will stay. Is that understood?'

Tina and Leticia shared a delicious moment of giggles.

It was only a moment later when Verity herself arrived, saw the constable in reception and, in a brief exchange, seemingly gave him short shrift. He didn't follow her when she strode up the corridor towards her office, but instead headed off to the gents'.

'He went into your office. I tried to stop him,' Tina said to her.

'Thank you. The case he was asking about isn't even mine any more, it's been transferred to Reading, something he could have discovered for himself if he'd read all the documents.'

It was only a few minutes later when Verity called Leticia into her office. She seemed to be in a good mood, and the young probation officer couldn't help but link it to the incident with PC Wickens.

'Take a seat. Can I get you a coffee?' Leticia watched her boss head off to the kitchen. It was quite unlike Verity to offer coffee to a subordinate. Although she was only one rung above Leticia, Verity radiated self-importance. But it was certainly true that she had an enormous caseload of her own, in addition to supervising her three direct reports.

'I just wanted to check that everything has gone according to plan with Wright,' she went on as she brought in two mugs and closed the door.

'Yes, everything went fine. DI Morgan has got him a house, rather better than I think he deserves. All the practical arrangements seem to be in hand.'

'You met Wright yesterday, didn't you?'

'Yes. He seemed quite ordinary, at first.'

Verity nodded. 'They often do. We always assume we can spot evil, but we can't. I've no need to remind you how important it is that we keep him on a short leash. I want you to continue to make it clear to him that every part of the conditions of his release under licence must be observed without exception. A single violation will result in him being sent straight back to a category A prison, not the cushy number he is on now.'

'Can I ask you something?'

'Of course.' Her pale green eyes locked on to Leticia's, alert.

'Why didn't you take the Rollason case yourself? You've got all the experience.'

'Jill offered it to me. But there were organisational reasons. You'll know soon enough why.' Verity put a reassuring hand on her arm. But even when the hand was gone, it felt like it was still there, chilling her blood, an image delineated in goosebumps.

'Now, I understand that DI Morgan has arranged for him to have a dumb phone, without Internet. They'll give it to him at the gatehouse as he leaves Spring Hill.'

'Morgan did mention that, yes.'

'The Parole Board approved stringent licence conditions, which include the monitoring of his call records. Morgan will oversee that on behalf of the Home Office, though I can't see how we can be sure that he isn't just using the Internet at the library or buying himself a burner phone. Our job is principally to oversee his rehabilitation and reintegration into society. However, Morgan has asked if you would make sure that he shows you the phone every time you meet him. Attendance of the weekly sexual offender treatment programme is also mandatory, and proof will be emailed to you separately by the organisers. Of course, because this is being run by a private sector rehabilitation company that does not yet have full Home Office security clearance, he will be registered to those classes under his new identity. I have to emphasise to you that you must be very careful not to disclose to them his real name.'

'But if he is undergoing SOTP under a fictitious criminal record, it won't do him any good, will it? The false record would surely have a much milder version of what he actually did.'

Verity Winter barked a short laugh. 'It's true. But with this particular offender, it would never do any good. Sometimes you just have to tick a box.'

Leticia looked shocked. Verity had a reputation of being even more principled than Jill Allsop.

'Leticia, you have to understand we can never achieve everything that we want to. The public want them all castrated or hanged, or both, while the government looks at the cost of keeping them all locked up and would rather they were dealt with quietly in the community. We can't win.'

'That's true I suppose.'

'There's something else I need you to see,' Verity said. She clicked on her computer screen, and brought up BBC iPlayer. 'Have you seen Monday's *Panorama*?' she asked.

'I haven't had a chance to watch it yet.'

'There's just one bit I want to show you.' Verity pressed fast-forward until she reached the scene with the vigilante and the threat of violence. They both watched it in silence.

'These are the people we are dealing with,' Verity said, then switched her screen to a website marked AVENGE. 'The Association of Vigilant Enforcers Getting Even. That's what it stands for.'

'They're nothing more than criminals themselves,' Leticia said.

Verity nodded. 'They have posted some videos here, of them confronting and beating up elderly paedophiles. It's pretty grotesque stuff actually. I'm only showing you this because if you see any evidence of threats to Wright, I want you to tell me. I'll be passing on any information to DI Morgan.'

'But they can't find anything out,' Leticia said. 'It's not on the case management system. Only on handwritten records, which go into the safe every night. Only you, me and Graham know his real identity.'

'These people are very clever, Leticia. And they have friends in high places. Jill took a phone call from the local MP, who had somehow heard that Rollason was going to be on his patch. He put a lot of pressure on her to disclose his new identity and address.'

'Why?'

Verity laughed. 'He's expecting to be appointed to the Justice Select Committee, and believes he should know. Jill had the measure of him. She said that if he was appointed, and the Home Secretary thought it appropriate, he would be informed by her department through the usual channels.'

'Everyone wants to know,' Leticia complained.

Verity gave a knowing smile. 'With that particular MP, it is most probably to fuel some drunken boasting to colleagues about the secrets he has in his possession.'

'Okay,' said Leticia. 'I have asked Wright to keep me informed if he receives any threats.'

'Yes. Tuesday is going to be an interesting day,' Verity said, and then suddenly turned away. A strange noise escaped her throat, and she began to heave. Before Leticia could say anything, Verity had grabbed a box of tissues and fled into the corridor. The young probation officer waited a moment, and then stepped outside. There was no sign of her boss. She must have gone to the ladies' toilet. After the way Verity had reacted last time, Leticia wasn't going to go in there and offer to help.

But finding herself in her boss's office, with the computer on and logged in, plus her mobile phone just lying there, was a huge temptation. She went to the PC first, looking for any information about her own appraisal, which was due soon. There was nothing obviously related to that. Leticia then picked up her boss's iPhone and checked her text messages, which just seemed to be a fairly lengthy and acrimonious exchange with her mother.

She was human after all.

Finally, Leticia stood, planning to exit the office and return to her own desk in the open-plan area. Before she could do so, she spotted desk keys hanging from the lock of one drawer in Verity's desk. It took only a few seconds to give them a quick turn and slide it open. It contained what Leticia expected. Papers, pens, a few feminine hygiene products, a bottle of vitamin tablets, some eyeliner and eyeshadow. The one unexpected item was a small brown medicinal bottle with an attached dropper. It was half full of some dark liquid and had a stained label written in some foreign script. Not Chinese or Japanese, because she thought she would recognise that, but perhaps a Middle Eastern or Indian tongue. Maybe that was the medicine she was taking for her sickness. She wouldn't be surprised if Verity was a believer in quack cures.

Then, she spotted something else. A pregnancy test kit. Now that was interesting. No one knew anything about Verity's love life. It might explain the sickness, too.

Chapter Seventeen

Claire Mulholland arrived at Mount Browne's CID building to see Gillard. He was sitting at his desk, eating a mid-morning sandwich, with the photographs of the body from the island laid out in front of him like some bizarre card game. Not too many people could sit and eat tuna and mayonnaise on granary bread while staring at the distorted features and blood-cyanosed flesh of a corpse, but she realised that his was the kind of familiarity that breeds, if not contempt, then at least decent digestion.

Gillard described to her what they knew of the man, now known irreverently as Mr Fang due to his one prominent gold-filled tooth. Claire could see the lack of progress was really beginning to bug him. The mitochondrial DNA tests had confirmed only what a simple glance at the man seemed to show, that he was mostly of Chinese origin. There were ancestral traces of Tibetan and Mongolian too, but Gillard wasn't sure how that would help. 'I'm looking for a more precise view of where the man had actually spent most of his life,' he said. 'That should come with the results of the stable isotope analysis, which shows the mineralisation in his body. It looks like that might yet be another week.'

'Well, here's a new line of enquiry for you,' she said. 'Baz is working on this private zoo owned by the Arab sheikh, just outside Walton-on-Thames.'

'Ah, is that the one on the old St Thomas's prep school site? Managed by that Zimbabwean.'

'Yes, Gus van Steenis. It has the makings of quite an expensive undertaking. There's not much detail online, but there's going to be a very substantial reptile house, including crocodiles, and they've got the famous injured rhino.'

'Ah, yes. Dennis.' The detective chief inspector stroked his chin. 'Interesting. Van Steenis went to the party on Tagg's Island the same night that everyone seemed to hear this splash in the river. If he was involved that would be very careless.' He turned to look at her with a smile on his face. 'Are you thinking along the lines that our victim was sat on by Dennis or something?'

'Well, it's possible isn't it? Maybe one of the constrictor snakes that he has.'

Gillard inclined his head sceptically. 'That would be one powerful snake to inflict the damage the body sustained. The rhino would be more like the kind of power we're looking for.' He began to Google Gus van Steenis. 'I remember reading about the guy in the local paper,' he said. 'Perhaps you can take a look around, Claire? Obviously, what I'd be looking for is a staff list, but I also want you to check they have all the legal permissions. Not just on animals, but for employing staff from abroad.'

'I'm giving Baz a lift tomorrow, so I'll do it then.' Just as she was about to leave she said: 'Craig, is the rumour true that Neville Rollason is being set up in our area with a new identity?'

Gillard shrugged. 'I spoke to Rigby about it, but she won't confirm. However, if you look at how busy and stressed Graham Morgan of Special Branch is, it's clear that something is going on.'

–

Teatime on a sunny Thursday and PC Andrew Wickens slid his patrol car into the car park at Mount Browne, killed the engine and took a deep breath. The young constable was based at Staines police station, but he did have an excuse to be here at HQ. CID had wanted to see some detailed notes that he'd made while interviewing witnesses to the splash on Midsummer's Night. The photocopies were in a folder on the passenger seat, with a sheaf of other relevant documents. It was the usual advice to a professional time-waster: always look like you know where you're going and have a piece of paper in your hand. The excuse for being there was covered.

The real reason was something else.

He'd been trying for days to figure out whether Special Branch was involved in resettling Neville Rollason. If so, he wanted the new identity and, better still, an address. A few days ago, when Jim Cottesloe had gone out for lunch and failed to log out, Wickens had used his colleague's terminal to do a search on the Police National Computer. It was a good precaution. You couldn't get access to the PNC without keying in your collar tag, and he'd used Jim's to cover his tracks in case anyone was checking up. He felt pretty safe, because there were bound to be dozens of enquiries from all over the country about Rollason, from disgruntled coppers trying to dig up the new name. All over the force, lots of officers were angry.

Special Branch was being cagey, though. There had been nothing on the system beyond the Parole Board decision and the release date. The details were bound to be on SB's own system, to which he had no access. So now, Wickens was going to enter the lion's den. He saw it as a crusade for truth and justice, against the *Guardian*-reading lefties who ran the Home Office and Parole Board, who would forgive anything a criminal did while forgetting the victims.

To right a wrong you sometimes have to break the rules.

He left the car, clicked the fob lock and strode across the car park to the main building. The male receptionist swallowed Wickens' excuse about the papers for CID and let him through. Directions were given. Follow the corridor to the CID block, through to the main ground-floor office. He nodded and set off, folder in hand. The place was buzzing. Two of the incident rooms in use, ranks of detectives on phones, looking at screens, piecing clues together. He suppressed his envy and climbed the stairs to the first floor. Much less busy here. He followed the corridor, past fraud, child protection and on to the Special Branch office. The door had a combination keypad, but was ajar. He could see a female receptionist inside on the phone but no one else.

This was no good. He was too early. Too many people about.

Trying to kill some time, Wickens left the CID block and made his way to the refectory. It was packed. The day shift for uniformed officers was just coming to a close, and many were taking the opportunity to load up on subsidised grub before heading off to the sports and social club for a pint. He paid for his pasty, chips and beans at the cash register, then turned to look for somewhere to sit. There were a couple of hot young female officers with a spare seat to either side of them. On any other day he would have been in like a shot, but he was looking for someone else. DI Graham Morgan, the Special Branch detective who hadn't been seen for weeks in the sports and social, and who according to rumour had a secret project to look after.

And there he was.

Wickens spotted him at the far end of the refectory, sitting alone on a table for two, eating a burger while reading a motoring magazine propped up against a bottle of ketchup, his coat and bag on the seat opposite. Off home afterwards, by the look of it.

The constable knew him only vaguely but did have one conversational hook that was guaranteed to work. He made his way across to Morgan and sat at an adjacent two-person table, so they were diagonally opposite each other. The Special Branch officer raised his eyebrows in acknowledgement, then returned to his magazine as Wickens cleared his table of the detritus of the previous occupant. Finally ready to eat, the constable asked Morgan if he could borrow the ketchup. As it was passed across he said: 'Crap performance in the rugby on Saturday, wasn't it?' Morgan was a known rugby fan and, after the disastrous England showing against France in a friendly last Saturday, Wickens guessed he would be happy to vent. For the next five minutes they talked through the game, the failings, the missed opportunities and the improvements that the coach should make.

Having put the world of sports to rights, Wickens asked: 'Word has it you've got a big project at the moment.'

Morgan sighed heavily and looked around the room. 'Too right. Drew the short straw on this one. Spending all my time on paperwork, filling out bloody benefit forms, council tax credit, you name it. Not what I came into the police for.' He chewed ruminatively on his burger.

'Some drug nark you've got to protect from the Albanians?'

Morgan shook his head and laughed. 'I wish it was. Someone worth saving maybe, someone with at least a shred of human decency.' He fixed Wickens with a glance. 'I can't say who it is.'

Wickens smiled. *You just did*. He finished his pasty, said goodbye, then headed out and back into the CID block. This time he was in better luck. The upstairs corridor was quiet, and he made his way along to the end to the Special Branch office. The door was shut, and from the lack of sound appeared to be unoccupied. He tapped and called hello. No reply.

He looked at the keypad. It was pretty old, requiring a four-digit code, plus the letter C to reset. He took out his LED torch and shone it at an angle. It clearly showed the four most heavily used digits on the keypad, because the black paint was rubbing off. Letter C, then five, nine, and particularly zero. In fact zero was almost unreadable. Most of the other numbers looked pristine. That was still a lot of combinations, but you could try as many times as you wanted. He tried a few but got nowhere.

Someone came past, so Wickens headed off to the gents', sat down in a cubicle and had a think. This was a bit like sudoku. He was fond of taking a paper with him into the loo and doing the brain-teasers. The last time he'd seen Morgan in the sports and social, it was his birthday. The Special Branch guy had bought everyone a pint, including him. What date was that? A birthday would make a memorable code, if not the smartest. It was some time in May. So let's assume that was the 05. He couldn't for the life of him remember what day it had been, but going for 09 would be a good start.

Of course, the door code might not be Morgan's birthday. It could be his wedding anniversary, the birthday of a grandson or something else. It could also be the receptionist's birthday, as she was probably in the office more than her boss. Wickens then realised that a six-digit date could be boiled down to four in two ways. One, by dropping the day or the year. Or two, by dropping preceding zeroes in day and/or month. Which to consider? Wickens returned to an observable fact, the worn zero. He decided to assume it was used twice in the code. He used a biro to write down some permutations on the palm of his hand, not wanting to sully the paperwork he was going to hand in shortly.

Wickens emerged from the gents' just as a female in civvies emerged from child protection and went down the stairs. He could hear activity on the CID floor, but on his floor it was quiet. He pressed in 0509. Nothing. He went through various permutations, and finally, at 0590, the door opened. Inside, he closed the door, sat at the workstation and checked to see if Morgan was still logged in. No. When he tapped return, the prompt came up to enter log-in details. No point trying that without the password. He looked on the desk for a Post-it note with the code on. Nothing. Even Morgan wouldn't be that dim.

He turned his attention to Morgan's in-tray. There was a stack of documents, most of which appeared to be irrelevant to the Rollason case. Right at the bottom was a blank council tax benefit form. Wickens cursed Morgan for having not yet filled it in. Maybe it had only arrived today. He looked in the bin. It contained a torn window envelope. Inside it he found a standard cover sheet from the council enclosing the benefit form he'd just been looking at. It was addressed to: The Occupier, 63 Wexford Road, Staines.

That must be the address where Rollason was going.

What a find!

He folded the cover sheet, then stuffed it in his pocket, left the office and quietly closed the door. He descended the stairs as quietly as he could. The CID office was almost empty as he made his way across.

'Wickens.' It was eagle-eyed DCI Gillard, sitting in his office with the door slightly open.

'Yes, sir.' Wickens made his way to the doorway.

'Got those notes for me?' Gillard continued to tap away on his keyboard, only occasionally raising his eyes to the junior officer.

'Yes, sir. They're here, sir.' Wickens walked into Gillard's office and set them on the desk.

'Thank you. What were you doing upstairs?'

Wickens paused for a moment. Playing dumb wasn't going to work. Gillard must have heard him. 'I was looking for you.'

Gillard continued to tap away. 'You walked right past my office. Got my name on the door.'

'So it has, sir.'

'I take it you have no ambition to become a detective then?'

'Sorry sir?'

'Not exactly Sherlock Holmes, are we? Can't read a name on a door.'

Eventually, Wickens extricated himself with another couple of apologies. He felt his face burning with embarrassment. The trouble was he really did have ambitions to be a detective. He'd dreamed of it since he was a child.

–

It was late afternoon. Baz Mulholland was tired and not in the best of moods, trying to finish the final stretch of wall in the herpetarium. Jakes was working on the other side, finishing off some edges. The bill for the van repair was much higher than Baz had anticipated, and then he had argued with Claire on the way in, about the death penalty and how to treat the worst murderers. He'd made the mistake of calling her a bleeding-heart leftie, and in the ensuing row she'd run rings round him. He was so annoyed that when he got out of her car he'd forgotten to take his radio. Now he was missing his music, and it didn't help that he knew that Jakes was continuing to listen to his own on his earbuds. The slight hiss of the classical music hovered at the edge of Baz's concentration as he swept one clear arc after another with his trowel. Baz hadn't often tried to engage his colleague in conversation. It wasn't an easy task, because Jakes took such an intellectual and philosophical approach to every subject. But today Baz, still needled over the subject of crime and punishment, wanted to provoke a conversation.

'So what about this bloke Rollason, getting out with a new identity courtesy of the British taxpayer?'

Jakes slipped off his earbuds, said nothing for a while, then ventured: 'Ethically it's a complex subject.'

'Is it bollocks. They should hang him.'

'Justice and retribution are not synonyms.'

'Eh?'

'Have you read any Nietzsche, Barry? The will-to-power concept has some interesting insights into the nature of good and evil.'

Baz knew he'd blundered into one of Jakes's many philosophical quagmires. He struck out for firm ground. 'Did you ever read what Rollason did to those children? Disgusting. One day they will be able to work out before birth who's gonna be like that and wipe them out with an injection.'

'Eugenics. Another tricky subject with no clear end point.'

'So why shouldn't they kill freaks like that?'

There was a tut, but no reply. When Baz looked across he noticed a careless crease like a wonky smile in Jakes's fresh plaster.

'You've got a line there, mate,' Baz said. He was aware he was still trying to provoke a reaction. Jakes was a perfectionist.

Again there was no immediate response, but as Baz looked up from his work he could see Jakes staring at him. The most amazing thing was that for the first time, both of Jakes's eyes were focused and unmoving, his mouth tight.

'No offence, mate,' Baz said, already regretting that his own petulance was causing mischief.

'You don't understand anything about it, Barry! Not a thing.' Jakes turned away and, with a sudden growl, gouged a great chunk out of the wall he was working on with his trowel. He flung the hawk to the ground, its full load of plaster splattering across the floor, and stormed out of the room. Plasterers' sacrilege.

For a full minute Baz carried on working, but then he realised his own arm was shaking a little. He'd never seen Jakes angry before and considered that an apology might be in order. Claire had often accused him of insensitivity. Once again she had been proven right. Perhaps Jakes had been abused as a child, something like that. Maybe that's why he didn't even want to discuss Neville Rollason. And he shouldn't have used the word freaks. Baz emptied his own hawk back into the bucket, set the trowel down carefully and set off to find his workmate.

The lower doorway of the herpetarium led out through a footpath fenced on both sides to a large open area, in which much construction machinery was stored. Baz could see Jakes off to the left by another enclosure. He made his way over towards him, passing through a metal gate and onto a metal walkway that traversed the edge of a large muddy pool. Baz held onto the handrails as the walkway led him across the edge of the turbid waters. Jakes was staring down into the water, seemingly unaware of Baz's approach. There was movement in the water, swirling currents, and then a shiny brown island surfaced for a moment before disappearing again.

'Is that a croc?' Baz asked, hoping for a safe conversational gambit.

As Baz leaned on the rail next to his workmate Jakes spoke, but kept his gaze on the undulating surface. 'Yes. It's not really warm enough for them to come out of the heated water. They need at least twenty-five degrees.'

'So that's why they are going to enclose the space, is it?' Jakes nodded.

'Good idea,' Baz said mildly. He was wondering how to apologise. His formula for apologising to his wife on the many occasions he upset her was to kiss her on the neck and offer to take her out to dinner. It didn't always work either. In any case there was no way he was going to kiss Michael Jakes on the neck.

Jakes saved him the trouble.

'Neville Rollason used to tempt boys into his car,' he said. 'He had a toy box in the boot. Tapes of rock bands for the older teenagers, and Lego for the younger ones. He had computer games and consoles, including the Super Mario ones which were huge at the time. He had sweets, chocolate, fizzy drinks and alcohol, all of which he had spiked with drugs. In the basement at his house he kept a huge model railway layout and a pinball machine. He kept photographs of his playroom in the car to show the boys he wanted to lure there.'

Baz didn't dare breathe.

'Daniel Cooper was the first victim. Thirteen years old, disappeared outside a sweet shop in Gateshead in 1984. Then Jason Harvey, seventeen, from Newcastle. He was last seen in a park in March 1985. Paul Sullivan, eleven, was the youngest, November 1985. Sullivan's body hasn't been found. Then there are the other victims, the suspected and the unknown.' He looked across at Baz, his eyes steady. 'Not all of them are dead.'

It seemed to him the pain of Jakes's childhood was being laid bare right before him.

'I'm really sorry, it was so insensitive of me.'

Baz saw a complex expression swarm across Jakes's face. The errant eye resumed climbing gradually, peering over Baz's head, and then, like a one-armed bandit, dropped back into its normal position.

'You have been to the police about this, haven't you?' Baz asked.

Jakes blew a sigh and turned away in exasperation. 'I'm touched, Baz, but I don't think empathy is your strong suit.'

Chapter Eighteen

Friday

Detective Inspector Claire Mulholland had gone the formal route in her approach to Gus van Steenis. The nine a.m. appointment meant she had to hang around a little after giving Baz a lift for his eight a.m. start. She left the car at the gate and, when Baz was buzzed through over the intercom, she walked in with him. The Holdersham Estate still boasted many of the stately-home attributes that had made it such an attractive preparatory school. A long ride of lime trees led up to the main house, and to the left were buildings that had previously housed the sports changing rooms. Between her and them were a series of substantial railings with padlocked gates. Beyond them, in front of a screen of bushes, she could see a woman in a green uniform manoeuvring a bale of straw in a wheelbarrow. Claire called her over, and after a couple of minutes she came to the other side of the railings. 'Can I help you?' she asked. She was in her early thirties, pretty and slim. Juliette, according to her badge, a name that seemed familiar. Claire had overheard PC Wickens going on endlessly about someone of that name to his mates in the canteen. Seeing the woman, she understood.

Claire flashed her detective ID and explained that she had an interview with the manager at nine. Juliette looked at her watch and plucked out the walkie-talkie radio clipped to her belt. 'I'll call him to let him know that you're here.'

'In a minute,' Claire said. 'I just wondered if I could ask you a few questions about the owner.'

'Sheikh Khalil? I've only ever seen him from a distance. He's hardly ever here.'

'Not here now?'

'We'd know. Comes in by helicopter. If you want to know anything about him, you should ask Gus, he's the manager.'

'I'm not after the official version. I'll be discreet and won't be making notes.'

'Okay,' Juliette said, her glance crawling sideways to the big house as if she could be overheard.

'How long have you worked here?'

'Just over two years.'

'How many members of staff are there here?'

'Is this about licensing, or something else?' she asked.

'Mainly licensing.'

'Well, four of us to look after the animals. I don't know how many work inside the house. Maybe two or three. He sometimes uses conservation volunteers too, to clear the scrub.'

'Has anyone left or been fired recently?'

'Not that I know of.'

'Any foreign nationals?'

'Only in the house, I think they all are.'

'Can I see the new building?'

'There's nothing to see yet. Just a bunch of workmen finishing off.'

'Humour me.'

Juliette shrugged, and led the way, up a ramp and through a pair of double doors. The building was a wide meandering corridor, lined with apertures on either side. Claire could hear the distinctive gritty sound of a trowel on plaster. She hoped Baz would keep quiet as she passed him.

'There will be glass tanks in here,' Juliette said. 'We've got anacondas, boa constrictors, pythons, and a bunch of other reptiles, many of them endangered species. They're currently in the old barn, which is difficult and expensive to heat.'

'There must be strict import rules.'

'Yes, but we don't import. The snakes are almost entirely rescues, sourced in the UK. They used to be sold quite widely in pet shops, and we buy them from owners who got bored or are incapable of looking after them. People don't understand that the constrictors have very precise requirements yet spend almost all their time asleep. They can live for decades and get very large.'

They passed Baz and Jakes, who were working on the ceiling of one of the spurs off the main corridor. 'All this work will be finished in a couple of days,' Juliette said. 'As you probably guessed, the building was designed to represent the sinuous shape of a snake.' She waggled her hips in illustration.

With that sixth sense that men have for a sight worth seeing, Baz's eyes flicked sideways at Juliette. Up, down, then a lingering glance at her breasts. It took a couple of seconds to register that Claire was there too. A splat of dropped plaster punctuated his surprise. He squeezed out a guilty smile and then went back to his work. His neck coloured slightly. Claire understood. She could read him like a dirty book.

Juliette led her on towards the end of the corridor, where the breeze-block construction was still visible. Claire looked to her left. A staircase, going down. 'What's down here?' she asked.

'I don't know. Nothing worth seeing, I'm sure.'

'May I?' Claire asked as she began to descend.

'What are you doing?' Juliette asked, following the policewoman down the stairs. At the bottom, an open door led to a small room, maybe ten feet square, on which the plasterwork had already been finished. On the floor there was a mattress, still in its plastic wrapper. A urinal-style gulley was at one end of the room. 'I really must ask you to stop,' Juliette protested.

Claire ignored her request and stepped into the room. 'What's this for?'

'I told you, I don't know. Now unless you have a warrant I must ask you to leave. If you have any more questions you should ask Gus.'

The detective inspector took a couple of photographs on her phone, and then complied. Juliette guided her upstairs and out of the building.

'Well, time for me to go up to the house,' Claire said. 'Thank you for your time.'

'I'm assuming the reason you're really here is to find out if the dead guy from the river used to work with us?'

Now it was Claire's turn to smile. 'Yes, that's part of why I'm here.'

'I think you'll be disappointed,' Juliette said. As she turned away, Claire could almost swear she heard the words the young woman spoke under her breath: *nosy bitch.*

-

Claire made her way up to the main drive and then strode towards the grand entrance of the house. She looked at the pictures she had taken. She wasn't sure that Michael Jakes had been correct about the function of that basement room. Yes, there was a big lock, and a sliding metal hatch. But it could equally be somewhere for an overnight security person to sleep. There was no smoking gun.

She rang the bell and a few moments later an Asian maid in traditional uniform opened the door and showed her in through the grand entrance hall. She was led into a wood-panelled drawing room. She had somehow expected there to be mounted heads of lions and tigers on the wall, but instead there were paintings of bewigged aristocrats that presumably had come with the property.

Gus van Steenis was wearing a white linen jacket over a crisply ironed pale yellow shirt. With him was a dark-suited middle-aged man, introduced as his lawyer. Coffee was ordered from the maid, and the manager beckoned her to a seat opposite his large walnut desk.

'So, Detective Inspector, you have come to check up on us,' he said.

'Not exactly. As you may be aware, we're trying to trace a man of Chinese origin who we found in the Thames last week.'

'I'm aware of that, in fact I gave a statement about my movements on the evening of his disappearance to PCs Wickens and Cottesloe,' he said.

'Yes, I have it here.' Claire opened her leather briefcase and took out the statement. 'That's fine for that line of enquiry, but I was just wondering if you had ever employed someone of that ethnicity.'

'Well, we had a Hong Kong Chinese chef here a few years ago. But he left back in...' He looked at the lawyer for help.

The suit rapidly flicked through a pile of documents. 'March 2017,' he said. He passed the document across to Claire, who made a note of the name.

'I understood that you were coming to check our various permits for the animals,' van Steenis said, his glance flicking across to the lawyer, who handed her a thick white envelope.

'It's all there,' the lawyer said. 'Local authorities and Defra zoo licence, planning consents, movement permissions, dangerous animal consents.'

'I'll take these away and have a look,' she said.

'Detective Inspector Mulholland, I understand that you have been asking questions of my staff.' He steepled his hands on the desk. 'You put Juliette in quite an awkward position, between her respect for the law and her duty of loyalty to me. I really prefer if you would ask me anything you want to know.'

'News travels fast,' she replied.

'Bush telegraph,' van Steenis said. 'Very reliable.'

'Have you ever had any accidents involving your animals?'

'Yes. I have the workplace accident book just here. There's been nothing serious for over two years.'

Claire picked up the book and saw that it was meticulously filled out. She was no health and safety expert but it looked like van Steenis took safety very seriously.

'Anything involving the rhino?'

'Dennis? No. He's incredibly gentle. It's much more likely to be Nora, our female saltwater croc. But we're very careful with her.'

Once Mulholland had left, and the lawyer too had departed, Gus van Steenis sat down in his private office. He checked the CCTV monitor to confirm the departure of the detective's car. He then changed into T-shirt and shorts, always his clothing of choice even in the cool British summers, and headed off to his personal workshop. It was a large and rather ugly metal barn well behind the main house, shielded from view by a line of leylandii. He unlocked the padlock, pulled open the corrugated metal door and switched on the light. The entire shed was turned over to tools of various kinds, from some ancient agricultural harrows and spanners right through to precision electronic kit. Van Steenis was a practical man and this was his chapel. Spread right in the middle of the shed was a large plastic dust sheet, and on it a gym mat. On this was a solidly built wooden dining chair. Van Steenis had built it himself and kitted it out. There were buckled canvas restraints on both arms and the chair's front legs, and larger canvas belts threaded through the back of the chair. A thick grey cable ran from a large junction box on the wall to the seat-back, where it split into six smaller cables, five of which were connected by brass plates to the arms, legs and back of the chair. The final small cable was connected to a circular brass strip, which hung loosely over the back of the chair like a discarded crown.

Van Steenis went to a toolbox, got out the voltage meter and once again began to test his contraption. It was almost identical to the one that he had made for Mobutu, when he was in Zaire back in '93, which was in turn modelled on Old Sparky, the Texas chair used until 1964. He rechecked all the connections. He wanted to be sure that it would work properly before Tuesday, when there would be a small select audience.

–

The small grey cat woke Michael Jakes just before noon on Saturday. Schrödinger was hungry, and clawing at the pillow and bedclothes, her insistent purr bringing him to consciousness. The cat showed no recognition that this was a day of rest. After stroking her for a few minutes, he clambered out of bed, ran his fingers through his hair and slipped into a bathrobe. Padding downstairs, he topped up the cat's biscuits and opened a sachet of the soft food that she liked to have in the mornings.

Coffee and *The Times*. Privilege of a day off. He picked up the heavy paper from the mat and saw that the post had come too, a large envelope in his sister's handwriting. That was a surprise, as he normally only heard from her on his birthday and at Christmas. They weren't close. She had the career, the car, the husband, the semi-detached house and the 2.4 children. But inside, Jakes knew that she was as screwed up as he was. The only difference was she didn't admit it and wouldn't talk about it. He tore open the envelope and saw that another smaller one was within, as well as a note from Sue.

> *Dear Michael,*
>
> *I hope you are well and taking good care of yourself. You can see from the enclosed that the day we feared is almost upon us. Try not to let it upset you. I promise you he doesn't know where you live.*
>
> *All my love*
> *Sue*

Jakes set the smaller envelope on the coffee table. It was neatly written and addressed to him, care of his sister. He didn't know if he dared open it. In the end curiosity overcame him, and he tore the envelope in his hurry, pulled out the one carefully folded sheet and began to read. But before he reached the end he broke down. His shoulders shook, and his vision blurred. The shadow of the past fell on him once again.

Chapter Nineteen

DC Rainy Macintosh was standing in the grand vaulted entrance of Imperial College in London, waiting for the academic to show up. This Saturday appointment was the culmination of half the morning and much of the previous day on a second piece of homework set by Gillard: trying to find what, exactly, the mesh or netting marks on the victim's body came from. Metal, wire, plastic, wire-in-plastic or something else?

She had soon realised she couldn't just email out the stomach-turning pictures of the dead body to all and sundry in her search for an answer. It had taken some of the technical expertise of young Research Intelligence Officer Rob Townsend to alter the CSI images and electronically bleach out the human details so that all that remained was the pattern. Rob's expertise on Photoshop had gradually turned the grisly image of a corpse into a rather beautiful 3D pattern, like violet wallpaper on a pale peach background. Looked at like this, there was a clear waviness that corresponded to the undulations of the now invisible flesh on which the marks were impressed. She had attached a scale to the side of the photographs, and then sent them off to the various obscure industrial academics who might know the answer.

The feedback had varied. Some blinded her with science, emailing back arcane papers and references without explanation. Others passed the buck to colleagues elsewhere, while a good half – this being the summer vacations – just didn't reply at all.

The person she was now waiting for, Dr Marcus Goetz, was a researcher here at Imperial. The first person who claimed to have a clear answer.

Plastic.

She had been waiting fifteen minutes when she spotted Dr Goetz, talking to a receptionist. She'd looked up his picture on LinkedIn anyway, but the threadbare blue suit and woollen tie were as much a giveaway as the tatty leather briefcase, smeary glasses and the few tendrils of greying hair that had been combed across his balding pate.

Rainy went straight up to him and introduced herself.

'Delighted to meet you,' Dr Goetz said. 'I think I've got something that will fit the bill perfectly.' He shook her hand in both of his, then led her quickly along the front of the building, down another street and to a basement entrance. Rainy's self-protection mechanism alerted her as the academic unlocked a steel door and showed her into a workshop the size of a triple garage. There were a few machines and consoles, but none of the presses or extrusion machines she had seen in her research.

'Plastics are wonderful,' he said. 'Light, strong, stable and enduring. They are also now incredibly cheap.' He went to a cupboard and brought out a few samples and laid them on a table in front of her. He produced an iPad and went to the sanitised victim photographs that she had sent him. 'This is really a fascinating conundrum,' he said. 'The distortion is relatively modest and I presume unrelated to the force that you mentioned was exerted on the body.'

He picked up a small sample of black plastic mesh and pulled at it. 'This is fish netting. I think it is too easily distorted to be the one you are looking for. At the other end of the scale is this.' He showed her a grey translucent mesh, with four large circular holes. 'You know what this is?'

'I'm from Glasgow, of course I do.' She laughed. 'It's the webbing from a pack of beer cans.'

'That's right. Now, the webbing is polypropylene and the other is polyethylene. This one, I think, is too rigid to be the mesh that you are looking for. I do wish you had a sample of it that I could test, then we could get to the root of the problem immediately. Think I'm going to need a lot more time.'

'I'm not surprised,' Rainy said. 'It's like starting with the suntan on a corpse and trying to work back to find the bikini she was wearing.'

The academic's eyebrows almost shot off the top of his head.

'I was actually thinking of hysteresis,' he said. 'The extent to which a stretched or deformed material will return to its previous shape.'

–

Saturday morning arrived gently, for once without the insistent ringing of the alarm clock. The first thing Gillard was aware of was the warm proximity of Sam, her dark hair resting on his chest, the red varnished nails of her fingers hooked on one shoulder. In theory Gillard had the day off, a rare treat during such a busy case. Claire Mulholland had volunteered for the weekend shift, to allow the detective chief inspector to spend a little time with his recuperating wife and visit his Aunt Trish, who was still in a coma in hospital. She had promised to ring if anything dramatic occurred, but Gillard knew she would take care of all but the biggest developments.

He kissed Sam gently on the cheek, slipped out from her arm and checked his phone. Good. Nothing important was notified. He slipped on a bathrobe and made his way downstairs to put the kettle on. Last night Sam had announced that if the weather was good they were going to go for a picnic at Box Hill, a famous beauty spot on the North Downs, a half-hour's drive away. Peering through the window, he saw a cloudless sky. He opened the fridge and found Sam had already cooked tandoori chicken drumsticks, along with home-made spicy samosas. There was chicken and ham pie from the local deli, and a home-made red cabbage coleslaw.

–

They had managed to find the perfect spot away from the weekend crowds. Sam had lain the tablecloth down in a field of buttercups not far from the spreading boughs of a horse chestnut tree, a mature beauty like a perfect scaled-up floret of broccoli. The view south was gloriously bucolic, a patchwork of fields and hedgerows little changed in hundreds of years. If he ignored the distant hum of traffic, it was possible to imagine he was in an England of the 1920s, with its traditional farm buildings and tumbledown cottages, rustic fences and horses grazing contentedly.

'It seems like years since we've had a picnic,' Sam said.

'I think we have Claire to thank for this. And the weather,' Gillard said. He stroked her dark hair, which was now shoulder-length, her fringe close to her shapely eyebrows. Sam had been quite quiet that morning, and he watched her as she laid out the food she had carefully prepared.

As they began to eat, he complimented her on the food, and rested his hand in hers. She smiled up at him. 'Just for today, Craig, I don't want to talk about the bad stuff. I want to forget it happened. I want to imagine we are in a time before it, okay?'

He nodded. 'That's absolutely fine by me. I would be happy if we never mentioned him again.' Sam had told her husband the bare minimum about her ordeal during the kidnap, but the group PTSD talking therapy courses and the one-to-one cognitive behavioural sessions seemed to be working. Her medication had already been lowered, which was a good sign. His own key metric with Sam was how receptive she was to affection. She adored being embraced, and was now kissing him back when he nuzzled her neck or cheek, which he did at every opportunity. However, their sex life had been non-existent for a while now, and she froze if he attempted to initiate. While he understood, it didn't make dealing with it any easier. He still desired her enormously but his main task, he felt, was to mask his frustration entirely so that she didn't feel guilty.

'Why don't you tell me about your new detective, the Scottish doctor?'

'Rainy. Ah, she's not so new now but she's doing very well. She's got a tremendous brain and is pretty good at keeping Carl Hoskins in order.'

Sam laughed. 'Someone has to, now that Colin's gone.' She knew DC Carl Hoskins pretty well from her time in the control room at Surrey police headquarters. The archetypal old-fashioned male chauvinist, softened considerably by his sense of humour. They both knew how much he missed his old mate Colin Hodges, who had died a few months ago.

'Rainy is a great self-starter, and I've given her the task of trying to narrow down the source of these strange marks on the body that we found in the Thames. We've considered wire mesh, chain-link fencing and industrial walkways, even a self-made playsuit.'

'But that wouldn't have asphyxiated him, would it?'

'No. Delahaye thinks there are two separate things – the force, which is probably mechanical, and the restraint that he was wrapped in.'

'Could it be a sex thing?'

'That's what Rainy mentioned. Sex games gone wrong.' He shook his head.

'I know people do bizarre things.' Sam giggled. 'But I can't get my head round this.'

—

A silver Peugeot with a missing hubcap crawled down Wexford Road until it reached number sixty-three. A parking space was miraculously available right outside. Two beefy men wearing hi-vis jackets and gloves and carrying paint-stained toolboxes emerged from the car. Nigel Chivers and Terry Dalton scanned the road, then walked up to the front door and rang the bell. As expected, there was no reply. Chivers crouched down and inspected the lock. 'Five lever mortice,' he said, and shook his head. 'We'll not get in here easily, at least not without leaving a mess.'

'We don't want to leave a mess, obviously, Nige,' Dalton said, keeping his eye on the street behind them. 'Don't want anyone to know, do we?'

'I'll go around the back,' Chivers said. Leaving his colleague to keep watch, the former bouncer found an alleyway a few doors up on the left. The narrow entrance led between the high fences of the rear gardens on either side, and then turned right to traverse the rear of the back gardens of a dozen homes. Chivers counted off the houses until he was certain he was at the back of number sixty-three. At first sight it wasn't good news. There was a six-foot-high holly hedge, broken only by a timbered gate. He pushed against it, and felt it flex as if bolted low down on the inside. He didn't like climbing, and even if he did, the rotten panels were liable to break. A hefty kick at the bottom of the fence did the trick, tearing out the hasp of the bolt retainer. He looked around to see if anyone had noticed the noise. There were no obvious signs that they had, so he stepped into the garden and closed the gate behind him. The short, tidy backyard led up to a UPVC window with locks top and bottom, and a matching UPVC back door. The door looked manageable. Chivers had never been a burglar, but a nine-month stint inside had given him the opportunity to learn from a man who did nothing else. Specifically, he knew how to snap the cylinders of the Euro profile locks used on most modern double-glazed doors. The most skilled practitioners reckoned to get inside in 15 to 20 seconds. Chivers was less well prepared. He had only tried to do this twice before, both times after a few pints when trying to get back into his ex-girlfriend's house after she'd thrown him out.

Using a large screwdriver, he levered off the exterior brass plate to expose the shank of the lock barrel. He then gripped the shank with a large adjustable spanner and twisted it to the left with all his considerable weight.

It took several attempts, as the spanner kept slipping, but it finally cracked. It had taken just under two minutes.

Chivers pushed open the door, and on his hands and knees searched the carpet on the inside for any metal fragments. None. There was no key on the inside part of the lock, but that didn't matter. The broken cylinder would still slide back into the gap in the lock, and even the brass plate would fit back on. Once he'd straightened the plate and glued it back with epoxy, it wasn't obvious that anything had happened. Any key used on the inside and turned could still apparently lock the door. It just wouldn't be secure.

He didn't need to go inside now. He had simply cleared the way to come back on Monday night and then lie in wait for Rollason as he arrived the following morning.

Monday

Gillard was expecting a call from Dr Delahaye, but when he picked up the phone the switchboard operator said it was someone from the Hyacinth Trust, who had asked for him by name.

The detective sighed and agreed to take the call. He knew the organisation, originally the Society of Murder Victims and one of the largest and most active of the many victims' organisations. He didn't catch the woman's name, but it was clear she had a prepared script. 'As you know, we have campaigned long and hard to make sure that those who commit the worst crimes are never released early from prison.'

'Well, perhaps if I could stop you there. I'm not involved with the decision. Perhaps you should direct your call towards the probation service—'

'I'm sorry, Mr Gillard,' she said. 'I'm ringing you because I understand it was you who originally caught Neville Rollason.'

'Where did you hear that?' Gillard wasn't aware that this was generally known.

'It was in the *Croydon Advertiser* back in October 1988. I've got a cutting. The article doesn't mention you by name, merely that a twenty-one-year-old new recruit made the arrest, but I was able to find out through some contacts that it was actually you.'

'I'm sorry, I didn't catch your name,' Gillard said.

'I'm the mother of Robert Fenwick,' she said.

'Ah, Mrs Fenwick, what can I do to help?' The detective realised he had spoken to her before, years ago. Thirteen-year-old Robert Fenwick disappeared from his home in 1986 and was never seen again. It was one of the coldest of cold cases in Surrey police history. His old boss Paddy Kincaid had reworked it several times but never got anywhere. Gillard recalled the slim and fashionably dressed redhead appearing at a press conference arranged by Kincaid during the early days of the search for her son. She would be in her late fifties now.

Mrs Poppy Fenwick had rung to speak to Paddy on numerous occasions, to see if progress had been made. But very often Paddy would ask Gillard, then simply a detective constable, to take the call and listen to her pour her heart out. He had, on his own initiative, sent a remembrance card on behalf of Surrey Police to Mrs Fenwick on the fifth anniversary of the boy's disappearance, assuring her that the hunt for the killer had not been forgotten. The trouble was it had been forgotten, and subsequently tucked away into a bureaucratic cul-de-sac. He was aware that the Hyacinth Trust had been pushing the theory that

Neville Rollason killed Robert and another boy, John Dawson, in the Croydon area. It had never been given much credence, despite Croydon being where Gillard had arrested Rollason, and where the murderer had been renting a flat from June 1986 to the moment of his arrest in 1988.

'Mr Gillard. I am a very patient woman, but I am not well these days, and I want to plead with you to reinvestigate the killing of my Robert.'

'I'm terribly sorry. I would love to be able…'

Mrs Fenwick's voice broke as she heard what must sound to her like bureaucratic buck-passing, certainly not for the first time. He knew it would be pathetic to have to tell her why his hands were tied. Following a reorganisation in 2010, the Met Police had been put in charge of the area where her son disappeared, and any reinvestigation would be down to them.

'Mr Gillard, please. I beg you. You have no idea of a mother's pain. It just never ends. It really never ends.' There was a long sniff at the end of the line, and then sobs. The caller who had begun so confidently, reading her prepared remarks, was now lost for words. Gillard waited out the tears, feeling utterly wretched that he couldn't help. He wondered what he could say to calm her, but realised it would take senior intervention to let him look again at what was now classified as a Met Police cold case.

But that didn't mean he shouldn't try.

'Mrs Fenwick. I'm rather tied up investigating who it was that was found dead in the Thames recently. You may have heard about that. However, I can promise you, that as soon as I have some spare time, I will personally ask the chief constable to let me look again at Robert's disappearance.'

After half a minute during which she struggled to maintain composure, she managed to rasp out one final croaky comment. 'Thank you for that, thank you. I've had more than three decades of grief, but not a single second of justice. I hope you can put that right.'

'I will do my best.' Don't get your hopes up, he wanted to say. Please don't get your hopes up.

'One more thing,' she said. 'Although I'm Robert's mother, I changed my name after he disappeared, and moved house to get away from the fuss. So I'm using my maiden name. Which is Tilling. Mrs Poppy Tilling.'

'Ah, I think I know your son, Gary.'

'Yes, he does very well in his laptop repair business. As you know, he's always helped the police with, you know, indecent images that he finds on hard drives.'

'Yes, we're very grateful.'

'He's a good boy, and though I've been bedridden for years, he looks after me.'

'I'm glad to hear it, Mrs Tilling.'

After he put the phone down, Gillard sat and thought about the woman, and the terrible suffering she had been through. Even now, nobody knew if Rollason had killed her son or if someone else had. The body had never been found. The official records showed that Rollason had been re-interviewed numerous times about it but had always denied involvement. Ahead of the murderer's release tomorrow, there was no chance to have another go.

He felt for Robert Fenwick's mother, but there seemed nothing he could do.

He would have to think about it.

Chapter Twenty

Monday, 1 July dawned as another warm and sunny day, and a dress rehearsal for freedom. Neil Wright was today being allowed an unaccompanied trip to Aylesbury, the nearest town. Three hours of liberty before his final release the next day. The sound of birdsong came in through the open window, along with a breeze. He eased himself out of bed and stretched. HMP Spring Hill really wasn't such a bad place, but he would be glad to get out of it all the same. There were things he had to do. A little to-do list with items to be ticked off.

He showered and trimmed his beard carefully. Applied some of his own special bleaching agent, three parts shampoo and two parts lemon juice, to his scalp and beard. It stung a little, but he knew it would deal with the iron-grey roots that were just beginning to show in a few places. He fixed in the last piece of dental bridgework, something organised and paid for by the Home Office. It complemented the implants made to replace the teeth knocked out by a cellmate. It made his jaw look California perfect, right down to being a little too white. Even as a youngster, he'd had bad teeth; jumbled and discoloured. Those were the ones immortalised in his mugshot. He polished the thick-framed plastic spectacles. He liked the Ferrari frames, which gave his face a more studious look.

Finally satisfied, he spent the last few minutes again practising writing with his right hand. His signature of the name Neil Wright was now utterly consistent and, he thought, rather elegant. At eight a.m. he headed off to the refectory for breakfast. He kept himself apart from the other prisoners, which was easy enough because there were always people leaving having finished their incarceration, and always new faces arriving. At this stage in their prison sentence they could feel and taste the freedom just beyond the gates. Very few wanted to jeopardise that by last-minute misbehaviour.

At nine, he was dressed and ready to be signed out. He had barely any money. The prison grant was being withheld until tomorrow, but he had plenty of things that he could do that wouldn't cost a thing.

He caught the bus, took a seat right at the back and kept his face close to the window for the forty-minute journey. He was thirsty to soak up all the details of the outside world, all those ordinary people going about their daily business. But underneath in his gut was a tight band of anxiety. Even though he knew it was very unlikely, he was terrified of being identified. He got off the bus at Market Square, with almost everybody else, and went straight into the shopping centre beyond. Waterstones, Clarks, Next, House of Fraser. There were plenty of big-brand chain stores that he knew, many he did not. Things had changed a lot in three decades.

He found the library and asked for help to use the Internet. He waited his turn, and then a librarian sat with him. He'd already been shown how to use a computer mouse at the Spring Hill computer room, but the teacher there had concentrated on word processing and getting the offenders to write job applications. There was no

Internet access at Spring Hill, so using a browser was completely new to him. He looked at the blank Google box and asked her: 'So can I just type any question I have in here?'

'Yes,' she replied. 'But you can't always trust the answer.'

Over the course of the next half-hour he managed to find his way around a bit, looking for addresses, phone numbers and so on. He got the librarian to show him how to use the printer, and took his two pages of carefully honed research with him. The information he had got was useful, but more limited than he'd hoped. He was shocked to be told that physical phone books were quite rare now, with many people not in them. He realised his task to track down his enemies might be a lot harder than he had expected.

With only half an hour left before his return bus trip, he looked for a phone box. There were hardly any. When he did see one, he found it wouldn't accept coins. He had for weeks been screwing up the courage to ring his daughter.

Perhaps it would have to wait until he got a mobile.

He looked around until he saw a mobile phone shop. He plucked up his courage and walked in. It was a peculiar place with bright white, largely empty tables, and was full of young women. He didn't even understand the questions they asked him about networks and payment plans. It made him dizzy, so he thought he would leave it for another time. Before he left, he asked one of the women, a blonde with ripped knees to her jeans: 'Did you fall over, pet?'

'I'm sorry?'

'Your jeans are all torn.'

She laughed. 'I bought them like that.'

'Didn't you check them first!' he exclaimed. 'You can take them back, you know.'

They laughed a bit together, and then he asked: 'Can I ask you a favour? Can I borrow a phone to ring my daughter?'

The woman hesitated.

'You see, I've not seen her for thirty years. She wouldn't come to visit me. You know, inside. I'll give you a pound.' He set down the coin.

The blonde nodded. 'Okay, so long as it's not international.' She handed her own phone to him. He had no idea what to do with the sleek black glossy device. There were no obvious buttons.

'Could you dial it for me?' he asked.

She seated him at a small desk towards the back of the shop and tapped out the number he gave her, before passing the device to him and walking away. His heart raced as the number rang out. The phone was picked up, and a familiar voice came on the line.

'Susan, it's me, your dad. Susan? I just wanted—'

A few minutes later, the blond woman looked up and saw the man moving towards the door of the shop. 'It's all right,' he said, 'I left your phone on the desk. Thank you.'

'So how is your daughter?'

'Ah, she's doing grand. Her job is going well, and she's got a house on the new estate. My granddaughter's going to big school next term. I'm looking forward to seeing her for the first time.'

'Ah, that's lovely. I bet you can't wait to be back with them,' she said.

'Yes, it will be great.'

She watched him go, and then looked back at her phone. She checked the call to make sure he wasn't one of those scammers who use the opportunity to ring a premium phone line. The number was a conventional landline. But her brow furrowed as she saw the call duration.

Four seconds.

—

On his way back to the bus station, he had a stroke of luck. He found a phone box that took coins, and took full advantage of it with three quick calls: a message left on the answerphone of Mrs Daphne Cooper, 73, a second on the mobile of Mr George Harvey, 78, and finally, a call to Mrs Rita Hollingsworth, 82, now in a hospice.

That call was picked up by her son, David. He listened, shocked, to what was said to him. 'If this is some kind of joke, I don't think it's very funny,' David said, slamming the phone down. All the families of the victims had suffered prank calls, anonymous letters and various other nuisances during the early years. News that the murderer was to be released seemed to be restarting the torment, this time on social media through a series of insensitive tweets and Facebook memes.

But this phone message was one of the old type. All the caller said, in a soft north-east accent, was: 'Are you afraid of the Bogeyman? Because he's coming for you. Tomorrow.'

Chapter Twenty-one

Tuesday, 2 July 2019

I'm not upset that you lied to me, I'm upset that from now on I can't believe you.

Friedrich Nietzsche

The fateful day arrived. Leticia Mountjoy was up with her phone alarm at 6:45 a.m., having slept badly. Anton was snoring lightly next to her, sleepily sliding his large arm around her shoulders as she extricated herself from the bedclothes. He rarely awoke before ten. Running a restaurant meant he was a night owl, her job made her a lark. But today she didn't feel full of the joys of spring. Neil Wright was being released from Spring Hill open prison today. In fifteen minutes in fact, and she was as nervous as hell. She would meet him later at his new house. Wearing her bathrobe, she leaned against the kitchen counter, holding a mug of coffee to her face for warmth and comfort, and listening to the early morning headlines on the radio. There was plenty going on in the world, and no mention of the prisoner who had been dropped into her care.

Verity had been off sick yesterday, an almost unprecedented event, but had phoned her in the evening. The call was terse, lacking the kind of support and empathy that Leticia felt she needed. Verity simply listed the essential documents and checks that had to be done. The only hint of human connection came right at the end. 'It's a big day for you, so good luck.' Then she had hung up.

The call just reminded Leticia that she was on her own. This morning she had opened the big fat metal briefcase, even before taking a shower. First there were the travel details. He would get the early bus into Aylesbury, then another, changing at High Wycombe for Staines, arriving if all went well shortly after ten. She would go to meet him at his house at eleven. For the umpteenth time she ran through the list: the contract for the house, letters of acceptance from the local GP surgery and a private dental practice, the application forms for a bank account, for housing benefit and for council tax benefit, all pre-filled by DI Morgan and simply awaiting Neil Wright's signature. She also had the details of his compulsory group therapy and individual psychiatric appointments, plus a copy of his formal licence conditions and agreed sentence plan in case he had left his own behind. The licence wasn't big, just a couple of pages, but few prisoners ever bothered to bring it with them. She wondered if there was anything else she should have. Of course – her own work phone, plus the iPad.

She breakfasted rapidly on an apple but couldn't face the usual cereal bar or banana. She was just gathering her bags together when Anton emerged sleepily into the kitchen wearing a pair of boxers. 'I just wanted to wish you the best of luck for today,' he said. Delighted and a little surprised he had managed to rouse himself to see her off, she flung herself into his arms, and inhaled the warm male sleep aroma that rolled off him.

'Anton, I am so nervous. My stomach is just full of butterflies. It's such a responsibility.'

He held her by the shoulders and looked down into her face. 'You are going to do a great job, Tish. Believe me. I have enormous faith in you. I'll be right behind you every step of the way, do you understand?' He kissed her hard and lifted her off the ground. 'Go to it, girl.'

Pumped by such a rousing send-off, Leticia had a smile on her face as she stepped out of her front door and stared up into the wide blue sky that promised so much. If she handled this case well, then promotion was a possibility. Verity had hinted as much.

She walked up the street feeling a few inches taller than she had felt when she first got up. As she clicked the key fob of her car and saw the welcoming orange blink she thought. *I can do this. I really can.*

—

As before, there was nowhere to park on Wexford Road or in the adjoining streets. In the end, already a couple of minutes late, she left the little car illegally, as before, on a single yellow line near the main road. After checking there was no traffic warden about, she tugged out the heavy metal briefcase, slid her leather shoulder bag on and began to march back the 300 yards to the flat. She stepped around a grey wheelie bin and walked the three steps that took her from the front gate to the front door. The curtains were drawn at the bay window, and the ornate bevelled glass in the front door gave no clear view inside. She pressed the bell, which gave a long satisfying buzz in the hallway.

There was no reply.

She pressed her face to the glass of the door and tapped.

It was beginning to rain, so she let herself in with the spare keys.

'Neil? It's Leticia,' she called. Getting no reply, she made her way into the kitchen, and dumped her bag and briefcase. The place smelled of fresh paint and cleaning products and looked pristine.

Except at the sink. There were fresh-looking coffee dregs around the plughole, and a plastic stirrer on the draining board.

So he had been here. He'd probably just gone out to get groceries. She breathed a sigh of relief, but found her anxiety replaced by irritation. It was already five past. She opened the briefcase and pulled out the various documents that Wright would have to sign. She occupied the next five minutes examining everything yet again. Finally, at ten past, she rang Wright's new phone.

It wasn't on.

She sighed, and then realised that of course, having served thirty years inside, he probably only had the haziest idea of how to use one. She left a voicemail message asking him where he was, then for good measure sent him a text asking him to reply. She went to the lounge and looked out of the bay window into the street. She couldn't see him, so she exited the front door and walked out onto the pavement, looking both ways. There were no pedestrians. She turned back, went inside and closed the door.

She kept busy answering her emails until she saw it was 11:25 a.m. Anxiety bubbled up. He wasn't coming back, obviously. What if he had never had any intention of co-operating in this elaborate and expensive resettlement programme? Would they blame her? Perhaps that was why Verity gave her the job – to be the fall guy, having suspected all along that something like this would occur. Perhaps he had gone to a pub and got drunk, like so many ex-cons on their first day out. That was a much more likely story. Alternate waves of optimism and pessimism swept through her.

What if he had immediately gone out to reoffend?

At quarter to twelve, she realised she could no longer delay calling Verity. But she was terrified to do so. Even though it wasn't her own fault, it would inevitably be seen that way. She had read enough coverage of high-profile failings in every aspect of social work to realise that there are always well-funded lawyers and officials with plenty of time after the fact to comb through the mistakes of even the most junior employees. But there were never enough people at the coalface to keep the workload to a reasonable enough level so mistakes weren't made in the first place.

Leticia decided to make the first call to a more easy-going authority, Graham Morgan. She got through and described what had happened. The Special Branch detective inspector didn't seem particularly worried at Wright's failure to show. 'You've got to understand, Leticia, that someone like him is always playing games with the system. I've seen it all before. They'll muck you about, being late, forgetting documents, and try to get under your skin. They have developed a pathological relationship with authority that almost demands being a pain in the arse. He's just asserting himself, particularly as you are less experienced than some.'

'This is serious, though. Missing his first probation meeting. And having the phone switched off!'

Morgan laughed. 'He's not missed it yet. Look, he is not a stupid bloke, far from it. If he's already shown up at the house, he'll be around somewhere. Betting shop, pub, something like that. He's not going to do anything so serious that we send him back. I guarantee you.'

'What about vigilantes? I saw a pretty a frightening documentary about them on Channel 4 last night.'

He chuckled. 'Look, most vigilantes are not the brightest sparks. It would be going some to have got hold of him on the first morning of his release, wouldn't it? Given that only you and I and a couple of others know which prison he was in, and where he was headed. Wait it out, love. I'm sure he'll be there.'

But Neil Wright didn't show. Some time after midday, Leticia phoned Spring Hill and spoke to the governor, a helpful woman who confirmed that, yes, Wright had been let out that morning. He had told the gate staff that he was catching a bus.

Leticia thanked her and hung up. Next she left a message for Verity, who had her own client visit scheduled for today. She next rang the office and was put through to Jill Allsop, who seemed far more concerned about it than Morgan had been.

'Good grief, Leticia. This is not good.' A click. The sound of Jill's office door, then the background noise disappeared.

'Look, Jill. I don't see any point in me hanging around here when he is clearly not planning to make the meeting.'

'Yes of course. I realise that your first inclination may be to report him for breach of licence. I would caution you not to do so immediately. An enormous investment has gone into creating a false identity here and to go official on this would blow it quite quickly. I think I need to make a call to the Home Office for guidance. Anyway, I'll see you back here as soon as you can make it.'

'Okay.'

'One more thing. No one is going to blame you for this, Leticia. It's not your fault.'

'Thank you.' Leticia could not put into words how grateful she was to hear that the departmental boss had her back. Still, whatever the reason, the shit was really going to hit the fan now. Especially if it turned out that he had gone out to commit a crime.

Some poor teenager. She couldn't bear it.

–

Gillard didn't get to hear about it until late that afternoon. The immediate summons from the chief constable, dragging him away from Mr Fang, was a clue that something important had happened. Alison Rigby's PA raised her eyebrows at the detective's approach.

'She's going ballistic in there, Craig. Tread carefully.'

It was true. Gillard could hear some poor sod getting the mother and father of all bollockings. It was unusual for Rigby to shout. With her intimidating height, she rarely needed to. She was quite capable of reducing officers to quivering wrecks with a quiet word here and there. The slam of the phone receiver was followed by a shouted, 'Craig, get yourself in here.'

Gillard took a deep breath and opened the door. Rigby immediately fixed him with her dazzling blue eyes. 'I'm afraid we're in crisis management mode here. As you know, Neville Rollason, multiple murderer, was released today under licence. It seems the bloody probation service has managed to lose him already. And as you had already guessed, he was released on our patch.'

'He's got a new identity, hasn't he? Are we allowed to know it yet?'

'No. Well, not yet. The probation service says yes, but the Home Office is dithering. They think that if the project has gone tits-up already, they'll never again be able to create a new identity for an offender. Which in turn would mean that some high-profile offenders can never be released.'

'I'm sure many people would applaud that,' Gillard said.

'Yes indeed, but it's been obvious for years that it can't continue. Prisons are universities of crime, turning out skilled criminals at an expense to the British taxpayer that would make an Oxbridge vice chancellor blush.'

'That's a good summary, ma'am.'

'So that's why the Home Secretary is desperate to be able to create some high-profile rehabilitation success stories, so we can continue to move lifers out of the system.'

'Ah, now I catch the drift.'

'Yes, Craig. There are only two ways to save money from the public purse in criminal justice. Execution or release.' She shuffled through her papers and sighed heavily before looking up. 'I'm not advocating the former, unlike some.'

'I can't do anything much, ma'am, until I know a name.'

She fixed him again with the blue stare of death. 'I've got the name, Craig, obviously. I've known from the start. But once it's out, it's out. Even if I mandate a total PR blackout, his new name will still leak within an hour.

Look, I'm aware how the rank and file feel about people like Rollason. It wouldn't surprise me if one or two have contacts with vigilante groups.'

'I'm not sure,' Gillard said cautiously.

'It's all right, I'm not asking for a list. Ideally as this is Special Branch's screw-up, it should be up to them to find him, and quickly. But having just roasted Graham Morgan, I don't have much hope they are up to it. You, however, might be.'

'I'm touched by your faith in me, ma'am.'

She smiled. 'I like a man who can look above him, and still admire the sharpness of the sword of Damocles.'

'Give me the name, I'll bring you the man.'

The smile she gave him was unusually warm. The man she could rely upon.

'Craig, I'm giving them two hours, then I turn it over to you, okay? In the meantime, I've got something that you can get Carl Hoskins to work on. I'll email you a picture of Rollason as he is now, and the bus routes he supposedly used. See if you can find him on CCTV.'

–

Gillard found himself almost running down the stairs to get back to the CID block. He found Carl Hoskins, sitting alone in the incident room eating a croissant and watching on his screen what looked like semi-naked women grappling with each other. He quickly flicked channels at the DCI's approach.

'Watching porn at work, Carl?'

'No, sir. I was doing my expenses.'

'What was on the screen?'

'Wrestling, I think.' He looked up as if butter wouldn't melt in his mouth.

193

'Women wrestling?'

'Not sure. Err… I think they may have some women,' he said.

Gillard seized the mouse and clicked on the search history, which clearly showed the oeuvre of Hoskins' artistic interest. 'I see it was "Battling babes in baby oil".'

Hoskins looked up quizzically. 'I don't know what it was called.'

'All right, I've got something a bit more important for you to do.' Gillard logged on to the local crime database and copied across two documents to Hoskins' desktop. First he showed the detective constable a bus map that ran from the Buckinghamshire village of Grendon Under-wood via Aylesbury, High Wycombe and Heathrow to Staines in Surrey. Then he opened a mugshot of an older white-haired man wearing red-framed spectacles. 'This man disappeared from Wexford Road, Staines, some time this morning. He would probably have arrived there on foot around ten thirty a.m., having caught a series of buses this morning on this route. Did he catch the buses or not? Get me an answer ASAP.'

'Who is he, sir?'

'Call him Fred Bloggs for now.'

'Righto. Are uniforms doing a local search on Wexford Road?'

'Not as yet, we'd rather proceed covertly to begin with. And Carl?'

'Sir?'

'If I find you watching stuff like that again at work, I'll send you to the headmistress for six of the best.' He pointed a warning finger at the detective constable.

'Yes sir.' Hoskins was smiling.

Gillard realised why. Hoskins would probably enjoy it.

The answer came within half an hour. Carl Hoskins shouted across the incident room to him. 'Sir, the bloke you are looking for never got on the bus.'

Gillard made his way across to Hoskins' desk. 'The service from Grendon is only once every three hours. I've looked at the onboard CCTV for the 07:45 and the 10:45 and he wasn't there.'

'That's a very quick answer,' Gillard said suspiciously.

'I was quite surprised myself. The bus company uploads its CCTV in real time to the cloud, and they were able to give me a password. Works like a dream.'

'George Orwell would be turning in his grave.'

'What, sir?'

'Never mind.'

'I take it our Mr Bloggs was a discharged prisoner from either HMP Grendon or HMP Spring Hill?'

Gillard tried to iron the surprise out of his face at this uncharacteristic intuitive leap. 'What makes you say that, Carl?'

'Stands to reason, sir. The prisons are the only things of any significance in the village. No one but a discharged prisoner or a car-less pensioner would be forced to take such a slow and obscure journey by rural bus.'

Gillard nodded. 'That's pretty good deductive reasoning.'

'So is this bloke Neville Rollason, then?'

Now the DCI was truly alarmed. 'No,' he said hurriedly. 'He's just an annoying fraudster.'

'Whose name you don't want me to have. Okay. It's just that Rollason got released today with a new identity. And this bloke looks a bit like him.' Hoskins looked up at his boss. 'So I'm wrong then, am I?'

'You've certainly turned speculation into a fine art,' Gillard said, and walked away, aware that he hadn't answered the question. He strode into his office, shut the door and rang DI Morgan.

'Rigby has asked me to give you a hand, looking for our missing person,' he said.

Morgan sighed heavily. 'I'm sure he's just playing silly buggers.'

'Let's hope so, but I think we had better assume the worst for the time being. From what I've heard, the proba- tion officer thought that Rollason had been to his new house. Is that correct?'

'Yes. She found a coffee stirrer that was still wet, and some dregs in the sink.'

'Hmm. Is she sure it wasn't the landlord?'

'No, she can't be.'

'Did she check to see whether there was any luggage? Did she go upstairs? Has someone been there to check?'

If there is a sound to scratching your head, DI Morgan was making it. 'The answer to all those questions is no, I imagine.'

'If it was him, he didn't get there by bus. The onboard CCTV proves it.'

This was news to Morgan. 'So you're saying somebody else gave him a lift?'

'I'm not saying anything. I just don't think we know enough about his movements once he'd left Spring Hill. However, in the meantime I would strongly suggest you check the Wexford Road house in person to see if he has been there.'

By four p.m. Rigby had given Gillard permission to reveal to a small special operations group that the person they were looking for was indeed Neville Rollason. The group included DCs Rainy Macintosh and Carl Hoskins, plus the one man who already knew, Special Branch's Graham Morgan. The group was to report directly to the chief constable and to maintain absolute secrecy about its work, even with family members.

The secret inquiry got off to a slow and discouraging start.

Morgan reported that he had visited the house on Wexford Road. 'There was no sign of any luggage. The probation officer seems to have rinsed away the dregs and thrown away the coffee stirrer.'

'Well, that buggers up the chance of any forensics,' Hoskins muttered.

'There is something else,' Morgan said. 'The back door of the house wasn't locked. It seems to have been forced at some stage.'

'Was that known?' Gillard asked. 'Did you speak to the landlord?'

'I left a message for him, but he hasn't got back to me yet,' Morgan said. 'The letting agent didn't know anything.'

'Maybe the vigilantes have got him,' Rainy said.

Morgan shook his head sceptically. 'I think it's more likely that Rollason forgot the keys he was given, didn't realise until he arrived, and just broke in.'

'He had no known burglary skills,' Gillard said.

'Yes, and it shows exactly that,' Morgan replied. 'The door was forced.'

'But having broken in he didn't hang around,' Rainy said. 'Was there anything in there to steal? I dinnae think so.'

'Well, we know less than nothing, it seems,' Gillard said. 'We don't know how he left Spring Hill except that it wasn't by bus, we don't know for certain if it was him that broke into the house, and we don't know where he is now. There's not much CCTV in the Wexford Road area, and the nearest ANPR camera is miles away.'

'But he was given a phone, wasn't he?' Rainy asked. 'We should trace it.'

'It seems to be switched off. We all took turns trying it,' Morgan said.

'So seeing as this is getting increasingly urgent, we might have to go public and blow his cover,' Gillard said.

Morgan shook his head emphatically. 'No, no, definitely not. He wouldn't have wasted this opportunity. He's not stupid.'

Gillard shrugged. 'It'll be Rigby's decision, and I have a feeling which way it will go.' Rainy threw her pen down in disgust. 'I cannae believe what's happened. How can the probation service have lost their most important client on the same day he left prison?'

'You've got to be fair,' Morgan said. 'Each probation officer has dozens of offenders they are responsible for. The Parole Board has taken the view for each offender that they are not a risk to the public, otherwise they would not release them. They are bound to be wrong on some occasions. There's only so much the probation service can do.'

'You wouldn't say that if Rollason had killed your child, sir,' Hoskins said.

'I'm sure I wouldn't,' Morgan said. 'But would you prefer it if national offender management policy was based on emotion?'

Hoskins' shrug indicated that he wouldn't mind if it was. 'One thing you can be certain of, sir, is that if he is not found quickly there will be plenty of blame to go around.'

'Aye, you're not wrong there,' Rainy said. 'A right shitstorm it'll be.'

'That's why we have to find him straight away,' Gillard said. 'And get some dabs checked for that door, and inside the house.'

–

The probation team's emergency meeting was called for five p.m. sharp. Jill Allsop was already there when Leticia arrived and DI Graham Morgan walked in shortly afterwards. Jill called them all into her office and closed the door.

'Where's Verity?' Jill asked, rolling her eyes.

'She's just coming,' Leticia said. It hadn't escaped her notice that her boss had spent a considerable time in the ladies'. That was puzzling. If she was pregnant she should be sick in the mornings, not the afternoons. Maybe it *was* the eating disorder.

Once Verity arrived, the four of them huddled round Jill's desk. 'Okay,' she said, setting out a tape recorder. 'This meeting is going to go by the book, as if the barristers were already cross-examining us about what happened. The client will be referred to by his assumed name only, is that clear? Leticia, let's start with you.'

Leticia recounted in detail the journey that morning, Neil Wright's no-show and the evidence of someone having been there.

'Graham, do you have anything to add?'

'Yes. Surrey police have already managed to obtain footage from CCTV, which shows that Wright did not board the bus from outside the prison. The landlord said he hadn't visited himself, and wasn't aware of a break-in, but we can't be certain the offender had anything to do with it. He may never have reached the house.'

'Someone must have given him a lift,' Jill said. 'He must have some friends still on the outside.'

'Not many, I would have thought, given the crimes he committed,' Verity said.

'Well, someone obviously likes him enough to save him a long bus trip,' Jill said.

Morgan nodded. 'A taxi would have soaked up most of his discharge grant and would probably have driven right up the lane to the prison. It would be on the CCTV.'

Verity turned to Morgan. 'Presumably you can trace cars that come along the road outside on those number plate cameras?'

He smiled. 'You mean automatic number plate recognition? No, the nearest ANPR camera is miles away. It's the first thing Surrey police looked at.'

Jill Allsop asserted herself. 'Look, our job isn't particularly to find him, nor to drag him from place to place in handcuffs. The Parole Board decided to trust him. That was their decision, based on dozens of psychological and psychiatric assessments. Although we had input, the decision was theirs.' She smiled. 'If he doesn't turn up voluntarily to planned probation meetings, or mandatory therapy, on time every time, he is in breach of his licence conditions and can be returned to jail. Simple as that.'

Everyone nodded, grateful for the context and logic that Jill's leadership always brought. 'Leticia,' Jill continued. 'When you last spoke to Neil Wright, did he seem content with the arrangements that had been made?'

'Yes. Well pleased, as he damn well should have been considering what a great house has been provided for him.'

'And in your view, did he seem to have come to terms with his crimes? Did he express any remorse?'

Leticia shrugged. 'We mainly discussed practicalities. Personally, I thought the decision releasing him was wrong – or at least premature.'

Jill looked down at her documents. 'There's nothing here in your meeting report about that.'

'Well, what would be the point? He just gave me the creeps. While we were sitting there in the interview room, he was looking around and even eyed up one of the younger male prison officers. He made some inappropriate comment...'

'What kind of comment?'

'Something about "downy little moustaches and long eyelashes". It wasn't so much his comment as the fact he felt the confidence to make it in front of me. I got the impression he couldn't wait to get back to the fray.'

'You felt he might reoffend?'

'It was just a hunch. I didn't know, and I didn't want to mark myself out as a dissident.'

Verity was now scrutinising Leticia very closely. 'Why was that?' she asked. 'You're paid for your judgement.'

Leticia sighed. 'Look, I was given this assignment when all the big decisions had already been made. I don't think anyone was interested in my opinion.'

'So what is your opinion?' Verity asked.

'I think Neville Rollason—'

'Neil Wright, please,' Jill interrupted.

'I think Neil Wright may have a new name, but he is not a new person and we must never forget that. I think he's dangerous, in some ways even more so now than he was when he was first imprisoned. Then, he was the perfect embodiment of the Bogeyman. He looked the part. Now, at first glance he looks like a sweet elderly grandfather. But he's only sixty-three, and I think he's quite fit and sexually predatory. The man is evil.'

The others looked at each other.

'I don't think we need to be quite so tabloid about it, Leticia,' Jill said. 'But your comments are noted.'

Just then Leticia's phone trilled. A text.

'Ah, it's from Wright's phone. Thank God!' Her face lit up.

There was a warm smile from Jill. 'Hopefully, we will all have been worried about nothing.'

But as Leticia clicked to the message screen, her jaw dropped open. 'Oh my God!'

'What is it?' Allsop asked.

Leticia showed her the phone.

> This is AVENGE. We have Rollason and the bastard is going to pay.

Chapter Twenty-two

Gillard was just tidying up the files when he got a call from DI Morgan. 'This is the news you didn't want to hear,' he said.

'Rollason has committed another crime already?' the detective said, leaning across the desk for his notebook.

'Er no, not quite that bad. We've had a message from AVENGE saying they've captured him.'

'The vigilante group? More than half the population would regard that as very good news.'

Morgan cleared his throat. 'Stop playing silly buggers, Craig, this is serious.'

'All right Graham, but is it true do you think, just a few hours after his release?'

'It was texted from his phone to his probation officer, so yes.'

'Are you sure it's not Rollason having a laugh? After all, it would be the perfect excuse for him to disappear from all the licence conditions, wouldn't it?'

There was a pause, as if the Special Branch detective hadn't considered that possibility. 'Leticia, his probation officer, tried to ring him back but the phone was already switched off again. Can you trace it for us?'

'I should be able to.' Gillard started making notes and then said: 'If this is a phone that he was given on release, I presume you would have put a tracker app on it to make it easy to follow.'

'No. His licence conditions preclude any use of the Internet, and so we could only give him a dumb phone. We can only trace it the old way.'

'Shame. That is going to cost us several hours. If AVENGE have even half a collective brain cell they will have sent the message from some obscure location and then chucked the phone away. Okay, leave it with me. I'll get back to you as soon as I can.'

–

It was seven in the evening, and the CID office emptied out, by the time Gillard was able to turn his attention fully to the vigilante group. Before taking any claim seriously, it should be verified. Standard police procedure. Gillard looked up the AVENGE website, saw there was a contact form, and filled it out. He was not optimistic about getting a return message. As he scrolled around the poorly designed site the detective got a clear impression of amateurism. The grammar was poor and there were spelling mistakes all over the place. It was certainly not as slick as that of Dark Justice, a group that used online entrapment to find paedophiles and then turn them over to the police. AVENGE seemed to be long on retribution but less focused on which areas it should be applied to. No spokesperson was quoted, but the threat of punishment was made again and again. Undoubtedly, it was operating on the wrong side of the law.

Looking around for bodies, he saw that the research intelligence officer's desk was unstaffed. Shame. He rang Rob Townsend at home. 'I'm sorry to disturb you, Rob, but I need a breakthrough tonight.'

He asked the research intelligence officer to use his technical brain to see if he could find any contact details or addresses hidden within the AVENGE site. Gillard then made a few calls to contacts in the Met, West Mercia police and to the National Crime Agency. He was looking for an insight into the vigilante organisation, to see if it had ever been penetrated by undercover officers and to ask what would be the best way to pin it down.

It was eight by the time he made some progress, a call back from Detective Chief Superintendent Nick D'Angelo of West Mercia. 'It's a very amorphous organisation, no obvious leader. We've got some passive monitoring of some of the Facebook groups they are connected with, which gives a hint of what they're up to. I did get a male officer into a meeting in Northampton a few times. However, my impression is that the actual cloak and dagger stuff is done informally by a few individuals acting on their own. The videos on their website are generally of the same three or four blokes, from up here in Birmingham to go by the accents.'

'Ever had cause to arrest any of them?' Gillard asked.

D'Angelo chuckled. 'Yes, once, unsuccessfully. Three of them badly beat up a convicted abuser in a pub in Selly Oak. There were several witnesses, but once they heard on the grapevine who the target was, no one had seen a thing. Even the victim refused to press charges. It was a bit frustrating.'

'What is your assessment of AVENGE's effectiveness?'

'Normally, six out of ten. But this, what you're telling me about Rollason, well it's incredible. Same day, and such a high-profile offender, with a new identity. I would say this is unprecedented. Inside job, you'd have to say. It's usually a screw. There's no end of them in AVENGE.'

'That's the way I'm leaning too,' Gillard said. 'I take it you have no intelligence about branches of AVENGE in Surrey?'

'Nope.'

As they were talking, an email popped up on Gillard's mobile.

'Ah, speak of the devil, AVENGE has got back to me,' Gillard told D'Angelo. 'They claim they don't know anything about it.'

'Not surprised,' he responded. 'Whoever did it probably wouldn't want the organisers officially involved.'

A minute later another email came through, about the trace on Rollason's phone. It showed that the AVENGE text had been sent from Walton-on-Thames. The phone had been on for less than a minute. Gillard passed on the news to D'Angelo.

He sighed. 'Well, given who it is they've abducted I think they would kill him. You'll be looking for a body pretty soon.'

'Thanks. I'll add it to my collection,' Gillard said and hung up.

It was almost nine p.m. Gillard, sitting in his office, rubbed his face in exasperation. D'Angelo had phoned around for him, and a whole series of emails from around the country were pouring into his in-box with bits and pieces of information about AVENGE. None of it amounted to very much. D'Angelo had agreed that West Mercia police would haul in the three Brummies who had been collared in the past for this kind of caper, but having looked at the videos on the website Gillard was far from convinced that they were responsible for something as crisply executed as this.

But who was? Perhaps this amorphous vigilante organisation had attracted new, more professional types, operating as freelancers. The trouble was it could be anybody. He looked again at the names of various prison officers who had been linked to AVENGE. There wasn't anybody at Spring Hill, but there was one at HMP Wakefield where Rollason had served most of the last six years of his sentence. He couldn't imagine getting a quick result by questioning him.

His gut told him that this was a local operation. Someone who knew Rollason was at Spring Hill. He wanted to bounce some ideas off the Special Branch officer. He walked upstairs and found DI Morgan in his office, on the phone. He waited out the call and then asked: 'Graham, I'm increasingly convinced this is an inside job. It's too damn quick for anything else.'

Morgan nodded in agreement. 'I've just spoken to Verity Winter, one of the probation officers, on exactly the same point. She told me that PC Andrew Wickens was sniffing around in their office just a few days ago without a reasonable excuse.'

'Wickens! I saw him mooching about here just a few days ago. He'd been upstairs, presumably to this office, looking for you.'

'I know he's interested in the Rollason case, because he made an attempt to talk to me about it in the refectory. But he's not alone. I set a flag on Rollason's PNC file so that I would get notified every time an officer accessed it. There's nearly 1,000 hits across the country in the last two weeks, including Cottesloe, Wickens' shift partner.'

'That flag was a good precaution,' Gillard said. 'I know Cottesloe. He is reliable and honest. I would trust that he had a good reason for looking. What I'd be looking for are any vulnerabilities in how we hold the data. I could get our chief geek Rob Townsend to have a look.'

Morgan, used to running his own fiefdom for many years, bridled at the suggestion. 'Well, the SB office is as rock-solid as I can make it. There's a tamper-proof log-in and the filing cabinets have dial locks that even I find a pain in the arse. We shred everything from the bins once a week before we put them out. I don't know what more we can do.' He sounded thoroughly defensive.

'What about in the probation office?'

'It should be fine. I audited their case management system before setting this up and decided to keep all critical details back from it. All the documents that identify Rollason or the address he was going to are solely on paper, and kept in the safe at Swan House, just to make things simple.'

'Who has access?'

'Jill Allsop as manager, and whoever is the duty officer. The safe logs entry. Allsop tells me there have been no unexpected accesses.'

'Which officer was in charge of resettling Rollason?' Gillard asked.

'Leticia Mountjoy. It was a bit of a surprise to me, actually, because she's relatively junior.'

Gillard rubbed his chin. 'Okay, let's split the work this way. You crank up an investigation on the quiet into Wickens, and I'll speak to Ms Mountjoy.'

As Gillard returned to his office on the ground floor, he couldn't help but think about the connection between a splash in the Thames, a man with the life squashed out of him and a missing serial killer. Leticia Mountjoy was cropping up in a few too many places.

–

Leticia lived with Anton St Jeanne in a converted flat in a quiet residential street in Kingston-upon-Thames. Gillard pulled up outside in his unmarked Vauxhall with DC Rainy Macintosh in the passenger seat. Ten o'clock at night would seem like a good time to get Leticia alone. Her boyfriend would probably be at work in his restaurant. The registration plate on the Mini parked outside the flat matched that which Morgan had given him, and the lights in the first-floor flat were on. Good, she's awake.

'I've checked through the statements the lassie gave to Cottesloe and Wickens,' Rainy said, putting her iPad down. 'It's pretty straightforward. And the location on her phone matched the bridge to Tagg's Island.' They both went up to the door and rang the bell. The woman who appeared was casually dressed in a T-shirt and jeans and looked sleepy. Having heard why they were there, she invited them in.

'I don't think I got much to tell you,' she said. The two detectives were offered a seat on the sofa in the tidy and tastefully decorated flat. A bottle of white wine was open on the glass table in front of them, a glass half empty beside it.

'The speed with which AVENGE seemed to have snatched Rollason rather beggars belief, given what we know of this organisation in the past,' Gillard said. 'They must have had help.'

'I can assure you it wasn't from me.' Leticia described her journey from work to the house where she was due to meet Neville Rollason, the delay while she rang colleagues and then her return to the office. It fully accounted for her day.

'Och, we're not saying that it was you, hen,' Rainy said. 'But if you cast your mind back, was there anyone you noticed asking questions or anything odd at all?'

She shrugged. 'Only the arrival of PC Wickens at the office,' she said.

'That's been reported to us already and we're looking into it,' Gillard said.

'And I don't know what else I can tell you,' Leticia said.

'When you went to the house, did you notice that the back door was unlocked?'

She looked baffled. 'Is that the door that leads from the kitchen to the garden? No. I just sat down and waited for him and checked through paperwork.'

'And did ye nae go upstairs either?' Rainy asked.

'No. I assumed he couldn't be asleep because of the number of times I rang the doorbell and the clatter I must've made coming in with heavy bags.'

'He could have been out of his wits on spice. Or he could even have committed suicide,' Rainy said.

Leticia looked rattled by these accusations. 'But he didn't, did he? Otherwise AVENGE couldn't have kidnapped him.'

'Well, we don't actually have any confirmation that they do have him,' Gillard said. 'Just the text you got.'

'What do you think has happened to him?' she asked.

Gillard shrugged. 'That very much depends on the whim of the individuals who have him.'

'They're nae going to take him for a wee pint and steak and chips, that's for certain,' Rainy said.

It was 2:57 a.m. Gillard sat with DC Carl Hoskins in an unmarked car outside a block of tatty council flats in Farnborough. They weren't alone. Squashed into a small unmarked van across the road were four uniformed officers in stab vests and baseball caps, with a door ram. The place they were keeping an eye on was on the third floor, number 302, a one-bedroomed apartment. Gillard looked again through binoculars. There was an apparently discarded settee and refrigerator on the balcony, and some flickering purple light from the curtained lounge. He had been hoping that the target would be asleep. The fact that a TV was on didn't prove he was awake, but Gillard would have preferred he was in bed. The target was a violent man with a criminal record, who in the past had possessed an illegal firearm. Nigel Chivers, former bouncer, sometime construction worker, divorced father of two, aged thirty-seven. Gillard consulted the flat layout plan on his iPad. The external door went straight onto the lounge with no hallway. The chance of surprise was still good if they could get up there quietly.

In three minutes, a hundred miles north in Birmingham, West Mercia police were going to raid seven known addresses of AVENGE members. They were coordinated with Gillard's raids, the one here and another being undertaken in Andover by Hampshire police for Chivers' mate Terry Dalton. The whole operation had been very rapidly pulled together by DCS Nick D'Angelo. As the seconds ticked down, Gillard leaned out the window and exchanged a hand signal with the uniformed sergeant in the van. He got a nod in return. Back up in the flat, the TV was still on.

The last time he'd been involved in a raid, the uniforms had forgotten to bring a locksmith. The good news was that this time Gillard's own reconnaissance had discovered that the block's external lock was broken. The bad news was that the tiny lift was barely big enough for two people, or one if it was the twenty-five-stone PC Tony Tunnicliffe with the door ram. Gillard had given clear instructions that instead of a manic charge up six half-flights of concrete stairs, waking everybody with the sound of constabulary beetle crushers and heavy breathing, it was to be a slow and stealthy ascent. That gave them a much greater chance of catching Chivers unawares.

At the appointed time, the officers exited their vehicles and carefully clicked the doors shut. They made their way silently twenty yards along the pavement and into the block. Gillard led them furtively up the stairs, but despite his own silent tread he was aware that some of the larger constables didn't seem to be able to move quietly, each heavy thud accompanied by wheezing. He was staggered at how unfit some serving officers were.

Finally, the gaggle of policemen were squeezed onto the landing. Gillard put his fingers to his lips, and rested his ear to the door of Chivers' flat.

The heavy breathing and groans were quite distinctive. Gillard found it almost impossible not to laugh. 'He's watching porn. I can hear it from here,' he whispered.

There was a cascade of barely suppressed giggles as the comment was passed from officer to officer. PC Tony Tunnicliffe took the door ram off his shoulder and rested it against his groin, giving some mock thrusts with the four-foot shiny red object against another officer called Craddock, who threatened to punch him by way of retaliation.

'Shhh!' Gillard hissed. 'You're like a bunch of bloody schoolboys.' He orchestrated the positions, with Craddock and Tunnicliffe on the ram.

Finally happy, Gillard pounded on the door and bellowed 'Open up, armed police.'

Tunnicliffe immediately responded with a falsetto cry of 'Ooh, give it to me big boy!' He slammed the ram hard into the lock, the door burst open first time, and Gillard raced in. Though the undulating and pistoning flesh on the forty-inch high-definition screen was an arresting sight, the truly unforgettable vision was Nigel Chivers' balding head wobbling from side to side as he, naked below the waist, ministered to himself. As he turned his face to the intruders he only managed to get two words out before being thrust face and erection down on his own leather settee.

'Oh fuck.'

Chapter Twenty-three

The previous morning

While his probation officer was waiting for him in Staines, the man now known as Neil Wright sat a few dozen miles away, at a rustic garden table at the Three Feathers pub in Great Missenden with a nearly empty pint of Old Hooky in front of him. It was 11:15 a.m. and the thatched Jacobean tavern, nestled among Buckinghamshire's Chiltern hills, had only just opened. There were a couple of drinkers at the bar, but no others in the garden. Wright had positioned himself so he couldn't be seen from the pub and sat with his arms folded and eyes closed to make the most of the sun, which warmed his head and neck. Birds were singing in the trees, and in the distance a motor mower could be heard. The remembrances of summers past stirred in ancient memory, together with more disturbing recollections.

He blinked and opened his eyes to banish those bad thoughts. Today was not a day for any of them. As the felon revelled in his freedom and thanked his lucky stars, he heard footsteps behind him, and the clinking of glasses on a tray. She had returned with another pint of Old Hooky for him, the packet of pork scratchings he had asked for, and her own glass of orange juice.

As she sat opposite him, and the lichen-scarred table resettled their respective weights, she looked at him, her large pea-green eyes assessing him. She was smiling, but it looked like something she had only just learned to do, and was trying out for size. The warmth certainly did not reach those eyes. 'So what are your plans, outside of the probation meetings?' she asked.

'Not too much, really. I've got forty quid of prison discharge cash, and I need to get the bank account open for my benefits. But after that, I shall probably spend most of the summer lying in my new garden trying to forget about everything.'

She hooked a hank of her long tea-coloured hair behind one ear and sipped her drink. She seemed even more nervous than he had been, looking left and right as more customers arrived at adjacent tables. Neville Rollason had only ever pretended to be attracted to women, even when he was married. It was only boys, and generally the subset that was slim, pale, shy and underdeveloped, that he desired. But now as Neil Wright he was able to see that slim, pale, boyish women were worth a look too. This one, he now decided, was beautiful, an almost ethereal Pre-Raphaelite. Late thirties, perhaps. He took a long draw at his beer, tipping the glass into the air, and felt the sweet cool malts caress his gullet.

He put the glass down and let his eyes wander her face. 'So, are you married?'

Her face tightened, and he feared he shouldn't have asked. She looked away as she muttered a reply. 'Not any more, thank God.'

'I'm surprised. I would have thought there would have been plenty of boyfriends.'

The flick of one eyebrow to no one in particular indicated that there was a story there of some kind, almost certainly a tragic one.

'No kids?'

She looked at her watch. 'I think we have to go soon.'

'What about my gammon and chips?' he asked. 'You ordered it, didn't you?'

'And I paid for it,' she said; then she leaned closer to whisper. 'But we don't actually have time. Plans have changed, and as I said, you are going to have to trust me.'

'Aw, pet, I thought you were going to give me a kiss.'

She bridled and pulled back a little. 'Neil, listen. As you are aware, there is quite a well-organised group called AVENGE, which is after you.'

'I know. Bunch of bastards.'

'We're having to move you at short notice to protect you, as your identity has been partly compromised. I don't think it's safe to remain here. In a moment we're going to leave, do you understand?'

He looked up at her and felt reassured. The sun behind her had produced a fiery shimmering halo around her hair. She was a saint from a stained-glass window, a woman who had come to rescue him. 'You are really quite beautiful, do you know that?' he said. 'Like an angel.'

'I'm no angel, I can assure you,' she said, gathering her bag and mobile phone.

He wasn't used to the beer, and his head was swimming a little. 'I'm sorry,' he said. 'I think I'm a little bit drunk. Must be out of practice. I used to be able to handle three times that, easy.'

'Listen carefully.' She instructed him as if he was a child. But then at the moment he did feel as if he was a child.

'Stand up gradually, Neil, I don't want you falling over and making a scene.'

He untangled his legs from the bench and stood up. He definitely felt woozy. 'I need to go to the toilet. All that beer.'

'No, not here,' she said firmly, sliding her own arm through his to steer him. 'We'll stop somewhere behind a hedge for you.'

He nodded. She guided him into the car park, and to her car, parked right at the far end. She opened the door and helped him slide into the passenger seat. She took her place behind the wheel and leaned across to do up his seat belt. The smell of her hair was intoxicating. Banana, avocado?

'You're lovely,' he said, as she began to reverse the car out. That sceptical eyebrow again, twitching. She seemed to be breathing heavily. Her diaphragm was moving. It was the kind of thing he had trained himself to notice, inside. To detect liars and to predict imminent attack. But that was inside, and he was out now. He trusted her. God, she was lovely.

They drove for only a few minutes before she took a left turn down a narrow country track.

'You can pee behind the hedge here,' she said.

He scrambled clumsily out of the car. For some reason he had trouble with his flies, and settled for undoing his belt and letting his trousers fall to his ankles. Hot urine poured out of him into the nettles behind the hedge, splashing his trainers. It took a while for him to hoist his trousers back up, and somehow he made a mess of getting the belt hitched correctly.

As he turned back to the car, he saw she was standing by the open boot.

'Come and have a look at this,' she asked. It felt like an order. He was happy to comply. He looked into the boot and saw a big canvas bag, a builder's bag.

'What's that for?' he asked.

'Did you not see the car, going past on the main road?'

'No.' For the first time a little tickle of anxiety pierced the swoon of well-being.

'Vigilantes. I recognised two of them. If they see you, you're finished. They have guns.'

'What can we do?'

'Hide in the boot, they won't see you. You'll be safe.'

He looked at the builder's sack and the cavernous interior. 'It'll be dark. I don't like the dark. I get panic attacks. Ever since I was in solitary and the power failed.'

'Just try it. There's a little light I can turn on. It will only be for a few minutes.'

He looked again. He wasn't sure. It felt wrong. Something cautionary was trying to emerge in his befuddled brain, to warn him. 'I will if you give us a kiss, pet.'

She hesitated. 'Okay, I will if you behave. Lean back against the car and close your eyes. Properly shut.' He did so, resting his hands behind him on the lip of the boot, and waited for contact from her lips.

Something was clamped over his mouth, and as his eyes flew open he saw her jump at him, her knee swinging. His groin exploded like a supernova. An enormous inhalation, to power a scream, was blocked by the damp pungent rag clamped tightly over his face. He sucked in some oddly perfumed liquid and the excruciating pain transmuted quickly into darkness. The last thing he felt was that he was toppling backwards into the boot.

Verity Winter tipped the unconscious man on his side and folded him up, knees to chest. She had hoped to persuade him to climb in, but had to admit to enormous satisfaction from using her knee, holding his shoulders down to get her full weight behind it. That one long-practised movement alone had justified the self-defence courses she had been forced to take in her teens, back in the darkest days when all was fear and foreboding. From a small plastic bag under the canvas sack she brought out a dozen foot-long cable ties. She bound his wrists and ankles, making them wickedly tight, so they cut into the flesh.

She had been fretting about every detail of this for days. The stress had been making her ill. But the plan she had been so dubious about had worked far more easily than she'd anticipated. She had seen him at the bus stop, and when she stopped the car he accepted the explanation that she had given him: that there had been a change of plan to keep him safe, and she was to give him a lift. The fact that he recognised her undoubtedly helped; she had met him briefly once before, when he was first moved to Spring Hill, and of course her probation service ID card and lanyard proved that she could be trusted. The thing she had fretted about most was the mobile phone, but he had handed it over immediately when she asked, claiming he didn't even know how to use it.

Trust. She permitted herself a small grin of satisfaction at having turned the tables. Rollason had himself enticed teenage boys into his car with a computer games console, and had doctored alcohol. She had lured him with the promise of safety.

Despite the flunitrazepam she'd dropped in his drink on the way back from the bar into the garden, and the liquid GHB in the handkerchief, there was a possibility he might wake during the journey. He'd have to be kept quiet. She stuffed his mouth with a rag, and gaffer-taped it closed, encircling his head three times. She was supposed to bring him in alive, but if Rollason came round and threw up before she delivered him, then he would drown in his own vomit.

Tough. She just hoped he wouldn't make a mess in her boot while doing it.

He was going to die anyway. But that wasn't her department and she didn't want to know any details. She turned Rollason's phone on and checked for messages. There were three, all left in the last hour by Leticia, asking where he was. She turned it off and dropped it into her bag. Now she had to make a delivery. That's when her involvement ended. She hoped it would finally be enough, and this thirty-four-year agony would be over.

Chapter Twenty-four

Wednesday morning

It was a quarter past four in the morning and the first glow of midsummer dawn was seeping above the horizon as Alan Wilson walked his black labrador on the verge along the A3050. He was heading for the Molesey Reservoirs Nature Reserve, hoping to get a good early walk for Lucky before the business trip to Scotland. He was in a good mood. The normally frantic road was almost deserted. The reserve would not be open yet, but Lucky had on a previous excursion found a good wide gap in the railings and seemed anxious to do some more exploring. What Wilson did not expect to see by the side of the road at that time of the morning was a young man wearing a bike helmet with a head-torch, bending over as if winded. Just a few yards away a bicycle was chained to a road sign. 'Are you all right?' he asked, from a safe distance, tightening the extendable dog lead. He hoped the man hadn't been sick. Labradors have a habit of eating anything, however revolting.

'He's dead,' the young man said, standing up, wiping a string of saliva from his mouth. He had a very odd movement in his eye.

'Who?'

'Through there,' he said, pointing through the gap in the railings that Wilson had intended to use. 'We need to call the police.'

Wilson peered through the fence. There was a dark shape ten yards away under the bushes. In the twilight it was hard to say what it was. Wilson considered going with the dog to investigate, but didn't quite trust this scruffy individual, with his dirty shirt, head-torch and a cycle clip on only the right leg of his grubby trousers.

'Who's dead?'

'The murderer, Neville Rollason.'

Wilson knew exactly who he meant but was sceptical of this young man's claim.

'Just killed him, then, have you?' He asked the question in jocular fashion, but the answer was straight.

'No, no, I found the body.'

'Is that his bike or yours?'

The young man stood up to face him. 'No, that's mine.'

He wondered quite how a passing cyclist could have made this alarming discovery. The body, if that's what it was, was not visible from the road. Lucky, sensitive as ever to the mood of her master, began to bark at the man.

'Are you sure that's actually a dead body?' Wilson asked.

In answer, the young man proffered his phone, a photo luridly displayed.

'Christ almighty!' Wilson recoiled at the image. 'Okay, I'll call 999. But I don't think you should go anywhere.' As he put the phone to his ear he knew there was zero chance now that he would be on time for his train.

–

It was just before seven a.m. when Baz Mulholland took the call. Claire was in the shower, and emerged just wearing a towel. 'Vince Babbage at Staines,' he said as he handed her the cordless phone.

The duty sergeant at Staines police station came quickly to the point. 'Sorry to disturb, ma'am. Control room picked up a 999 call. Two witnesses reported a body found in the Molesey Reservoirs Nature Reserve, and you're the closest senior detective. I know you're not on duty for another hour in theory, but CSI is already there and I thought…'

'That's no problem at all, Vince.' She put the phone on speaker, walked into her bedroom, tossed the phone onto the bed, dropped the towel onto the floor and began to dress rapidly. 'Do we know anything about it?'

'Well, the cyclist who first spotted it says it's definitely Neville Rollason.'

'I'll take that with a pinch of salt,' she said, as she buttoned up her blouse. 'Almost nobody knows what he looks like these days. I certainly don't.' She slid on a pair of jeans rather than work slacks, thinking of mud, blood and mess at a nature reserve.

'That was my feeling, ma'am. Wishful thinking maybe. Still, the witness was very distressed and the control room operator didn't feel it was a hoax.'

'Okay, I'll be there in ten minutes,' she said. 'Do me a favour. Email DCI Craig Gillard, and DI Graham Morgan in Special Branch. If there is even a chance it's Rollason, they'll need to know.'

'Righto, ma'am.'

Claire hung up and yelled for Baz. On his reply, she shouted: 'Sorry, no lift today. Can you grab me a couple of cereal bars?'

There was an answering grunt from downstairs. She made a pout, grabbed a lipstick and with a rapid and practised movement circled her mouth. She squirmed her feet into a pair of pre-laced trainers. She'd settle for rubbing some toothpaste round her mouth with her finger in the car until she had time to use the toothbrush she kept in her desk at work.

She thundered downstairs, scooped up car keys, phone and briefcase from the hall table and then glanced at herself in the mirror. Her hair was a post-tornado haystack. She gave a brief scowl and looked for her brush. Not there, so she attacked it with Baz's own plaster-spattered comb. Better than nothing. 'Baz!' she called again. He emerged from the kitchen, a slice of toast jammed into his face, a plastic bag with her on-the-go breakfast in his hands.

'Time to clean this,' she said, swapping the dirty comb for the bag. 'Have you fed Dexter?'

'What d'you think that chomping noise is?' he replied cheerfully.

'Don't forget – when you pick up the car, there's my dry-cleaning to get too. The ticket's behind the clock. Make sure they got rid of the stain on the trousers, blood on the left knee. Pick up Dexter's tablets from the vet, and don't forget to wheel the bin out. Recycling not green waste.'

'Right.' She watched her husband's face veer to panic at the prospect of inheriting this Gordian knot of multitasking. 'See you later, love.'

She kissed him on the cheek and stopped in the utility room to pick up her grab bag. Wellingtons, torch, and fresh packets of plastic gloves and booties.

Once in the car, routine returned. She checked in on the comms system, hit the blue lights and left rubber on the road. At least the blues would get her past the roadworks on the main road.

–

Traffic on the A3050 was stationary in both directions. Claire had to take ownership of the middle of the road with sirens and lights. Motorists were hanging out of their windows taking photos on their phones, and others had even parked on the verge in order to get a closer view. A couple of uniformed officers were dealing with it. Two patrol cars and a CSI van were also parked on the grass. Crime scene tape ran back from the forty limit sign a good fifty yards, and a crime-scene tent was already visible inside the nature reserve. She recognised Yaz Quoroshi, talking to another CSI technician.

As she added her own vehicle to the melee, she spotted PC Jim Cottesloe talking to a scruffy young man wearing a cycle helmet while a middle-aged man with a black labrador stood by. She got out and went over to the group. The younger man turned to her. It was Jakes, her husband's colleague on the zoo job.

'Small world, Michael,' she said. 'Are you our witness again?'

'Hi, er...' He clearly recognised her but was struggling with her name.

'Claire Mulholland, Barry's partner. Detective inspector.'

He nodded. 'I remember.'

'So, you were a witness on Tagg's Island the other week, and now you're here.'

'Bit of a coincidence, I'd say,' Cottesloe volunteered, staring hard at Jakes.

'Yes.' There was a waft of vomit about him.

'And you are a witness too?' Claire turned to ask the dog walker.

'Not exactly. I just found this young man in a state of distress. I haven't seen the body, just his picture of it.'

Claire called over a uniformed officer to look after him and turned back to Jakes.

Cottesloe handed Claire a phone. 'Mr Jakes took these photographs of the dead man.' Claire recoiled at the graphic images. The entire face and neck was purple and swollen, the eyelids inflated and the eyeballs themselves almost popping out of his head. Clearly, he had sustained very similar injuries to those of the body on the island, though this victim was still clothed. The pictures showed a short-sleeved shirt and blue trousers.

'May we keep this for now to help with the identification?' she asked Jakes.

'No need. I'll tell you who it is, it's Neville Rollason,' Jakes said.

'Did you know Mr Rollason then?' Claire asked.

'Not exactly *know*, seeing as he has been inside for decades,' Jakes said. 'But I know what he looks like.' He reached for his phone, and she gave it back to him. He swiped through, and then turned the screen back to her. 'This is him,' he said. The picture was of a smiling white-haired pensioner with red-framed spectacles, resting his chin winsomely on one hand. The interior background was more convincing than the subject. It looked institutional, with just the kind of unbreakable plastic furniture she had seen in prisons.

Claire had only seen the same historic images of Rollason as every tabloid reader. The scowling goblin was stuck in every mother's imagination and she was one of those, too, as well as being a cop. She'd seen nothing recent. This picture could be anybody. She doubted Jakes and had growing concerns about his mental stability. She reached for his mobile and, before bagging it for evidence, took a snap of the image of the older man with her own phone. She left Jakes with the uniforms while she made her way over to Yaz Quoroshi inside the crime tent.

Quoroshi greeted her warmly, then added. 'Looks like he's struck again.' The snap judgement from the CSI chief was that the body had been at the site only a very short time, the time of death probably a few hours before.

'So that fits with the witness who claims to have seen a car with its boot open just before?'

'Yes,' Quoroshi said. 'On the face of it. But I gather our principal witness is a little on the tainted side.'

'And not just by puke,' she said. She was going to make sure that he was taken to Staines police station in a patrol car. She didn't want him in hers. Especially before she had a chance to finish her breakfast. The first thing she had to do was to send off Jakes's pictures of the older man and the body to Special Branch to see if either of them really were Neville Rollason.

–

Michael Jakes was brought to Claire after he had been swabbed for DNA, fingerprinted and had his phone sent for analysis. Sergeant Babbage had given him the opportunity to sponge his shirt and trousers down before bringing him into the interview room. Jakes, while not exactly fragrant, looked less like a vagrant now. He still had his cycling helmet on, as if he was expecting to leave in a couple of minutes. He stared around at the two low settees, the potted plants, and the view of shrubbery through the partially drawn venetian blinds. Claire had chosen the rape suite on a hunch. She sensed a vulnerability in him and thought quicker progress might be made via a more sensitive approach.

She patted the sofa opposite. 'Sit down please, Michael.' She got Babbage to bring in a coffee and offered him one of her own cereal bars. 'I expect you need breakfast before telling me everything you've seen.' Claire tried not to stare at his errant eye.

He thanked her.

'So how did you discover the body?'

'Like I told the PC, I was cycling back home when I saw a car on the other side of the road with its boot open.'

'The nature reserve side? So you were heading towards Walton.'

'Yes. There was a man at the boot. I thought nothing of it as I went past. About a minute later, the car overtook me, and I noticed the indicator flashed a bit fast. So I turned around...'

'Sorry, what was the significance of the indicator?'

'The car I saw at Tagg's Island also had a defective indicator. I thought it might be the same one.'

'So you stopped cycling?'

'Well, not at first. I tried to give chase but he was too fast.'

Claire smiled, imagining a bicycle trying to overtake a car and force it off the road. The ultimate have-a-go fantasy.

'I went back to where he had been parked. There were fresh tyre tracks. I saw there was a gap in the railings, so I went through.'

Claire looked up from her notes. 'I'm sorry, Michael, I don't quite understand what led you to turn around, cycle back and go into the nature reserve just because you'd seen a car with a defective indicator.'

Jakes was wringing his hands. 'When I saw the car at Tagg's Island the other week, I thought the splash I heard was a man dumping a body. So, when I saw the man at the boot so early in the morning, I thought he might be dumping another one.'

Claire put down her pen. 'That's quite an intuitive leap. Why were you expecting there to be another body?'

'I wasn't, particularly.'

'You just said you did. All right, did you recognise the man at the boot?'

'No.'

'Could you describe him for me?'

Jakes rubbed his chin. 'He was big.'

'Just big? Anything else?'

'No. That's all I remember. I wasn't suspicious when I first passed him. It was dark.'

'I still don't get why you had this brainwave. I mean, it's enough that you assume a vehicle with a defective indicator light is the same one you saw before, but an even bigger leap to assume that every time you see this car and this man he's got a body to dump. Wouldn't you say?'

Jakes just wrung his hands, only stopping to pick at tiny lumps of plaster on his knuckles.

'Did you get the number plate of the parked vehicle?'

'No, I didn't.'

'What make of car?'

'I don't know. I can't drive, because of my nystagmus. I've never really taken an interest in mechanical things.'

'Come on, you must have noticed something. Was it an estate car or a saloon? A big four-wheel drive? Was there a trailer?'

Jakes's eye set off on one of its heavenward journeys. 'There was no trailer, that's for sure. And the man was at the boot. He was taking off gloves.'

'Gloves, you didn't mention that. It may be significant.'

'It didn't seem to me a big car and I thought it was old from the sound of the engine as it overtook me.'

She turned back to her notes. 'But the thing you most clearly noticed was the faulty indicator?'

'That's right. Because it was just like the other vehicle I'd seen in the distance at Tagg's Island.'

Claire put her pen down again. 'Can I ask why you were cycling around at four in the morning?'

'It's a habit of mine. I can't sleep sometimes. I have a circuit that goes through Hurst Meadows park, along the edge of the Thames and back to Walton on the A3050 or back the other way along Hampton Court Road. During the summer I do it four or five times a week. It would be far too busy during the day. But ever since the splash I'm always keeping an eye out for the car I saw at Tagg's.'

'Can I ask again, what made you start looking around in the bushes?'

Jakes didn't answer.

'What about this photograph that you say is Rollason? Where did you get that from?'

He stared down at the floor, wringing his hands again. Getting no reply, Claire left him in the suite and went into the corridor to make a phone call. She got through to Gillard, who was still at the site of the Farnborough raid.

'Just following up from the email earlier, Craig,' she said.

'Is it Rollason?'

'Could well be. Quoroshi thinks so. Same MO as the previous body, worse if anything.'

'The witness said it was Rollason, that was the message I got,' Gillard said.

'Yes, Michael Jakes. The splash witness at Tagg's Island.'

'How on earth would Jakes know what Rollason looks like now?'

'He has a photograph that he claims is him. It looks recent, but I've no idea if it is him. I sent it to Graham Morgan, but no reply so far.'

'Didn't you copy me in? I have seen the brand-new Rollason. He's got a bit of white hair and wears red specs.'

'That's what I saw in the pic. So it is probably him.'

'How did Jakes get that picture?'

'He won't say.'

'All right. Keep him there, Claire. There's only so many coincidences in life. We should probably interview him under caution.'

'Well, I can't if it gets formal. I know him. He works with Baz.'

'Okay, if I ever get finished here, I'll get Hoskins to sit in with me while we interview him. But first I've got to go to the mortuary to see the body with Delahaye. Hoskins is going to contact any family Rollason has who would do a formal ID.'

'Okay. Well, I can come along for that.'

–

By the time the body bag was pulled out on the slab in the mortuary at Kingston Hospital, there was little doubt

231

that the corpse still zipped inside would indeed turn out to be Neville Rollason. DC Hoskins had found an address for Rollason's daughter, but hadn't managed to track her down by phone.

Dr David Delahaye was there with Claire and they were both poring over his iPad, where the two photographs from Jakes's phone and those from CSI were enlarged. The forensic pathologist swiped to a CSI close-up of the corpse's face and spread his finger and thumb on the screen to further enlarge it. 'Dentition is remarkably similar,' he said. 'Clearly reconstructed, bleached and so forth.'

'Yes, looks the same to me.'

Delahaye looked up. 'I thought Gillard was going to be here.'

'He said he'd be here by nine,' Claire said. 'He's on his way back from a joint operation with West Mercia Police.'

The forensic consultant looked up at the clock. Ten past. 'I think I'm going to start anyway.' Delahaye positioned the overhead mic, suspended by its cable, and the extractor hood. He pulled closer a trolley of wicked-looking medical instruments, some with hooks or curved blades. Another trolley had an electric saw and accessories.

Claire's mouth went dry as he undid the zip. Her gasp was involuntary.

She had seen plenty of dead bodies and been to a few post-mortems, although she usually preferred to leave before the electric saw or scalpels began their work. The grisly photographs of this one had hardly prepared her for the reality. She had never seen a corpse that looked anything like this. The chest, a florid purple, was crushed to half its normal depth on one side; the eyes and mouth were wide open, seemingly caught in a final rictus of agony.

'There are obviously some startling similarities between this case and the body found in the Thames. The cyanosis in this case is even more starkly visible.' Delahaye leaned close and used a magnifying glass to briefly inspect the eyes. 'Profuse petechiae in the conjunctiva and strong cyanosis in the head, neck and chest. Compression on the thorax was sufficiently intense to reverse blood flow in veins and arteries, some of which can be seen in the upper body. The jugular vein in the neck is horribly distended, almost serpentine, which again would be caused by excessive pressure.'

The pathologist pressed gently on the chest with his gloved hands. 'Both collarbones are broken.' He pressed and counted. 'Yes, we have five detached ribs, and another three broken, all on the left side. Unlike the other body, this one seems to have been subject not just to pressure but acts of violence.'

He shone a torch into the mouth, where Claire could see dried blood. 'The securing screws for the dental implants have been torn out through the upper jaw, and the lower mandible has been fractured. This is consistent with some hard object being thrust with great force into the mouth,' Delahaye said, looking at her over the top of his square metallic spectacles. He then gestured at the crushed ribcage. 'This alone might well have been sufficient to cause death. My guess at this stage is that he had already passed out through lack of oxygen.'

At that moment Gillard walked into the mortuary, accompanied by a hospital technician. After brief greetings, the detective chief inspector peered at the body.

'Good grief. Just like the other one.'

'Not quite,' Delahaye said. 'This time he was clothed. The body is fresher, no water to muddy the evidence, and in my view considerably enhanced pressure was applied. This time we don't have the diamond pattern of impressions.'

'Proving that the mesh wasn't instrumental in the pressure,' Gillard said.

'It looks that way,' Delahaye said, extracting an arm from the body bag. 'Ah, now we're getting somewhere. Look at this contusion.' He displayed the corpse's wrist, with a thick band of indentations around it.

'Tied up?' Claire asked.

'Yes, cable ties. Tight enough to break capillaries. It is clear that at some stage he was restrained.'

'That doesn't surprise me, if he's conscious and about to get squeezed to death,' Gillard said. 'He'd fight, wouldn't he?'

'Indeed. I'm going to start on the formal post-mortem in a few minutes; did you want to stay around?' Delahaye asked.

'Thank you, but no, I've got an incident room meeting at ten,' Gillard said, then paused. 'How did things turn out with the cyclist, David?'

'Michael Jakes?' Claire asked.

'No, I knocked a cyclist off the other day while talking on the hands-free,' Delahaye said. 'He threatened to punch me but settled for breaking the Tesla's wing mirror. Serves me right, I suppose. I have to watch where I drive unless I want to make more work for myself.'

Once they were in the car park, Gillard said to Claire: 'Normal cases, you get more evidence, it begins to make sense. This one, the more we discover, the crazier it gets.

Two bodies killed in similar ways. One we've barely got a clue about and the other a notorious murderer just released from prison. The involvement of Jakes doesn't seem to me to explain what's going on.'

'He must have some useful information.'

'Maybe. But can you see him as part of AVENGE? I struggle with that. I mean, whoever managed to abduct Rollason knew exactly what they were doing, even if the disposal of the body seemed a bit amateur.'

'Does it link with the raids you were on?'

Gillard blew a sigh. 'We found plenty of people who would undoubtedly want Rollason dead. But I'm sceptical as to whether any of those we got hold of were involved. The two we arrested, Terry Dalton and Nigel Chivers, had a consistent story. Dalton even had an alibi.'

'What about Andrew Wickens?'

'That's gone up to Rigby,' Gillard said. 'I wouldn't want to be in his shoes.'

—

Mount Browne was a hive of activity as the two detectives walked into the CID block. Whiteboards were being set up and dozens of chairs set out. Research Intelligence Officer Rob Townsend had set up a videoconference call with West Mercia police for 10:15 a.m.

After being up most of the night, Gillard had managed to squeeze in a quick shave and clean his teeth in the staff bathroom. He raided his upstairs locker for one of his emergency clean shirts. Once freshened up, he came down to see most of the team assembled in the largest incident room: DCs Carl Hoskins and Rainy Macintosh, financial specialist DC Shireen Corey-Williams, Christine McCafferty from PR, and Special Branch's Graham

Morgan. The one absentee, who would surely arrive at some stage, was the chief constable herself.

Gillard stood at the front between two whiteboards, each dedicated to a murder victim. Rainy had filled them out with bullet points in marker pen and beneath them taped on photographs of each of the bodies.

'Good morning everyone, I hope you all had a better night's sleep than I did. We now have two corpses. Men who died in similar fashion, almost two weeks apart, the bodies being found within a mile of each other.' He pointed to a large map pinned to the wall, then went over the circumstances of the discovery of the first body and the numerous witnesses to the splash, and referenced their witness statements, which were contained in a prepared pack on each person's desk.

'We still do not know for certain whether the splash was relevant to the body. Up until the discovery of the second body we did not in fact have any significant leads. That has now changed.' He turned to the second whiteboard and described how Rollason's body was discovered.

'We're awaiting a formal ID when we can get hold of his daughter, but there is little doubt from dental records who it is. I think we can all agree that with a common MO we can rule out accidental death in both cases. Neville Rollason looks to have been killed within twelve to fifteen hours of his release from prison. There are impressions of cable ties on both wrists and ankles, indicating he was bound for at least part of that time. Someone used his phone to claim he had been abducted by AVENGE.'

'Are you now doubting that, sir?' Rainy asked.

'Yes. I'll cover that in more detail when we have the conference call. The biggest immediate challenge is going to be a public relations one.' He glanced at DI

Morgan. 'The Home Office in its wisdom sanctioned the creation of a new identity for one of Britain's worst child-killers. The process that was used was one that had been used several times before and should have been foolproof. When we go public with the news, and I'm afraid we will have to do that within the next few hours, we're going to need a clear narrative.'

At that moment the double doors to the room opened and the chief constable walked in. Alison Rigby's effect was, as usual, to chill the atmosphere. She folded her tall frame onto a seat right at the back of the room.

'Christine, what would you suggest?' Gillard asked.

'We have to be as transparent as we can,' the PR officer replied. 'The coverage is more likely to focus around why he was released in the first place and why we ever use the public purse to build someone like him a new identity. The tabloids will undoubtedly react with glee to the news that he is dead. It's a huge embarrassment, clearly, but my instinct is that it is the Home Office and the probation people who will get it in the neck more than us.'

Morgan could be seen shaking his head slowly, more with regret than disagreement.

Christine continued: 'The fact that raids have taken place against AVENGE even before the public knew of Rollason's death makes us look reasonably proactive, which should mitigate criticism.' Gillard noted a slight nod of agreement from the chief constable.

The conference call began, and the face of DCS Nick D'Angelo of West Mercia police appeared on the screen. Gillard introduced some of the key players from his team and asked the detective chief superintendent to summarise what had occurred overnight.

'A force of eighty-five officers raided sixteen addresses across the Midlands, with some additional arrests made in Farnborough, Andover and Gateshead. We can call it a truly nationwide operation. Twenty-two people were arrested, including four known active vigilantes. Charges have already been preferred on seven of those people for possession of unlicensed firearms, including a police-issue taser, for assault and for resisting arrest. A number of those held have now been released on police bail, but three are being held in custody pending further investigations.'

'Alison Rigby here,' the chief constable called out from the back. 'You probably can't see me but I hope you can hear me on the speakerphone. Do you have reason to believe that any of those arrested were involved in the abduction of Mr Rollason?'

'No ma'am, in fact we are increasingly convinced that they were not,' D'Angelo responded.

Rigby turned her attentions to Gillard. 'Craig, I believe you arrested one of the AVENGE members here in Surrey. Are you telling me he wasn't involved either?'

Gillard smiled and pointed a remote control at the TV screen suspended from the ceiling. 'This is a short clip from my interview with Nigel Chivers at Aldershot police station just a few hours ago. I think we can judge for ourselves.'

The black-and-white CCTV image showed a square windowless room with four people around an interview table. Chivers was easily the largest, splayed belligerently across a chair, thighs apart, meaty arms folded across his chest. Next to him the duty solicitor looked like a pale shadow of a man. Opposite Chivers sat Gillard and DC Hoskins, documents open in front of them.

The clip began with Gillard asking a question: 'So you are telling me, Nigel, that you tried to get Rollason, but failed?'

'Yeah. As God is my witness, I sat upstairs in his house from seven in the morning until midday waiting for the little bastard, but he never showed up. All I heard was the sound of this woman downstairs, who'd let herself in.'

'How do you know that Rollason wasn't with her?' Hoskins asked.

'Because when she came in she called out for him. I hid under the bed as I thought she was gonna come upstairs and look, but she never did. I was trapped in there for a good hour until she left. It was obvious that she was expecting him to be there.'

'What did you do next?'

'I waited until she'd gone and then slipped out the back way. Terry was waiting outside in the car.'

'That is Terrence Dalton, in the Peugeot you previously identified?' Hoskins asked, looking down at the documents.

'Yeah.'

Gillard clicked the screen off and turned to his audience. 'Under interrogation Nigel Chivers readily admitted that he and Dalton had planned to abduct Rollason, with the assistance of others they have so far refused to identify. Somehow, they had obtained the address where the offender was going to be living. Chivers had effected an entry to this property on the Sunday two days in advance of Rollason's release from prison and, as you heard, was waiting upstairs for him to arrive on the morning of his release.'

'Chivers' story stacks up,' Hoskins said. 'He recalled details of the arrival of the probation officer at Rollason's address that correspond with her story. Right down to the fact he had a takeaway coffee and left the stirrer and some dregs in Rollason's kitchen sink. Only somebody who was there would have known that.'

Gillard took up the story. 'As we know Chivers was at the house all morning, by definition he couldn't have been involved in the abduction, because we know Rollason never arrived. There is not a single dab of his DNA anywhere in the house. Likewise, Dalton's story, that he was in the Peugeot in Wexford Road waiting for Chivers, is consistent and is backed up by the timings on ANPR images.'

'So what happened?' Rigby asked.

'As we already guessed, Rollason was abducted by somebody else before he even got to his new home,' Gillard said.

'Who?' Rigby asked. 'Any ideas, DCS D'Angelo?'

'I think it was a freelance operation, ma'am,' D'Angelo said.

'Our errant cyclist, Mr Jakes?'

Gillard demurred. 'There are problems with that theory, ma'am, which I'll come on to.'

Rigby didn't look happy. 'I have an urgent meeting, so I have to go now.' She stood up. 'I suppose we can say that we were pretty quickly onto it, if nothing else. Okay, Christine? We'll have a breakout meeting on the PR angle we take. You, Morgan and Gillard in my office at noon. Thank you.' She stood up and left the room.

The conference call was wrapped up. The next phase of the meeting focused on that morning's arrest.

'As many of you will have heard, we detained Michael Jakes near the site of the discovery of the second body. He's a thirty-four-year-old plasterer, no criminal record but has had some mental health issues. He was a witness to the splash associated with the first body and claims to have discovered the second. His statement is in the folder on your desks.'

'And a bigger pile of codswallop you will never read,' Hoskins muttered.

'He also had on his phone a recent photograph of Neville Rollason, sitting at a table in what appears to be HMP Spring Hill refectory,' Gillard said.

'All that just can't be coincidence,' Morgan said.

'Agreed. He seems to be cropping up in rather too many places for comfort. He's under arrest, and I'm hoping to get to interview him under caution as soon as this meeting is over. However, while the temptation might be to think we have solved this case, I need to point out a few awkward facts about Jakes. One, he appears to have arrived by bicycle at the crime scene, which obviously precludes him having just dumped the body himself. Two, Jakes cannot drive. Three, according to the second witness, the dog walker, it was Jakes who first suggested calling the police. It's only a tentative conclusion, but it's hard to believe that this man had more than a peripheral involvement in either of these crimes.'

'That photo on Jakes's phone must have been Rollason's own doing,' said Morgan. 'We told him not to do anything stupid to compromise his new identity.'

'I thought he wasn't supposed to have a phone under his licence conditions,' Claire said.

'It is an open prison. He is allowed out.' Morgan shrugged, his expression returning to the defensive pout he had worn throughout the meeting.

The next phase of the meeting covered some of the forensic details, comparing injuries and marks on the two bodies.

'We would really like to pin down the method and location of the killings,' Gillard said. 'Rainy, do you want to expound on your work on that?'

'Aye, sir.' Rainy Macintosh came to the laptop next to the projector and hit a few keys. 'The biggest mystery we have in both these cases is how exactly so much pressure was applied, gradually, to asphyxiate these two victims.' She displayed photographs of the two bodies, to gasps from those present who had not seen them before.

'The marks on Rollason were made through clothing, but do not include the diamond pattern we saw on the first, which we now see as irrelevant to the cause of death.'

'How much pressure?' Hoskins asked. 'Do we have an exact figure for that yet?'

'Och no, Carl. There is no such thing as a standard human body, with mechanical tolerances. Doctor Delahaye's guesstimate was half a tonne or more. With Rollason it may be higher still. That led us to look for industrial locations. To be honest, we're not making much progress on these. While we've eliminated any premises within a mile of the site of the first body, there are hundreds of possibilities further out, including enormous industrial estates around Heathrow and Slough. It could take months.'

'What about the mesh suit on the first victim?' asked DI Morgan.

'Plastic, seems to be the received wisdom. I spent an afternoon with Imperial College's own resident expert, learning everything there is to know about tensile strength, durability and hysteresis on industrial meshes.'

She winked. A ripple of laughter washed around the room. 'Aye, it was fascinating, but as I mentioned, probably not involved directly in killing him. But we don't know who made it or why.'

'What about the zoo angle? That seemed promising,' Hoskins asked.

Gillard inclined his head sceptically. 'DI Mulholland had a good look round. There wasn't anything conclusive. When she was there, she did some random DNA swabs in bathrooms, on locks and gates, but we found nothing to match either of our victims.'

Rainy was looking down at her phone. 'Hold on a minute,' she said. 'We just got a result, sir, from the stable isotope analysis. They know where our first victim lived.' She scrolled down through the document on her phone.

'Come on, don't leave us all waiting,' Gillard said.

She looked up. 'Taiwan, sir. That's where he grew up, but the minerals in his teeth and bones showed he spent some time in New York in later years, before returning to Taiwan.'

'Right, now we've really got something to get our teeth into,' Gillard said.

Chapter Twenty-five

The incident room meeting broke up and the detectives gathered round the email now showing on Rainy's laptop.

'That's good news. It seems quite conclusive,' Gillard said, reading through the list of minerals present in the bones of the man found on the island. 'Carl, would you email the Border Force to see if any Taiwanese nationals arrived in Britain in the last three months. Then contact the national police headquarters in Taipei, and ask them about missing persons, copy in the British Embassy there. In fact it would be a good idea to get a complete list of anyone who bought an air ticket from Taipei to Britain in the last few months. The embassy might be able to help clarify who we need to speak to.'

'Yes, I'll get right on to that,' Hoskins said.

Gillard turned to Rainy. 'I still want you to put more work into the MO. If we solve that I think we crack open the entire case. It seems baffling to me that someone who may just have been a visitor to Britain happens to be slowly crushed to death.'

'Aye, sir. It's not just the method in common but the perpetrator. I can quite understand why someone would want to kill Neville Rollason, and presumably there might be someone who hates our Taiwanese fella enough to want to kill him. But who could possibly be involved in killing them both? It just doesn't make sense.'

Hoskins leaned forward. 'And if he did want to kill 'em both and had 'em tied up, why use some elaborate crushing technique? Why not try a simple whack on the head: easy to arrange, simple tools, job done.' He shook his head ruefully, as if critiquing some botched DIY home repair.

'It has certainly baffled me right from the start,' Gillard said. 'My gut feeling since the discovery of Rollason's body was that we would have far more leads about who might have killed him than the Taiwanese guy. But who knows, we might make more progress once we get to know a little bit more about the first victim.'

–

Alison Rigby's office seemed quite crowded. DI Graham Morgan, DCI Gillard and Christine McCafferty sat around the coffee table with the chief constable.

'Okay, Christine, let's have your take on this,' Rigby said.

'Well, as I mentioned, we have clearly shown a proactive approach. We should steer press enquiries towards the details of the coordinated national raid, it's the sort of thing they love. What we don't want and should refuse to comment on is any involvement in the creation of the false identity.'

Morgan nodded. 'I second that, Christine.'

'We can in any case direct any queries to the Home Office,' Rigby said. 'We have good operational reasons for saying nothing about how we protect those who leave prison, as this debacle clearly demonstrates. To do so would jeopardise future efforts, not only with people like Rollason but supergrasses and gang informers.'

'I take it none of the shocking images of Rollason's body will be released to the press?' Christine asked.

'No, absolutely not,' Gillard said. 'We mustn't allude to the nature of the injuries either. As with the first victim, we just mention asphyxiation as the cause of death.'

'They won't take no for an answer,' Christine said. 'If you thought there was a lot of media interest in the first victim, you've seen nothing compared to what there will be for Rollason. We haven't yet officially confirmed that it is him, but I'm already getting deluged with questions. By tomorrow the crime reporters will be digging out their old contacts in the Met and elsewhere who are happy to share off-the-record titbits in exchange for a big boozy lunch.'

'We'll just have to hold the line as best we can,' Rigby said.

'Can we use the picture of Rollason the witness already had on his phone?' Christine asked.

'We could release that, I suppose,' Rigby said. 'Though in theory we need Jakes's permission.'

'Tabloids won't like it,' Morgan said. 'They want the picture of a monster, not some sweet old grandfather with Hollywood teeth.'

Christine conceded the point. 'It's true. They have a story to peddle and want an up-to-date illustration that fits the evil-murderer narrative.'

'Tough luck, is the answer,' Rigby said. 'They'll get what we give 'em.'

As Rigby and McCafferty nailed down the final details of how the press would be handled, Gillard watched Graham Morgan's fists unclench along with the rest of his body. His shoulders must have dropped a good couple of inches during the conversation. He would have been the first to admit that his arse was on the line. But if your boss is willing to cover it, everything is fine.

Once Christine had departed, Rigby held back the two detectives for one further subject.

'I'm sure you won't be surprised to hear that I have ordered the suspension of PC Andrew Wickens. I'm turning him over to the not-so-tender mercies of Detective Chief Inspector Sarah Bracewell of the ACU.'

The two detectives exchanged a glance. Sarah Bracewell practically *was* the anti-corruption unit that covered Surrey and Sussex police forces. Gillard had never met her, but she had previously been a commercial lawyer and was recruited at a senior level rather than rising through the police ranks. Such recruits were rarely popular with the rank and file, who saw them as incompetent queue-jumpers to the best senior jobs, but Ms Bracewell was different. She had a reputation that preceded her for intelligence, toughness and diligence. Naturally enough, officers she had investigated had far worse things to say about her. In ACU you needed a hide like a rhinoceros. The word was that she could charge like one too, and make those charges stick.

'That's good, ma'am. If anyone can find out who he was working with, she can,' Gillard said.

'I want him to be made an example of,' Rigby replied. 'I'm aware that many serving officers are uncomfortable protecting ex-offenders. This will remind them where their duty lies.'

—

DC Hoskins drove Gillard from Mount Browne to Staines police station. The detective chief inspector had been almost hallucinating with tiredness by the end of his meeting with Rigby, but still had an urgent interview to conduct with Jakes. Gillard reclined the front passenger seat and dozed for half an hour during the journey. He awoke to Hoskins' dulcet tones announcing that they had arrived.

After gulping down two coffees in quick succession, and introducing himself to the duty solicitor, Gillard reread Jakes's witness statements while Hoskins set off to read him his rights and set up the tape recorder.

The detective chief inspector felt much more alert by the time he stepped into the interview room. Jakes was still wearing his cycling helmet and generally looked truculent.

'Why won't you let me go?' he asked.

'Quite simply, Michael, because of all the unlikely coincidences you are involved in. You witness the splash on Tagg's Island. A few days later you are hanging round there again, in the middle of the night, frightening the woman who discovered the body. Next thing we know you are found right next to another body, that of the recently released prisoner Neville Rollason...'

'Did you kill him?' Hoskins asked.

'You think I did it? But it was me that asked the dog walker to call the police.'

Hoskins chuckled. 'Many murderers call the cops. It's the guilt.'

'I didn't kill him!'

'But you would like to have seen him dead?'

Jakes said nothing for a moment. 'Well, it's complicated actually.'

'The final coincidence,' Gillard said, 'is that you just happen to be about the only person in the country to have a recent photograph of him, on your phone. How did you get it?'

Jakes folded his arms and looked into his lap. He said nothing.

'Come on, Michael. Only half a dozen people in the country knew what Rollason looked like today. How come you are one of them?'

No reply.

'Did he abuse you?' Hoskins asked. Gillard was surprised that the detective constable had come out with this one. He obviously hadn't read up on the statements properly. Rollason was caught in 1988. Jakes would only have been a toddler. It wasn't impossible, but it didn't fit Rollason's known MO.

Jakes stared back at Hoskins. 'No, he didn't abuse me. He's my father.'

The two detectives stared open-mouthed, then looked at each other and declared a short recess.

—

Michael Jakes sat and stared at the duty solicitor. The middle-aged man, grey suited, grey-haired and wholly undistinguished, started talking at him. Something about his rights and what he should and shouldn't say.

He didn't take in a word.

When he was an adolescent he had listened to his older sister, an assertive sixteen, badgering their mother to find out about their dad, Noel, who had died when they were both infants. Susan wanted to know where he was buried or if he had been cremated when they lived up in Newcastle. Why were there no photographs of him? Why was she being robbed of her childhood?

Michael, just fifteen, had long been told he was the man of the house. He had come to his mother's rescue, holding her in his arms while she cried and cried under Susan's relentless verbal assault. Eventually his mum blurted out that their father was a bad man who would knock her about and had threatened both of them. 'He ruined everything in our lives,' she had said. He had accepted this but his sister kept on, harrying their mother about inconsistencies in her story. Eventually, just a few weeks before his eighteenth birthday, with Susan back from university for the summer holidays, their mother called both children together and laid out a stash of family photographs on the dining room table. They'd not seen any of them before.

'I've lied to you, but only because I love you and wanted to save your childhood,' she said. 'Now I'm going to tell you the truth, because I want to save the rest of your lives. Lies are corrosive, and I'm being eaten up by them.'

Then she began a tearful tale of their loveless marriage, in which domestic violence seemed to take a central place. 'He loved children, that's what I'd always thought, even though I could see pretty soon that he didn't love me.'

To him it all seemed a tragic tale, and he didn't share his sister's fury. 'So when did he die?' he had asked.

His mother faltered before speaking. 'He's not dead, pet. He's in prison.'

It took a whole minute for this to sink in. 'Because he hit you?' he had eventually asked.

'No, not for that reason,' Susan interjected. She had been looking through the photographs and documents. She brandished one in her mother's face. 'He's not even called Noel Rogers, is he? He's called Neville Rollason.

It's written on the back of his photograph. You've lied to us in every way!'

Only then did he hear the horrible truth. While their mother, having locked herself in the bathroom, cried piti-fully, Susan turned to him. In her pain, she revealed a spiteful side: 'Our dad is that man who killed all those boys for fun. Boys about your age. What do you think of that?'

That was the beginning of a downward spiral. The void within him filled with a darkness that only Niet-zsche could explain. The very next day his mother was found dead, having taken an overdose. He felt his life was over, and abandoned hopes of going to college. The next dozen years passed in a haze of misery, antidepressants, therapy and loneliness. Plastering, which he learned while doing casual jobs on construction sites, gradually became his saviour. Attending to surfaces allowed him to bury the depths. Eventually, he felt well enough to try for a qualification in philosophy at the Open University.

Now, coming to terms with the death of his father, having seen the body, Michael Jakes felt that he was finally purging himself of all the twisted lies and deceits on which his life had been constructed. There was nothing to fear any longer. As the detectives came back in, he felt ready to tell them his story.

Gillard and Hoskins sat opposite him.

'You said the victim is your father.'

'Yes.'

'I suppose we should offer you our condolences,' Gillard said. 'Did you ever meet him?'

'No, I never visited him because I didn't know he was my father until I was fifteen, and then I discovered exactly who he was.' Jakes relayed the story.

'Did he make any arrangements to visit you after he was released?' Gillard asked.

'He sent me a letter recently, via my sister. That included the photograph. My mother had changed our family name to Rogers soon after he was sentenced, and moved us away from the north-east down here. That kept the press away, but somehow he'd tracked her down. After she died, Susan got married and I changed my name again, to Jakes, my maternal grandmother's name. But in the last year or so my father managed to find out where Susan was. He wrote to her, a couple of times,' he said, staring around the room. 'He wanted to meet us both. I wasn't ready, the whole thing just made me really anxious. Neither of us were keen.'

The two detectives sat back and looked at him.

'In some ways this raises more questions than it answers,' Gillard said, turning briefly to Hoskins. 'According to your story, you saw a man who may have been dumping a body. Don't you think it's a bit of a coincidence that the very person who stumbled across a body in the middle of the night happened to be the victim's son? Especially if, as you maintain, no arrangement to meet up had been made.'

'What do you mean?'

'I think it's pretty obvious,' Hoskins said. 'We're detectives, and we add up the clues. You already had the opportunity to kill this man, given that you were found by the body. Now you say he is your father, we have a motive too.'

–

Michael Jakes was released on police bail. He had to catch the bus back home, as the police had retained his bicycle in the search for evidence; and he was told to phone them from home every evening. The police seemed to think it was a coincidence that he had stumbled across the same car that he had seen that first night on the bridge. But it wasn't that much of a coincidence. He had had a feeling that he was on to something right from the start, from the first splash. It was a premonition that came into his dreams that very night. Nietzsche had come to him, in the darkness: *You will be the instrument of salvation, not just for yourself but for others. But you must look.* He had cycled every night, sometimes twice a night, in a big figure of eight from Walton-on-Thames to Hampton Court Bridge looking for that car, looking for a murderer. And in the end he had found him. And in doing so he had found himself.

–

Leticia was on the lunch run, queueing for sandwiches at Eileen's Deli in Staines High Street, enjoying the cafe radio. A couple of regulars, painters and decorators by the look of their overalls, were ahead of her, ribbing the woman behind the counter, who hadn't yet finished making an elaborate salad for someone sitting down. 'Come on, Eileen,' one muttered, echoing the 1980s hit that had just been playing. The woman, whose name was Pat, rolled her eyes at the tired and endlessly repeated joke. The hourly news bulletin kicked in, announcing the discovery of another dead body between Staines and Walton-on-Thames.

> *The police for the moment are declining to give details, but a source close to the investigation told Surrey FM that the victim was the notorious*

> *murderer Neville Rollason, only released from*
> *prison yesterday.*

The two tradesmen ahead of Leticia turned to each other in apparent joy. 'Yes! Fucking result, my son,' one said, proffering a clenched fist. His mate clapped him on the shoulder and said: 'Sorted. In double-quick time.'

By the time Leticia got back to the office, the news had already electrified the place. She distributed the sandwiches she had got on behalf of Tina, Jill and Adrian. An impromptu meeting was called in Jill's office while they all munched through their lunch. 'So they really did have him,' Leticia said.

'It certainly looks that way,' Jill said. 'We of course must institute an immediate and thorough enquiry into our actions and re-evaluate our procedures. As I said yesterday, please continue to refer all press calls to the Ministry of Justice media team in London. If you're asked a question, just act dumb. Pretend to be a temp. Don't give your name, but most importantly, at no stage should any of us confirm Rollason was on our books.'

They all nodded in agreement.

'This is a better result, frankly, than the other kind of surprise, which would be to discover that Rollason had reoffended,' Richards said.

Jill turned to him. 'Adrian, a man we were supposed to be rehabilitating is dead. It is absolutely not good news.'

Richards shrugged, his indifference lost in the noise as Verity crashed through the door, late as usual, and dumped her bag on the table. 'I got caught in a half-hour jam near the crime scene. There were half a dozen police cars. There were people picnicking by the roadside to watch.' She looked excited, her face lit up.

'People are nothing but ghouls,' Richards said.

Leticia then relayed the reaction of the tradesmen in the sandwich queue. 'They were delighted.'

Jill shook her head. 'I think we have always recognised that the great British public do not appreciate a lot of our work. It only makes it harder.'

Thursday evening

Gillard's wish to learn a bit more about the first victim was answered sooner than he had expected. The detective chief inspector was still sitting at his desk at 6:45 p.m. the same day when an email arrived in his in-box, headed 'missing persons' and written by the chief international liaison officer at Taipei police HQ. There, in excellent English, was a list of the several thousand male Taiwanese citizens who had bought air tickets to London since March. The liaison officer had helpfully flagged up those who had already returned, which left 485. Even more useful was the appending of the date of birth of each person, based on passport details. That allowed Gillard to exclude those who were clearly too young or too old to be the man they had found. Leaving a wide age window of 40 to 65 gave them 117 citizens. The officer apologised profusely for not yet having linked the supplied list to those who had been reported missing but promised it for the next day.

DC Hoskins came over to see what his boss was so excited about. 'That's fast,' he said. 'We haven't got an answer from the Border Force yet about who arrived in Britain.'

'Well, we can help them,' Gillard said. 'Send Border Force those 117 Taiwanese passport numbers, see which of them did indeed arrive and how many have left. I want it by tomorrow morning. I'll ring Rigby at home to see if she can add her authority to it.'

Chapter Twenty-six

By the time the main incident room meeting was convened the next morning a lot more information had arrived. Only one of the Taiwanese travellers had been reported missing, and that was quite recently. He was Dr Wei-Ling Chen, a well-known academic in the field of nanotechnology who was supposed to be attending a conference in Oxford early in June.

He had never checked in.

Gillard had appended printouts of everything he'd received from Taipei, and the confirming information from the Border Force onto the whiteboards that had for so many days only had speculative information scrawled on them. 'Hopefully, we can make a very quick break-through on this,' Gillard said. 'Dr Chen was reported missing by his sister just a couple of weeks ago. She said that her brother had been depressed and might not have caught the plane to Britain at all. In fact, as we can see here, he did arrive at Heathrow on June seventeenth.'

'Do we have a mobile phone number for him?' asked Rob Townsend. 'That would be the quickest way of checking where he went.'

'Yeah, way better than trying to wade through CCTV cameras at Heathrow,' muttered Hoskins.

'That would be a great start, Rob. We've got one additional line of enquiry,' Gillard said. 'Attached to the documentation of the e-ticket he bought is the booking of a hire car through Avis at Heathrow. Rainy, I'd like you to follow that up and see whether the car was ever returned.'

'Okay boss.'

'The Taipei police have been incredibly thorough already,' Gillard said. 'They have given us an entire data dump from the phone service provider for his work and personal phones. That includes all the messaging by text or email, although not WhatsApp. Most of what we have now is in Chinese, but they have offered to translate it into English.'

'Top marks,' said Hoskins. 'That's above and beyond.'

'I get the impression that considering the prominence of the man, they want to get a fairly rapid result,' Gillard said. 'I told them we did too.'

–

Gillard was waiting for Rainy Macintosh to get off the phone to Avis car rentals when Research Intelligence Officer Rob Townsend beckoned him over to his computer, on which was displayed a high-resolution map showing a faltering yellow trace heading west from Heathrow airport. 'This is the journey of Dr Chen's phone on the morning of June seventeenth,' he said. 'The mobile was on presumably from the moment he arrived. He headed down behind Heathrow, through Hounslow and Feltham. He certainly looks like he was heading for our patch. But then the signal stops, and never goes on again.'

'I'm pretty sure that's not the way that the satnav would take you if you're heading to Oxford,' Gillard said. 'And I'm guessing, but I don't think he would have known the backroads and rat runs in that area.'

Before Townsend could give his own response Rainy called over, having just finished her call. 'He booked the hire car, but cancelled on the day by phone,' she said.

Gillard and Townsend stared at each other. 'So maybe someone gave him a lift?' Townsend said.

'Seems the most likely. With luck, we'll know when we get the contents of his phone.'

'How long do we have to wait for the translation?' Rainy asked.

'They promised us a day,' Gillard said. 'But you know, if he was messaging somebody about a lift from Heathrow, it would probably be in English, wouldn't it?'

The three of them crowded around Gillard's screen while he downloaded a PDF from the Taipei police email. Most of the messages were in Chinese script, but as the data was sorted by date and time, he was able to home in on a message sent soon after the Taiwanese man landed at Heathrow.

> Dear Mr Chen, the driver will be in arrivals with
> a card with your name on it.
>   Looking forward to seeing you.
>   Penelope

The only later text messages in English were ones from the Oxford conference, welcoming him to the country, and some from the phone service provider about roaming services. Gillard scrolled back in time, looking for anything from Penelope in the preceding days. There was nothing.

'There must have been other messages on other phones, or emails, something like that,' Gillard said. 'Arrangements must have been made before he set off.'

'It might be easier for us to trace Penelope's email,' Rainy said.

'Rob, I'd like you to make that your top priority,' Gillard said. 'First of all to see if we can find out who sent the email, and secondly to see if anyone called Penelope is connected with the conference organisers.'

Townsend nodded. 'It's probably a false name,' he said.

—

It was only another hour later when another raft of translations from Dr Chen's laptop arrived from Taipei. 'Oh, this is it, the motherlode,' said Rainy Macintosh, who was sitting next to Carl Hoskins.

'What have you got there?' he asked.

'An English precis of each of the twenty most significant Chinese-language documents from Dr Chen's laptop. It's a canny piece of work. They must be working into the wee hours over there in Taipei.'

Hoskins called up the master list of all documents on the laptop. 'There are still thousands of others they haven't done. And they could have done it on Google Translate.'

Rainy looked at him over her glasses. 'Och, Carl, I've got a new career for you: gift horse's dental consultant.'

'What?' Hoskins said.

'Never mind. The value is in the precis as much as the translation. Look at this one: "personal correspondence with sister arranging lunar New Year holidays." That saved translating a 600-word email.'

'See what you mean,' Hoskins conceded.

'I'll send half the translations to your terminal, for you to take a wee look.'

'Like I didn't have enough work to begin with,' Hoskins muttered.

The two detectives sat in silence scanning through the list. Hoskins found a document that was already fully in English. He started to read it.

Memorandum of agreement

Charon Stichting, Singel 893 Bis, Amsterdam (the agent)

Chen, Dr Wei-Ling of San Shia Campus: 151 University Rd, San Shia District, New Taipei City, 23741 Taiwan. (The client)

1. This agreement concerns an arrangement made under the auspices of Dutch and European law to govern a private and confidential contract between the client and the agent.

2. The agent agrees to fulfil the client's requirements as set out in the addendum ('The service'). The agent will locate, brief and introduce the supplier of the service. The agent will check that the supplier is qualified, prepared and able to provide the said service in a timescale compatible with the client's requirements.

3. The client agrees to pay in advance by banker's draft the full and final fee

for the service without deduction, and agrees to indemnify without limit the agent, for any additional costs incurred in transferring the said amount. This fee will then be held in escrow pending confirmation that the service has been provided.

4. The agent will retain thirty-five per cent of the fee, plus any applicable taxes.

5. The agent agrees to oversee the execution of the post-provision codicil, including without limitation the return/and or disposal as stipulated of the client's corporea, possessions and effects by international courier.

The document went on and on. Hoskins' eyes glazed over, and he moved on to something less dull. The cogs must've been grinding slowly because he suddenly realised there was something significant in point five: client possessions and effects. Was this an international removals agreement?

'Rainy, take a look at this would you? I'm no good on legalese, but this looks to me like a physical transference, maybe a removal job.'

The Glaswegian detective looked over his shoulder and scanned the wording.

'Do you think he was going to live in Holland?' Hoskins asked.

'Sweet Jesus,' Rainy breathed. 'There's one word there that does not belong at all. I did enough Latin in my medical training to know what we're talking about here.'

'Which word? I don't know what half of them mean.'

'Corporea, Carl. It means bodily remains. This contract appears to be about the movement of a dead body.'

'Time to get the boss back in,' Hoskins said.

-

Gillard had just returned from a meeting with the chief constable and DI Graham Morgan when DC Macintosh called him over.

'What is it, Rainy?'

She showed him the screen and pointed out the fifth clause. 'I agree it looks strange,' he said. 'Where's the nearest lawyer? There's bound to be a duty solicitor somewhere in Mount Browne who can explain this contract.'

It took fifteen minutes, but Rainy managed to find a solicitor from the Crown Prosecution Service who was at police HQ for another matter. The South Asian-looking woman agreed to leave her meeting for ten minutes to assist them. She looked at a printout of the contract and agreed that it was extremely strange. She backed up Rainy's interpretation of the word corporea. 'Do you have the codicil, the legal appendix referred to?' she asked. 'That would certainly shed further light.'

'No,' Rainy said. 'There don't seem to be any of the other documents here.'

'Hmm. There's an unidentified third party referred to, the supplier. It could be a funeral home or crematorium I suppose, though I have to admit it would be an unusual contractual arrangement to go through a third party.' She looked at her watch, and said she had to be getting back to her meeting.

'The third party, is that Charon?' Hoskins asked, as she started to walk away.

'Yes. Now that in itself is interesting,' the lawyer said. 'In Greek mythology, Charon is the ferryman of the dead. He carries the souls of the newly deceased across the River Styx into the underworld.'

Gillard thanked her, and turned to look at the other two detectives.

'The ferryman of the dead! It's no' P&O and that's for sure,' Rainy exclaimed.

'Yeah,' Hoskins said. 'Roll on, roll off, roll over and die.'

Gillard rolled his eyes. 'Rainy, ask the Taiwanese if they have any more related documents. I'm going to get Rob to investigate the Dutch firm.'

Suddenly Rainy gave a sharp intake of breath. 'I wonder if the man knew he was dying. That might explain everything.'

Gillard looked at her quizzically.

'Dr Delahaye's post-mortem report mentioned a huge tumour in the man's liver,' Rainy said. 'Delahaye assumed that he wouldn't have known, because liver cancer can get quite far before you notice it. But maybe he *did* know. Maybe he was making arrangements in advance.'

Gillard conceded that this was an interesting new angle. 'Why come to Britain to do it though? Was there some special requirement?'

'Maybe the Oxford conference,' Rainy said.

Hoskins leaned back in his typist's chair with his hands behind his head, and yawned. 'So are we really talking about a funeral firm that squashes people to death? And then takes it upon itself to squeeze a particular murderer who has just been released from prison?'

'Yes, I admit as a theory it doesn't exactly hang together. At least not yet,' Gillard said. 'But I'm sure Charon, ferryman of the dead, has the answers.'

–

A Skype call with Dr Chen's sister in Adelaide, Australia promised to clear up some of the contradictions. Mrs Wendy Ho had first requested to speak to British detectives early that morning, but because of its multiple addressees the email had dropped into Gillard's junk mail folder. Although it was three p.m. in Britain when the detective responded, Mrs Ho got straight back to him. She had clearly been awake even though it was 11:30 p.m. in Adelaide.

The woman who Gillard saw on the screen was a bespectacled middle-aged Chinese lady with a kind face. Behind her was a wall hung with family photographs.

'Mrs Ho, thank you so much for agreeing to talk to us at such short notice. I hope you don't mind but I am recording this to help with the case.'

'No worry,' she said, with a twang of Australian showing through the Chinese accent. 'I no sleep so well since I told he dead.' The woman lifted to the screen a framed photograph of a handsome and confident-looking naval officer in a white uniform and peaked cap, with golden epaulettes. 'This is my brother Wei-Ling. Is this man you found?'

Gillard could see that the portrait had been taken decades ago. 'Do you have anything more recent?' he asked.

She picked up a phone and after swiping a few times showed him a picture of a dapper grey-haired fellow, smiling, standing under a cherry tree heavy with blossom. It was hard to say for certain if it was the same man. Gillard needed a comparison. He carefully slid one of the gory CSI pictures face down back along his desk, only lifting it face up behind his screen to be sure that the Skype camera didn't pick it up. The two images side by side were not conclusive. A little elasticity with the truth was required.

'It certainly could be him, Mrs Ho. What have you been told about your brother's death?'

'Just that he found in River Thames. Maybe suicide.'

'Did your brother have suicidal feelings?' Gillard asked.

'He depress, since he heard about cancer. No cure. But I no think he kill himself. He very brave man.'

'I'm sure he was, Mrs Ho.'

'Mr Gillard, how long Wei-Ling been in UK?'

'He arrived at Heathrow Airport on June seventeenth, his body was found on the morning of June twenty-second. We don't know much about what he did between those two dates. Is there anything you can tell us?'

'He planned to go to nanotech conference in Oxford, I knew that. But I thought he not go, because of cancer.'

'As far as we know, he didn't go. In fact, we don't know what he did do. Did he have any friends in Britain or any contacts here that you are aware of?'

'I send you list. I email to them already to ask. They say he no tell anybody what he plan.'

Gillard nodded. 'I understand from the police in Taipei that he isn't married, and that you are his only living close relative. I assume since you live in Australia that you didn't see him that often.'

She nodded. 'He divorce, long time ago. No woman for long time. But I no sure. We too far apart. I live here with my son and daughter. Better with no big communist next door like in Taiwan.' She smiled.

Gillard knew that the next part would need to be done with the utmost delicacy. 'Mrs Ho, were you aware of any plans that your brother had made for his own death?'

There was a pause at the other end and he saw her blink numerous times. 'One time when he depress and call me, he said he go to Switzerland and go out nicely. I beg him no, there always hope. He had money. Could go America for treatment. He no mention it again.'

The detective noted down details of when Dr Chen's sister had last seen him and any friends and neighbours he had in Taipei who might have a better insight into his mood immediately before he departed for Britain. He once again thanked Mrs Ho, asked her to forward the details of any local police liaison officers who were helping her in Australia, and said he would be in contact again. He knew that it was likely there would be upsetting details that would reach her at some stage, and he was anxious that she shouldn't have to deal with it alone.

–

While Gillard was on the call DC Rob Townsend had found a website for Charon Stichting. 'It's a charitable health foundation. Stichting just means "foundation",' the research intelligence officer said.

The detective chief inspector looked through the English-language version of the website. It was glossy and professional, with many photographs of trustworthy-looking white-coated male medics. They all had perfect smiles and good hair, stethoscopes resting over their shoulders, often conferring with gorgeous but studious female researchers at their microscopes in pristine and modern-looking labs. It wasn't immediately apparent what specific services Charon undertook; if he had not read the text, Gillard would have assumed it was some Florida cosmetic surgery outfit. After five minutes of skimming, looking past the euphemisms and corporate-speak, it was clear to him that the organisation was involved in end-of-life care. Helping afflicted individuals make difficult choices and guiding them on their chosen paths. Much was made of the charitable end of the organisation, in which those with incurable diseases and limited means were, in one memorable phrase, 'offered pain-free off-ramps from the highway of suffering.' Buried within the website was a section with its own email address that offered to connect those wanting 'bespoke services' with others willing to provide them.

The detective sent a message to the site explaining that he was looking into the case of the Taiwanese man who had been found dead in Britain, and who appeared to have been in contact with them.

While he was waiting for a reply, Gillard wandered across to Rob Townsend's desk to see how he was doing tracing the email address for Penelope, whoever she was. The research intelligence officer looked frustrated. 'It's been well disguised. Proxy servers, and probably more. I can pass it on to the specialists in the City of London police if you like. It won't be quick,' he warned.

The detective chief inspector looked around the CID office and saw how many good detectives on the team were working hard, using their initiative trying to crack this case. Unlike the early days, there were plenty of leads to follow even if none of it really made sense yet. Tomorrow was Saturday, but he had already made a formal request to Taipei police headquarters for a Skype call with a liaison officer. Brief translations of the documents found on Dr Chen's laptop were still arriving in dribs and drabs by four p.m. UK time so someone in Taipei must have been working late into the night. The call would probably be early in the UK morning, but he could do it from home if necessary. In the meantime, he set off for the canteen to buy the entire crime team coffees and Eccles cakes, which had recently become a bit of a late-afternoon favourite. Crispy sugared pastry filled with currants. Probably not good for you, but he had never seen a detective get as excited over a grated carrot salad as Hoskins did over this confection. Hoskins' late colleague DC Colin Hodges, equally overweight and equally fond of something sweet, would have been proud.

Gillard was just making his way back with a full tray, backing his way through the double doors into the main office, when Rainy Macintosh called for him. 'We've just been sent part of Dr Chen's will, apparently found on a different computer.'

'Okay, what have we got?'

'We've only been sent the covering letter, but it tells us a lot.'

> *My dear friends,*
>
> *I know a number of you have been curious about my unexplained absence, and I can finally now explain my apparent rudeness in not replying to your messages. A few of you may be aware that I have an untreatable liver cancer. Three months ago I was given six months to live. Rather than just let my life slip away painfully at the pace dictated by my affliction I decided to seize control*

*of my destiny. Therefore I arranged to end my life
in the manner of my choosing, enjoyably rather
than painfully. I was already scheduled to go to a
conference in Oxford in the UK, and I anticipate
that I will rejoin my ancestors at the end of June. I
apologise for not sharing my plans before, I realise
some of you will be hurt, but I dared not risk being
dissuaded from the path I had chosen. After the
return of my body, I have arranged for my funeral
to take place here in Taipei on 7 July.*

    My love to you all
    Chen Wei-Ling

Gillard and Rainy Macintosh looked at each other.
'Whatever he thought he was getting, I'm sure he
didn't sign up to be asphyxiated and dumped in the
Thames,' Gillard said. 'Apart from everything else he's
been defrauded. His body was presumably to be returned
to Taiwan. The contract says so, as does this letter. Right,
I'm phoning Charon. They have some explaining to do.'

Two hours after his email enquiry, Gillard was speaking
by telephone to Dr Ernst Molenaar, the chief ethicist of
Charon.

'Our charity is, as you will have seen, based in
Amsterdam and merely acts as a global facilitator for those
who want to end their life. Like Facebook, we do not
take responsibility for the interactions over the network.
It's really no more difficult to understand than contacting
a plumber online.'

'These people are generally terminally ill, yes?'

'Often but not necessarily. The obvious choice for those who are suffering pain or have terminal illnesses is a Swiss organisation called Dignitas, which for about £10,000 will get you brought to Switzerland where your life will be ended painlessly and, as you can tell by the name, in a dignified fashion. We go above and beyond that in our offering.'

'So some of your clients are healthy? Do you not check their motivation?'

'Of course not. Everybody has a reason. My reason may not persuade you and your reason may not persuade me. We've had clients who are so depressed about our inability to face up to climate change that they want their lives to be ended now in a calm and organised manner rather than face the chaos of civilisation's collapse. It's not my job to question it.'

'I'm calling about one of your clients, as I mentioned in the email.'

'I'm sorry, we are simply not able to disclose the details of parties to the transactions, nor to give you access to our network.'

'At this stage all we are asking you to do is to confirm that you helped arrange a contract involving a Taiwanese man named Dr Wei-Ling Chen.'

'I'm sorry, I can't do that.'

'We believe that Dr Chen was murdered by someone who got access to him through your network.'

'That's a very serious allegation, Detective Chief Inspector. I cannot comment on individual cases but you should remember that those who contact us are requesting that their life be ended. It thus cannot be murder if the contract is fulfilled.'

The detective felt a wave of frustration with this slippery man. 'All right, the contract we have seen indicates that Dr Chen had arranged with the service provider to have his body returned to Taipei. Instead it was dumped in the Thames. Whatever you think of his death, that's still a breach of contract. Even by your own standards, it should concern you.'

'Yes, it does. If what you say is true, that would be a serious matter. If a complaint is to be made it would be up to the client—'

'Who, might I remind you, is dead,' Gillard interjected.

'—or their next of kin to contact us. We have a thorough complaints procedure open to either party, with compulsory arbitration.'

'We're talking about something a bit more serious than a flawed purchase.'

'Not so far, we're not. The client expressed a wish to die, we can prove that.'

The detective was clenching his fists in frustration. 'If you don't co-operate, we will get a court order,' he said.

'You may certainly try, but it would have to be under Dutch law, which gives the parties significant privacy protections against such oversight. These, after all, are confidential commercial contracts.'

'And I'm sure they are illegal in many of the countries that your clients come from.'

Molenaar laughed gently. 'In a few, possibly. In most it is simply a grey area, and for good reason. After all, if it is a crime, then who would the victim be? A person who has just paid many thousands of pounds for a service that took some time to organise could not be said to have lacked volition or power over the process. Laws that deny us the ability to control our own bodies stand in stark contravention to the usual laws of contract and property.'

'It's the law's job to protect people.'

'The law won't stop people dying. The figures for suicide show that. What it does do is remove the possibility that someone wishing to end their life can discuss their wishes with family and friends and move to a conclusion without threat of legal intervention. Instead what you get is the discovery of a loved one having taken an overdose, hanging themselves while you're out, or being gassed in a car with the exhaust pipe taped inside. As with abortion, the law doesn't change the outcomes, it just makes the process a whole lot more unpleasant and undignified.'

Gillard blew a sigh, feeling he had got nowhere. Time to step back. 'All right, Dr Molenaar, can you tell me what kind of suppliers you have on your network?'

'You mean what kind of termination? Well, we only police them to make sure they do what they're supposed to do. Which is kind of difficult – you can hardly ask a dead person to fill out a customer satisfaction survey. Many provide a death by the sea. The pounding of tropical surf nearby, a glorious sunset, a fantastic hotel. However, we are aware of numerous erotic and sex-related outfits. Our research indicates that it's mainly men who are interested in these. One of our most popular is right here in Amsterdam, a farewell party for one, involving three very beautiful, uninhibited and imaginative escorts.'

'That's little more than prostitution, then.'

'It's a lot more, believe me. Remember that the orgasm was always termed "the little death". *La petit mort* as the French say. Everybody wants a bigger bang, of whatever kind. A couple of years ago we arranged a personal crucifixion surrounded by hired worshippers, which turned out to be one of the most awkward and thus expensive arrangements we have ever tried to source. Overall, there are as many variations in how people want to die as in how they want to live. Some clients just want to be cuddled, sometimes by two or three others, as they die. Occasionally, one wants to be eaten. There was quite a famous cannibalism case in Germany years ago. And if that's your thing, why not?'

After Gillard had hung up, he realised that he'd learned an awful lot about assisted suicide, but almost nothing about the case he was investigating. Could Dr Chen really have paid to be killed in that extraordinary way? Or was the reality simply that he had paid for one service and received another, entirely different? He couldn't imagine anybody would pay to have the breath squeezed out of them, but then he would have never guessed that anyone would pay to be crucified. In one respect, he had to admit, Dr Molenaar was right: any court case to try to force Charon Stichting to disclose details would take months to arrange.

He needed answers more quickly than that.

Chapter Twenty-seven

It was breakfast time on Saturday morning when Gillard got a call at home from DCI Sarah Bracewell of the anti-corruption unit.

'Sorry to disturb your breakfast,' she said. 'I've got some information that you might find useful in the hunt for the killer of Neville Rollason.'

'That would be much appreciated.'

'I've been interviewing PC Andrew Wickens, who as you know is being investigated for feeding information to the vigilante group AVENGE. For the first two days he refused to say a thing, so I set in motion a rolling series of interviews with the minimum rest period between, and just hoped to grind him down. I'm aware that we need a quick result here. We finally broke him just before dawn this morning.'

Gillard had occasionally deployed intensive interviewing practices and witnessed how gruelling it was to face the same questions again and again. The best results were often gained by going back right to the beginning each time, even down to getting the interviewee to spell his name and address each and every time. He wasn't surprised that it was in the small hours that Wickens' resolution had finally collapsed.

'He confessed to attempting to gain information on behalf of AVENGE, which dovetails with what we discovered from Nigel Chivers and Terry Dalton. He also admitted that he'd logged onto the Police National Computer using a colleague's ID.'

'Ah, that would be PC Jim Cottesloe.'

'Yes. The final nugget was that he finally coughed up who the mister big behind this abduction attempt was. A man named Gus van Steenis.'

'That makes sense,' Gillard said. 'We've been sniffing around Holdersham Hall and Estate on a number of occasions related to the murder of Dr Wei-Ling Chen.' He thanked Bracewell, finished the call and abandoned the rest of his breakfast. It was time to make another visit to the Zimbabwean.

—

Within an hour, three patrol cars were screaming their way to Holdersham Hall. Gillard himself hung back, driving more slowly, on the hands-free phone to the duty magistrate who was to issue the search warrant. The female stipendiary seemed to want to ask a lot of lengthy but not unreasonable questions before granting Surrey police the full range of rights they were seeking. Gillard hung on the line, even as he could see on his mobile text messages from uniforms who had come to a screeching halt outside the stately home's main gates. It was another fifteen minutes before permission was granted, but even as Gillard relayed to the officers on the scene that they could now effect an entry, he was aware that any element of surprise would probably have been lost.

Gillard finally arrived at Holdersham Hall, to find only a rather disconsolate Rainy Macintosh standing at the entrance to the main building, while officers ferried out plastic bags containing computer equipment.

'The wee bird has flown, sir. The house manager confirmed that Gus van Steenis left on Friday afternoon to catch a flight to Harare.'

Gillard cursed under his breath. 'So we were already too late. Never mind, let's search this place from top to bottom.'

A team of thirty officers began combing through the zoo, aided by the staff and keyholders, while Gillard sat behind van Steenis's rather grand desk and started checking up on flights to Harare. He made some progress quite quickly, discovering that Zimbabwe was a signatory to the 2003 Extradition Act. Of course, that may not be van Steenis's final destination. He was an old Africa hand and there must be many places on that continent where he would be welcomed. The detective was just making his second call, to British Airways to see if van Steenis had been on Friday night's flight to Harare when a grim-faced Rainy Macintosh walked into the office.

'I think you better come and see this, sir.'

Gillard ended the call and followed her. She led him around the back of the main building to a large ugly barn. Officers had already forced the corrugated metal door and switched on the light. The entire shed was turned over to tools of various kinds, ancient and modern. Spread right in the middle of the shed was a large plastic dust sheet, and on it a gym mat.

'The bastard built an electric chair, probably for Rollason,' she said.

Gillard walked over and inspected the hefty hardwood chair with buckled canvas restraints on its arms and front legs.

'Just pop yourself on here, Detective Constable,' Gillard said. 'I just want to check if it's connected.'

'With all due respect, boss, kiss my arse,' Rainy replied cheerfully. The male uniformed officer by the door, who had been chuckling at Gillard's suggestion, gasped at the Glaswegian's insubordination. Gillard playfully pinched her cheek. 'What would we do without you, eh?'

'Shocking behaviour, sir,' the male uniform ventured.

'Don't you start,' Gillard retorted.

'It's clear van Steenis went to a huge amount of trouble, but never got to use his wee chair,' Rainy said.

'How do you know?' Gillard replied.

'Have you ever read accounts of the effect of electrocution on the human body?'

'No, I haven't, but I'm sure you're going to tell me.'

'I dealt with a man who was badly burned trying to steal part of the live overhead cable going from Shotts into Glasgow Central. Aye, he wasn't a pretty sight. Not to put too fine a point on it, sir, you'd never get rid of the smell of piss and shite from this place, if van Steenis had used his machine.'

'Point taken, Detective Constable. Trouble is, someone did kill Rollason. If van Steenis had hold of him why didn't he use the chair?'

The phone call came at eight thirty on the Sunday morning. Gillard was having a rare lie-in, holding a still-sleeping Sam close, his arm around her shoulder, her warm breath against his neck. It had been a bad night for her, with nightmares and a feeling that she was being suffocated. He had sat up with her in the small hours talking it through. In any PTSD recuperation, he'd been told, there would be setbacks. This was one of them.

He reached for his mobile with his free arm and answered softly. 'Gillard.'

It was DC Hoskins. 'Sorry to disturb, sir. We've had a missing person report this morning. Rather a curious one.'

'Really?' He gradually and carefully extricated himself from Sam's embrace.

'It's the probation officer who was in charge of Rollason.'

'Leticia Mountjoy?'

'Yes, sir. Her partner Anton St Jeanne reported her missing a few minutes ago. He's not seen her since yesterday morning. Normally, as you know, we wouldn't be that concerned within twenty-four hours, but I thought you should know.'

'Okay. I'm not due in until this afternoon but keep me informed. Try to trace her mobile, car number plate if relevant, that kind of thing. Make it a priority.'

'I've already started.'

Gillard ended the call, sat on the edge of the bed and rubbed his face. Leticia Mountjoy, Anton St Jeanne, Leroy Ceejay. Leroy was a crook, but of a known type. St Jeanne seemed straight despite his entanglement with Ceejay, while he had no reason to believe that Leticia Mountjoy was anything other than a responsible professional. Yet something here was worrying him.

He rang Graham Morgan. The Special Branch detective inspector reacted with horror to the news Gillard gave him.

'You know her better than I do,' Gillard said. 'Any theories?'

'No. She's reliable, capable, level-headed. Though there are others with more experience than her, I think she is doing a good job.'

'We have two killings to solve, both carried out the same way, but only a motive for one of them. Someone wanted Neville Rollason dead. Whoever had the skill to find out which prison he was leaving on July second could only have got that information from a very small number of people. She is one of them. You are another. If it was her, then that creates a motive for getting her out of the way.'

'That's plausible except for the timing,' Morgan replied. 'If she provided the information, wittingly or unwittingly, and the killer needs her out of the way, why not act before Rollason's body was discovered?'

'That's a good point. But perhaps the opportunity hadn't arrived. I don't know. Can I ask you to make enquiries among her colleagues?'

Gillard had no sooner put the phone down than it rang again.

Hoskins again. 'Sir, further to the missing Ms Mountjoy: her car's just been found, burned out on waste ground in Feltham.'

'Okay. I'll be in as soon as I can.' Feltham was just a few miles from Leticia Mountjoy's home. Gillard rubbed his face. He was beginning to fear for the young woman's life.

Chapter Twenty-eight

Two days previously

That Verity waited until last thing on Friday afternoon to announce she was leaving took almost everyone by surprise. Leticia knew something was up the moment her boss, having been absent all day, walked into Swan House at four p.m. carrying a large cake. She had never seen Verity with such a flamboyant hairdo or wearing so much eye make-up. The high heels and the black dress gave her the look of a catwalk model, glamorous but undernourished. And she was grinning like a Cheshire cat. She rattled the metal forks in her hand to get everyone's attention, and declared that today was her last day and after a short holiday she would be taking up a new post in Nottingham.

'We hadn't even heard you were going,' said Adrian Richards.

'Well, it took a long time to confirm the details of the new post. Jill has known for some weeks but I asked her not to let the details out until it had been confirmed,' Verity said.

'What is the new job?' Leticia asked.

'I'm going to be head of special services for the disabled in Nottingham City Council.'

'Ah, I saw that job advertised,' Richards said. 'I was thinking of going for that myself.'

Verity then called out to the rest of the staff in the open-plan office that there was carrot cake. 'Once you've finished this, I hope you can all come and join me in the wine bar across the road after work,' she concluded.

Leticia and Tina exchanged wide-eyed glances. They had never known Verity to go drinking. They weren't going to miss this for the world.

–

The wine bar was already thronged with the after-work crowd when Leticia and Tina got there. Verity was talking to a couple of young men at the bar. She refilled three glasses with a bottle of something fizzy from a silver wine cooler. The only other person from the office who was there was Adrian. He must have sneaked out early from the senior team meeting. She didn't know most of the rest. As soon as they got to the bar Verity greeted them warmly and called to the barman for another bottle of cava. She seemed genuinely pleased to see both Leticia and Tina.

'Leticia,' Verity said. 'I think you are going to do very well. I know I'm late with your appraisal, but I'm going to tell Jill that I think you should replace me.'

'Wow, that's very kind of you,' Leticia said. It was clear that Verity was already a little bit tipsy, but if that meant she would confide in her that was no bad thing. Leticia was far from sure that she was ready for such a hefty promotion, and her face must have reflected that.

'No, I mean it.' Verity leaned close until Leticia could smell the wine on her breath. 'That little slip-up with you-know-who seems largely to have bypassed our department, I'm glad to say. Bloody Parole Board got it in the neck, if the newspapers are anything to go by.' She laughed.

Verity was called back to the bar. Two men from the private-sector probation firm downstairs at Swan House were well down the cava, and were clearly interested in her.

Leticia was drawn away by Tina. 'I can't believe this,' she said. 'Verity is like a new woman.'

'I suppose she's just delighted to leave,' Leticia said. 'She was under a lot of pressure, and it's a clean start for her.'

Tina nodded. 'So maybe she's not pregnant then. Maybe it's just the eating disorder.'

Leticia glanced at Verity, still as thin as a rake. 'Perhaps. She'd be too early to show, but sickness is worst in the early months.'

'Yes, but she wouldn't be taking another job just to go straight on maternity leave would she? There's no better way to get off to a bad start with a new employer.'

Leticia shrugged and turned back to watch Verity, who was clearly flirting with one of the men.

'Well, there are a lot of firsts today,' Tina said.

'Drinks, cake. What else?' Leticia asked as she sipped her cava.

'Men, at least in public.'

'Did you ever meet her ex?'

'No. But I heard the arguments on the phone, before Verity got her glass box. Now she just rows with her mother.'

Leticia nodded. Tina leaned in to her ear and whispered: 'Her older brother disappeared when she was young. Never been seen since. Her parents' marriage broke up, and she and her younger brother don't really get on.'

'All that and a bad divorce,' Leticia said.

The evening wore on. Eventually, at nine, Tina announced she was heading home. Leticia was tempted to follow suit but then thought of her empty flat. Anton would be at the restaurant for hours yet; he rarely got in before one a.m. Jill Allsop had been and gone, and the two hunky guys from downstairs had disappeared too. Verity was leaning on the bar, talking with two women and a guy who were dressed as if heading for a nightclub. Leticia was pretty sure they were nothing to do with the probation service, but they seemed happy enough to guzzle Verity's cava.

Leticia rejoined the group, thinking perhaps she should rescue her boss. The first thing she did was dissuade her from ordering another bottle. 'Actually, Verity...' Leticia said, gently tugging back her arm, which was waving a credit card towards the barman.

'What?' She eyed her subordinate quizzically.

'I think you've had enough, don't you?' Leticia said.

'No, s'all right,' Verity slurred. 'I can afford it now. I've come into some money. And I need a drink.'

'Actually, Verity, it's been a lovely evening, but it might be a good idea to think about heading home.' She could immediately feel the chill of disappointment among Verity's fair-weather friends. 'Are you getting a taxi?'

'I've got my car.' She pointed vaguely in the direction of Swan House.

'You can't possibly drive in this state. I'll ring for a cab. Where's your gift?' Leticia recalled that Jill had secretly bought Verity a beautiful Italian soft leather briefcase on behalf of the department, and had presented it just before she left the office.

Verity looked puzzled for a minute, then said: 'In the boot.'

'If you give me the keys I'll go and get it for you,' Leticia said. She smiled icily at Verity's new friends, who were reluctantly draining their drinks and getting ready to leave.

Keys now in hand, Leticia walked back to Swan House and found Verity's Nissan in the car park. She clicked the fob, and the lights flashed orange. She flipped open the boot and saw the new briefcase still partially in its silvery wrapping paper.

As she lifted it up, she felt it snag. Something was stuck to the trailing sticky tape on the parcel. She peered underneath, and gasped. A slender object was caught in the recessed catch for the boot. She recognised it immediately, but could not imagine how on earth it came to be there. If she was right about what it was, it would change everything that had happened since Tuesday.

Absolutely everything.

Chapter Twenty-nine

Leticia set down the parcel and tore off a strip of the silvery wrapping, then carefully untangled the tiny metal hinge of the broken spectacle arm from the threads of the boot liner. She held up the slender red plastic for a closer look. Yes, it looked just like his. She wrapped it carefully and put it in her pocket.

The young probation officer was in a quandary as she walked back to the bar. Verity wouldn't have had any official contact with Neville Rollason, and there could be no good reason for part of his glasses to be in the boot of her car. She simply couldn't think of an innocent explanation; but neither could she imagine that her boss would have had anything to do with his abduction and murder. Who should she turn to?

Pushing open the door of the bar, she saw that Verity was slumped at a table, her head resting on her arms. A female member of the bar staff stood over her, trying to wake her. Leticia sensed that her boss would hardly be able to talk, let alone give a good answer to the questions she desperately wanted to ask. Leticia told the staff member she would take care of Verity. 'I've rung for a taxi, it should be here soon,' she said. Verity's head nodded but no sound came.

Leticia herself had drunk three glasses of wine, but seeing Verity sobered her up quickly. She had a more immediate problem than what to do about the spectacle frame: Verity herself. Part of her just wanted to be shot of the woman – to bundle Verity into a taxi and get her own cab home. They would probably never see each other again.

When the taxi came, she and the Sikh driver eased Verity in. Looking at her, helplessly drunk, Leticia realised she couldn't just abandon her like this. She sighed, then got in the back seat with her, the new leather briefcase between them. Verity gave an address in Walton-on-Thames. During the journey Leticia tried to keep her talking and stop her falling asleep.

From out of the blue Verity said: 'Stop the car. I'm going to puke.'

The taxi was on a dual carriageway and stopping immediately wasn't easy. Leticia groped in her shoulder bag for a plastic carrier that she knew was in there somewhere, but she was too late. Verity had grasped the briefcase, opened the clasp and vomited profusely into her new gift.

Soon afterwards the taxi, driver muttering, all the windows wound down and joss sticks burning in the front, turned at speed into a tidy tree-lined street in Walton. They pulled up outside a neat stuccoed terrace.

'Come in for coffee?' Verity rasped to Leticia.

'No thanks. I'd better be getting home,' Leticia said immediately. She'd done her duty; that was more than enough. 'Don't forget this.' She gingerly passed across Verity's now weighty briefcase.

'Oh God,' Verity slurred. She fumbled in her pocket for her purse and waved three crumpled twenties. 'To getcha home. Sorry about everything.'

By the time she got home, Leticia had convinced herself that she must be mistaken about the spectacle frame. She opened up the package of wrapping paper on the coffee table and stared at it. The plastic was intact, though a little bent. The arm had been broken off at the little hinge, which was fractured. It needed a new screw, too. Normally she wouldn't wait up for Anton but tonight she really wanted the benefits of his wisdom and perspective. It had only been a few days since she had disclosed to him that Neville Rollason had been her client. Anton had been shocked but supportive of her. 'That's a mighty big job you had to do,' he had said.

It was a quarter past one when he finally walked in, looking exhausted. Leticia, now sobered by black coffee, said she had something she needed to ask him. First she described her meetings with Rollason and then what had happened that evening. The tale of the briefcase full of vomit had him holding his sides with laughter. 'Oh man, that is so bad. So bad.'

When she finally pointed out to him the small red plastic object he said, 'Letty, baby, they could be anybody's. It's not proof.'

'Yeah but those little yellow shields with the black horse on, it's quite distinctive.'

Using the paper, Anton picked up the frame and looked closely at it. 'That's the Ferrari symbol. There's millions of them out there.'

'Oh. So maybe I am wrong.'

Anton set down the frame, took both of Leticia's hands and looked into her face. 'I've heard you describe your boss as a bitch, but do you believe she is capable of murder? She's skinny, right? Could she lift a body to dispose of it?'

'I wouldn't have thought so, not easily. But Rollason was quite small. Maybe she had help. Look, I just don't know what to do.'

'Well, I'll tell you something for nothing. Assume you're right. If the cops get to know we have Rollason's specs here in our flat they are going to think you and me killed him. Ain't no evidence now they were ever in your boss's boot.'

'I think you're being a bit paranoid.'

'Really? Go up to that mirror, have a good look and tell me what colour face you see.'

'Colour is not everything.'

'When shit gets bad, it is, I'm telling you. Especially where cops are concerned. How many times have I been stopped in that car? Think on that.'

'So what should I do? I thought about showing it to Jill Allsop. She's full of good sense.'

Anton shrugged. 'Or you could post it anonymously to the cops, say where you found it.'

'But if I'm wrong that would just drop Verity in it. She's starting a new job in a week's time.'

He shook his head in amazement. 'You're overthinking everything, Letty. You can't be nice to everybody. What about that guy from Special Branch you work with? You could just leave it in his in-tray. Make it his problem.'

Leticia sighed and put her hands over her face. 'That would just get back to me.'

'Well then maybe you should just throw it away.'

'Anton! That's destroying evidence.'

He stood up, clenching his fists in exasperation. 'Look, baby. It's a high-profile case. They will get the murderer eventually. I don't care what you do, but don't leave it here. The cops have a habit of turning up uninvited.'

Leticia awoke just after six the next morning. She hadn't slept well. The spectacle arm had been hidden under the cutlery tray in the kitchen, but she had kept dreaming that the police arrived and found it. She had lain awake after each dream, pondering where would be a better place for it, but failed to come to any conclusion. Meanwhile Anton had slept soundly beside her, provoking in her a little nugget of resentment.

There was one thing she had decided during her long hours tossing and turning. She would ring Verity and simply ask her about the glasses. If she had a good explanation, that would be the end of it. She made herself a coffee, went online and looked up Ferrari brand glasses. She found that there were many different versions. As Anton had said last night, she was probably making a lot of fuss about nothing. But on the other hand she couldn't just afford to do nothing about it, and she knew she wouldn't be able to get on with her day until she had put this particular anxiety to bed.

It was cruelly early after a heavy night out, but she rang Verity at 8:30 a.m. The phone was off, so she left a message asking how she was. She made no mention of the real reason for the call.

For the next hour she paced about. Anton would probably eventually give her a lift to go and get her own car back from the office car park, but he was still asleep. There was another way. She could get a bus to the office now. It would take twenty minutes. Once she had the car it would be quite possible to drop in to see Verity at her house in Walton. That wouldn't be far out of her way. Yes, that's what she'd do.

Leticia had never been invited to Verity's home, but like many at the probation unit she had been party to the drama of its purchase a year previously. They had all overheard her many phone calls to solicitors and estate agents, the agonisingly long process always seeming close to collapse. She had to admit that she was looking forward to seeing what it was like inside now that she had an excuse.

She found the address easily enough. As she had glimpsed last night, the house was a tidy white bay-fronted Victorian terrace, with a neat front garden and recently clipped box hedge. Leticia parked the car outside and picked up her handbag, which contained the carefully wrapped spectacle arm. It was just gone ten, not too uncivilised a time.

She rang the doorbell. No reply. She pressed the bell again and eventually a very pale Verity in T-shirt and shorts pulled open the door, squinting against the light.

'Oh, hi, I just sent you a text,' she said sleepily. 'How did you know where I lived?'

'It was the address you gave to the taxi driver last night. I was in the cab with you.'

'Of course. That's all a bit of a haze. Come in, I'm just making some coffee.'

'I just wanted to find out how you were.' Leticia could see pristine pale carpets, a recently decorated hall with several mirrors. All very tasteful. She slipped off her shoes, and padded after Verity in her socks. She was led into a spacious kitchen with a view out over a neat garden.

'I'm not too bad,' replied Verity croakily, sweeping her hair back. Without make-up she looked younger and almost androgynous, like a perfect plastic mannequin. 'I drank a pint of water before bed and that helped. The briefcase is utterly ruined though. I feel terrible about it, but I've had to throw it away.'

'Oh no.' Leticia hadn't even made her own contribution to buying it yet. Jill's hurried whip-round email was only sent last thing yesterday afternoon. Everyone had been asked to put in a tenner.

'I feel awful, Leticia. Please don't say anything.'

'I won't. Your secret's safe with me.'

Verity smiled. 'I really must thank you, too, for bundling me into a cab and looking after me. That was really kind.' She began to prepare coffee.

After a couple more minutes Leticia decided now was the moment.

'Look, Verity, there's something I need to ask you. When I was fetching your bag from your car yesterday, I found a piece of broken spectacles in the boot.'

The silence was enormous and stretched-out. Verity turned back from the coffee mugs. Her face seemed to tighten, her eyes narrow. 'Sorry,' she finally said. 'What did you find?'

Leticia repeated what she'd said, then added: 'I know this sounds really stupid, but they look just like the glasses that I saw Neville Rollason wearing.' She fiddled in her bag and brought out the tissue-wrapped arm, and opened it on the kitchen table in front of her.

Verity didn't look at it, but stared straight at Leticia. 'I've never met him.' The hangover voice had transmuted to the work voice. Emphatic, crisp and incontrovertible. 'So it's impossible, isn't it?'

'Of course,' Leticia said. 'As I say, I'm probably mistaken.'

Another silence. Verity glanced down as if even seeing the object would implicate her: 'Ah! I think I know. The Ferrari symbol is the giveaway. They're my brother's. He borrowed my car last week. It's probably from his spare pair. Keeps all sorts of junk in the boot.' She gave a high little laugh that sounded forced. Back to the old Verity who didn't know how to smile. Crapped-upon bathmat Verity.

'I think it's broken.' Leticia pointed to the bent hinge wire. 'He'll probably need a new pair.'

Verity picked up the plastic arm and inspected it. 'Why did you wrap it up like this, with a tissue and everything?'

Leticia laughed. 'Actually, to preserve any fingerprints.'

'*What?*' Verity's mouth hung open in shock.

Now it was Leticia's turn to give a high-pitched nervous laugh. She rolled her eyes and said: 'I was thinking, you know, it was in case you had bumped him off and I had to go to the police about it. I know, I know, it was stupid. I watch too many detective dramas.' She was aware she was flapping her hands about nervously. 'I wasn't thinking straight.'

'No, I can see that. You obviously don't have a very high opinion of me.'

Verity's complexion was ashen, her lips almost pewter. Leticia realised that even to have someone casually consider you capable of murder was not very nice. Verity turned away and fiddled with the coffee things. She spilled some milk, and tutted. A teaspoon jangled and fell onto the floor. They both bent to retrieve it, their heads almost clashing. She could smell Verity's breath, last night's wine mixed with something a little bit sour. The stare she gave her on the way up was hostile.

Coffee was made, and while Leticia sat at the kitchen table Verity turned away and fiddled with her phone, tapping out a text.

'Did you mention this to anyone? You know, thinking you had discovered Rollason's spectacles in my car?'

'Only my boyfriend. He thought I was imagining things.'

Verity's forced laugh again. 'Sensible boyfriend.' She was still standing by the kitchen counter working her phone.

Leticia laughed again. She was feeling very uncomfortable and unwelcome now. She wanted to go but the coffee was too hot to be drunk rapidly. She didn't want to be rude and leave her drink untouched, but she was getting fidgety. They made small talk for a few minutes, then Verity asked casually: 'So you've been to pick up your car have you?'

'Yes, it's outside.'

'Right. Did you say you were coming here?'

'To Anton? No, he was still asleep.'

'Right,' Verity said absent-mindedly. 'Late hours at the restaurant, huh?'

'Yes, always.' Leticia sipped her coffee and suddenly felt a real chill in the atmosphere.

Verity turned to her, licked her lips and gulped. She looked paler than ever.

'Are you all right?' Leticia asked.

Verity nodded. 'I'm fine.' She wasn't. Leticia could see her flat stomach flexing, as if she was about to heave.

There was the sound of a key at the door. A deep male voice called something out, and Verity replied: 'She's in here.'

The door from the hall burst open. A large scruffy man wearing a camouflage jacket strode in, a huge sports bag in hand. His brown eyes were focused wholly on Leticia, and she immediately sensed he intended her harm. She stepped back and opened her mouth to scream, but before she could take a breath, a pale chill hand was clamped over her mouth, with a handkerchief in it. Verity's hand.

She fought like crazy but the struggle was unequal. The man was enormously strong and she couldn't breathe properly through the smelly rag. Oblivion came quickly.

Chapter Thirty

Verity watched as Gary folded up the unconscious woman, tying her wrists behind her back with cable ties and binding her ankles. He then unzipped the holdall and pulled out a very large canvas builder's bag. Quite gently he lifted her up and placed her inside the bag.

'I can't believe it's come to this,' Verity said. 'I never wanted to do it in the first place.'

'Until you were offered the money, as I recall.'

'Yeah, thanks for reminding me. It wasn't my idea. I said it was stupid. We're going to get caught.'

'Not if we keep our heads,' Gary said. 'It's quite straightforward. We've got her car keys. I'll carry her out to her own car. I think she'll just fit in the boot.'

'It's a Mini!'

'They're bigger these days.'

'But then what? Kill her as well? She's a colleague!'

'I'll have to see what the boss says,' Gary replied.

'None of this would have happened if you'd been more careful when you moved Rollason. Why didn't you check the boot?'

'Why didn't you check it?' he retorted. 'It's your car. I've got enough to do.'

'What are you going to do about her phone? I can't get into it.'

Gary smiled. 'I can. I'm going to reply to any messages, so that it appears she has left here. I'll drive near to her place, so it looks like she's gone home, then I'll turn off the phone. Then I'll nip back home through some back routes away from the road cameras. I'll leave the car in Mum's garage, and we can move her to the shed without being seen.'

'You can't leave that car at Mum's! She'll go spare.'

'She doesn't have to know. It'll only be for a few hours. When it's dark, I'll take it out somewhere and burn it.'

Verity nodded.

Gary looked up at her and said: 'I saw a pair of water voles at Hurst Meadows yesterday.'

'Do I look like I give a fuck?'

'You can be horrible sometimes,' he said, shouldering the heavy bag.

Verity folded her arms. 'Yeah, says the man who is going off to kill my colleague!'

–

The first Leticia knew was coldness, dark and pain. Everything hurt, especially her head. The next was the discovery that she was bound and gagged, still clothed, but spread-eagled on an old single bed frame. There were cable ties on her wrists and ankles that held her to the metal grid. There was something in her mouth too, hard like a golf ball, which made her jaw ache and rattled against her teeth. She couldn't push it out because of the gag. The darkness settled out into shadows and shapes, radiating from a skylight above her, where a faint orange glow indicated streetlamps not far away. It was set in a pitched wooden roof full of cobwebs. Turning her head a little, she mapped out a large wooden shed. Spiky silhouettes distilled into a lawnmower, a rake and a hoe, plus smaller tools hanging from nails in the walls. Her head was muzzy, as if she had been drugged. Yes, the handkerchief.

Every one of her senses had to be put to use. The shed looked fairly new and smelled of creosote. She could not detect any other odour. She listened intently and heard the distant hiss of traffic, plus the movement of the occasional vehicle nearer by. A woman was talking to herself as she walked, her heels clicking on a hard surface, no more than twenty yards away. Two discernible words. 'Steve' and 'pizza'. She was on a mobile. Leticia envied her freedom and her voice. After a fading minute the clicks and voice attenuated to nothing, leaving Leticia bereft, as lonely as an astronaut on the moon as the last Earthbound ship departs. She didn't even know where she was. Still at Verity's home or somewhere else? She tested her bonds, rotating her feet and narrowing her hands, checking to see if she could slide them back. No. She was firmly attached to this squeaky bed frame, unable to move even an inch. She bucked her body and found that the frame rattled. But it did not move along the floor.

Oh God. She had been so stupid. She should have gone with her first instinct, which was to tell the police. But when she'd seen Verity that morning, so hung-over, skinny and pallid, it had seemed ridiculous to suspect she was capable of abducting anyone, especially a dangerous man. Only then had she got up the courage to admit to Verity what she had found in the boot. The frosty response, she had assumed, was because her former boss was insulted to even fleetingly be considered a murderer.

Everything changed the moment the big scruffy man arrived. Of course Verity hadn't been working alone. She was the brains, he the brawn. Someone powerful to seize and kill the captive, and dispose of the body. She had called him Gary. One of the last things she had heard before losing consciousness was: 'Not so tight, Gary.' It was when he was tying the gag around her mouth. He was a lumbering scruffy individual, with a bald patch and a mane of long greasy hair around it. There was dandruff on his shoulders. She distinctly remembered seeing it. He couldn't possibly be her boyfriend. Her brother perhaps? Tina had said they didn't get on.

Then there was someone else. Someone referred to as the boss.

Leticia's thoughts returned to her own safety, and to realising that everything hinged on Anton. She had no idea what the time was, beyond knowing that it was evening and all of Saturday had slid away while she was unconscious. If this Saturday was typical, her partner would have been up by eleven and probably wouldn't have thought anything of her absence. He didn't have to hurry to the restaurant. The sous chef at J'adore Ça would handle the lunch preparations and Anton would have gone in for midday, just to check things over. She had been in a hurry to catch the early bus and had just texted him a quick greeting while she was on the way, saying she was going to pick up the car and then some groceries. She had implied that she would be back before he left, but stupidly had not mentioned she was going to Verity's. The reason? Because Anton would have thought she was wasting her time spending even another minute on this daft theory of hers. Worse still, he knew that she had a fairly elastic weekend schedule. He would probably have sent her a quick text during the afternoon, but it would have been early evening at least before he started to get concerned that he had never heard back from her. The first time he would be really worried was if she was not back by the time he got home from the restaurant.

Which could be one a.m. or later.

She didn't think it was that late yet. Too much traffic noise. But at this time in the summer it must be after eleven to be so dark.

Would Anton report her missing even then? His distrust of the police was so ingrained and his faith in her common sense so robust that it might well be Sunday morning before he seriously got round to thinking she was in danger.

In the meantime, they were probably going to kill her. She had information that would implicate them. Verity and this other man hadn't just killed Neville Rollason, but presumably the other person whose body was found on the island. She couldn't get her head round why, but that didn't matter so much now. Something else made sense, too: Verity's vomiting episodes. They could well have been stress and anxiety. Maybe someone was forcing her to be part of this. Even after what she had experienced, Leticia still couldn't quite accept that her former boss was a cold and calculating killer. She had known her for long enough to be sure of that. She must be doing this under duress. Her unique access to the details of Neville Rollason's new identity could have led someone else to put pressure on her.

Leticia caught herself, making excuses for a woman who might well kill her. Even now, she didn't want to believe the worst of anybody. Anton had said he liked this quality in her, but right now it looked like it was going to cost her her life.

Verity would have her phone. It was locked, so at least she wouldn't be able to tamper with her messages. The police would be able to trace it, but only if someone reported her missing quickly. She had no resources and she knew it. She was entirely at the mercy of her captors. She wanted to cry, and she could feel the tears welling up. But she couldn't afford to feel sorry for herself. She had to think, to put her brain to use. Right now, there was no one to rely on but herself. And that meant she had to keep it together.

–

At the same time a few miles away, Anton was hard at work in the restaurant kitchen trying to coordinate hors d'oeuvres for a late booking of a table for ten when Saskia, from front of house, came to the kitchen hatchway.

'Anton, is Leroy around?'

'No. I've not seen him tonight.'

'There's a woman asking for him. He said he would be here, apparently.' Saskia gestured to a tall pale woman with hair the colour of weak tea. She was wearing a raincoat with the collar up, as if she was cold, despite the warm evening.

'I can pass on a message. Who is she?'

'She said her name was Verity.'

Anton was suddenly totally focused. He wiped his hands on a tea towel and emerged from the kitchen. He'd never met Leticia's boss but she matched the description, with that prim moue of superiority. He'd had no idea she knew Leroy, though he could guess why.

'Hi. I'm the owner, can I help?' The image of her vomiting into her leaving gift, so graphically described by

Leticia, fired a smile that threatened to turn into a chuckle. He quelled it by thinking of the other story Leticia had told him, about the spectacle frame. Anton had in his early life known quite a few people capable of killing. This pallid stick insect was not one of them. Surely the only thing she could justifiably murder would be a steak and kidney pudding.

'I was looking for Leroy. He said he would be here.' Her big green eyes roamed the restaurant as if her contact was somehow hiding there.

'I can text him for you,' Anton said.

'It's okay, I've already done so.' She looked behind her, and to either side, still apparently not believing what Anton was saying to her.

'I'm Anton,' he said. 'I think you know my girlfriend, Leticia. Nice to meet you.'

A look of horror swam across Verity's face, and her eyes widened. 'Oh, yes of course. How are you?' She looked away, seemingly uninterested in the answer.

He was used to such looks from white people. Looks of superiority, disbelief that he could be running his own restaurant, and sometimes just fear. Several years ago in south London he had picked up a purse that an elderly white lady had dropped outside a newsagents. He chased after her, calling out. When she finally turned and he held out the object, she had flinched as if he was about to strike her. After taking the purse, the first thing she had done was to check the contents. The gratitude when it came was perfunctory. He was upset about it for days.

So Anton was used to strange expressions on the faces of white people. But this one he didn't know how to categorise. Maybe it was racism. He was darker than Leticia and had inherited from his Windrush generation parents some long Jamaican vowels. She could pass for white English on the phone, he couldn't. To her it seemed a small thing, but when you see small nuances in attitude on a daily basis it confirms your fears, and those tender spots eventually become calluses.

There were only two reasons this woman might be here to see Leroy. Anton knew most of Leroy's women, but there were always new ones. She was probably his type, skinny and high-class, but didn't seem quite young enough. So it must be the other reason. Her anxiety and edginess confirmed it to him.

He looked forward to telling Leticia all about it. Her boss wasn't a murderer. But she *was* a drug user.

--

Anton St Jeanne arrived back at the flat a little before two a.m. He wondered what it was that he had said to so upset Leticia. She'd replied to only one of his texts, just a terse *be home soon* around noon. Nothing after that. And she wasn't answering the phone at home. When they had a row, he could normally see it coming. The time two years ago when the female customer made a pass at him. Another time, his failure to show for a play because of a crisis at the restaurant. She had bought expensive tickets, and one went to waste. But this, he just couldn't fathom. She had a bee in her bonnet about her boss being a killer. It was crazy. It just didn't make any sense at all. Having seen the woman, he was surely right to have dismissed the idea. Still, maybe he had been too heavy about the way he did it.

He climbed the stairs quietly, slid the key carefully into the lock and turned it. Put on the lounge light. She had left no note. He tiptoed into the bedroom. The curtains were open, and in the harsh light from the streetlamp he could see that she wasn't there.

This was serious. She must have gone back to her mother's. That had only happened once before. Leticia had always labelled him a procrastinator, but everyone had their triggers. He was really worried about his girlfriend now, but he'd ring her mother in the morning. It was much too late now.

Chapter Thirty-one

Leticia awoke to direct sunlight on her face, a headache and a raging thirst. The cold had turned to warmth. She could hear birds. The coo of pigeons. For what felt like an hour she suffered the discomfort, trying to focus on the birds and their freedom. Finally, she heard footsteps and the sound of a key in the lock to the shed. The door was opened slightly and the big man who had overpowered her edged his way in. He didn't meet her gaze, but just scratched his head. 'Are you hungry or thirsty?' he asked.

Leticia nodded, and made a low groan through her gag, the only sound available to her. He glanced at her, then looked away hurriedly as if he had found her naked. She was too scared to eat but at least if he removed the gag she might be able to shout for help.

The man said: 'If I take the gag off you mustn't scream. If you do, bad things will happen. Understand?' She followed his gaze and saw the many tools pinned to the wall, including a mallet and a hand scythe.

She nodded again. He crouched down and carefully untied the cloth around her face, and removed the golf ball that was in her mouth.

'Please don't hurt me,' she croaked. He nodded. She could already feel that her captor was quite uncertain and lacking in confidence.

'I need to go to the toilet, Gary. That's more important than food.'

He looked surprised. 'How do you know my name?'

'Verity called you Gary.'

He nodded as if this made sense. Close up, his unwashed odour was pervasive.

'I need the toilet. And something to drink. And headache tablets.'

'Wait,' he said and squeezed out of the door, leaving it slightly ajar. The small visible slot of the outside world was an unkempt and weed-strewn garden. She wondered if Gary really would hit her if she screamed. He didn't radiate criminality. At least, not in the way that Neville Rollason and many other of her clients had. If she had to guess, she would put him down as somewhere on the autism spectrum. She'd done a course on the various types of disability she might come across with ex-offenders, but it was two years ago and she couldn't recall the details. But anyway, common sense dictated that screaming now wasn't a good idea. It might make him panic, and he might well kill her without meaning to, just to stop the unsettling noise. Now was not the time to risk that, not if her life wasn't in imminent danger.

She could hear him outside on the phone to someone. She couldn't make out what he was saying but from the tone, he was clearly taking orders not giving them. Probably from Verity. The conversation stopped and he squeezed back into the shed, stuffing the mobile into his pocket. He reached up to a shelf and pulled a dull metal object down. He knelt down, looked at her intently for the first time and, grasping her wrist, slid out the triangular blade from the Stanley knife. Leticia started to scream, but his big hand clamped over her mouth.

'Don't worry, I'm only cutting the cable ties.' Gradually he worked round, freeing her from the bed frame. He allowed her to come up to a sitting position and then re-bound her hands with tough plastic baler twine from his pocket.

'What time is it?'

He looked at his watch '9:37 a.m.'

'And where are we?'

'No. Don't ask that.' He shook his head. 'I can't tell you.'

'Gary, did you murder that man Neville Rollason?'

'No.'

He eased her off the bed frame, pulled her to her feet, then blindfolded her with a scarf. Her legs protested at taking her weight, her shoulders an agony of cramps. She was led into the outside world of sound. Blackbirds, pigeons, distant traffic. Faint music, and voices, perhaps in an adjacent garden. No, it was the muffled bass of a car stereo in the street. She wasn't sure if Gary had taken a tool from the shed with him. If so, it was probably the knife. Something small. She would play for time. He led her through a door, and up a step. The change in noise levels made it clear she was indoors. Somewhere stale. Unemptied bins and unwashed bodies. She heard flies. She was guided carefully up a staircase. The smell became a stench, and there was a rumbling snore, like a blocked drain trying to empty. Eventually she was manoeuvred into a small room that reeked of air freshener, the blindfold removed and the door shut behind her.

'Be quick,' he said through the door.

She was in a tiny traditional bathroom, woodchip wall-paper painted mauve, a horseshoe-shaped pink acrylic rug snug round the base of the WC. A big jar of potpourri on the floor. Black mould furred the ceiling edges and the rotten window frame, held shut with rusty screws. The cistern was old-fashioned cast iron, high on the wall with a dangling chain and a black rubber pull. She shot the flimsy bolt and used the facilities. Sharp glossy toilet paper, more like baking parchment. The spare roll sat wrapped on the floor, in a green wrapper. Izal Strong Medicated. She'd heard of the stuff – almost wartime vintage, she thought – but had never experienced it. Surprised it was still available.

She finished up and rinsed her hands at the tiny grubby basin. Not cleaned in a long time.

Gary tapped on the door and she unlocked it. She submitted to the blindfold as he said: 'I'm going to introduce you to my mother.' She took just a few guided steps. Gary knocked on another door. 'Mum, I've got her here.'

'Brrnnghn.'

The low growling sound from within didn't seem female nor quite human, more like the voice of several people at once. It took a moment to realise what had been said: 'Bring her in.' The door was opened and the odour almost overpowered her. She could hear the whine of an extractor fan, hard put to match its task.

A dead body. That's what was in here. It couldn't be anything else. She was suddenly very frightened. If she hadn't heard the voice, she'd have thought Gary's mother was actually dead in here, perhaps with others. She felt her knees go weak, and reached out for a wall as she was ushered into the room. Gary steadied her hand until it found something vertical. A door frame.

'What's your name?' the voice gasped. Leticia realised this person was reaching desperately for every breath. Each vowel a suck or a gasp.

'Leticia Mountjoy.'

'I'm Poppy, well, Penelope really. Vee mentioned you.'

'Vee?'

'Verity, my daughter.'

'Why are you holding me prisoner here? You have no right to do this.'

A great wheezing noise rocked the woman, and she could feel the floorboards vibrate with her movement. A laugh. 'The trouble with you, Leticia, is that you are too observant for your own good. Too inquisitive, too nosy. You've made this all very difficult, and it wasn't easy to begin with.'

'Neville Rollason was my client. I was responsible for him.'

'And did you like him?'

'It's not a question of like or dislike, I had a job to do.'

'How very professional of you.'

'Verity is a professional, just like me. Our job is to guide—'

The throaty rasp interrupted. 'Verity took some persuading, it's true. Never happy with the plan.'

'So you took it upon yourself to punish this man? Just like the vigilantes.'

'He killed my firstborn, Robert. Verity's and Gary's older brother. He killed my son and he destroyed my family. He disappeared on Wednesday, 4 September 1986. It's a date carved into my heart. His body was never found.'

Leticia had suspected something like this. 'I didn't think that was one of Rollason's murders.'

'Yes, it was.'

'Not officially. Did he admit it?'

The wheezing laugh again. 'Oh yes, he did. Eventually, almost with his dying breath.'

309

She felt Gary shifting uncomfortably beside her.

'Excuse me, I need oxygen. I lose my voice without it,' Poppy said. There was a pause, the hum of a machine. When her voice returned two minutes later it was higher and more melodious. 'You see, Leticia, I'm a grieving mother and I have very little time left. I needed the truth, and I needed justice. Your lot let him out. Removed what little justice there was in my life. Disgusting. You gave him a new name, bought him a nice little house...'

'Rented, actually.' *And not so little.*

'...Applied for his benefits, his council tax benefit, his Jobseeker's Allowance. No one filled out a form for my Carer's Allowance, my Personal Independence Payment. Your lot built him a new life, while I lay rotting in my old one.'

'I take your point.' Leticia could not deny this woman her grief, her grievance. 'The justice system is so imperfect. But that doesn't mean to say you're entitled to get Gary to exact revenge on your behalf by killing him.'

The big man shifted uncomfortably beside her but said nothing.

'Gary? No, Gary didn't kill him. I wouldn't ask him to do that. It's not really in him to end a life. Won't kill a spider, will you Gary? It was my job and I did it. Gary brought this despicable man up to the room when he was still unconscious and tied him to the single bed. The same one you've been using. I didn't want to touch him, so Gary put a plastic sheet on him. I use the hoist to get myself from my bed to that one, and I gradually lowered myself onto him, right close, face to face. I needed to see him suffer.'

Leticia struggled to imagine how big this woman must be. 'You squashed him?'

The laugh again, interrupted by a hacking cough and then a long suck of oxygen. 'Not all at once. I had some important questions to ask him, so I did it a little at a time. I used the remote to gradually lower myself in the hoist. Sat on him, then lay on him. Hard to get it right. Eventually, I knelt on his hips. My forearms were across his chest. Lifted the hoist, then set it down. Squeeze, hold, hold, hold, then relief. Squeeze then relief. I must have done it a hundred times. Taking him to his final breath, saw the flush on his face turn to purple, blood fill his eyeballs. I wanted him to find it as difficult to breathe as I do. When you have 489 kg on you, it's very hard to take a breath.'

'You weigh half a tonne?' Leticia squeaked.

'Just recently, yes. I didn't always. When I was young I was a dancer, believe it or not. On a cruise ship. Ballet was my thing, though there is no call for that on a cruise. When I was sixteen, I weighed less than eight stone, around a hundred pounds. My weight was quite normal for as long as my life was normal. Then on 4 September 1986 my Robert disappeared on the way home from playing football. Verity was only four and Gary just a baby. I struggled with it for a few months, depression, anxiety and worst of all, hope. Hope is the bitterest of all emotions because of its falsity, its nagging chirpy unwarranted optimism. My marriage failed, my husband divorced me, and I found my solace in eating. You see, when hope died I took to my bed and I have not left it since.'

'I'm so sorry.'

'Sorry? Words are cheap. You can't imagine the pain. I promise you that. It never goes.'

'But you can do things about your weight, you always can.'

'I know. I've been on a diet recently.'

'It didn't work?'

The laugh again and some more oxygen. 'Yes, it worked perfectly! I was 350 kg and I didn't think that was enough to do what I had to do to that wicked man, so I stepped up my intake and added more than 150 kg in the final two weeks before his release. My peak weight was eighty-seven stone, or 1,200 pounds. If I was so minded I could get a place in the *Guinness Book of Records*, at least for the UK.'

'May I look at you?' Leticia asked.

'I wouldn't recommend it. I don't look my best in the mornings. Takes me three hours to get ready for my fans.' A great gasping sigh escaped her. 'And of course, I have yet to decide what we're actually going to do with you. When Vee let me know what had happened, and I decided to talk to you, I was hoping that you would volunteer that Rollason was one of the most evil men who ever lived. I hoped you would agree that he deserved to die, and that what I had done was a service to the great British public. We need to be sure you would keep our secret. But now I'm not so sure.'

Leticia was terrified, but principle stuck uncomfortably in her throat. She couldn't just swallow it. 'Just because somebody might deserve to die doesn't mean to say it's our job to do it. Or your job to do it.'

'How wonderful to be so moral. You know I could sit on you and you would agree to anything. Rollason took three minutes eight seconds to die, once I'd got my full weight on him. Oh, how he begged. Wept, and in the final moments called for his mother. There's nothing like not being able to get air. You're young, so you might last another half a minute. Or maybe not.'

Leticia felt a wave of fear but steadied her voice: 'I can tell from talking to you that you are not that kind of person. You felt the loss of your son. You're not a psychopath.'

'Don't be so sure. I killed a stranger for money, just a few weeks ago.'

'No!'

'I did. It was easier than I thought, but then he wanted it.'

'You've no need to kill me. It won't help you.' Leticia knew she was sliding into desperation. Soon to be begging for her life, just like Rollason.

'I haven't decided. Look at it from my point of view. I've achieved my aim, which is to find out who killed my son and to exact retribution upon the murderer. My body is gradually collapsing under its own weight, my spine is crumbling. I don't have long to live, so for me it wouldn't matter if I'm caught. But what point is there getting justice for my beloved missing son if I sacrifice the future of my remaining son and a daughter? They're both implicated. If you open your mouth they'll both be imprisoned long after I've died.'

'I can keep that secret,' Leticia said. Principles began to crumble.

'No, I don't think you can. Gary, undo her blindfold.' The scarf was removed and Leticia found herself gazing at the largest person she had ever seen. The top half of Poppy Tilling's head was normal, the hair held back in a short greasy ponytail. But from the dark deep-set eyes downward, a blotchy mottled skin expanded in a series of viscous jelly waterfalls, with a sagging basketball-sized wattle hanging beneath her chin. The nightdress was like a tent, a protruding arm a giant plaited brioche of blubber.

Her hand and fingers were incongruously normal, heavily ringed, the nails neatly trimmed and varnished in red.

'You see, I need to make sure my babies are okay. Gary has Asperger's and would be bullied in prison. Verity, well. She's had an eating disorder since she was nine. While I ate myself to a huge size for some kind of comfort she has binged and purged and made herself sick on and off for many years. Bulimia. Families, as we all know, are complicated, and react to trauma in different ways. I gave her most of the money from the Chinese guy. She is flying to South America this evening to start a new life.'

'I thought she had a job in Nottingham?'

The woman laughed. 'A cover story.'

'None of you can escape your problems like that,' Leticia said. 'You just take them with you.'

'Not where I'm going,' Poppy said.

'I was brought up a Catholic. So I'd say especially where you're going.'

'If you've been through what I've been through, you can never believe in a God.'

'If you believe in justice you should release me,' Leticia said.

'No.' Poppy was consumed by an enormous hacking cough that went on and on and shook the room. Finally, she was quiet. 'Gary, you know what to do.'

Leticia screamed, but Gary's hand was quickly over her mouth, the gag in place shortly afterwards.

Chapter Thirty-two

Gary seized hold of Leticia, blindfolded her again and marched her carefully down the stairs. Her hands remained tied behind her back as she was manoeuvred out of the house and to the shed. Once there the blindfold was removed but her wrists and ankles were secured again by cable ties to the bed frame. 'Not so tight, Gary, it hurts,' she said. The big man responded by loosening her ankles a little but kept the wrists taut.

He was about to put the golf ball in her mouth again when she said: 'I'm hungry.'

He scratched his head, releasing a cloud of dandruff. 'I forgot,' he foghorned. 'I was going to get you some food.' He settled for tying the gag around her mouth, told her not to make any noise and slipped out of the shed, closing the door behind him.

He was back within five minutes with a steaming Pot Noodle. 'This one's my favourite flavour, but you can have it. Macaroni cheese.' He untied her, allowed her to sit up, and removed the gag.

'Don't you have anything else?' she asked, wondering how far she could push him. 'Something with vegetables. Do you have any fruit?'

'I don't eat fruit. Mum does sometimes. I do have a Skittles winter fruit pouch in my anorak. And a raspberry doughnut. I like to eat them when I go wildlife spotting.'

That didn't sound like much of an improvement on the Pot Noodle. 'Okay, I'll stop being fussy.' She gestured for the snack pot and he passed it to her, together with a plastic spoon and fork. She was so hungry she almost burned her mouth gobbling it down. He looked at her as she ate, gradually risking brief eye contact.

'That was so fast, you could go on *mukbang*, like Mum.' She risked a smile and carried on eating.

'Good, isn't it? I like Sundays because I always have macaroni cheese flavour. On Monday I have Vietnam street food flavour. The cupboard holds exactly two weeks' worth, so I know what day it is just by looking at what flavour is next.'

'You're very organised, Gary.'

'Thank you. I mend laptops for my job. Monday to Friday, nine thirty a.m. to four p.m. with half an hour for lunch.'

Leticia needed to coax him to talk but wanted to divert him onto something a little less tedious.

'What sort of wildlife do you like, Gary?'

A grin lit up his face. 'I like night creatures most. You don't see so much during the day. I go to Hurst Meadows by the Thames and use my tent as a hide. I often hear owls.'

'I adore owls! Two years ago, I went on a trek to northern India and we saw lots of beautiful birds of prey and lots of owls. Some of them were really big.'

'I like water voles. Some people call them water rats but they are not rats. They have got the wrong kind of tails for rats and they just live in the riverbank. There aren't many in the Thames, because mink eat them. Do you want to see some pictures of otters?'

'I'd love to,' she said. This was going better than she dared hope.

He got out his phone and started to fiddle with it.

'It would be good to see a nice big picture of an otter,' she said.

Gary thought for a minute. 'I have to tie you up again while I fetch my laptop.'

'I have a better idea. Why don't you take me into the house so I can see your laptop there?'

'I'm not supposed to. You are supposed to stay in the shed.'

'Who's going to know? I certainly won't tell.'

Gary considered her for a minute, sitting on the edge of the bed frame. One of his knees started to move rapidly up and down. A sign of stress or anxiety. She'd covered it on the mental health course.

'If you keep tying me up and untying me like this you're going to run out of cable ties.'

He shook his head. 'I got a carton of 1,000 on eBay. Enough for a long time.'

'I'd like not to be tied up. It hurts my wrists. Please.' She gave him her most winning smile. It always worked with Anton.

He looked away and both his legs started to tap, tap, tap on the floor. He caught her looking at his oscillating knee.

'Mum hates it when I do this. She says "Stop throstling, Gary, it's doing my head in".'

'Throstling?'

'It's just her name for it. When I get nervous. With my legs.'

'I don't want to make you nervous, Gary. If I promised not to run away, would you untie me?'

He shook his head. 'I can't do that. Mum would be angry. She's not well. I'm not to upset her. She shouts at me, and then gets out of breath. I hate it when she can't breathe.'

Leticia realised she was trying to move too fast. 'All right. Would you free my feet? Then I can walk in with you to see the pictures of the otters.'

He considered this for a long while, a frown deepening on his face.

'We could look at some videos of otters on YouTube as well,' Leticia said. 'That would be fun.'

'I'm not sure. I should phone Mum.'

'She'll say no, Gary. And she'll be angry with you.'

He nodded. 'I've got some good meerkat videos.' He looked at Leticia quizzically. 'Verity wouldn't watch them with me.'

'I will, Gary. I adore meerkats.'

'We will have to be quiet,' he said. 'But I've got some spare headphones, and a two-into-one audio jack that I bought for £3.75. Half price.'

'Okay, Gary,' she whispered, and held out her wrists in front of her. He tied her up loosely with the baler twine. Previously her wrists had been tied behind her back, which was much more difficult to deal with. She was confident that with three or four minutes unobserved she could be free of her last remaining bonds. She was already much freer. No gag, no blindfold, nothing around her ankles.

Gary led her into the house, through the lounge and into his den, which was piled high with computer equipment, cables, modems and all sorts of things she didn't recognise. The carpet was filthy. Obviously no one had vacuumed for months. He picked up a couple of long cables and some big over-ear headphones, and spent a few minutes connecting the laptop to the big TV in the lounge. Five minutes later they were sitting side by side on the grubby sofa watching videos of otters. Her captor had stopped his throstling and appeared to be quite relaxed. He was so focused on the animal images that Leticia was able to work away, rotating her wrists and loosening the knots.

In half an hour the first long video, about otters in Scotland, ended. Gary turned to the laptop beside him to select the next. Leticia knew that he wouldn't hear much with the headphones still on. This was her big moment. She slid one wrist from the twine, then the other, but held it loosely over her hands. Then she slipped off the headphones and eased her weight gradually off the low settee. He was still busy at the laptop.

Leticia stood and then ran. The front door was just a few short strides away. She got there just as Gary looked up.

–

Gary bellowed his anguish and levered himself clumsily from the sofa. The security chain on the door was on, and Leticia fumbled trying to remove it. What she hadn't counted on was that it was locked too and she couldn't see the key. She had no time to look for it, so had to retrace a couple of steps to go for the side entrance into the garden. She ducked through with a second to spare as Gary's huge arm reached out for her. Seen properly for the first time, the garden was not an easy escape prospect. A large unkempt leylandii hedge fifteen feet high ran around three-quarters of it, where it abutted neighbouring properties. The lowest point was where a pair of five-foot-high wooden gates barred the driveway from the street beyond. They were padlocked.

Leticia was twenty-eight and had last done any serious athletics at half that age. Hurdling had been one of her worst disciplines at school though she was a decent enough runner. An hour a week on a treadmill or an exercise bike was all she managed these days.

But nothing steels the body for action like fearing for your life.

She scrambled her way over those gates in a couple of seconds, landing in a heap on the other side. The short drive led to a curved suburban residential street of tired-looking semi-detached homes, many of the front gardens paved over for parking. As she stood, she heard the rattle of wood, and behind her the looming form of Gary, attempting to reach over the gates for her.

She jumped away and sprinted down the short drive.

'You promised me you wouldn't try to escape,' he called after her.

A car had just stopped ten yards away to the right, and she pelted towards it, sensing rescue.

She was wrong. Verity Winter emerged from the vehicle, sunglasses balanced on her head, car keys in hand, a big suitcase on the back seat. She hadn't seen Leticia at first and froze.

Leticia ran straight at her former boss, targeting the keys. Verity hid her hand behind her even as Leticia grabbed. The two struggling women smashed into the side of her car, where the driver's side door was still open. The creaking of wood and some male shouting signified that Gary had clambered over the gates and was now lumbering down towards them at the kerbside just thirty yards away.

Time to abandon the fight. Leticia shoved Verity, who fell backwards against the car, then began to run. She didn't recognise the area at all. She sprinted around 200 yards to a suburban T-junction. She was looking for a rescuer, preferably a solidly built one. One old gentleman working his garden and an elderly lady pushing a shopping trolley didn't quite fit the bill. However, a beefy middle-aged man in rugby shirt and jeans did. He was just getting into his Audi when Leticia basically threw herself onto the bonnet.

'Please, please help me,' Leticia pleaded. 'Call 999.'

The man emerged from the car and saw the bulky figure of Gary Tilling lumbering up the road towards them.

'He after you?' the man asked as Leticia got to her feet.

'Stop her,' Gary bellowed, having stopped some distance away. 'She's a thief.'

The man looked from one to the other and then said. 'Not many thieves would ask to ring 999. Get in the car, love. I won't let him get at you. We can sort it all out when the Old Bill arrive.'

Chapter Thirty-three

The unmarked grey Vauxhall swept into Linden Avenue, Gillard having turned off the blue lights a couple of minutes before. Gillard slewed the car to a stop across the front drive of Tilling's home. While Carl Hoskins went around the back, the detective chief inspector banged on the door. Before he got a reply the first of two patrol cars arrived in the street.

Through the reeded glass, Gillard watched the shuffling shambolic figure of Gary Tilling fumbling with the locked door. The moment he opened it, Gillard put his foot inside and grabbed his wrist. 'You're under arrest in connection with the abduction of Ms Leticia Mountjoy. We've got a warrant to search your home too.' Tilling didn't resist and nodded as if he'd expected it.

While two uniformed officers handcuffed Tilling, Gillard directed others to the den to seize the many laptops there. Hoskins read Tilling his rights, while Gillard began to climb the stairs. He was soon struggling against the stench.

'Please don't disturb Mum,' Tilling called out to him. 'She's taken a turn for the worse recently, and the doctors say she is not to be disturbed.'

Gillard located the room, knocked lightly on the door and called out: 'Mrs Tilling, it's the police. I'm afraid we need to come into your room.'

There was no reply, but the detective was aware that this was where the penetrating smell emanated from. Twisting the handle, he pushed, and shed light on a stinking darkness.

–

The curtains were drawn, but a faint light seeped into the room. In the centre was a large double bed, which groaned under the movement of its large occupant, whose suppressed hoarse breathing filled the room. The detective groped for the light switch, but a powerful gravelly voice said: 'Leave it.'

Gillard flicked the switch anyway and flooded the room with light. 'Turn it off!' It was an almost feral growl. Emerging from under the duvet was a head, greasy hair loose around the face, a small feminine hand shielding her from the light. The entire bed creaked and squealed as the woman adjusted her position. Leticia Mountjoy had not exaggerated. The woman was gargantuan.

'Are you Mrs Penelope Tilling?'

Machinery whirred and the far end of the bed began to tilt, lifting the upper body of the woman into a sitting position. A finger pointed directly at Gillard, and its owner rasped: 'What right have you to come in here?' She reached for something on the bedside table. An oxygen mask. Placed it on her face. A uniformed police officer joined him in the room, took one glance at the woman within, and almost gagged.

Gillard said: 'Mrs Tilling, you are under arrest for the abduction of Leticia Mountjoy. You are not obliged…'

She set the mask aside. 'Detective Chief Inspector,' she said, her voice now at a more conventional register. 'I have been confined to my bed for nearly thirty years. Whatever it is that you are investigating, I'm afraid I can't help you.'

Gillard completed reading her rights.

'Are you going to arrest me then? Drag me out of my sickbed? Squeeze me into a police car? Leave me overnight in a cell? The truth, Detective Chief Inspector, is that if I resisted, even ten of you couldn't get me down the stairs.'

Gillard had no answer to that. She was right. The staircase was steep and narrow, obstructed even further by the stairlift screwed into the floor that was clearly far too insubstantial for this woman.

Her small deep-set eyes stared out at him from her fleshy face, like two currants from a bun. She gathered her hair up and tied it into a ponytail, the wobbling dough of her numerous chins flopping from one side to the other as she did so.

'I can tell that you are repulsed by my appearance,' she said. 'Most people would be. But I wasn't always like this.'

'I remember. I met you, briefly.' The wall was hung with framed photos, including a large studio portrait of a slender young woman with a 1980s-style perm.

'That was another life,' she said. 'Before I got married, before I had any children, before my eldest son was murdered.'

'Robert. Yes, we talked about him. I remember you from the public appeal, and the reconstruction.'

'If you are investigating a murder, Detective Chief Inspector, let's start at the beginning, with my son.'

'The disappearance of your son has been investigated many, many times—'

'Without result. Now it seems you prefer to persecute the victims of murder, the vulnerable and those with disabilities.'

'I'm not persecuting you. I'm investigating two murders. Rollason, and a man called Dr Wei-Ling Chen.'

She said nothing, sucking on oxygen, her eyes boring into him.

'Mrs Tilling, did you kill Dr Chen?'

'I didn't murder him, if that's what you mean. He had terminal cancer. I helped him.'

'The Charon Foundation sent him to you, didn't they?'

'That's right. He was willing to pay a big woman to dominate him, to smother him. They tried a lot of the professional dominatrices, the so-called big beautiful women. They couldn't find anyone who would go right through with it, to the ultimate conclusion.'

'How did they find you?'

'Through my *mukbang* channel.'

'Your *what*?'

'I eat, professionally. People watch me on the Internet.'

Gillard tried to hide his amazement. 'Who pays you?'

'It's advertiser-funded. I have my own channel on YouTube, with 16,719 followers at last count. They're mostly from South Korea, but there's a smattering from all over the world. I get paid, by noodle manufacturers mainly, to display, eat and promote their products. I do three one-hour shows per week. I'm an influencer, and the bigger I get the more followers I attract.'

'That's incredible.'

'Yes, it certainly is. I stumbled on it by accident when researching bariatric diets. But it's been great for me. Fat faming, instead of fat shaming. I make even the biggest people feel slim. I'm a normaliser, if you like. It empowers them to know how wide, how broad, is the range of human sizes. I'm famous, successful and earning a good living. I show them there's hope. A twenty-stone woman emailed me to say she was so happy to realise she's in the slimmest quarter of humanity's size scale.'

'You're paid to make people feel good about themselves?'

She giggled, an incongruous process that made her chins jiggle. 'Not all of them. I'm sure for some casual viewers it is Elephant Man syndrome, a circus freak show. But the Internet means I don't have to watch them stare at me. And it paid for all this.' She lifted an arm, serried folds of blubber dangling, and pointed to a large blue wheeled frame on the far side of her bed. He saw that it was a medical hoist: stabilising legs that would slide under the bed and an arcing jib that suspended a sling. Further to the left was a bath-sized bariatric toilet, only partially screened by a curtain, and beyond it what appeared to be a wet room.

'And it covers my care bill.'

'If you had money, why kill Dr Chen?'

'Just to help him out.' Another giggle. 'Actually, I needed more money, but I also needed to practise asphyxiation techniques before Rollason's release date, before I tried it for real. Poor Dr Chen. I emailed a photo of someone else, a plus-size model, when Charon put him in contact. When he saw me in the flesh, he changed his mind. Boy, did he change his mind! He panicked and cried out and didn't want to go through with it. But Gary had already fixed him to the bed. He wore this weird plastic mesh bodysuit that he'd had specially made so that he would feel helpless, and it was firmly cable-tied to the bed, so he couldn't move an inch.'

'That means it does not count as consent.'

'Maybe he just got a treble helping.' She smiled. 'A lot more woman than he bargained for! Of course, he had wanted a lot of disgusting sex things that I wasn't willing to do. But by then of course he was already tied up, so he could hardly contest the matter.'

Gillard could hardly imagine the horror of Dr Chen's final minutes. 'And after everything, you had Gary dump him in the Thames.'

She shrugged, a mountainous tremor beneath the nightdress. 'Who would know?'

'When did you dream up this idea of revenge against Rollason?'

'The moment the Hyacinth Trust was notified of his release. I was totally disgusted that it could be allowed, but then I realised Verity would be a great asset. She was reluctant at first, of course. Too professional.'

'And where is she?'

'Gone off to Nottingham.'

Gillard had heard enough. 'Mrs Tilling, investigations are continuing. You are likely to be charged with murder. And you'll be going to hospital, to get you in shape for a visit to court. They'll look after you better than Gary can.'

'I won't go.'

'You will. In fact, if you'd had appropriate treatment at the start, proper therapy, exercise and mental health assistance after Robert first disappeared, this festering fantasy of vengeance would never have been necessary.'

'You have no idea.'

'Social services will be here soon.'

She flapped a hand dismissively, all varnished nails and chunky rings. 'I've seen them all before. All of them. Mr Ahmed, a consultant from Kingston Hospital, came to visit me last year, to persuade me to go into hospital. He was a bit surprised. "You've got a touch on the chubby side, Mrs Tilling." That's what he said. Offered me the full à la carte: sleeve gastrectomy, gastric bypass, gastric band, intra-gastric balloon; but I said no. At that time, I was a little below 350 kg. That still exceeds the tolerance on their largest hoist. He looked around and admitted that I had more facilities here than the bariatric ward at his hospital, but he still wanted me in. I said no. Mr Ahmed went away and called in social services to assess me. They undertook a capability assessment, to see if they could section me. Could I look after myself? They could see that I had money and was earning enough to employ two private carers to come three times a week. They saw I already had a specialist bariatric toilet in a wet room, an industrial hoist that will get me from my bed to the wet room and back, the only journeys I have made in more than thirty years. Their only concern was assessing my diabetes and the sores on my legs and feet that refuse to heal. They had noted the fact that three months previously a carer had found maggots in a sore on the back of my left ankle.' She pulled up the duvet to reveal a leg the size of a side of pork. A hand-sized dressing was taped on the enormously swollen and blotchy limb. 'It's a lot better now, but I have acres of eczema and other skin conditions between the folds of flesh. My carers find it extremely hard to keep me clean.' She dropped the bedclothes back.

Gillard shook his head. 'If you don't go to hospital, you'll die, it's as simple as that.'

'No, it's not as simple as that. I showed my fan mail to the assessor from social services. Like I told her, if I went into hospital, I'd lose it all. My online show. All that affirmation. All that positive mental energy. I'd be depressed, less mobile, and with inferior physical care too. Social services agreed. I was fully capable and there was little they could do for me in hospital that could not be done here. In the end we reached a deal, the NHS and me. They simply stepped up the visits from the district nurse, who comes now once a week instead of once a month.'

Gillard looked again at the photos on the wall. There were many aged portraits of a smiling gap-toothed child, his hair carefully combed, freckles on his face. 'Is this Robert?' he asked.

'Yes.' Her voice was no more than a whisper.

'He looks like a nice lad.'

'You cannot understand a mother's grief if you have not experienced it. It tears the soul into shreds, hour by hour, day by day, week by week. His father abandoned us a year after Robert disappeared. But a mother has to keep going, to bear the daily pain of waking and recollection, for all eternity, to be there with open arms. Just in case.'

Gillard nodded. He'd seen too many such cases over his career. No mother ever truly recovered.

'On the first anniversary of Robert's disappearance, I took to my bed. I told my two remaining children that I would remain here in this room, until he was found, or until I could touch his forehead and bless him on the journey to the great beyond. I would eat, but would not go out into the cruel world that had taken him from me.' Her voice broke, and she reached again for the oxygen mask. It was a couple of minutes before she was able to continue.

'You look at me, and I see disgust in your eyes.'

'It's not what you look like, Mrs Tilling, it's what you have done. You could have chosen another path.'

'But eating, in my confinement, is my only remaining pleasure.' She laughed, a high tinkling sound quite at variance with the body it came from. 'Don't you understand, Detective Chief Inspector, even now? I am grief, made flesh. Only when you see how much of me there is, only when I have been weighed on the scales of anguish, can you measure the depth of pain from which it all comes.'

Gillard turned off the light, closed the door and returned downstairs, having made only a cursory inspection of the woman's room. For now he was stumped. This was a woman who could never manage to be a fugitive from justice, or indeed from anything. He could return when he had more information. He was clearly going to need help from medical professionals.

All the computer equipment had been removed from Tilling's home office and was being ferried in large plastic bags out to waiting police vehicles. 'What have you got?' Gillard asked Rob Townsend, indicating the stack of plastic-bagged laptops and computers.

'It's too soon to say,' the research intelligence officer said. 'He really knows his stuff. A lot of his devices have very strong passwords, but we were lucky to catch one laptop that hadn't yet shut itself down. So we might be able to find out what we need.'

Gillard beckoned Hoskins outside so that he could talk.

'Has Gary Tilling said anything?'

'No. He claims to know nothing about our Dr Chen. But we've got his mobile phone now, and we'll be able to check. There is also a satnav in his car, so we should be able to double-check his movements.'

Gary Tilling was sitting on a sofa giving a statement to a uniformed female officer. He apparently didn't have much to say, and kept asking if he could go and attend to his mother. The officer looked up at Gillard enquiringly. He called her over and lowered his voice so Tilling couldn't hear.

'What's the mother like? How big is she?' she asked him, indicating the upstairs room with a flick of her eyes.

'I promise you have never seen anything like her in your life.'

Gillard started searching his phone contacts. Justice required that the woman be taken to hospital, urgently. It was the only type of custody that would be safe for her. It was beyond his experience, but he guessed he would have to involve the woman's doctor and care providers. He would ask a family liaison officer to coordinate whatever was required. This was certainly going to be tricky. But before that, he needed to secure the scene.

'I need to have the room searched thoroughly before we let Tilling up there. That includes the bed itself.'

'Really?' asked Hoskins.

'It's the perfect place to conceal evidence. I'll need two female officer volunteers, but we'll wait until we can get a neutral observer, maybe a district nurse. I've got a call in to social services. I just want to make sure that no evidence gets flushed down the loo, chucked out the window or smuggled out. We don't yet have enough evidence to charge either of them with the murders, but there's plenty for the abduction.'

There was one other person who had managed to evade arrest. Verity Winter. Where on earth was she?

–

Back at Mount Browne, Gillard was quickly presented with compelling evidence from Gary Tilling's laptop of his mother's online *mukbang* business.

'It's not for the faint-hearted,' Townsend warned.

The production values of the YouTube video were pretty slick, the camera steady and a backdrop projected that made her look like she was in some luxury penthouse apartment, a glorious city nightscape in the background. Mrs Tilling had put on make-up, a wig and jewellery, though she was still in bed. The officers had crowded around to watch the Youtube video, but, after the product introductions had ended and the eating began, almost every detective turned away. The slurping of noodles, the juice running down her chin – it was all too much.

'What else have we got?' Gillard asked Townsend.

'Some finances and bank account stuff. Gary Tilling has done a good job of deleting incriminating material. But there is this.' The research intelligence officer brought up an early draft of the contract, drawn up by Charon Stichting, that the Taiwanese man had been offered.

'He paid them £87,000 to be killed by "gradual and protracted intimate suffocation",' Townsend said. 'The bank account details do show that it was paid.'

Gillard looked over Townsend's shoulder at a PDF of Mrs Tilling's bank statement. 'I see that payment, but there are many others for smaller amounts.'

'Yes. I can't be sure what they are yet – *mukbang* maybe – but I've asked the banks to forward the counterparties behind these IBAN codes.'

'Let's look at the contract again,' Gillard said. 'Wouldn't it have stipulated that he have some kind of proper funeral arrangement afterwards?'

'Yes. It's right here. In fact, the breakdown of the quote shows that most of the money the Tillings were paid was to cover arranging for repatriation of the body to Taipei. They saved £25,000 by just dumping him in the Thames.'

Gillard shook his head. 'Chisellers as well as murderers, eh.'

'A civil matter,' Townsend said, looking up at his boss. 'I can't quite see it coming to court.'

Gillard returned to the Tillings' home to find a considerable press presence outside. One young woman with a microphone pushed it under his nose as he was making his way to the door.

'Why are the police harassing this disabled lady? A woman who believes she lost her son to a man just released from prison. What have you to say about that?'

The detective brushed past the reporters, and greeted the female uniform who had been posted at the front door. 'When did this lot arrive?' Gillard asked her.

'About half nine this morning, sir. Just to let you know there are two of Mrs Tilling's regular carers inside, and a manager from social services in Sunbury.' Gillard thanked her as she let him in. He immediately saw Gary Tilling sitting on the sofa watching daytime TV.

'How are you doing, Gary?' Gillard asked.

'I've got loads of work to do and I can't do any of it because you've got my equipment. I don't understand why.'

'Two men have been murdered, Gary. If you weren't your mother's principal overnight carer, and if she'd agree to anyone else looking after her, I'd have put you in

custody yesterday instead of on police bail. Think on that.'
Gillard looked upstairs, where a conversation could be
heard on the landing. He climbed up, easing his way past
the stairlift.

A dark-haired bespectacled woman in her fifties was
talking to two younger women, who from their overalls
were clearly from a specialist social care company. The
older woman seemed pleased to see him. 'I'm glad to make
your acquaintance, Detective Chief Inspector. I'm Helen
Cathcart, head of social services outreach.'

Gillard guided her to a spare bedroom as the two care
workers continued with their tasks.

'Mrs Cathcart, I'm trying desperately to do this by the
book, though from everything I've heard this particular
chapter has not yet been written.'

'No, indeed, we're all rather feeling our way along,'
she said. 'The crucial thing here is that Mrs Tilling is
quite within her rights to refuse medical treatment, even
though it would undoubtedly be good for her. She passed
her capability assessments quite easily. She has Attendance
Allowance and some other benefits, but they are not sufficient to cover the cost of two carers. It is only because
she is able to continue her self-employed work from bed
that she can afford the care she needs. I'm afraid she has
constructed rather an elaborate legal construct that makes
it hard to prise her from her home.'

'Well, Mrs Cathcart, I'm going to have to arrest her as
we now have most of the evidence we need.'

She gave him a wintry smile. 'That is an arrest I really
have to see.'

'I don't even know how I'm going to do it.'

Chapter Thirty-four

Gary Tilling sat in the dock at Staines Magistrates Court looking bewildered. He was the only representative of the Tilling family present for this first stage in the legal process. Leticia Mountjoy, watching from the public seating area, saw him look first to his solicitor, a young woman whose eyes were fixed on the paperwork in front of her, and then roam the room looking for some kind of ally, someone to explain what was happening. His eyes found hers, and Leticia risked a brief smile. He blinked and looked away.

The grizzled stipendiary, who had spent several minutes in close conversation with court officials, looked over his half-moon spectacles at the defendant. 'I think you are aware, Mr Tilling, that these committal proceedings are not to examine your guilt or innocence. They are merely to ascertain that all the instruments of law and the required evidence are present for the case to be referred to the Crown Court, which in terms of the severity of the crimes alleged is its right and proper venue. It is at this stage that you are required to confirm your name and address.'

After being prompted a second time Tilling did so.

'Now where is Ms Verity Winter?' the magistrate asked, looking at the ranks of legal officials at the modern desks in front of him. Two approached him, and there was another whispered huddle around the magistrate's desk.

'Mr Tilling,' the magistrate asked. 'Are you aware of the whereabouts of your sister?'

'No, sir,' he replied.

'The police seem to think that she took a flight from Heathrow to Buenos Aires several days ago. If you have been in contact with her, Mr Tilling, can I ask you to request that she return immediately? An international arrest warrant has already been issued and the consequences will be much more severe if she seeks to hide from justice.'

The stipendiary turned to address the court. 'Now, Mrs Poppy Tilling.' He looked around as if expecting her to magically appear. The clerk of the court leaned across his desk and fiddled with a console in front of him. A large TV screen in one corner of the courtroom flickered into life, revealing a startlingly close-up image of the florid face of Mrs Tilling, in bed. Her hair was neatly arranged in a ponytail, and she was wearing some kind of shapeless leopard-print top that almost filled the screen. A female officer stood at the bedside.

'Mrs Tilling.' The magistrate then asked her about the whereabouts of her daughter Verity and repeated his request that she be persuaded to return of her own will.

'I've no idea where she is.'

'Now, Mrs Tilling. I understand that you have mobility issues. I'd want to ask you to co-operate with those attempting to improve your health to allow for your attendance at Crown Court.'

'I'll come to Crown Court if it's a case about the murder of my son, Robert.'

'Mrs Tilling, may I remind you that it is not up to you to decide which cases you would wish to attend. This is not, if I may choose a particularly apposite metaphor, a Christmas box of chocolates from which you pick only those that appeal most.' The magistrate permitted himself a small indulgent smile before he continued. 'You are required to attend in person, and I expect you to make whatever physical adjustments are required to ensure that happens.'

'I'm not coming unless it's about Robert,' she said again. She banged a huge arm right in front of the screen, and the image jumped. 'I am a victim. I have suffered grief that you would not believe for more than thirty years. I demand justice.'

'Mrs Tilling, I am sure everyone has the greatest sympathy for your loss. However, you are in no position to make demands or reset the legal agenda. You are accused of three extremely serious offences for which a custodial sentence would on conviction be inevitable. You seem to think that you are able to treat this as something no more serious than dropping a chocolate wrapper in a park.'

'Then I'm not coming.'

'You most certainly will attend, Mrs Tilling,' the stipendiary told her, his face bristling with indignation. 'You will be seized and brought to face justice, even if you have to be moved with a crane. Your comments are already close to contempt of court.'

The video call was ended and the formalities of the hearing concluded. Leticia watched as Gary was escorted by two burly prison officers out of the courtroom.

–

The operation to remove Mrs Poppy Tilling from her home had been a number of days in the planning. A huge crowd had assembled in Linden Avenue to watch the contractors on the cherry picker removing the window from her bedroom and then using angle grinders to cut down through the brickwork to create a space big enough to remove her and her bed. An eight-wheeled crane with a large jib that soared high above the house was standing by. Two uniformed police officers were in her bedroom together with two contractors and a paramedic. Everything seemed to be going fine, even though Mrs Tilling was repeating that she was not going to co-operate and had no intention of leaving the room that she had occupied for over thirty years. Just as the contractors had secured webbing underneath her bed, she decided to wriggle off it. The sight of her in enormous leopard-print pyjamas, lying on the floor, was extraordinary. The paramedics spent a long time trying to persuade her to get back on the bed but she said she had no intention of allowing herself to be removed from her home. She then complained of breathing difficulties and had to be reconnected to her oxygen machine.

A group of demonstrators had been maintaining a vigil outside the house for some days. Justice for Poppy, it was called, and they were selling pink poppies to anyone who would contribute to her fighting fund. 'This was a woman who suffered for justice. Why on earth should she be persecuted by the police and the courts for doing the job that they should have done?' said a grey-haired spokesman for the group when interviewed by the BBC.

The operation had to be abandoned for the day when it became clear that Poppy Tilling's pulse was racing, and it would no longer be safe to move her.

Gillard, who had been outside watching the operation, was later called into a meeting with Chief Constable Alison Rigby, the head of Staines adult social care, the chief lawyer for the CPS and a specialist bariatric consultant from St Mary's Hospital in London.

'This woman is making a laughing stock of the justice system,' Rigby said. 'There has to be a way to arrest her without making her have a heart attack.'

'It's going to be difficult,' Gillard said. 'Some of the news organisations have rented rooms in the house opposite so they have a good view with telephoto lenses into the bedroom. Effectively that means any forcible attempt to remove her will be filmed and risks us looking brutal.'

'This new Justice for Poppy outfit seems to have got itself organised fairly quickly.'

'By the woman herself,' said the head of social care.

'I thought we'd taken her mobile phone away?' Rigby said, looking at Gillard.

'We have, ma'am, but she has a landline. While we can take the mobile away in the search for evidence, there is no equivalent justification to removing the landline. We've been advised that we cannot disconnect it. She now seems to have got herself pro bono a rather effective lawyer who has been making life difficult for us in front of magistrates every time we apply to broaden the warrant.'

'But she can't continue to stay there, surely, with a window missing and a section of brickwork removed? The house isn't fit to live in.'

'It's arguably been that way for many years,' the head of social care responded. 'As she couldn't be moved, polythene sheeting has been rigged up to protect her from the elements.'

It was on the fourth day of the stand-off, which had become a national TV spectacle, that the sad news came through that Mrs Poppy Tilling had suffered a massive stroke. This time the process of removing her was unimpeded, and after her condition was stabilised, the crane winched a platform with her, her bed and some essential medical equipment out of the first-floor window of 32 Linden Avenue. A team of ten paramedics then moved her onto a specially made gurney. Her departure by helicopter was witnessed by thousands thronging the streets, many of them carrying pink poppies.

Her death at the age of fifty-seven was announced that evening. Craig and Sam Gillard were sitting at home watching the news and it was the first item. The Home Secretary, caught by a press pack leaving a Whitehall meeting, said: 'I am of course extremely sad to hear this news and extend my sympathies to the family. However, it is very important that we bear in mind that we should never take the law into our own hands.'

The final words were almost drowned out by a demonstrator nearby yelling: 'Murderer! What about Justice for Poppy!'

Epilogue

Verity Winter didn't stay long in Argentina. She was eventually tracked down to neighbouring Uruguay, from where she was extradited and sentenced to twelve years for abduction, assault and conspiracy to murder. Gary Tilling, having pleaded guilty at an earlier stage and co-operated with the prosecution, was sentenced to fourteen years, ten of them suspended, for conspiracy and manslaughter. Leticia Mountjoy submitted a statement of mitigation on his behalf, which was read out in court. The judge agreed that Gary was very much in the shadow of his domineering mother.

Leroy Ceejay was arrested in a National Crime Agency drugs raid, in which 1.6 million amphetamine tablets were discovered in a lock-up garage in south-west London. Six members of his group were convicted of dealing and possession, though Ceejay himself was cleared of all of the major charges. Anton St Jeanne's restaurant won its first Michelin star, and now you can't get into the place at anything less than a month's notice. Leticia Mountjoy succeeded Verity Winter, and very much enjoys her new job. While moving in to her former boss's office she discovered a bottle of what turned out to be Rohypnol solution in a locked drawer. Andrew Wickens was fired from the police and jailed for three and a half years for perverting the course of justice.

Gus van Steenis made his way north from Zimbabwe via Zambia and Angola to the Democratic Republic of Congo, where he remains beyond the reach of British justice.

Poppy Tilling was buried in a grand piano case at Sunbury Cemetery, the closest cemetery to the place where her son Robert was last seen playing back in 1986. Her last resting place is something of a place of pilgrimage for those who have lost children, and is looked over by an alabaster angel paid for by her supporters from Justice for Poppy.

The body of Robert has never been found.

The body of Neville Rollason was cremated. Michael Jakes, the only attendee at the private ceremony, took the ashes and one night, at midnight, dropped the urn containing them into the Thames from the bridge to Tagg's Island.

It made just a small splash.

-

It was Midsummer's Night, exactly a year after the discovery of the body in the Thames. Leticia had gone to meet Anton at his restaurant, and after he had finished up, they drove along Hampton Court Road. Anton took the left turn to Tagg's Island and parked on the bridge. It was very quiet and they both stood looking down into the water, not speaking, but reflecting upon the year that had just passed.

Suddenly there was a movement off to the left near the bank, and a splash.

'Oh no, not again,' said Anton.

Leticia grinned at him and looked back at the dark water. There was a silvery V sliding across the faintly rippled surface. 'I wonder if that's an otter,' she said, peering out over the surface of the great river.

'Better that than a body,' Anton said.

'I've got a good mind to come back tomorrow night with my camera and see if I can get any pictures. I know someone who would love to see them.'

Acknowledgements

I'd like to thank Kate Mitchell and Andy Lynch for their wealth of experience on the probation service. Hester Russell, Head of Crime at GWB Harthills, expertly guided me on legal procedures. Dr Stuart Hamilton once again was kind enough to look over the forensic aspects, and retired detective inspector Kim Booth helped with many issues on police procedure. Other police sources have asked not to be identified, and I have respected their anonymity. Particular thanks to John Sanders for his help on Nystagmus. Shaun Foggett of Crocodiles of the World, near Burford in Oxfordshire, advised me on the construction of reptile houses, while Craig Surfleet's knowledge of plastering was invaluable. Rebecca Napier was kind enough to share her nursing knowledge of bariatric patients. Thanks to Tim Cary and Sara Westcott for reading the early manuscript. I am indebted to all of them, and any mistakes remaining are my own.

Tagg's Island and Ash Island do exist, but I have simplified their geography a little for the purposes of the plot. My thanks go to Alessandra Thorbjorn for the map.

The rather surprising world of *mukbang* can be found on YouTube, for those with a strong stomach.

Michael Bhaskar and the Canelo team as always were enthusiastic backers of the book. Jacqui Lewis did an excellent editing job. Of course above all is my wife and first reader, Louise, to whom this book is dedicated.

Do you love crime fiction and are always on the lookout for brilliant authors?

Canelo Crime is home to some of the most exciting novels around. Thousands of readers are already enjoying our compulsive stories. Are you ready to find your new favourite writer?

Find out more and sign up to our newsletter at canelocrime.com